GETTING *TOO* PERSONAL

Ice Man was like a funhouse: full of surprises, some nice, most not. But this time, when he let out a mellow chuckle that made his gray eyes dance like shooting stars and . . . well, it *was* almost pleasant to be in his company. And she must have been tired, because a second later she was giggling with him, like they were a couple of little kids up past their bedtime and down with a bad case of the sillies.

"You should do that more often," he said at last.

"What?"

"Laugh."

"Well, look who's talking. I'm not the one who wanders the halls with a scowl on his face."

"No. You're the one who wanders the halls with a chip on her shoulder."

Alayna's smile blew off her face faster than a hanky in a hurricane . . . and Ice knew *exactly* how mad she was. That's why he was smiling that funny little white boy smile.

"Back to your usual insulting self, I see. Do me a favor, will you, Richards?" She leaned forward, enunciating each word carefully, just in case. "Just . . . stick . . . to . . . work."

"Just calling them like I see them," he answered, pretending not to notice that she'd stuck the menu up between them like a shield.

KARYN LANGHORNE

a personal matter

HarperTorch
An Imprint of HarperCollins*Publishers*

This is a work of fiction. Names, characters, places, and incidents are products of the author's imagination or are used fictitiously and are not to be construed as real. Any resemblance to actual events, locales, organizations, or persons, living or dead, is entirely coincidental.

HARPERTORCH
An Imprint of HarperCollins*Publishers*
10 East 53rd Street
New York, New York 10022-5299

Copyright © 2004 by Karyn Langhorne Wynn
ISBN: 0-06-074773-0

First HarperTorch paperback printing: September 2004

HarperCollins®, HarperTorch™, and ❦™ are trademarks of Harper-Collins Publishers Inc.

Printed in the United States of America

Visit HarperTorch on the World Wide Web at www.harpercollins.com

10 9 8 7 6 5 4 3 2 1

Chapter 1

ord, she was one *ugly* white woman.

In her sixties, probably, though with white women, who could tell? The chick's lank, bleached hair was running away from her forehead like it stole something. Skin leathery yellow from cigarettes and drawn tight around her lips like the strings of an old laundry bag. Trixie McCoy frowned deeper into her computer, attacking her keyboard . . . anything to avoid giving Alayna the common courtesy of looking up.

Didn't matter, since Alayna already knew what she'd find in Trixie's flat, hard-featured face anyway: the image of a hundred Confederate soldiers on the march, whistling Dixie with every step, ready to lay down their lives for slavery and the virtue of white womanhood. You could dress up the Trixie McCoys of the world, educate them, sit them outside or inside the offices of the powerful. But if you turned their collars . . . their necks were still red.

And of all the legal secretaries in the city of Atlanta, this particular model was sitting outside the office of the managing partner of this law firm and had been ever since Alayna had joined the firm five years before.

Kinda made a statement, so Alayna folded the corners of her mouth a little tighter and gave the hag a "she who must not be ignored" look that would have made Queen Nefertiti jealous.

"He in?" Alayna shrugged toward Mr. Boss Man's closed door.

Trixie lifted a scrawny shoulder: universal trailer park code for "Don't know, don't care." Alayna's fingers twitched to slap the woman's tongue loose, but she just muttered, "Thanks. Thanks a lot," and turned to find out the answer her damn self.

Of course, when Alayna raised her cocoa-colored fist to rap on lily-white Boss Man's door, Trixie remembered her job was to keep the uninvited out. She heaved herself away from her terminal and snatched up the phone.

"What you want to see him for?"

None of your damn business.

Trixie read it in her face, but Alayna answered sweetly, "A personal matter," and Trixie dialed.

A personal matter. Of about nine thousand six hundred and eighty dollars, Alayna added to herself, thinking again of the tuition bill folded at the bottom of her purse. *Martine's college tuition and my own personal contribution to the United Negro College Fund.*

From the crimson flush burning the tips of her ears, it was obvious Trailer Trixie was annoyed as shit that Mr. David R. Weston, Esq. acquiesced to Alayna's admittance.

Alayna swung her round, young hips a little as she stepped across the corridor. *Take that, you shriveled old prune,* she thought, and pulled on the handle of the managing partner's heavy wood door.

With a last-word mutter, Boss Man slammed down his phone and wiped a hand over his temples as if mopping up the remnants of his annoyance. He was one of those Humpty Dumpty–shaped white men: all soft in the center, with big jug ears and thick brows over fox-quick brown eyes. When he was in a good mood, his voice was syrupy with Southern "good ol' boy" charm. When his mood wasn't so good, his voice dropped to grunts and barks that would have made many an impatient New Yorker envious. And when he was mad, he sounded like he'd been raised in the jungle with Tarzan: "Me boss, you . . . *work!*"

"Six o'clock. All hell's breaking loose. As usual," he grunted as Alayna let the door click shut behind her. "Glad you came by. Wanted to talk to you anyway."

"Oh?" Alayna approached his desk, arranging her face in pleasant solicitude so her dislike wouldn't show. "Something new with the Williams matter?"

Weston grimaced. The Williams matter was one of *those* cases: big-buck potential at the early stages, nothing but headache and trouble by the end. Scheduled for trial in a week, the opposition's sudden interest in settlement had ground Weston's patience and Alayna's trial preparations to an absolute halt.

"No, no." The pricey black leather of his chair squished wetly as Weston leaned back. "A new matter."

At his nod, Alayna perched on the arm of a side chair opposite his desk and gave him a faceful of what she hoped was deferential "you first." But the truth was . . . now that she was sitting here in the Boss Man's office, she was in no great hurry to launch into the I-need-a-raise song and dance. Almost automatically, her mind ran through the arguments she'd been practicing for days: how hard she worked, the number of big cases she'd managed alone, the strength of her last performance review. And, as an absolute last resort, she'd play the "race card." Remind him that of the paralegals who had worked at the firm five years or longer, she—the black one—was the only one yet to be promoted to senior paralegal.

But mentioning race would give him permission to bring up the ugly incident with Greta Jennings two years ago. Of course, Greta was an idiot who would have been fired eventually if Alayna hadn't helped her quit, but Alayna wasn't sure she'd come out on top with Boss Man if *that* was going to get tossed into the mix. Slender white girls with long blonde hair and doe-wide blue eyes always got away with being ignorant in ways a Sister never could.

Lord . . . we need this money. Mama, if you're listening . . . ask Jesus to send a few dozen angels to help me bring this crazy white man around . . .

Boss Man still hadn't spoken, just sat there, staring at her, those shrewd brown eyes narrowing in his tired, fifty-something face. Measuring her, that's what he was doing. Running her skin tone against a paint store colorwheel. Ginger brown? No. Nutberry? Maybe. Pricing her white off-the-Macy's-sale-rack blouse—$19.99, two for $29. Slipping a mental tape measure from her waist to the widest curve of her hips beneath the navy blue skirt.

"How would you feel . . ." he began at last, speak-

ing so slowly he sounded like he'd hurt himself,
". . . about a raise?"

Only the grace of an ever-present God kept her hand
off her hip and her head from doing the She-Nai-Nai
swing on her neck. She stared at him for a long second,
openmouthed in shock. When she did manage to
speak, what came out was a fresh-from-the-Ghetto:
" 'Scuse me?" that made Weston grimace. It was pretty
clear he didn't want to use the dreaded "r" word again.

"I want to *persuade* you to take a senior paralegal
position," he repeated, and the subtle emphasis he
placed on the word *persuade* snapped Alayna back to
reality.

Uh-oh. Danger, Will Robinson, the little robot in
her head warned, arms flailing, lights flashing. *White
man talking.*

Weston punctuated her concern by standing up,
pacing toward the large windows of his spacious
office. For a few moments all was calm and bright
except for the low hum of the air conditioning circu-
lating through the room. Then he started talking.

"Martine graduates from high school when? Next
week?"

It wasn't a question: it was a reminder. He knew
her situation, knew it very well, and Alayna cursed
the day she'd ever told him she had a sister. It wasn't
good for white folks to know too much of your business. Push come to shove, they'd use it against you
every time. Before answering, she tried to read his
eyes, but he was hiding them from her, staring out of
the large windows as though something in the street
below were suddenly captivating.

"Two weeks from Sunday," she said at last.

"She's going to . . . ?"

"Howard University."

"That's right. Washington, D.C. Good school—private school. Not cheap," he told the street. "Well. Her timing's perfect, because we've got a new case. Big technology case. Software infringement. Lots of hours, tight deadlines, complex issues . . . and . . ."

And what?

Men as cheap as Weston didn't start conversations with the word "raise" unless the "and" was the size of the Grand Canyon.

And . . . and . . .

And you'll have to travel to Alaska.

And you'll have to retrieve the evidence from the local landfill . . . with your bare hands.

And if we lose, you're fired . . .

"And . . . ," Boss Man continued, "you'll be working for Ben Richards."

Alayna heard a rush of air and realized it was her own breath trapped in a gasp of surprise.

Ben Richards? Ice Man? The Freezer? Great. Give me the landfill.

Weston took one look at her face and started talking a little faster than before. Important case for the firm . . . needed someone of her intelligence and experience . . . Joel's unfortunate resignation making it necessary to assign Richards a new paralegal. . . .

"Joel *quit?*"

Weston scowled like a lunatic axe murderer.

"About an hour ago. No notice . . . no nothing. Hope he never needs a reference from *me* . . . ," Weston grumbled, stopping just short of adding ". . . *the little faggot.*"

Alayna let this latest news soak into her brain. Joel Mitchum had *quit*. Not that he hadn't been threatening—he'd been threatening *forever*. Alayna could almost hear him, lisping his complaints over hurried lunches at the sandwich shop around the block. *The Freezer* called in the middle of the night last night with more assignments and requirements. *Ice Man* found one typo in a client letter and hit the roof. The Freezer, this. Ice Man that. But she hadn't expected the guy to actually quit. Joel's lamentations about his workload were nearly overshadowed by his raptures over Ice's beautiful gray eyes, perfect physique and thick dark hair. "Girl," Joel had said a dozen times if he'd said it once. "He's an *asshole*. But he's the most beautiful asshole I've ever *seen*." Then he'd close the bitch session by wondering if The Freezer were really straight, or just so comfortable with his closet that only the Second Coming would bring him out of it.

And it was true, The Freezer wasn't bad looking . . . if you liked white boys . . . but he had the personality of a bowl of soggy potato chips.

"Mountains of work, of course," Weston was saying to the windows. "But I thought you might be better suited to his . . . temperament . . . than Liz Gordon. She's a little . . . timid . . . while you're . . ." He hesitated, searching for a politic word with the heft of *insubordinate* but without its punch. "Well . . . let's just say you're no shrinking violet, are you? It will be great learning experience. He's one of the best lawyers we've got . . ."

Lawyers.

All lawyers were the same: They wanted what they

wanted when they wanted it. They all thought they were just a little bit better than everyone else because they could put "Esq." behind their name. Even that Barbie-doll Greta Jennings had had *that* much on the ball.

But at least The Freezer wouldn't insist on that phony-baloney we-are-the-world office camaraderie. From everything Alayna had observed, he really *was* an asshole—and an equal opportunity asshole at that. The kind who could walk right past you in the hallway and not even nod. The kind who answered "How was your weekend?" with "None of your damn business."

And . . . if the price was right . . .

She thought of Martine then. Martine happy and free at Howard. Free in a way Alayna had never been as a college student, saddled with two jobs, a house and a little sister who looked for—and found—trouble under every rock on the playground. Martine, who, in spite of all the struggle and tussle, had managed to grow up, graduate from high school and get accepted to a very good college.

"How much?" she asked, determination at the edge of her voice.

Be careful what you pray for, girl, Mama warned in Alayna's head. *You just might get it.*

Chapter 2

The May sunset shot crimson streamers through the sky as Alayna parked her aging red Jeep in the driveway of 555 Magnolia Street, unstuck her back and skirt from the sweaty cracked leather of its un-air-conditioned interior and hurried toward the house.

But Martine was already standing on the porch, shooting out evil red streams of her very own. Her sister's slender arms crossed her chest like a shield, her lower lip hung down to her chin. With a spear and some face paint, she could have doubled for a *National Geographic* Bantu warrior princess.

"Where you been! I plan something special you get caught up with that stupid job and nearly ruin everything! Honestly, Alayna." Martine tossed her bone-straightened-ironed-flatter hairdo like a white girl on a shampoo commercial and pouted. "He'll be here any minute."

"Oh, joy of joys," Alayna muttered and let the screen door squawk birdishly as she pushed into the old house.

Martine had been busy.

The ancient hardwood floors gleamed slick with new polish. The decrepit living room sofa, jacked up with a couple of textbooks from Alayna's college days and festooned with a throw fashioned from a colorful old bedspread floated in the center of the room facing the fireplace instead of in its customary spot against the wall. In the dining room, a white tablecloth covered a candlelit table.

Alayna eyed her sister.

"Is all this necessary?"

"What's wrong with making it nice for him?"

"Did you do everything *else* you were supposed to today?"

Instead of answering, Martine headed for the kitchen, talking trash.

"I could have used your help with dinner," Alayna's little sister sniffed. As if the I'm-gonna-be-pissed-to-change-the-subject tone was going to shake Alayna off her tail. "Thank God Nalexi had some time to help out with the cleaning this afternoon or—"

Nalexi. A little wisp of a teenaged girl with a high, babyish voice and sly, lie-in-your-face eyes. If Martine knew the effect the word "Nalexi" had on her credibility, she'd have renamed the girl every week.

Alayna put on her kill-the-bullshit voice and a face to match. "What the hell is going on, Tiney?"

"Why you always gotta think—"

"Because I know you. Been listening to you dish up tales since you were a kid. Am I gonna have to call the office of McPherson High School? Cause you know I'll do it—"

"Okay, okay!" She shook her dark brown eyes like

a roller looking for sevens and coming up craps. "I cut school today—"

"Cut school!"

"So what? What's the big deal?"

"You know what the big deal is. I promised Mama—"

Martine groaned. "I'm going to *graduate,* Alayna—"

"But Martine—"

"We have two weeks left. One. Two," she flashed a couple of fingers at her sister, then snapped them under Alayna's nose. "What am I going to learn in two weeks that I haven't already learned? Yeah, I cut school. And it's a good thing I did," she said as she stuffed a yellow duck-shaped mitt on her hand and bent to the oven. "Considering all the help *you* turned out to be. Where you been?"

"Getting a raise."

Martine hoisted a black roasting pan out of the oven and filled the kitchen with the aroma of baked chicken. "That's good," she told the bird. "How much?"

"Eight thousand dollars!" Alayna couldn't stop herself from doing a happy dance around the kitchen.

"Sweet."

"Wait, there's more!" Alayna joked, imitating the announcers in those late-night infomercials. "Sign now and you get the title senior paralegal and a five-thousand-dollar bonus! Five thousand, cash! Can you believe it? Weston was desperate, and all Mama's angels were whispering in my ear! I just kept pushing up on Mr. Boss Man 'til he gave in and gave me what I wanted."

"Mama's angels. Right. That's nice," Martine said, sounding as placid and disinterested as Marian Cunningham on a rerun of *Happy Days*. "Get the salad out of the refrigerator. Please. And go change your clothes."

Alayna stared at her.

"Nice? *Nice?* It's better than any 'nice.' Especially considering the deal with the devil I had to make to get it. Remember me telling you about the lawyer they call The Freezer?"

"Hmmpf," Martine grunted. "You talk about those white people so much it's hard to keep them all straight. Which one was he?"

"The one no one can work with."

"I don't see how you work with any of them." Martine sighed. "I said it was good, Alayna. What do you *want?*"

"I want you to come up with some new adjectives, girl." And before she was conscious of it, her hip hand was in place and there was a finger waving beneath Martine's nose. "Terrific . . . fabulous! The jam! You can hug my neck and jump up and down, if you can't think of anything to say. Your tuition is paid! You hear me? Paid!" Alayna slapped her hand against the counter. "Paid in full!"

"Well . . ." A tight smile crimped Martine's lipsticked lips. "That's good." Then she poked attentively at the chicken as though she'd never made one before in her life, which was far from true.

Uh-oh.

"What's the matter with you, Tiney?"

"Nothing."

"Nothing, my brown butt. You ain't acted right since you got the information packet from Howard—"

"What's the matter with *you?*" Martine snapped. "I said it was good. I'm thrilled. See look," she bounced halfheartedly on her carefully pedicured toes, exactly twice, then stopped. "What do you want? A parade?"

Alayna swept her eyes over her sister again. Same height, same slim little figure of perky breasts and firm round behind. Same cinnamon brown skin, same fresh mouth. And yet . . .

"I'm talking 'bout *money,* here, Martine. Cash. Dinero. Bucks. Green. You can spend your summer job money on clothes. And you won't have to get a job as soon as you get to Washington. You can spend your first semester getting to know the place—"

"Yeah, yeah," Martine waved the topic away with an impatient flutter of nails. "Are you going to change your clothes or not?"

Naw, baby. Now, this ain't right. You might look like Martine and sound like Martine, but there's no way you're my sister. Considering the whines and protests Martine put up about how she WAS NOT gonna get caught dead on Howard's campus in some work study cafeteria job with her new hairdo under a hair net, this news should have her shaking her little round booty around the room.

The look-alike Martine must have decided to play it cool, because she didn't say a word and didn't look up, even though Alayna's eyes were burning Superman holes in her underwear.

"Well, *I'm* happy," Alayna grumbled, deciding to

let it go for the moment. "Even if I'm gonna spend the next year with this weirdo lawyer they call the Ice Man, it's worth it to know you'll be up there without having to worry about money like I always had to. You'll get to pledge a sorority, go to homecomings and step shows. Maybe we can even afford a couple of spring break trips. Might meet yourself some fine brother studying medicine or law—"

"That's another thing," the Martine Thing interrupted, swinging flashing eyes on Alayna. "Don't talk about them people you work with tonight. Lord. You'll bore him to *death*—"

"But—"

"And go change! I ain't having you at this table looking like some corporate buppie, okay?"

For a long second, the Clash of the Titans raged between them in the little kitchen. Zeus had out his thunderbolt and Poseidon was thinking about one serious tidal wave. Between fire and flood . . . well, mere mortals wouldn't stand a chance. Alayna, still doing a hands-on-hip-hop that now had some major Medusa overtones, stared hard into Martine's face until at last the girl caved with a loose raspberry of exasperation.

"Well . . . ," she said as though Alayna had demanded an explanation out loud. "You been whining on and on about how you hadn't met him, so I finally invited him. And now he's coming any minute and all you want to talk about is college and money and them dumb white people you work with. Ice Man and the Boss Man and Trailer Trash Trixie—"

Alayna inhaled the few molecules of available tolerance and put her lightning bolts back in their quiver.

"Oh, all right," she said and left the kitchen, making sure her pumps clicked staccato annoyance on Martine's fresh-polished floors.

The three bedrooms of the home parted off a central hallway like tributaries off a river. Alayna passed the closed-door sanctuary-stillness of their mother's room on her right, then turned into her own room on the left. Martine's room lay a little further down, connected to hers by a common bathroom.

"You know what I think?" Alayna called as she stripped off her work clothes and tossed them into a jumbled corner for Saturday's trip to the dry cleaner. "I think we should go ahead and pay the whole year's tuition up front with this money. The bonus plus what I got in savings over at Peachtree Federal is just enough. That way—"

The doorbell rang.

"Hurry up!" Martine yelled, and Alayna could hear her sandals slapping her heels as she raced out of the kitchen to the front door.

He's just another boy. Be another one next month, or the month after, Alayna thought, wiggling into a short skirt like Martine's and a crisp white tee. She grabbed the white Keds resting neatly under her bed and a pair of white socks from the top drawer of her dresser. *What's the big damn deal?*

Shoes tied, she paused at the mirror, smoothing stray black hairs off her forehead and into the clip that held the other strands in a ponytail on her neck. The dark shadows under her deep brown eyes made her look old. The Williams trial was taking its toll, and the recurring dreams of Mama's dying request were back, brought on, Alayna suspected, by the weight of raising nine thousand six hundred eighty dollars.

"*It's handled now, Mama,*" she told her reflection. "*Martine's gonna go to school. Just like I promised you she would. And after she's out of school, I'm . . . I'm going to . . .*"

She wasn't sure how to finish that. Not yet. Her reflection blinked wearily back at her as though saying, Whatever you're selling, girl, I ain't buying.

The suspicious silence from the front of the house drove Alayna from any further self-persuasion. Instead, she tested out a smile of welcome, deemed it acceptable and left the bedroom.

Martine's visitor was a young man of barely eighteen, around six feet tall, with cocoa brown skin and hair cropped so close to his skull that Alayna could see his brain working. As Alayna approached, Martine lifted her face, and she and the boy kissed full on the mouth—apparently the latest in a string of kisses they'd shared since Martine had opened the door. The boy's hand strayed to Martine's buttocks, squeezing. When the pair broke apart, he draped his hand lazily over Martine's shoulder, fingers grazing her breast. He didn't know it, but those wayward fingers had just reached across the room and snatched off Alayna's welcome smile, twisting it into an ugly scowl.

"This is my boyfriend, Jamal Preston." Martine's voice went all babyish and silly, while her face lit up like the star on a Christmas tree.

Mr. Jamal Preston stuck out his hand. "Nice to finally meet you, Ms. Jackson. I've heard a lot about you."

"Wish I could say the same." Alayna didn't bother to re-paste a smile on her face. "Tell me, uh, Jamal. Just how long have you and Martine been together?"

"This weekend's our seven-month anniversary."

"Really?"

Alayna shifted her gaze to Martine. The girl looked at her sandals, at the floor, at Jamal—everywhere but into Alayna's steely eyes.

"Come on out into the dining room," Martine coaxed her Mr. Man in a syrupy-sweet tone Alayna was sure had never come out of her wise-ass sister's mouth before. "I've made all your favorites."

With great flourish, Martine seated Jamal at the head of the table, then swished into the kitchen, reappearing with the platter of roasted chicken, which she placed in front of Jamal.

"Will you carve, honey?"

Alayna watched the boy's chest inflate like a rubber inner tube.

"Sure, baby," he answered, taking the utensils awkwardly and starting to saw at the breast like he was taking up the violin. While Martine made two more trips to the kitchen for wild rice, dinner rolls and salad, each of them got a raggedy slice of chicken breast.

Alayna offered a quick blessing, and they ate.

Silence was queen of the table until Alayna said, "Well. Graduation in two weeks."

"Yes, ma'am." Jamal pushed a bit of chicken around his mouth to answer.

"What will you be doing after high school?"

Martine shot her an angry, furtive look.

"Getting a job, I guess. My grandparents—they

raised me—they want me to go to college, but—" He gazed at Martine. "I've had enough school for now. It's time for me to start my life."

And the two joined hands and looked at each other all lovey-dovey. A small warning light flashed in Alayna's brain.

"Well, I guess you'll want to spend as much time together as you can," Alayna continued after a short pause. "Martine will be leaving for Washington before we know it."

Jamal's Adam's apple bounced suddenly in his gullet. His round head swung from Alayna to Martine.

"You didn't tell her?" he asked, his tenor climbing to a soprano.

"It's not the sort of thing you just blurt out—"

And even though she didn't know *what* wasn't the sort of thing you just "blurt out," Alayna felt some unseen Dennis the Menace drop an ice cube down the back of her shirt, and she knew that whatever it was was bad enough to have been a secret. That alone was enough to make her voice as hard as a slap as she demanded, "Tell me what?"

Jamal took a breath so deep he couldn't have left much air for the rest of the planet. His fingers laced Martine's more tightly.

"Martine's not going to Washington," he said as forcefully as his youth could muster.

"Oh no?"

"No," Martine piped in. "We getting married after graduation. Just as soon as I turn eighteen." Martine rolled her pretty head around on her neck, ending her little stretch by raising her chin at her sister.

At the neighborhood block party late in the summer they still had those booths where folks try to throw a ball and dunk some poor fool under water. Most people don't have good enough aim to do it, and the fool stays dry a long, long time. Then some kid who's the star pitcher for the local little league hits the bull's-eye and *whammo!* Pity the poor fool, 'cause there's cold water all over, filling his ears and lungs and blocking out his vision. Everything that was the whole rest of the world fades to black and there he is: shivering and wet.

Whammo!

Alayna was submerged, stunned, shocked as shit. Couldn't think of words to say because she was too busy trying to scramble upward, out of cold water and into air.

While far away back in the dry world, the phone jangled. Before Alayna could come up with a response to her sister's announcement that didn't involve a string of profanities, Martine thrust the handset under Alayna's nose.

"Some white dude."

She recognized his voice immediately.

"I need you here." Then a second's pause before Ice Man added as a hasty afterthought, *"Now"* and hung up.

Chapter 3

It was after 9 P.M., and even the cleaning crew had bounced by the time Alayna got back to the office. In corridors as creepy as *The Blair Witch Project,* she crept toward the War Room—an ugly little shoebox reserved for trial preparation. That was where Ice the Freezer Man said he'd be waiting—just before he left her listening to the dial tone.

Alayna flicked on a couple of hallway lights just so she wouldn't be like some stupid white chick in a horror movie, feeling along in the dark, too dumb to turn on the lights. *Hell no. With the lights on, whatever's out there, at least you see him coming.*

Only not this time.

Because as Alayna turned from the long, lighted office corridor to the short dark hallway of work rooms, she ran full-tilt into The Freezer himself and let out a scream loud enough to shatter glass. It took a couple of seconds to shut up and realize she hadn't met the Boogeyman and that the surface she was up against wasn't anything more dangerous than a normal man's chest. Torso, really. He was pretty tall . . . and the said chest was hard as a rock. But he didn't have a knife. The most dangerous thing about him was a medium-bad case of b.o., but when you run face-first into a man's armpit, it had to be expected.

"Sorry," Alayna muttered, backing up. "I—"

"Pay attention to where you're going," he snapped.

Alayna grimaced. The collision was probably her fault, but there was no need for him to get nasty about it.

"I said I was sorry," she responded, managing to keep her tone below a 4 on the Bad Attitude scale.

"Don't waste time being sorry," Ice Man muttered. "Hassled" was written all over him, from the tousled tip of his head to the conspicuous lack of both jacket and tie. "Just *move*." Then he put his big, ham-fisted hands on her and shove-shifted her out of his path before barreling around the corner and up the hall toward his office, like that was the end of the matter.

Wrong.

Wrong Sister.

Wrong night.

Wrong move.

"Mr. Richards!"

He spun around again.

"Ms. Jackson I'll deal with you later. I've got a problem here of some magnitude, and I don't have—"

"A problem of some magnitude." Only a person who thought he was smart talked like that.

"This won't take a second—"

But he'd already turned away, resuming his break-neck pace up the hall.

When she caught him by the arm, a pair of clear

gray eyes snapped to her face. Joel was right: They were startling. Intense. So was the scowl on his face.

"Mr. Richards," Alayna began again, her own voice pretty hassled and pissed off in its own right as it climbed from 4 to 5 to 6 on that little B.A. scale. "Is there something wrong with your hearing?"

His eyebrow shot up, but his chilly voice stayed level and low.

"What?"

"Your *hearing*. Do your ears work?"

"What—"

"You walked away from me in the middle of a sentence just now. And I didn't want to jump to the conclusion you were just rude, so I had to ask. And now that I have, I think we can both reach a safe conclusion on *that* score."

"I don't have *time* for—"

"Look, I've heard about you. About your schedule, about your demands, and all that's fine with me. But let's just get one thing straight from jump, okay? I expect *respect*, get it? So come correct or I'll just go home right now."

His mouth opened and closed as fast as his eyes blinked. But when a full three seconds went by and he still hadn't said anything, Alayna leaned close and let her lecture finger fly.

"And keep your hands off me. I'll be in the War Room." Then she pivoted as sharp as the drum major of the Grambling Marching Band and took herself on down the hall.

White Boy training session number one: concluded.

The Freezer, Alayna thought, feeling him still standing there, staring after her in silent, stunned surprise. *Perfect name for an ice-cold jerk with a stick up his butt.*

By the time he got back to the War Room, Alayna had already read the papers he'd spread out on the monster worktable beside the remains of a large pizza, slick with cold, greasy cheese.

The top sheet was the summons requiring their client's presence in court, through his attorneys, tomorrow morning at 9 A.M. The next sheet was the pleading, filed in federal court, the parties' names identified in a little computer-generated block.

"Preliminary injunction," Alayna read, flipping to the twenty-page brief behind it, in which their opponents had outlined six different reasons why the court should stop their client from marketing a computer program used to track employee internet use. For all the legalese, the bottom line was pretty simple. Their brand-new client was being accused of stealing some other corporation's product. If these papers were to be believed, she and Richards faced the monumental task of digging some very bad guys out of some very deep shit.

"These people are in a *mess*," Alayna muttered just as Ice made his entrance.

He didn't say anything for the long minute it took him to give her the once-over with those eyes.

And now that she really took the time to look at him, she had to agree with Joel. Those gray peepers *were* his best feature . . . but that was an easy enough choice, considering. At this moment, anyway, the rest of him looked *beat down*. Something red and gloppy stained his wrinkled white dress shirt, which he wore with the shirttail hanging out and sloppy sleeves rolled above a pair of forearms dusted with dark brown hair. He was giving her a faceful of stubbly shadow that looked closer to ten o'clock than five, puffy gray circles under the startling slate eyes, and a pair of little round glasses that gave him an unbecoming "geeky smart boy" look. Still, with a shave, a little more sleep and something stylish to wear, he'd still be *white*, but *GQ* would probably give him a job. Provided he could dig down deep in that itty-bitty Grinch heart of his and find a cover boy smile.

Something stylish to wear... she sounded just like Martine.

And then all *that* was back. Not that it had gone far, anyway. The nasty little noose that had been spinning in the pit of Alayna's stomach since Martine and Jamal had announced themselves "engaged" tightened another twist.

Here I am, busting my butt with this jerk for the money to send this girl to school, and she'd rather spend her life cooking poultry for some skinny-scalped little brother. Lord, don't You ever make an even trade?

A fragment of the thought must have stuck to her face, because when she focused on him again, Ice Man was staring at her like he wanted to hear the rest of the story.

Then he sat down next to her, reached for his pizza and took a quick, wolfish bite like a man about to starve to death. That's what the red stuff was. Tomato sauce. Chewing, he waved a hand toward the pizza in impatient invitation, but Alayna shook her head. Just looking at that mess of cold fat made her churning stomach turn.

"No . . . thanks. Look, I've got . . . a personal matter . . . to sort out at home, so . . . can we just get started, okay? I read this and I think I already have some of the research you'll need for your brief in response, so why don't I just get started on that, Mr. Freeze—I mean, Mr. Richards."

A little smirk crimped his lips, the same I-got-you-one-up look Alayna would have given him if she'd caught him about to use the "N" word.

"No," he said simply and took another big mouthful of pizza. "Let's not do that."

"What?"

"What's the matter? Don't your ears work?" he asked, and she could tell he was enjoying himself at her expense. "I said no."

And then he just sat there chewing for what seemed like an eternity. Just as long and as rude as he pleased. Like he knew it would drive her absolutely nuts, and that was reason enough for doing it.

Alayna folded her lips and swore to herself that she'd sit there until the Archangel Gabriel's call before she'd say another damn word to this cheese-chomping fool.

"Our conversation in the hallway has me thinking," he said at last in a voice so crisp and soft it was like he didn't want to waste any more words or air than was absolutely necessary. "Since this is the beginning of our working relationship, I want some *ground rules*—"

He was interrupted by beepings. It took Alayna a

second to decipher them as the faint tone of a cell phone—her cell phone—announcing incoming.

She grabbed her purse.

"What?" she hissed into the phone.

"Since you ruined our dinner, Jamal's taking me down to Dairy Queen for dessert, that's what," Martine said, challenge resonating in every syllable.

"No. You stay home 'til I get back—"

"I'm not asking for permission, Alayna. I'm telling you. So you'll know. In case we're not back by the time you get here. So you won't be calling the police or chasing around the neighborhood like some kind of damn nut."

"Martine—"

"Have fun with your Ice Dude."

"Martine!"

But she was gone.

"Dammit," Alayna cursed, forgetting Ice Man, *again*. "That girl's gonna have me doing time for manslaughter, I swear."

"How old is she?"

"Seventeen."

He shrugged. "Old enough to make her own decisions."

"Her own *bad* decisions."

"Good . . . bad," Richards said indifferently. "Where was I? Yes, our working relationship—"

"Do you have any children, Mr. Richards?"

Those laser eyes centered on her as if she were a strange new species to be dissected for high school biology class.

"No," he answered at last.

"Then you don't know what you're talking about,"

Alayna snapped. "Martine is my sister, but I been taking care of her since she was eight years old, so she's
like my daughter. *You* may not care if she makes good
decisions or bad ones, but it matters a lot to *me*."

Another crimp of a smile tucked the corners of his
mouth.

"I see I've offended you again. Good."

"*What?*"

"No. I meant . . ." He wiped the sentence away
with a sweep of his hand. "Ms. Jackson, you seem to
be a rather . . . *prickly* woman, with an excess of confidence and no difficulty in speaking your mind.
Admirable qualities in measure," he continued, seem-
ingly unaffected by the deep scowl of dislike now
marring Alayna's face. "In short, let's say, I've heard
that you are the sort of woman who appreciates a
good contract."

Alayna threw an eyebrow toward the ceiling and a
lip toward the floor.

"What kind of a contract? My contract is with this
law firm. I don't need to make any kind of contract
with you."

"Yes, you do. To avoid anything like that little
episode with Greta Jennings."

Alayna jack-knifed out of her chair.

"What do *you* know about that? You didn't work
here then! You didn't even *know* her! She was an
incompetent—"

"Don't be so sensitive, Ms. Jackson. I'm sure she
was incompetent and I'm sure she didn't know what
she was doing, and that she was a 'stupid little white
girl who was costing her clients thousands'—yes, I
heard that story."

"Who?"

"This firm is like a small town. I hear everyone's business even when I don't care to. The point is, if you want the right to *read me* like you just did"—he put a faint emphasis on the slang, like he wanted to assure her he knew what it meant—"then I want a few rights of my own. And rule one is this: Don't ask me to abide by rules you ignore yourself."

The Freezer spoke softly, emotionlessly, completely rational and detached. The snake probably sounded like that when it talked Eve into the apple. Napalm. Quiet, chilly, napalm.

Alayna glared at him.

"And what is that supposed to mean?"

"It means, don't ask for *please, thank you, excuse me* and other conventions of polite society then turn around and wave your finger in my face. Either we're going to be polite or we're going to be ourselves. Period. You want to cuss me out, fine. Cuss away. I doubt I'll burst into tears and run to the managing partner like Greta did." He stared at her for just a second, and when he spoke again, there was a nasty little hiss in his voice. "Just don't ask me to cram my nature into your little box. Either we both 'keep it real' or no one does. You pick. I'll abide, either way."

When he said "keep it real," Alayna had to work some to suppress a smile. The expression sounded utterly ridiculous in his mouth, and yet he didn't seem to be attempting that pathetic simulation of black culture some white people felt obliged to perpetrate in the presence of their ethnic colleagues. He said it like he'd just said "it's raining," which made it even funnier in a way.

Alayna looked him over again. Just your average, everyday, tired-looking lawyer. Okay, a better-than-average-looking everyday lawyer.

"Well?" he grumbled. "Decide. I haven't got all night."

"How do I know you won't pull a Greta?"

"Will you accept my word?"

Alayna rolled her eyes.

That made Ice Man smile. Actually smile. And when he did, something warm and alive slipped out of him, skipped across the table and pushed the corners of Alayna's mouth up, too. Hard.

He grabbed a notepad and started scribbling.

"We, the undersigned, Benjamin J. Richards" he muttered, "and Alayna . . ."

"M."

"Alayna M. Jackson," he continued, writing quickly, "agree to abide by the following rules during the term of our working relationship. In consideration of our mutual promise, we both accept these rules unconditionally and abandon any recourse to authority flowing from this agreement—"

"Hold up," Alayna interrupted, showing him a traffic cop palm. "That last part. *'Abandoning recourse to authority.'* What if you're some kind of freak and I need to have you arrested?"

"The agreement is no good against illegalities. We're not talking about things that are otherwise against the law. Harrassment, battery, theft. You can't contract away your right to pursue justice for things like that. It won't hold up in court."

Alayna nodded, Martine and all the problems of home fading to the back of her mind.

"Okay then," she said, peering over his shoulder as the words appeared on the page. "Clause one: We both get to be ourselves and no one complains about it."

The Freezer wrote it down, then added one of his own.

"Clause two: We both stay out of the other's personal business. No comments, no questions. No exceptions."

Alayna nodded. Keeping folks out of her business was her second career.

"Fair enough," she agreed. "Clause three: Give me as much responsibility as I can handle."

Ice Man gave her another long, measuring look.

"I mean," Alayna murmured, feeling her ambition hanging out like the edge of a frilly slip, "as much as is appropriate."

There was no way to decipher his expression on that one; it was as flat and blank as the frozen tundra. But he wrote it down.

"Clause four: We call each other by our *names*. No nicknames."

Alayna blinked her surprise. Ice Man cared about what he was called behind his back? The Freezer had feelings?

"To anyone? I mean, suppose you're talking to your wife or something—"

"I'm not married, but I see where you're headed. You want an 'intimate conversation exception.'" He paused, tapping the pen against the paper thoughtfully. "But then we'd have to define who's an intimate and who's not."

"Blood relations?"

He shook his head. "How close are you to your

great-aunt in Chicago? Your cousin Marcus in Detroit? They're blood relations, but—"

"Okay, okay," Alayna muttered. "No need to lawyer it to death. Let's just go with a strict prohibition. No nicknames. No gossip."

The Freezer wrote it down while Alayna racked her brain.

"Clause five: We tell each other the truth, the whole truth and nothing but the truth."

Now it was his turn to blink.

"The truth about what?" he asked, sounding suddenly as guilty and nervous as a man with bodies buried in his basement.

"Our expectations of each other, what we think of the work, how we're measuring up," Alayna clarified. "I don't want you telling me I'm doing great on this matter to my face, and keeping a file on me behind my back."

"Suspicious, aren't you?"

"Call it suspicious if you want to. I call it taking care of myself."

"Well, provided it's limited to our working relationship, as agreed per clause two, the truth it is. So help me God," Richards added, his head rocking back and forth in a nod so definite it was like he was saying amen in his mind.

And then neither one of them could think of anything else.

"Subject to amendment," Richards muttered, signing his name in an illegible flourish and passing both the paper and pen to Alayna.

Alayna read it over carefully. It was all there, faithfully recorded in Richards' odd combination of print and script, letters bumping up against each other like ramshackle tenements in the poor section of town. Alayna added her own name in her even, orderly script. Two contracts regarding the same man and the same job in the same day. Must be some kind of record.

"I'll make a couple of copies," Richards said, rising.

"I'll go pull the injunction research files."

"You want coffee?"

"You making?"

He nodded solemnly. "My specialty. How do you take it?"

"Enough milk to make it my color," she said, stretching a hand toward him so he could get the shade straight. "One sugar."

"Thanks for the visual aid," he muttered, flicking an eye over a cinnamon brown arm. Then he held the door, letting her precede him out of the War Room like it was a formal ballroom and she were its belle. Then he stalked toward the firm's small kitchen.

Alayna hurried toward her cubicle, pulling open the metal filing cabinet with one hand and pounding on the phone's speed dial for Martine with the other.

No answer.

She tried the girl's cell phone but got that annoying little recording that meant the thing was turned off.

How long did it take to get a banana split?

She hoped they were talking. Just talking and not doing the other things an unsupervised teenaged boy and girl who were already talking at playing house might be doing at ten o'clock on a Thursday night.

But then, maybe The Freezer's interruption had been one of God's favorite kind of blessings: the kind that came in disguise. The kind of blessing that removed her from a volatile situation long enough to calm down and get her head on straight. The kind of blessing that would give her time to come up with a strategy. An argument. A plan. And that could only be a good thing.

And even more, it had given her the chance to see the man in a new light. He was capable, it seemed, of being . . . She didn't know what word to put there. Fair? Honest? Direct? Human? People had a way of getting a bum rap in this firm, she knew that from experience.

She heard his voice in the hall, gathered the research file and headed up the corridors toward the sound.

He was in his office, a cellular phone at his ear, prowling the cluttered space like a caged lion.

"Look . . . let's just . . . stop arguing . . . and . . . why don't you just go to sleep, okay? Go to sleep and I'll be there when you wake up in the morning, okay?"

The person on the other end clearly wasn't buying it.

"Because I have to work, that's why!" Richards snapped into the phone. "Look, Doug. Doug . . . calm down. Go to sleep. I'll be there in a few hours—" His voice softened to comforting, as though he were talking a small child out of an extra bedtime story and into sleep. "There . . . just . . . I love you, too . . . just go on to sleep . . ."

He turned and saw Alayna standing in his doorway listening avidly to every word.

Two seconds flat.

That was how long it took him to cross the room,

grab the door and slam it so hard that the sound echoed down the empty corridors. Alayna had to jump to avoid being reduced to little more than a scrap of flesh caught between door and jamb.

Sure. This assignment was going to work out great.

Chapter 4

If the slammed door left any doubts that clause two of their contract was now fully in effect, The Freezer removed them when he returned to the War Room.

He handed her a couple of sheets of paper that had been ripped hastily from a legal pad and muttered, "Facts." Then he collapsed into his chair and flipped open his laptop without so much as a second glance in her direction. Here, in all his glory, was the man Joel Mitchum had griped daily about: a rude, cold, nasty son of a bitch.

She read the papers. In a crimped, sloping scrawl across the top were the words "Notes Telephone Conversation w/Alan Graves, General Counsel, Cybex" and the day's date. The rest was a series of almost indecipherable jottings that would barely pass for sentences in an inner-city first grade. Some words were circled or underlined, but most were just unrecognizable. Alayna called the man sixteen different brands of sloppy in her head, sighed, and read the notes the best she could.

They just worked after that: Alayna pulling court case after court case, Richards hunched over the laptop, typing a brief in opposition to a motion for preliminary injunction (a.k.a. "Why My Client Isn't the Bad Guy") as fast as any secretary she'd ever seen. No wonder he couldn't keep one. He said not one word about what she'd overheard, or about nearly taking her nose off her face. He even forgot about the coffee.

Alayna called Martine a dozen times over the succeeding five hours. Nothing. No answer. Anywhere. It was like Martine and The Freezer were two little girls on a junior high school jealousy check. *Alayna thinks she's all that. Let's not speak to her. You don't answer the phone and I— Well, I won't even look at her if I don't have to.*

Whatever, Alayna told herself. As long as they both still needed her—and they both clearly did—they could play whatever little games they wanted and she'd still smell like flowers at the end of the day.

"The Georgia Trade Secrets statute was recently amended," she announced, breaking the silence after a particularly rewarding hour of research in the library.

He pulled his face out of the computer long enough for Alayna to read the words *"Brief in Opposition: Argument Three"* and stretched.

"So?"

Alayna sat down beside him, opening a heavy law book on her lap to the page she'd marked. "I found this case, a successful constitutional challenge to the last amendment in 1997. The language is different, but I wondered—"

"If the same kind of challenge might be made to the new law," he finished for her.

"I don't know if it will work, but it was an interesting argument and I thought you'd want to know."

For a moment his slate eyes held hers, then he grabbed the book and scanned the case quickly.

"You're smart, you know that?" he said when he was through.

"Of course I'm smart. What were you expecting— 'Lordy, Mr. Lawyer Man, I don't know nuthin' 'bout filin' no injunction'? Please," Alayna muttered and got up and left before the urge to bring that fat tome down on top of his skull became too overwhelming.

She glanced back at him from the War Room door. He was grinning something contagious and reading the case like it held an antidote.

The hands on the round, institutional-style clock on the wall above them were hiking toward 3 A.M. when Ice Man Richards printed his magnum opus and handed it to her.

"Proof. And check my citation form," he commanded, plopping into the empty seat beside her and rubbing his face wearily.

He was a good writer, one of the better ones at the firm, from what Alayna had seen. Clear and straightforward, making his points in logical progression without unnecessary verbiage or flourish, the language persuasive without begging for the reader to see his point. When, on page 13, she read, "Argument Four: The Trade Secrets Act As Amended Is Unconstitutional" she couldn't stop herself from murmuring,

"Yes!" and was a little surprised at how good it felt to see her idea laid out so well in black and white. That little nagging *go to law school, girl* voice started niggling the back of her brain, but she checked it with reminders of the weight of current obligations and kept reading.

She corrected a couple of typos, suggested a sentence be moved, crossed out an incorrect citation and prepared to hand it back to him . . . only to find him leaning toward her, reading her notes as she made them and typing them into the computer without reservation.

Then he printed again, tossed the sheets of paper onto the table without looking at them and pronounced, "We're done."

At four o'clock in the morning, not even Martine and her forsaking-college foolishness could have kept Alayna's eyes open a second longer. Or at least they wouldn't have if Martine had been *home* at four o'clock in the morning when Alayna reentered the old house on Magnolia Street. But the place was empty. And it was pretty damn clear from the dishes still in the sink and food left out on the kitchen counters that her sister hadn't bothered to come back after a double scoop at the local DQ.

Alayna surrendered exhaustion to pure, unadulterated fury, wishing she'd paid attention to the boy's last name. Then *his* parents could have gotten a wake-up call that, unless they were idiots, would have had them standing by her side in this living room waiting to kick his scrawny butt. But no such luck. At the time she'd shaken Jamal's hand, she hadn't expected to ever have need of his *first* name again, let alone his last.

So, after a short, breathless excursion into tearing the house apart looking for a clue to Martine's whereabouts, Alayna screwed the top off a bottle of the pink stuff and sat down—lights off—in the silence of the living room. *The better to catch you with, my dear,* she thought, tossing her head back for a swallow deep enough to earn the respect of corner winos all over Atlanta. But it was not to be: The antacid bottle was empty except for a chalky dribble that didn't even reach the back of her throat, let alone the stinging in the pit of her stomach. Muttering and cussing, Alayna yanked her tired self out of the chair and stalked down the hall to the bathroom.

She didn't even bother with the medicine cabinet, bending instead toward the cabinet beneath the sink. Here was the stockpile: a couple of twelve-rolls of t.p., soap in thick, banded eight-packs, antiperspirant and sanitary napkins in specially priced doubles, as yet unopened generic brands of aspirin, cough syrup and somewhere, she thought, extra antacid.

When a minute of visual tracking failed to locate it, she had no choice but to go in. She sank to her knees on the yellow fluff of the bathroom rug and leaned head first into the darkness of the cabinet's interior. Alayna started pulling out the contents, grabbing first at the big stash of toilet paper. But of course it was open, and before she could catch them, several fluffy two-ply rolls spilled out and knocked over three tall shampoo containers and several other smaller bottles of lotions and potions.

"Dammit," Alayna muttered, collapsing from her

knees to her butt. It was a job now. She'd have to reorganize the damn thing just to close the cabinet doors again. With a sigh, she gave the remains of the toilet paper package a tug.

At first she thought it was one of those double-sized relaxer kits. But something about the box didn't look right. She couldn't remember the last time she'd bought one of those anyway, preferring to pay a visit to one of the neighborhood salons, if there was any cash to spare. Alayna grabbed the cardboard rectangle for further inspection. If the contents were as old as she suspected they might be, it was time to introduce them to Mr. Trash Can.

It was a double-size, all right. Just not hair relaxer.

A pregnancy test.

Open.

With one testing wand missing.

A strong man could have punched her in the gut and left more air in her body than the implications of an open, used pregnancy test . . . here . . . in the bathroom cabinet Alayna shared with her baby sister. But of course, in the miraculous timing that is God's Universe, before she could process this latest development, she heard the *click* of the front door as it tumbled from lock to unlock.

Martine was home.

She was creeping across the living room when Alayna shut her down with the bright heat of the lights. Then she stopped dead, letting what Alayna supposed was Jamal's leather jacket slide from her shoulders to the floor without retrieving it. Her eyes widened when she saw the pregnancy kit in Alayna's hand, then narrowed in preparation. As her sister squared her shoulders in readiness, Alayna realized with a sudden, painful heaviness of heart that the ten years' difference between their ages had closed to nothing of any consequence. A young woman old enough for a pregnancy kit was an equal adversary, not a child.

"Which first?" Alayna began. "Where you've been . . . or this?" She held the little box toward her sister.

Martine rolled her eyes and hitched her mouth to the side like she tasted something nasty.

"I don't have to discuss this with you, Alayna. That's my business. Mine and Jamal's—"

"Are you pregnant, Martine?"

The smile that crept across her sister's lips said the devil made me do it as clearly as if Martine had spoken the words out loud. Instead, though, she said, "You'd hate that, wouldn't you? Me having a baby? You'd lose your rep for having done such a good job raising me. You'd have to settle for 'she done the best she could' and know it wasn't good enough every time those little old ladies whisper behind your back at church."

"Hey, don't worry about me. I'll live," Alayna snapped. "You're the one who'll be cutting yourself short. Because if there's a baby now—marriage or no marriage—college is gone for a long, long time. Do you know how hard it is for a black woman without an education to get anywhere in this world? I had to fight every step of the way for my degree. Fight for every credit hour, you hear me? Rushing from dead-end job number one to dead-end job number two, worrying about who was watching you, trying to study and keep food on the table—"

"Whatever."

A single word. A single, everyday word. Who would expect it to be as powerful as "Abracadabra." Full of enough magic and monstrosity to stir the Something Ugly that had been sleeping between them for a long time.

Two people who need each other always have one—an Ugly—bewitched by mutual agreement, a stone neither person turns, a door neither one opens for the common good. To turn, to open, doesn't just rock the relationship boat, it upends it. And for all either person knows, that boat might not ever, ever float again.

Now, their Ugly shook itself and stretched, blinked its eyes and scanned the short distance between them. The boat was listing dangerously to one side.

"What does *that* mean?" Alayna hissed.

"It means," Martine said, choosing to seize Ugly by the tail and pull, "I'm sick and tired of hearing about your suffering and your sacrifices! It means I'm sick of living up to your expectations! It means I'm sick of *you*, Alayna. You and your rules and your requirements and your uptight, old school attitudes about every damn thing. You're worse than Mama would have been—"

"Mama's *dead*."

The words fell from Alayna's lips as hard as a slap. Martine's head rocked her neck with their impact, and Ugly shifted the boat violently to the other side.

"She's dead," Alayna continued, unable to stop. "And I promised her on her *deathbed* I would take care of you! That I'd look after you—"

"Well, you're finished," Martine hissed. "*Over*. From now on, I look out for *myself*—"

"Really? Is that why you need to get married? Because you can look out for yourself? Or is this little boy supposed to look out for you now?"

"We gonna look out for each other."

Alayna sighed. Why was it always this way with Martine? Why was she always afire with some scarcely-thought-about idea? And why was Alayna always cast as the dirt to put it out? She pushed aside the image of herself for once cut loose of the tight bonds of maternal duty, acting foolish and wild and crazy enough to make Martine play the role of dirt just once.

"Tiney . . ." With effort, Alayna lowered her voice to gentle, hoping to coax Ugly back beneath his rock before he did any real damage. "If there's a baby, there's a baby. But you don't have to get married . . ." Martine shot her a look just short of violence and Alayna backtracked to, "All right, you want to marry this—Jamal, fine. But later, baby. Mama wanted you to go to *college*—"

"College, college, college!" Martine stepped to her, screaming fully in her face, breathing hard and heavy as her voice crested in tenor and volume. "I'm so sick of hearing you talk about college! Mama never went to college—"

"And she worked herself to death!"

"You went to college! I don't see things getting all that much better for you! All you do is work and worry, work and worry—"

"About you! For you—"

"See! Back to the recording!" Martine spat. "Alayna the martyr! Alayna who worked twelve jobs and marched through ten miles in the snow—"

"Stop it, Martine."

"Alayna the long-suffering older sister who went without—"

"I said stop it Martine!"

"Poor Alayna—"

"Stop it!"

"What about *me,* Alayna?" Martine wailed, and the anguish in her voice was like a pinch on that Ugly Thing's tail. "While you were off putting food on the table and clothes on my back, where was I? I was just a little kid, and you just left me alone here in the house where Mama died for hours and hours—"

"What else was I supposed to do! Let you starve? They left us nothing, Martine! Nothing but bills! Nothing but debt! What was I supposed to do? Where else was there for you to go? Who was there for you to go to—"

"I don't know!" Martine shouted. "I don't know!" And now the tears fell. Her thin chest heaved with great big sobs that mirrored great big hurts of the great big ugly unfairnesses life sometimes dealt. "But Jamal—Jamal loves me! Finally, someone loves me! You don't know what it's like . . . this feeling . . . Like you want to crawl up inside someone so you can see what they see, feel what they feel. I'm not going back to being all by myself in this world! I love him!"

Alayna sighed. "Martine, Tiney, listen to me. Can't nobody fill up what you think is missing inside you. Nobody but you. A baby . . . this boy—"

"You're just *jealous!* You're jealous because I have

someone and you got no one. Never had no one. Never gonna have no one. You always been alone and you're gonna stay that way, 'cause you don't know nothing about loving anyone! You're mad 'cause I'm gonna have some love in my life and you—you still alone!"

Ugly reared up, fangs bared, smelling meat. There was no controlling it now, no way known to either man or woman. It took a chunk out of the little boat as it struck.

"Well maybe I wouldn't be if I didn't have your ungrateful butt to take care of!" Alayna spat back, watching her sister's tears dry under the heat of the words. "You're not the only person here who didn't get what she wanted! I've been your mother for all intents and purposes since I was seventeen years old! You've put me through more crap than a little, and I'm tired of it, Martine! I'm tired of *you!*"

Martine studied her sister coldly for a moment.

"Well, you won't have to put up with it much longer," she said. "As soon as school's out, Jamal and I are going to get married! And you'll be free of my ungrateful butt for the rest of your days!"

Then she pushed past Alayna toward her room. For the second time in one night, a door slammed in Alayna's face, and she was shut up, put out, uptight and alone.

Her fingers had curled into tight fists, and her stomach throbbed like a neon sign. She sank into the armchair, her heart pounding and her thoughts whirling and Ugly coiled at her feet, its fangs stuck deep in bone. The wound was as sore as it was deep, and now that the heat of battle had passed, Alayna wished for nothing more than to undo it. Better to be aboard a leaking boat than to be cast upon the water, miles from dry land.

She sat there, her knees shaking and her mind racing, trying to compose her thoughts into some kind of prayer God might actually answer while night ticked through its final hours and the first light rose over the world outside. She might have closed her eyes for a minute, but not long. Because before she knew it, it was time to shower and be-suit herself and get back to the office. The Freezer would be waiting at seven.

Chapter 5

At seven in the morning there was no one at Hughes Weston and Moore but The Freezer, cool as a cucumber on ice, in a charcoal suit that Alayna might have noticed complemented his eyes—if she'd felt like paying him any attention whatsoever. This office might have her body, but her mind was still at Magnolia Street, tussling with Martine.

Benjamin "Freezer" Richards, Esq. watched as she compiled the appropriate attachments for the almighty brief, made the copies and handed them to him. He kept his lips pressed shut until she was almost done.

"I want you at the hearing," he said just as she finished packing him up for court. "I think you should meet Alan Graves, Cybex's general counsel."

Alayna sighed. "Mr. Richards . . ."

"We can take my car," he added, sounding almost like some brother trying to get into her panties with his fancy ride. Only since he didn't even *like* her, she was pretty sure that was just her imagination.

But it was a fancy ride. An elegant black box of a sedan without flash or adornment, the very simplicity of the buttery tan leather interior whispering *I got the power and I got the money.* No black man she knew would have picked it—it was a little too square—but it suited Ice Richards perfectly, Alayna decided, as she slid inside.

He settled into the driver's seat, traded a pair of slick-looking designer sunglasses for the little nerd glasses he usually wore and started the car, all without saying a word to her. They were pulling into the garage beneath the federal courthouse before he said abruptly, "You look tired."

"Well, I was up all night," she snapped, rolling her eyes at him like something out of *The Exorcist.*

He didn't say anything else, and, when she thought about it, if their positions had been reversed, she probably wouldn't have either. *Take that,* she thought, feeling angry with him all over again. *Your clause one ("gotta be real") and your clause five ("the whole truth") live and in person.*

As for clause two, neither one of them needed any reminders. That door was still slammed tight.

Alan Graves looked just like she would have expected the general counsel of a technology company to look: a lanky Bill Gates wannabe right down to his goofy glasses and ill-fitting blue suit. As the two men shook hands, Alayna couldn't help but notice how fit Freezer Boy was by comparison. His shoulders were nearly twice the width of Graves's, and his brown hair lay neatly around his ears. On second gander, even the glasses were cool. Probably cost as much as she made in a week.

Rich, arrogant and vain, she concluded, heaving the heavy case of documents out of the middle of the corridor where the Ice Man had dropped it when Graves had approached. Richards turned toward her just as she'd got a good enough hold on the case to drag it up the hall toward the men.

"My associate, Alayna Jackson."

"Hello," Alayna murmured, nearly dropping the box altogether. A moment later, she felt The Freezer's warm hand cover hers, prying the document case from her fingers. He lifted it like it was a hatbox and strode into the courtroom, talking an unprecedented blue streak about how "the court usually finds for the other side on motions like this." He kept talking, too, warning Graves not to get his hopes up since the real work would come in preparing for the full-blown hearing in about sixty days.

Graves yapped back something about his people preparing the documentation, and the two of them forgot all about her.

Rich, arrogant, vain . . .

And strong.

Alayna took a seat at the far end of the defense table and pulled the copies of the brief out of a red-brown expanding file. She glanced quickly at her watch: just enough time to file one with the clerk's office before the hearing started.

"Mr. Richards?"

He turned immediately, abandoning his sentence like a leaky-bottomed boat.

"Ms. Jackson?"

"I'm going to . . ." She waved the brief at him and nodded toward the doors.

"Yes. Thank you, Ms. Jackson."

Graves laughed like a loose donkey on a rerun of *Hee Haw*.

" 'Mr. Richards'? 'Ms. Jackson'? So formal! Hell, in our office the copy dude calls me Al! Didn't realize Hughes Weston and Moore was still in the Dark Ages! Or is it just you, Ben? You always were a stiff— even back in law school."

The Freezer looked annoyed but didn't say anything.

"Wouldn't you rather he called you Alayna? Such a pretty name."

"What's the 'copy dude's' name, Mr. Graves?" Alayna said, smiling the last of her fragile cool.

He took a quick couple of blinks before he spoke.

"Uh . . . Dwayne . . . I think . . . no. Darrell . . . I think. . . ."

"You think," Alayna repeated. The grin on her face felt gooey and sticky and made of something not entirely real.

Graves darted a querying glance at Ice Man that asked about two dozen questions topped with, What the hell . . . ? But Ice, Alayna was surprised to see, had his own cheesy smile going.

"Ms. Jackson takes no crap," he offered breezily, grinning like he had a secret. "A difficult quality, but one which is gaining my increasing admiration."

Increasing bullshit.

Thank God her own smile was already stuck there

so the eye-roll she gave him looked like cheerful banter and not like she wanted to knock his block off.

He must have gotten his rocks off on her annoyance, because the big, fat grin on The Freezer's handsome, humorless face widened a smidge more as Alayna made her way out the door.

The clerk's office was open, and there were already people in line. Most were there to submit the documents that moved the legal system, a few to obtain copies of similar papers already filed. They all had the look of veterans: lawyers and paralegals in suits, couriers with names like ASAP Legal and DocuDelivery emblazoned on their uniforms. Scattered among them were those who did not fall into either category, wearing the more casual clothing of non-legal civilians. Folks who had the bewildered expression of those hoping to get the 411 on how to get the legal system out of their lives forever.

Alayna took her place behind a tall, brown-skinned boy with a skinny haircut who wore khaki pants and a long-sleeved rugby-style shirt. Even if his clothes hadn't given him away, she'd have known this child had to be lost. He was too young for anything else.

Alayna tapped the kid lightly on the shoulder. "Need some help?"

He turned.

For a second they both stared at each other in wide-eyed surprise. Then he stumbled back a step like he was afraid she would smack him across the head with her copies of the 29-paged brief.

And the possibility *seriously* crossed her mind.

"Jamal! What are you doing here?"

"I . . . uh . . ."

"Is Martine with you?" Alayna craned her neck, canvassing the room.

"No-no, ma'am. I'm doing this myself."

He paused, hanging his little round head guiltily for just a second. Then he swallowed hard, Adam's apple bobbing like a buoy lost in his neck.

"I came to find out about a marriage license."

"Marriage license!"

Heads turned. Jamal backed up another step.

"I know you don't like it, ma'am, and I'm sorry 'bout that," he said, keeping his head and his voice low. "But this is the way it's gonna be. Martine's gonna be my wife in three weeks. I just need to know what we gotta do."

"I don't believe this. I don't *believe* this," Alayna muttered, shaking her head. "This is . . . this is . . ." Lunacy? Idiotic? Foolishness? Crazy? Alayna took a deep breath, then dove into him head first. "First of all, you are *not* marrying Martine in three weeks, so you don't need a marriage license. Second, you *both* need to go on and get college degrees before you think about drawing another *breath*. Third, I haven't even had the chance to discuss this properly with Martine, and, finally, you are not only in the wrong *line* you are in the wrong *court*. You want the state court. This is the *federal* courthouse. They don't do marriage licenses here—"

But Alayna had said too much. Jamal was already ducking out of the line and heading for the exit.

"I'm marrying Martine, Ms. Jackson, 'cause I love her and it's the right thing to do," he said quietly, his sneakers squishing on the floor tiles. "Peace."

Peace in heaven, boy. 'Cause if you marry Martine, trust me, you're in for Hell on Earth.

But even more troubling was the phrase "right thing to do." For the first time since Ugly had entered the picture, Alayna realized that Martine had never explained the pregnancy test or answered the baby question.

They'd had the "safe sex" talk a dozen times if they'd had it once, Alayna pushing every button Martine had so it would stick. The talk was short on morality and long on vanity: get AIDS and die ugly. Get pregnant, lose that cute little figure. Add a couple of pictures of Kaposi's syndrome and sweaty, hair-gone-back teenagers in hospital nighties grunting out ten-pounders and Martine had sworn herself grossed out enough to carry a condom everywhere she went.

But last night she was talking about crawling under this boy's skin and all kinds of stupid nonsense. Sounded like the birth control beatdown had gone in one ear and out the other. Like a sledgehammer of self-evident truth, the next thought cleaved what was left of Alayna's composure from her body in a single stroke.

If Martine was pregnant at seventeen, Alayna was pregnant at twenty-seven—without having had any of the fun of making the kid. She'd just get the pain of rearing both of them. For the next eighteen years.

A vision of herself at forty-five—a skinny shank of used-up old maid—flashed terrifying in her mind. And like a sudden bolt of jagged lightning, Alayna knew exactly what she'd have to do next.

That is, as soon as she could escape from the Ice Age.

* * *

Ice really *was* a good lawyer: calm and smooth-tongued, utterly unruffled by the judge's interruptions, coolly belittling to his opponent—a bushy-haired white woman with Buckwheat teeth and a fortyish figure—and forcefully persuasive in the presentation of his own point of view. All executed with a kind of Rico Suave charm, which, considering the whole image was made for TV bullshit, was truly exceptional. Too bad he couldn't translate even a teaspoon of it into his everyday interactions with regular human beings.

And they lost anyway, just like he'd said they would. The judge asked for briefs on the constitutional theory, set a hearing on the brief in forty-five days and a trial on the merits for sixty days hence, pounded the gavel and disappeared. Ice excused himself, heading over for a word with Bushy Hair Woman who, in spite of her boxy black suit, lifted eyes of definite attraction to Ice's face.

Alayna had forgotten all about Graves standing beside her until he started talking.

"That was great. But then I expected it to be," Graves said, speaking with an enthusiastic eagerness that generated far too much spit to stay comfortably in his mouth. He sprayed Alayna with a little, then wiped his mouth with his sleeve apologetically. "Richards is top notch. Always was. Even in law school. Probably because of his father and all. The kids who had lawyers in the family always had a leg up on the rest of us. And Richards' dad was a freaking federal *judge!* I mean, give me a break!"

This was an interesting piece of 411.

"So his parents are still living?"

Graves shook his head.

"Mother's been dead for years. Since Ben was a kid, I think. But old Judge Richards is still around. Retired from the bench a couple of years ago, I think. But I'm not sure. He could be hearing cases every day for all I know. So—" He stopped short as Ice strode back to them looking teed off. "What's *she* talking about?"

"Being a contentious asshole," Ice muttered, unaware that he was the proverbial pot calling the kettle black. Then Ice and Graves started going back and forth using "kill" verbs. How to *squash* the part of the judge's ruling prohibiting distribution, marketing and sale of one of the company's most popular software products. How to *slam* their adversaries in discovery. The best way to *massacre* the opposition's experts in deposition.

Then they gentled into their own housekeeping. When to schedule interviews with Cybex's software designers. How to retrace the development of their product from concept to test market. Who had the documents. On and on in low voices, while Alayna did the grunt work of restoring all their materials to the heavy black box.

"Still, it went better than I expected, Richards. That constitutional thing was a stroke of genius. The judge was intrigued."

"Ms. Jackson discovered it."

With barely a pause for breath, Graves transferred a mouthful of abundant, flowery praise to Alayna until she wished she had some cotton to stuff in his mouth. Richards seemed to be taking advantage of his moment of liberation to think about something else. Like he was the only one who needed some mental privacy, the dirty dog.

Finally, Graves said, "A working breakfast?" and rubbed his hands together eagerly.

Ice answered before she could frame an acceptable excuse.

"Excellent idea, Alan. I'm sure Ms. Jackson is starved." He hefted the document box with one hand and commandeered Alayna's arm with the other.

Alayna gave those pale fingers curled around the fabric of her dark blue suit the hard stare, then looked up at Ice like she was considering pressing charges.

The man just stared back, blank as a board.

Crap, she remembered with a flush of annoyance. She'd forgotten to put "hands off" in the contract.

Chapter 6

The fluorescent clock on the dashboard flashed 1:10 P.M. in bright green digits.

"Crap," Alayna muttered.

Ice Man certainly knew how to ruin a day. A hearing, brunch with the client, a trip out to Cybex's corporate headquarters, and the high point—a near-miss accident with a wayward bicycle courier. The Freezer had swerved sharply to miss the kid, sending Alayna careening toward the passenger door so hard even the seat belt couldn't stop her shoulder from making hard contact with the window. And Ice Man had thrown his arm across her chest like that had been extra protection. It had felt like getting felt up by a mechanical restraint.

"Okay?" he asked, all concerned. Like he thought she might sue him right out of his fancy ride and that expensive suit.

"Sure," Alayna muttered, rubbing her arm. At her feet, the contents of her purse rolled all over everywhere. "I *love* nearly getting killed. Try to do it every day."

He wrinkled his nose. "Are you always so sarcastic?"

"Are you always so reckless? And don't forget clause one, Richards. You get to be obnoxious and I get to be sarcastic."

He nodded grimly. "Gotta be *real*."

She couldn't tell if he was joking or what.

After another eternity of silence, he finally dropped her off in front of their office building, popping the passenger door open with the unceremonious announcement of "I have an appointment." Translation: Get out.

With pleasure. I've got an appointment of my own.

Alayna nearly said the words out loud, but that was asking for a clause two inquiry, and she no more wanted The Freezer in her business than he wanted her in his.

Not bothering to go up to the office, Alayna used her cell phone to check for messages, headed straight for the garage and hightailed it out of there.

Once the Jeep was rolling, she dialed the number for the next step on the ladder of her own private business.

"And why does your sister need to see the doctor?" the nurse asked. A routine enough question. It took every fiber of her being to respond, "A pregnancy test" in a voice so flat and emotionless The Freezer might have asked to borrow it.

When she arrived at home, Martine was sitting in the living room, eating a dish of raspberry ice cream and watching *All My Children*. On the couch beside her was Angel Wilkes, a bubbly chunk of teenaged girl with thick dark hair braided into a ponytail atop her head. On the floor sat Diamonique Borrells, a dark-skinned girl with a hint of blue Caribbean waters in her speech, and beside her, the infamous Nalexi Davis, a twiggy mite of a girl with a hairdo identical to Martine's in cut, but streaked with reddish highlights.

The Cabinet was in session.

They shushed the minute Alayna stepped into the room but not before Alayna heard, "This one sounds like a cute little place—"

"Girl, that's over in Techwood. Some serious 'hood, you know what I'm saying? Mmphff. I had a man as fine as Jamal, I wouldn't put him nowhere near those ho's."

The newspaper was spread out on the coffee table, open to the Classifieds. The red circles around several ads for cheap apartments in lousy sections of town made the newsprint look like a game of ring toss.

"You ain't nothing but a snob, Nalexi," Angel said, laughing.

"Maybe so, but I tell you one thing: Tiney don't know how to fight well enough to scrap with *those* girls. She *way* too Bougie for that—"

Then they saw Alayna, and the room got quiet enough for a challenging game of chess.

Every last one of them was supposed to be at school—graduation in a couple of weeks or not—as the guilty looks on their faces attested.

Martine didn't even try to play it. She squinted annoyance, rolled her eyes at her friends and shrugged as if to say, "So what?"

Alayna heard the high whistling steam of fury rise in her ears.

"I think you'd all better go home now," she said, meeting the eyes of the three visitors one by one, speaking to them in a silent language they were sure to understand. *Get out. NOW.*

Angel and Diamonique didn't have to hear the words aloud.

"Yes, ma'am," Angel muttered. She held her ice cream bowl uncertainly, hesitating between the mannerly route of taking it back to the kitchen or the expedience of leaving it on the living room table. Diamonique didn't even bother: the girl brushed past Alayna at the speed of light. Her brown hand was already on the doorknob.

Nalexi, on the other hand, hadn't so much as blinked.

"Y'all don't got to go because she say so," Martine muttered.

"Uh . . . I . . ." Angel made a quick decision and set the bowl on the table. "I . . . got to go anyway. 'Bye, Alayna."

Alayna nodded at her. A second later the screen door slammed, and Angel's and Diamonique's feet thudded down the front porch.

"Goodbye, Nalexi," Alayna said quietly, fixing the remaining girl with a look of steady dismissal.

Nalexi stood up, stretched casually so her skin-tight white micro-shorts could crawl out of the crack of her young butt, and blinked a sly wink at Martine. Then she sauntered to the door.

"Hey, Alayna?" she said at the door, swinging that asymmetrical bob of reddish black like a model. "Tiney's grown now. When you gonna get that?"

"Run your smart mouth in your own damn house, Nalexi, and stop disrespecting mine."

"I always heard it's Tine's house, too," the girl said slyly. "Or had you forgotten that?" Then she let herself out of the house, giving the slamming screen door the last word.

Alayna grabbed Martine by the arm and jerked her up and off the sofa before the girl could open her mouth.

"Get in the car."

Maybe it was the look on Alayna's face, or the steely band of fingers circling her forearm, but for once in her life, Martine clamped her lips together and did what she was told.

"It's finally happened," Martine said. "You've finally lost your damn mind."

She sat in one of the plain gray chairs, an old issue of *Vibe* open on her lap. A scrawny pop diva with too-light lipstick stared vacantly up from the page, looking for all the world like a crack head, rehab or not.

Wound too tight to sit, Alayna prowled the space, narrowly avoiding the little plastic cars left out for the younger children with every stalking step. After all, this *was* a pediatrician's office. For a few more days at least, Martine was a minor, and her pediatrician was her primary care provider.

The irony of seeing a pediatrician for a pregnancy test was almost too much for Alayna to stand.

On the drive to the doctor's office, Alayna had put the question to the girl over and over again, getting only eye rolls, sighs and petulant cross-armed silence in response.

Kinda like the girl in the magazine was shooting out now.

Alayna closed her eyes against the dull throb of a headache. Her whole body felt tight, as though she were straining to move an obstacle three times her size.

"Martine Jackson."

Alayna opened her eyes. A familiar nurse, a rotund Jamaican with lips pursed in a perpetual bad attitude, tapped her clipboard expectantly. She surveyed Alayna and Martine with round, black, disapproving eyes, as though she'd always expected the two of them would end up like this.

Martine rose, tossing the magazine back onto the low table in front of her. "I think I can pee into a cup by myself," she sniffed, pushing Alayna aside. She switched down the corridor after the nurse, her little round behind bouncing atop her long, camel brown legs as the door swung slowly closed behind them.

Alayna stared after her, a rush of troubles flooding back to her in a nasty black wave. The arguments they'd had when Martine had wanted to fly off to New York to pursue a modeling career, the night Martine had got arrested when she'd snuck out to go to some party Alayna had forbidden her to attend; the daily struggle to get Tiney to do her homework, to get Tiney to do her chores, to get Tiney what she wanted for Christmas, to get Tiney the latest haircut, to get Tiney . . .

To take care of Martine. Like she'd promised.

When she closed her eyes again, she could almost

hear Mama, whispering in that faint rattle of her dying breath.

Promise me . . . you'll take care of . . . your baby sister . . .

"I promise . . . I promise . . ." Alayna whispered, fighting back tears, fighting to shoulder it all, no matter how heavy. So that after all, her struggling Mama could go on to God in peace.

And promise me . . . you'll . . . take care . . .

But the woman's strength had failed her then, and she'd never finished. Alayna had held her hand, promising to take care of it . . . whatever it was.

Mama . . . please ask God . . . Mama. It's been hard enough being Martine's mama, I don't want to be her mama and her baby's mama, too. But she's my sister. My only family. You know I could never just let her—

"Ms. Jackson?"

Alayna looked up.

The same beady-eyed nurse was standing in the open corridor.

"De doctor tinks you should come, too, now."

Martine was sitting across from Dr. Gerson with tears streaming down her face.

"But it came up negative before, Alayna. I swear. I knew I was late, but the home kit . . ." Her voice trembled, cracked, broke, washing away defiant rebellion in the tears of a little girl.

"But Jamal—"

"I told him it was positive . . ." Martine's shoulders quivered with the force of her sobs. "I love him . . . and . . . I just wanted . . . You won't tell him that I lied . . . will you?"

"But *why*, Martine? Why did you *lie*?"

Tears or no, Martine's words were crisp with devastating female logic.

"How *else* was I gonna get him to do what I want?"

Chapter 7

The only luck of the day was pulling into the garage beneath the office at four o'clock in the afternoon and finding an empty parking space right at the elevator.

But the spot was right next to The Freezer's black automobile, and of course The Freezer was sitting right in the car like he was waiting for her.

Damn.

The window was down and he was reclining in the driver's seat. At first she thought he'd been on some kind of deliberate stakeout, trying to catch her slipping into the building after all this time. Then she noticed that his tie was a limp, loose noose around his neck and his sunglasses rested crookedly on his worn face. His chest rose and fell slowly. But what really gave him away was his mouth. Slack, half-open, silent, a ragged exhale bubbling through it every now and then.

Ice Man was asleep.

If this don't beat all, Alayna thought, marveling at him. What was he? Sick or something?

As automatically as she might have checked Martine's forehead for fever, she reached in through the window and lay her hand on the sleeping man's head. His skin was cool, and the wisps of dark brown hair beneath her fingers were dry. Not sick. Just bone tired. He stirred slightly at her touch, seeming to nestle under her hand for a moment, and Alayna felt something distantly related to compassion for him for a hot second. But the feeling was a relation so far removed that she forgot about it and gave his shoulder a rude shove instead.

"Wake up."

And with a jerk that sent his sunglasses skittering to the floor, Mr. Freeze was back among the conscious.

"What—" he croaked. "What is it? What happened?" He sprang up and out of the vehicle, urgency and confusion written all over his face.

She was halfway to the elevator before it occurred to her to ask him if he was all right.

"I'm just tired," he snapped. "I was up all night."

Alayna rolled her eyes.

"Fine, great, good," she muttered, pressing the button for the eleventh floor. "I could go for forty in the Jeep myself about now."

"In your Jeep? Don't you have a bed?"

"Don't you?"

Score one for the sisterhood, because the next words out of his mouth were a tight, "First, you're toeing clause two. Second, you think it's easy to stand before a judge like that? It's not. It's exhausting."

"Whatever," Alayna shrugged. "Look, when my

mother was dying we took care of her at home. I also went to school, had three part-time jobs, and did all the cooking and cleaning. And of course there was Martine. There's *always* been Martine. . . ." Just saying the girl's *name* made the air around her scarce. Grimacing, she plundered on. "Worse years of my life. You think arguing a motion is hard? Being a caregiver is worse. Raising a kid when you're a kid yourself is no picnic either. Family, I tell you what . . . give me work any day of the week." She lost the point for a moment, mired in memory up to her neck.

Ice pulled her out of it.

"Family," he repeated in the same worn-out exhale she had used, sounding like he was ready to testify his damn self. "Why did you tell me that?"

"Because," Alayna used the word to climb out of the clause two pit. "People have reasons for the stuff they do. And all I'm saying is, so you fell asleep . . . so what? I'm sticking to our deal: no questions, no gossip."

When she looked over at him, he was staring at her like she'd been the one caught sleeping in the parking lot.

Ada Mae Potter, the firm's ancient receptionist, looked up from her station as they entered.

"Alayna Jackson, you are in so much *trouble*," she began, but before she could elaborate, Weston came snorting out of his office. He stuck a plump white finger in Alayna's face.

"Where the hell have you been!" he screamed. "The hearing ended *hours* ago!"

"I'm sorry, sir, I had to—"

"The settlement just fell apart," Weston fumed, already pacing back toward his office. "The Williams matter goes to trial next week. And that means I needed *you*," he jerked his thumb at Alayna. "On this case. *Yesterday*." His eyes flipped to Richards. "Heard about the hearing, son," he grumbled. "I'm not worried. You'll pull it off at trial. You're a chip off the old block. Your father's son." He paused, getting himself together a little. "How is Judge Richards?"

"Fine, last I heard," Ice answered in a flat, mind-your-business-tone. "Golfing. Florida. Sends his regards."

"That's the life," Weston chuckled. "He's earned it."

The Freezer's head bobbed once in acknowledgement, then he strode past the managing partner toward his own office without so much as an *excuse me*.

Weston watched him, his expression darkening by the instant.

"That stuff's gonna cost you, Richards," he muttered, dislike pulsing and palpable on his face. "Come on, Alayna. Whole damn day wasted. Let's get to work."

"The whole ten thousand dollars."

"No."

"Seventy five hundred—"

"No."

"Then at least five—"

"No."

"I want my money, Alayna."

Alayna rubbed at her head, trying to remember the last time she'd felt this tired. Over thirty-six hours without sleep, enough work and stress to beat down a strong man, Weston yelling and screaming over the Williams matter—that on top of The Freezer and Cybex. Trial preparation could drag on for years, but Ice's was scheduled for a little less than two months from today.

And of course, Martine. There was always Martine.

"It's not your money. It's *my* money," she said, trying for strident and coming out only a cut above exhausted defeat.

"But you were saving it for me. Like in trust—"

"I was saving it for your college."

"So you telling me what's yours is yours? Even though I went without, too, so you could save it? I been getting the same amount of spending money since I was fifteen! I never have enough for the things the other girls got—"

"Don't look like you're hurting to me. When'd you get that perm, last week? Those shorts?"

"Alayna! These aren't even name brand!"

"Get out of my face with this crap, Martine," Alayna sighed. "I'm *tired,* you hear me? I was up all night, I gotta work all weekend. Let's talk about this later—"

"There is no later," Martine spat. "You heard the man. I'm *pregnant* and we getting married and we're gonna be a family. We're gonna do this right. Now, how you expect us to take care of this child without any money?" Martine paused to make a grab from her junk food fiesta: a couple of kinds of chips, sour cream, melted cheddar cheese, salsa and a great big bottle of caffeinated soda. Not exactly a meal for fetus-growing, but Martine jammed her hand deep into the bag of tortilla chips, then swirled a big square one with enough hot sauce to choke a few dozen Mexicans.

"Did you take those vitamins the doctor gave you?"

Martine sighed. "You ain't even listening. As usual."

"You're right, I'm not listening. 'Cause what you're saying doesn't make any sense. You're saying I'm-grown-stay-out-my-business in one breath and take-care-of-me-'cause-we-ain't-ready in the next." Alayna pulled herself out of her chair, and the room spun crazily for a dizzying bit of a second. "Wake me up when you decide."

Martine grabbed her hairbrush, stroked a hank of hair straight and smooth, then jammed a bobby pin as long as a steak knife flat against her head. The only curl in the business was the curl in her lip.

"You want to hear the truth, Alayna? I'll tell you some truth."

The pounding two-alarm headache of fatigue in the back of Alayna's brain ratcheted up to a full five.

"The truth is I'm pregnant, we're in love, he asked me to marry him and I'm going to. The truth is we need that money, and at least some of it is mine by rights anyway. The truth is you need to stop putting up all this resistance and give it to us so we can raise our child as we see fit."

"No! Not one red cent," Alayna muttered, as Ugly shifted and stirred again. "First of all, you might still go to school one day. Second, you should have thought about how you were gonna pay for the child before you opened your legs without any protection, Martine. And third, you never should have lied to that boy, so you're getting what you deserve, okay? Now, you so grown, you figure out a way to raise your baby and leave me alone, you hear me?"

Martine glared at her. "All right. But I'm gonna do what I'm gonna do, Alayna," she hissed, giving her neck an evil little snap. "I'm gonna do what's best for me, this baby and Jamal and I don't give a damn if you like it or not."

The doorbell chimed. Before Alayna's tired brain fully registered the sound, Martine swept a colorful do rag around her half-done head, leapt off the sofa and skittered toward the door.

Only it wasn't Jamal.

Standing on the other side of the screen door, live and in the flesh, was none other than Ice Man Freezer.

He was dressed casually in a pair of khakis, white polo shirt and sneakers. The cool sunglasses were pushed off his forehead, revealing those searching, steely grays.

"You must be Martine," he said. "Is your sister home? Oh—"

Alayna was at the screen door faster than a cat can pounce.

"What the *hell* are you doing here?"

It was impossible to tell what this man found so amusing, but he gave her his weird little smile at this greeting.

"Good evening, Alayna." He leaned against the door like he was striking a pose or something. "Are you . . . missing anything?"

"Missing anything?" Alayna pushed open the screen and stepped onto the porch. "Missing my privacy, for one thing. Why are you—"

"Something important, by any chance?"

"What are you talking about?"

He pulled something long and navy from his rear pocket and fanned himself with it like he was Blanche DuBois and the heat of the evening was unbearable to his sensitive constitution.

Alayna recognized it instantly. "My wallet!"

"Found it underneath the passenger seat. Must have fallen back there when your purse spilled. Surprised you hadn't missed it."

Her fingers twitched to open it, check to make sure everything that ought to be in it was still in it. But doing that right in the man's face was ignorant beyond ignorant and tacky beyond tacky. And he'd be gone in another minute anyway.

"Truth is, it's usually just about empty," she said, trying to sound casual. "I don't use credit cards, and I keep money in other places."

"Tucked into her bra like an old grandma." Martine muttered, ignoring the dark glance Alayna shot her.

Anyone else might have laughed or at least cracked a polite smile, but Ice acted like he hadn't heard anyone speak at all.

"I would have called, but I left your number at the office, and I've had enough of that place for one day. Tried information, but—"

"It's unlisted."

He nodded.

"But the address was on your driver's license and we were out for a ride anyway, so I—"

"We?"

She was dying to crane her neck toward that sleek black car and see who he had in there, but that would have been just about as obvious as obvious too, with him standing right in front of her like this. She prayed Martine would have the good sense to look, and she settled for checking his expression for a hint.

"Yeah. I have . . . someone . . . with me." Every word sounded ripped from him involuntarily.

"Well. It *is* Friday night."

He shook his head. "Nothing like that. Just a friend."

And his face told her there was no way the person in the car was just a friend.

"Well, thanks for bringing it. Going out of your way and everything. I would have noticed eventually—"

"And totally freaked out," came the comment from the peanut gallery on the other side of the screen.

"No problem," Ice said, ignoring both Martine and her commentary. In fact, he was already halfway down the steps and ready to bolt from the porch to the yard. "Get some rest, okay?"

"You too."

Alayna thought she saw a small, silver-blonde head in the passenger seat as the car pulled away, but between the setting sun and the dark-tinted glass of the car's windows, she couldn't be sure if it belonged to a male or a female.

"You know who he look like?" said the voice from the other side of the screen. "That movie star. The one that used to be on *ER*. You know the one?"

"Yeah," Alayna muttered, turning slowly from the porch to the house under Martine's heavy scrutiny.

"So?" her sister asked at last.

"So what?"

"What gives?"

"Nothing gives, Tine."

"That's not what it looked like to me."

"Oh, really? And what did it look like to you?"

Martine heaved a loud sigh. "You know something? You play one of them double standards. You been all up in my love life my entire *life,* but you don't tell me nothing—not one damn *word*—about what you got going! Maybe if you could just, you know, *talk* to me or something—"

"Talk to you about what I got going? With The Freezer? You must be hormonal, Martine."

" 'Get some rest,' " Martine mimicked, tossing in all the drama and syrup of a bad soap opera. " 'You too.' I didn't know you were into white boys."

"I'm not into white boys and you know it. Now I'm tired. I'm going to bed."

Chapter 8

Weston wasn't there when Alayna dragged her exhausted butt back to the office Saturday morning. But, of course, The Freezer was.

He was sitting in his office with those nerdy glasses on, a big box of donuts atop the papers cluttering the entire surface area of his desk. He held his microcassette recorder curled in his fist and had apparently just taken a long enough pause from dictation to stuff a monster filled with jelly and powdered sugar into his mouth.

"Hi," Alayna mumbled, feeling sick and tired and pissed off. "I'm just going to . . ." She jerked her head toward her office down the hall.

"The Williams matter."

She nodded.

He studied her for a minute, then stood up. "Donut?"

Alayna shook her head, remembering how, about an hour after she had tumbled face first onto her bed and sunk into an exhausted sleep, she'd been awakened by the sound of her name coming from the adjoining bathroom.

Maybe it had been the potato chips or the vitamins or the combination of the two, or maybe it had been the fact that her pregnancy had now made its way from Martine's brain to her body, but something had grabbed hold of the girl something fierce. Martine had spent the rest of the night with her head hanging over the toilet bowl, and her eyes wide with realization. She'd finally gotten it, had finally understood that what was happening was real and not just the script from a television program in which she'd been cast in a starring role. Her body really *was* changing. Her life really *would* be different. So that meant it was time for Martine to change, too. And just like a snap, she had.

Changed into a full-blown pregnant diva, that's what she had. Shed that wimpy diva-in-training stuff with the first roll of her guts.

"Call Jamal," she'd muttered.

"I am not calling that kid at midnight to tell him you're throwing up!"

"Then I'll call him." And Martine had heaved herself up, ashy as chalk, and marched for the phone. Sure enough, Jamal had shown up a little later, and Alayna couldn't help but feel sorry for him. If he really did marry her sister, this little brother wasn't going nowhere. Not for a long, long time.

Alayna had padded back to her own bedroom and let him assume the role of comforter-in-chief to Martine's petulant damsel, but the noises of retching and crying and comforting had kept her up half of yet another night. This morning, her head felt like a logging camp had taken up residence inside it.

Freezer was staring at her.

"What did you say?" Alayna muttered, realizing she'd gone deep *Twilight Zone* on him.

"Fresh coffee. In the kitchen."

"Oh. Thanks," she mumbled and left him to his work.

It was after three when she saw him again, hurrying through the library like the building was on fire.

"There you are," he said, stopping short when he saw her sitting alone at a table in a corner of the room, nearly buried under a pile of jury instructions.

She frowned what-do-you-want at him.

"Get your notes from our trip to Cybex and meet me in the lobby?"

Say what? Alayna looked back at Ice blankly.

"Notes. Lobby. Now." he repeated, pulling her chair away from the table with her still in it. "Come on."

Alayna balked, staring at him like Farmer Brown's intractable mule. "Why? What's the rush?"

"I'm hungry," he grumbled. "Weston's gone, you're not. Since you're on this assignment all week, I have to manage Cybex's work by myself on top of my regular cases. So bring your notes. You can help me make a plan while we eat." He quirked an eyebrow at her. "Well? You haven't had lunch, right?"

She would have lied had her stomach not picked that very moment to execute its betrayal.

"I'll take that grumbling noise as no," Ice replied.

"Get your notes. I need you, it's billable time and Weston's not here to complain about it, so we're going. Besides, you look like you could use a change of scenery. Now."

He was already striding out of the room when Alayna's fist found her hipbone and nestled itself in its favorite spot.

"Is there something wrong with you?"

He stopped still.

"Why?"

"You're being—"

"What?"

"Almost . . . nice," Alayna grimaced. "Driving over my wallet last night and . . . this. What happened to clause one?"

To her surprise, he pulled their contract from the pocket of his jeans and shook it out of its folds.

"Clause one: We both get to be ourselves," he read. "So. You've decided that restricts me to behaving like an asshole."

"That's pretty much your precedent," Alayna muttered.

"Well apparently there's more to me than you've assumed, isn't there?" he said in a snotty voice. "Come on. I'm hungry and I've only got a couple of hours."

"Why?"

He shook the sentence away.

"Never mind. Get your notes. Let's go."

After a short, silent walk among the bustling Saturday tourist traffic near Atlanta's famous Underground, they arrived at a diner with a city-goes-country atmosphere.

"We'll stay," The Freezer told a desperately slim young hostess who looked like she needed to eat some of the food the joint served. Before Alayna could protest, they were sitting in a romantic little corner booth.

Alayna closed her eyes, hearing Martine's "he likes you" repeating like a bad recording in her ear.

If you think something's gonna happen between me and this dude that's gonna solve all your problems, Tiney, you need college even more than I thought.

When she opened her eyes he was studying the menu like it was Shakespeare and he had a test in the morning.

A pasty-faced young waitress with too much eye makeup and hair dyed tangerine nearly broke her neck trying to get to them.

"How ya doin', Mr. R?" She gave him a big-toothed grin of what appeared to be genuine pleasure. "Where ya been?"

"Working." Ice gave her a reserved smile. "How's school?"

She gave him an eyeroll Martine would have been proud of. Come to think of it, for all the pencils and paint, she was probably about the same age.

"Boring," Tangerine Girl answered, snapping Alayna back to the present moment. "Cokes?"

He nodded.

She stared at Alayna a beat longer than was strictly necessary, and the smell of something burning told

Alayna Tangerine Girl's mind was working overtime checking out everything from the length of Alayna's hair to the cup size of her breasts. Skin color wasn't this chick's issue. She wanted to know one thing and one thing only. It was written on the lenses of her contact-blue eyes.

Even Ice Man had picked up the vibe.

"Alayna Jackson, Gina Dorsett. Gina Dorsett, Alayna Jackson. Ms. Jackson and I work together."

"Oh. Hiya," the girl said. She seemed satisfied with the answer, and without further contemplation released Alayna from her skeptical eye. She flashed another high-powered smile at Ice Man. "I'll be right back with your drinks."

"Thanks, Gina," he said and shut back down, turning toward the window. The rugged outline of his jaw made him look like he had been cut from stone.

Ice had women grinning up in his face everywhere he went. That bushy-haired lawyer back in the courtroom. This little waitron. When he'd first joined the firm, half the women in the office—and at least one man—had dropped their work to rhapsodize about how gorgeous he was. Of course, then they'd gotten to know him and the text of the rhapsodies had changed considerably. Still, it was funny that a man could attract so much female attention and seem to be so uninterested in it.

Curious as hell and sick of silence, Alayna put a toe on the line of clause two. She made her voice light and playful, like they were buddies from way back when. "She has a crush on you, you know."

"You do?" He presented her with a face stamped

with the dictionary definition of utter amazement and frowned.

"No, fool!" Alayna spat, forgetting herself and lapsing into friendly fire. "Open your ears! The waitress. She likes you."

"Oh." He shook his head. "No. Gina's a little young for me. Been encouraging her to finish getting her associate's degree. She's too smart to wait tables for the rest of her life."

"Tough job," Alayna agreed. "Hard on the wrists, the back, the legs. And people don't realize how difficult it is to deal with the public every day. But in a place like this, you probably get decent tips. Right in the heart of Hotlanta tourist heaven."

"Clearly you have firsthand experience."

"Name a job and I've done it."

That got Ice's attention.

"Seriously?"

"What do you think? I just stepped out of Vassar and into the law offices of Hughes Weston and Moore? Please. I've had just about every kind of blue or pink-collar job you can name: dishwasher, janitor, babysitter, lawn mower, housekeeper, courier, dog walker—"

"Dog walker?" A slight smile unfroze The Freezer's features, and genuine interest sparkled in his eyes.

"It's harder than it looks, believe me."

"How?"

"To make any money, you gotta walk more than one dog at a time. Which means you have to be able to manage multiple leashes, as well as the paces and habits of different dogs. And sometimes the dogs are more interested in . . . well . . . getting to *know* each other than in walking. If you know what I mean."

"I think I do." Another smile.

"The trick is knowing which breeds walk well together and which ones don't, and then being lucky enough to have clients with the right combinations."

"I can't imagine you in Piedmont Park with half a dozen dogs," he said.

"Neither could I when I got the job. I was scared to death of dogs!"

Ice Man was like a fun house: full of surprises, some nice, most not. But this time, when he let out a mellow chuckle that made his gray eyes dance like shooting stars, it *was* almost pleasant to be in his company. And she must have been tired, because a second later she was giggling with him, like they were a couple of little kids up past their bedtimes and down with a bad case of the sillies.

"You should do that more often," he said at last.

"What?"

"Laugh."

"Well, look who's talking. I'm not the one who wanders the halls with a scowl on his face."

"No. You're the one who wanders the halls with a chip on her shoulder."

Alayna's smile blew off her face faster than a hanky in a hurricane. Ice knew *exactly* how mad she was. That's why he was smiling that funny little white boy smile.

"Back to your usual insulting self, I see. Do me a favor, will you, Richards?" She leaned forward, enunciating each word carefully, just in case. "Just—stick—to—work."

"Just calling them like I see them," he answered, pretending not to notice that she'd stuck the menu up between them like a shield. "Since you're out of commission, I'm thinking of spending most of next week out at Cybex interviewing some of the key players. Where's your list? What was that guy's name? The chief software designer?"

And things went on like that, until his pager beeped.

Ice Man pulled one of the tiniest devices Alayna had ever seen from deep inside his pocket and frowned at the incoming number, then he was up and was outta there without a word.

Bam.

He whipped out his cell phone and slid out of the booth, the thing already pressed against his ear. As he disappeared around a corner, Gina approached with their food at last.

"Where's Mr. R.?" she asked, setting Alayna's salad on the table.

Alayna shrugged.

"Pager."

"Oh, God." Tangerine Girl's face turned a whiter shade of pale. "Hope it ain't like last time."

"Last time?"

"Yeah," the girl began, sliding the biggest, greasiest cheeseburger Alayna had ever seen and about six dozen potatoes' worth of French fries in front of Ice Man's place. Add those to the donuts, and no matter how fit he looked now, the man was clearly hoofing toward an extra forty pounds and his first heart attack at age forty.

"Breakfast. About a month, six weeks ago. I work

mornings most of the time, y'know. And he was sitting here reading his newspaper, waiting for his eggs—three, sunny side, with lots of Tabasco. Anyway the pager goes off. He grabs his cell phone, cancels the order, pays for his coffee and flies out of here like a bat out of hell. Scared me to death. Thought somebody had died or something!"

"What was wrong?"

"Dunno," she shrugged. "Saw him on the street a few days later and he said everything was okay. You don't know anything about it, do you?" The young waitress's face was furrowed with genuine concern.

"I don't know a thing about him, really," Alayna said slowly. The girl was right. Sounded like somebody was dying. Or at the very least seriously ill. But then, there could also be a dozen other explanations. Some stupid case out of control or a client having a panic attack. "I just started working with him a couple of days ago—Wait, here he comes."

The tight lines of frustration on his pale face told Alayna there was no way he was staying to eat. If there had been a door around to slam, he probably would have taken if off its hinges.

"I have to go," he told them, reaching into his pocket for his wallet and handing the young server a bill.

"Want me to put your burger in a to-go box?"

He shook his head. "No time."

"Maybe I should go, too. If it's the case, I might be able to help—" Alayna began.

"Clause two," he muttered, bid them both a chilly good-bye, and hurried out of the restaurant.

"What's clause two?" Gina asked when she recollected herself enough to stop mooning after him like a lovesick schoolgirl.

"A personal matter." Alayna responded, watching him book back toward the office at a walk so fast it might as well have renamed itself run and been done with it. "Wrap up the food. I'll take it back to the office. Maybe he'll eat it tomorrow or something."

A few minutes later, Tanger-Gina handed her two big Styrofoam boxes, and Ben Richards' problems were sitting on Alayna's plate beside Jamal Preston and Martine.

Chapter 9

Jamal was still there when she returned to the house Saturday evening. Sleeping on the couch, big socked feet resting on the bolster of the old sofa, Martine's little head nestling on his chest, the television blinking one of those funniest home video shows with the sound so low that it might as well have been off altogether.

Martine awoke with Alayna's entrance, rising to follow her toward the kitchen with sleepy eyes. Jamal snored on.

"You look like hell," Martine muttered, yawning. "You need to get some sleep. Your white boy might not mind how bony you're getting, but no decent black man wants no hag."

Then she disappeared up the hallway. Alayna heard the door to her room open, close, and then silence.

When Alayna returned to the living room, Jamal had stretched himself out a little more comfortably, but other than that, Martine's exit had changed nothing.

Alayna shook him.

"Jamal."

He stirred but didn't wake.

"Jamal!"

He blinked at her blearily.

"Go home. Your grandparents are probably worried."

It took a while for the words to register. When they did, his eyes circled the room for his Lady Love.

"Gone to bed."

He nodded.

"She's okay?"

"She's as okay as she ever was," Alayna muttered, ignoring the look the boy shot her. "You want me to drive you?"

"Naw. I be all right."

He unfolded himself, stretched, hesitated.

"Can I say something to you?"

Alayna let her head snap, crackle, pop a bit on her neck.

"Can I stop you?"

To her surprise he grinned a little.

"You and Tiney. You a lot alike. You both gotta play so tough."

Must be Psychology 101 Day. First a Vanilla Ice, now a Round-headed-Boy.

"Say what you want to say, Jamal."

He paused a second, stroking the little fuzz above his upper lip like some sober grown-up with years of life experience behind his next words. All he needed was a pipe and those little professorial patches on his jacket. And, of course, the jacket.

"I know you don't like me, Ms. Jackson. I know

you think we're too young, that we can't make this work." He paused. "But that's my baby she's carrying, you understand. *My* baby. I never knew my own father, but I know I gotta do better than he did. I gotta support that kid with my money and my time. Marrying its mother's a good start toward doing that."

He straightened himself a little after this declaration, as if the words had given him a running leap into manhood. Maybe they had. Compared to Martine, the boy was at least talking sense. Alayna had to give him his props . . . and a grudging grimace of respect.

"Marry her, then, Jamal. I'm not gonna try to stop you. Not anymore. But go on to college. Get yourself a good job so you can really provide for them. There's no reason both of you should abandon—"

But the round-headed man-boy wasn't having *that*, either.

"When and how we go to school's our decision," he said firmly. "Not yours, not my grandparents', not anyone's. Ours. It's time for you to back off, Ms. Jackson, before you get yourself hurt. I know you don't mean no harm, but you holding on too tight. If I have to, I'll make like Moses on you."

"What you gonna do, boy? Send a plague of locusts? Part the Red Sea?"

"I'm gonna make you let us go . . . ma'am."

He stared at her hard, and even when she gave him the one-more-word-and-I'm-gonna-slap-your-silly-face look, he stood his ground.

When she didn't hit him, he gathered himself together and made a pretty damn dignified exit, considering everything.

* * *

Between the sounds of Martine vomiting up her dinner in the adjacent bathroom, the nagging memory of things left undone at the office, and the image of Ice Man's ashen face as he'd leapt from the table, Alayna suffered nightmare after nightmare. With the first light of morning shining in the windows, she awoke, still exhausted, her heart thudding desperately in her chest and a sick feeling in her stomach. Martine was still throwing up in the bathroom next door.

"Alayna . . . ," Martine muttered thickly from the bathroom. "You up? I . . . really need . . . a glass of . . . water . . ."

Alayna rose. The floor from the bedroom to the kitchen and back was cold beneath her feet, as if the wood had been powdered with snow while she'd slept, but she filled the glass and headed back up the hall without complaint.

With the water delivered, sleep shattered and peace in dubious supply, there wasn't much else to do but get ready and get on. To work. Again. Martine had the bathroom on lockdown, so Alayna grabbed her things and dragged herself back up the cold hallway.

At the closed door to her mother's room, she paused, turned the handle and pushed inside.

Except for the growing light of dawn feinting at the night through the white curtains, the room was dark. Mama's big, old-fashioned four-poster bed sat high in the center of the room where it always had, a white cotton spread and an old-fashioned quilt scrunched against the smooth dark wood of the footboard. Across from the bed, the dresser loomed stoically in its usual place, still adorned with her mother's collection of family photographs. From a scarred old frame, Big Mama, Alayna's grandmother, frowned down at them a little disapprovingly. Mama had said Big Mama's expression meant she didn't see what the big deal was about either living or dying, having already done both herself many years ago. Like the newest branches sprung from the family tree, the pictures of Alayna and Martine sat in front of these elders, including two fancy studio portraits of them posed together: the last taken when Alayna was sixteen and Martine was about six. Alayna stood over her younger sister, her hand resting protectively on her shoulder, looking serious, while Martine blinked a coy smile into the camera.

The pictures of Mama and Daddy were pushed toward the back, more dim, almost hidden. Alayna let her eyes rove over the frames, knowing each one even in the darkened room. Nearest the wall in the heavy silver frame sat the wedding picture: Mama in her white dress, as short as a miniskirt, her hair a wild Donna Summer mane behind her, showing her spirit in every one of her white teeth, no hint of the trouble to come in the chestnut oval of her face. Daddy stood by her, dapper in his police uniform, an arm around her waist almost like the tether on a bright balloon, his smile more reserved but happy nonetheless. Alayna could never look at it without wondering if it all might have been different if a desperate convenience-store-robber's bullet hadn't taken Daddy away when Martine was just a baby.

But Daddy, too, was long gone, and it was all as it

was, right down to Mama's dying whispers floating in the stillness of this very room, audible with the heart's ear, if not the body's.

"Laynie, this is gonna be hard for you."

"We'll be okay, Mama."

"I know that, sweetie. You're a smart child. Always was. Not sure I did the right thing . . . lettin' that court 'clare you an adult, but if it'll help you an' 'Tiney stay together—"

She had paused then, her breath wheezing raggedly in the silent room.

"House . . ."

"We're behind, Mama, but I'm going to try to keep it, if I can—"

Mama's head moved in something that looked like a nod.

"Sister . . ."

"I'll look out for her, Mama," Alayna said, taking the feeble brown hand. *"I promise. Don't worry about Martine. I'll take such good care of her . . . it'll be like you're here with us. Promise."*

Mama drew a tight breath, grimacing with effort.

"School . . ."

"I'll finish, Mama. I'll finish high school, don't worry. And I want to go to college . . . maybe even law school . . ." Mama's chest lifted in a small sigh. *"I'll find a way, Mama. I will. And I'll make sure 'Tiney does her homework, just like I do now. I'll keep her out of trouble and I'll send her to college when the time comes—"*

Mama nodded, her eyes closing heavily.

"Come here . . . Alayna," she murmured with her last bit of voice.

Alayna leaned close enough to her mother's lips to feel the feathery kiss on her ear.

"*Forgive me . . . stealing your . . . childhood . . .*" Mama whispered, and for the first time Alayna saw that the glittering lights in the woman's eyes were tears.

"*Mama . . .*"

"*Say . . .*"

"*I forgive you, Mama,*" Alayna whispered, blinking hard to bury her own tears deeper inside.

"*And . . . don't . . . forget . . . to . . . take . . . care of . . .*"

She choked, eyes wide, and Alayna watched her strive against death for a breath they both knew would never come. Mama's hand clamped tight on Alayna's, holding her fast with the Reaper's terrible strength. In the agony of the end, Alayna said over and over again, "*Mama, I promise. I'll take care of it . . . all of it. I promise, I will. Whatever it was, I will . . .*" as the final tears of farewell streamed down her cheeks.

Yeah, the room was the same as it ever was: white curtains, washed twice a year, same big, high, old-fashioned four-poster bed with its white canopy, the old rocking chair beside the nightstand. The dresser. The photographs.

"Alayna!"

Martine. All high-pitched and urgent. Alayna sighed.

"What?"

"Where are you?"

"In here."

Martine presented a washed-out and sick-looking face that didn't stop her eyes from darting around the room, taking in its undisturbed sameness before settling on Alayna's flat bed hair, bare feet and night T.

"What is it?"

"Nothing . . . I just thought you were gone already."

"It's six o'clock on a Sunday morning."

"So? You work all the time." Martine's eyes narrowed. "I mean, you *are* working today, right?"

"Why? So you can invite Jamal over for the day?"

Martine frowned. "I'm gonna do what I'm gonna do, Alayna."

"Yeah." Alayna rounded on her sister like a tired Jackie Chan in the final rounds. "Can I ask you something? Just what did I do to you? What did I do that makes you so . . . so . . . evil all the time? What are you so mad about? Do you even know?"

Martine's wan face shot her hardness and spite. "What are *you* so mad about? Do *you* know?" Before Alayna could answer, Martine said, "You going to work or not?"

"In a couple of hours."

Martine nodded. She took another long, lingering glance at their mother's room, then turned on her heel and headed for the kitchen.

Suspicion should have planted Alayna's butt in the house when Nalexi and Diamonique showed up just as she was leaving, but she was just too tired to question them.

"Birthday presents," Nalexi said happily to the big boxes in their arms. "Tiney got lots of friends."

And just what was Martine expecting Alayna to do

this year? Write her name across the sky? Send her and Jamal to Disney World for their honeymoon? Adopt her unborn child? Or just write her a check for ten grand?

One thing was certain: the beautiful designer nine-piece luggage set Alayna had bought two months ago would be about as out of place as a white girl in the Delta Sigma Theta Step Show.

The Freezer didn't make an appearance, and Weston was in a lousy mood, clearly not wanting to be there any more than she did. Everything Alayna handed him was the wrong thing, every point she offered was the wrong point. Nothing could suit him. After he finally went home, leaving her with his request to review some obscure deposition references, Alayna almost wished for Ice Man. *Almost.*

She retreated to her office, sank into her chair and buried her face in her hands. An avalanche of thoughts shifted and swirled in her mind: Martine and Jamal, school tuition payments, marriage plans, birthday presents, juggling research files and deposition transcripts, trial exhibits . . .

This is stupid. Martine's not going to go to college. What's the point of this promotion now? I should just tell Boss Man I've changed my mind. Get out of the way of all this work at least. Pardon my French, God, but this is all fucked up. All . . .

A few tears slid out of her eyes and rolled down her face. Alayna batted them away, but another couple wanted in on the act, then a few more. Alayna reached for her purse, rummaging around in its black depth for a tissue, but there were none. The lack of tissue made more tears fall, hot and fast on her cheeks. Two more seconds of this and she'd be a one-woman sob-a-rama.

Inhaling, she pressed her lips tightly together to keep sobs inside, where they belonged, then exhaled slowly just as some damn fool with no life and a screwed-up sense of priority had the nerve to start knocking on her damn door. Without waiting for her response, the idiot outside turned the handle.

"Alayna?"

The disappearing Freezer Man stood on the threshold of her small office, a computer disk in his left hand. His eyes swept over her red eyes, nose, and the two big, fat tears presently making their course down either cheek.

"What are you doing here—" she snapped.

"I'm *always* here . . ." he snapped back. "Or at least it feels like it, anyway," he continued in a softer tone.

Alayna swallowed hard, slapping at her face. "Can't you wait for a person to say come in—"

"I—"

"What do you want?"

He paused a long time, like he was trying to figure out if he should do something or say something. Finally, he just stuck to the point.

"Message from Graves. He's having a truckload of documents delivered to us. Friday afternoon. Hopefully Weston's trial will be over by then. A lot of material. Might have to clear additional space—"

"Okay," Alayna muttered, looking away.

She expected him to leave then. After all, he'd delivered his message and gotten the added bonus of seeing her cry, which she expected he would probably enjoy. But he didn't leave. He just stood there, straight as a sentry guarding her gate, staring at her. To add insult to obnoxious injury, another tear slipped down her face.

"I'll handle the documents, Richards. Okay?"

"Okay."

But he didn't leave. Just stood there. Looking all . . . all *nice* . . . and *compassionate* . . . and *concerned*. He reached into a pocket, pulled out a wad of crumpled tissues and stretched them toward her.

"They're clean . . . unused . . . whatever," he stammered, all loose-tongued and idiotic. Gone was the silver-tongued advocate. This guy needed a dot-to-dot book just to finish a sentence. "Just been in my pocket since, well I'm not sure how long. But these jeans are clean. Well, I wore them yesterday, but—"

Alayna stood up and took the tissues from him, then dropped them directly into the trash. "Don't you have a pager to answer or something?"

That should have pissed him off, sent him spinning on his heels muttering about personal matters and looking for doors to slam, but no such luck. Instead he chuckled a little, like he was having a good time. And still didn't leave.

"Why are you so damn angry all the time?" he asked after a second's pause.

"Why are you so damn rude!" Alayna exploded. "You barge into my office, when . . . when . . . I'm obviously . . ."

"Upset."

"Yeah, upset! And since you're not gonna ask me what's wrong any more than I'm gonna ask you where you ran off to yesterday at the diner, why don't you just go on about your business and leave me alone!"

And she pushed him a little, enough to get his self out of her office, and this time she got her own, well-deserved door slam, right in his pale, tired, surprised-looking face.

Chew on that, Ice.

But he knocked again a second later.

"What?" Alayna screamed, ripping the door open.

"Feel better?"

"No!" she shouted and slammed the door again.

This time, he got the message and left, or stayed waiting out in the hallway until his stomach or his bladder or his pager or whatever got the better of him, because when Alayna opened the door hours later, he was gone.

Chapter 10

Some weeks have brakes and some have wings, and this one flew toward Friday like an arrow from the Unseen Archer's bow.

So busy she could barely keep on top of it all, Alayna found that her hours were a round of must dos: organize deposition summaries, collate trial exhibits, coordinate documents and testimony, research the last-minute issues Weston kept throwing at her as they approached Friday's trial date. Boss Man was working pretty damn hard, too, and it was obvious from his foul humor that he wasn't particularly happy about it. And no one else was going to be happy, either, or at least so it seemed. Trixie McCoy could barely get out from under Weston's hot breath long enough for a smoke break before he was screaming about something else that wasn't done, or something else he couldn't find, or someone else who needed to be contacted. Meanwhile, Boss Man went around muttering under his breath, "I shoulda rammed that settlement down that fool's gullet" and littering them both with tasks faster than they could finish the old ones.

Too bad Trailer Trixie didn't find Alayna worth speaking to. At least they'd have had company in their mutual misery.

"Tyrant," Trixie hissed after one particularly long Weston tirade. "I only got two hands and he knows it."

"That's all you need," Alayna quipped before she'd thought about who she was quipping to.

Trixie quirked a straggly brow at her.

"One to smack each of his heads."

There was a long blank second before the woman smiled, then made a hoarse chuckling sound that sounded like the original motor of a hard-driven Model T.

"Yeah," she chortled huskily, flopping a bony wrist through the cuff of the ubiquitous red sweater she wore around the office. "Pow! Most of these guys could do with a good smack. Your Freezer 'specially, huh?"

Especially, Alayna was about to add, but since Weston had reappeared with something else, she settled for a mental agreement and the quick smirk Trailer Trixie flashed her before diving back into her work.

And as for The Freezer, she hadn't seen him since the PLTE—Pocket Lint Tissue Encounter. As good as his word, he'd headed for Cybex to conduct some interviews and no one had seen him since. He made sure Alayna didn't get lonesome for him by leaving rambling voice messages: "Alayna, it looks like we'll have to track down a few former employees who might have leaked confidential information, more later"; "Alayna, add restrictive covenants to your research list, more later"; "Alayna, this woman named Denise Stinson is arranging the delivery of the relevant documentation on Friday afternoon. Leave a message on my dial if that's still good"; "Alayna, Graves says hello."

He'd sounded like he was laughing a little on that last one, and she smiled herself. Richards and Graves were one of the more unlikely pairs she'd seen in a while: Graves goofy-talking a mile a minute, Richards staring at him like he was trying to figure out where they'd hid the man's Off switch.

And on the home front, Jamal was AWOL, too. Alayna hadn't seen hide nor hair of him, but the Cabinet was in full effect. With graduation a week from Sunday, high school was all but out for the seniors who would march the stage, except for a few widely spaced rehearsals.

Angel, Diamonique and Nalexi congregated at the house on Magnolia Street so frequently that Alayna strongly considered charging them rent. They answered the phone when she called to check in or were sprawled across the living room when Alayna dropped by to shower and change before a long, late night of work. Several times they'd arrived suspiciously early in the morning, dressed in sloppy shorts and unbecoming baggy T-shirts totally contrary to their fashionista reps. Queries got her nothing but wide innocent eyes and big, toothy denials. Alayna got the feeling that she'd interrupted something as big and significant as preparations for thermonuclear war, but there was no hard evidence of it. And no hard evidence meant her case was circumstantial at best—and Martine had Johnny Cochran-ed circumstantial cases long ago. The girls just sat with Martine in the living room, like they always did, watching TV or listening to their Alisha Keyes CDs or cooking or talking. The house looked as it always did for the most part, though Alayna noticed that some of the furniture here and there had been rearranged. Usually for the better, she had to grudgingly admit.

"My friends are helping me with a little spring cleaning," Martine said coyly on Alayna's query.

"Just stay out of my room," Alayna answered, and that was the end of it.

It was a real production, getting to court on Friday morning with half a dozen witnesses, forty-eight trial exhibits, several document cases full of books and papers. Alayna loaded up two hand trucks and rolled most of the stuff out that way, careful not to get any stray cardboard fibers on her crisp, gray, gotta-see-the-judge suit. The way Weston struggled to help her unload it all made her think of Ice. How he'd lifted a heavier box so easily when they'd been together just a week before.

Ice was like a different species compared to this flabby, floppy specimen, sweating and straining and wheezing just to push a stack of boxes on a rolling cart. Of course, he was fit now, but with his eating habits, Ice was a Weston in the making. The image of Ice gone all doughy in the middle made a sudden smile curve Alayna's lips.

"What?" Weston snapped, still mad as a wet cat in hell.

"Opposing counsel," Alayna murmured, dropping the smile immediately and nodding toward the hallway behind him. "On his way, at nine o'clock. Not too late to ram the settlement down his throat. Sir."

In the split second Weston stared at her before he spun a military half-turn and jackbooted it up the hall, an absolutely wicked gleam of mischief sparked his mud brown eyes that could mean only one thing: He intended to do the opposing lawyer some serious damage.

Weston *did* ram a last-minute settlement down the other lawyer's throat, and that was why, at a little before noon on Friday, Alayna was free to stop by 555 Magnolia.

Unexpectedly.

The settlement had provided the time. As to the reason, Alayna had no idea what had possessed her when she'd left the courthouse and made a beeline for the house. Had she and Martine been on better terms, it might have been to hear a little bit about the graduation rehearsals or discuss graduation parties and weekend plans. But they weren't on those kind of terms these days. Not by a long shot.

A late-model Honda station wagon of a forest greeny color was sitting in the driveway. Definitely not a teenager's dream car, but not one Alayna recognized either. Somebody's mother—or grandmother—drove that car, but a teenager desperate to go would borrow anything in a pinch.

The passenger side door hung open as wide as Alayna's mouth as she peered inside.

The little vehicle was filled to the gills with trash bags stuffed with clothing, books, CDs and DVDs tossed aimlessly and hurriedly inside. Someone was making a quick, if not exactly organized, getaway.

Alayna's heart skipped like Jane and Dick in one of those old-time readers: see Jane skip, see Jane run. See Jane kick her little sister's ass if she's even thinking about running out of town with some round-headed boy in his grammy's station wagon two seconds after she accepts her high school diploma.

"Martine!" she yelled, charging up the steps and into the house. "Martine!"

The living room was a mess of video games and crates of athletic gear and other young man stuff mixed with a few tightly taped boxes labeled "Mama's Stuff" pushed toward the door.

Yelling, Alayna headed up the hallway toward Martine's bedroom, stopping short outside her mother's room.

Or at least what had been her mother's room.

Now, fresh curtains sprinkled with a light pattern of greenish bamboo shoots hung from the windows, contrasting with walls painted a masculine avocado with fresh white trim around the door and window frames. The big bed, almost unrecognizable with half a dozen bright throw pillows and a duvet matching the shade of the walls, had swapped places with the old dresser, whose drawers hung wide and ready and empty, the photographs that had topped it for so many years . . . gone. Even Big Mama's rocker wasn't sacred. No longer squatting dourly at bedside, its new port was beside a charmingly impractical-looking white bassinet decorated with a shiny yellow bow.

"What do you think?" Martine appeared, her arms defining *satisfaction* in a fold across her chest. "My girls helped with it."

"Where's . . . where's . . ."

Martine shrugged toward the front of the house. "Some of it's in boxes, some of it we gonna take to the Goodwill later. Some of it, I threw out."

"The pictures . . . ," Alayna gasped, barely able to finish her sentences.

"Oh, those. Your room. You the one attached to all that old stuff. Jamal and I are working on some memories of our own."

"Jamal?"

Like Aladdin's genie, Jamal appeared behind his fiancée.

"Well," Martine said slowly, an unholy alliance of mischief and determination tangoing on her face. "Seeing how neither you or Jamal's grandparents will help us out with any cash, we looked at our money, and we looked at our jobs and we made a decision. We can't afford to stay on our own just yet. And it wouldn't make no sense for me to try and move into Jamal's little room at the Prestons' house. Especially when we got this big old empty bedroom in *this* house. This house Mama left to *both* of us."

Alayna gripped the four-poster bed to keep from falling flat out on the floor.

"So," Martine finished triumphantly. "Jamal and I gonna move in here 'til we get ourselves straight.

Shouldn't take more than a year. We gonna fix up my room as the nursery for the baby and make ourselves a little family. Me, Jamal and our baby. And you, of course."

Chapter 11

Alayna didn't remember how she got back to the office. When she finally graced the corridors of Hughes Weston and Moore, still shaking with anger, exhaustion and another emotion too complicated to even name, Alayna wanted nothing more than to slink back to the silence of her tiny little cubicle and put her head down. But a woman with a headache the size of Texas, a week's sleep deficit and a doozy of a personal problem couldn't catch a break. She stepped out of the elevator and into office chaos.

The documents.

The reception area was lined with piles of boxes four feet high, almost blocking her view of the receptionist. As Ada Mae dealt with one caller, another line bleated impatiently from the panel at her elbow. Two men in brown uniforms bleeding Business Archives, Inc. in red letters wheeled a dolly up the corridor toward her. One of them, a wiry man of indeterminate age, approached the reception desk and leaned against it, casually dangling his dirt-stained hands over the counter.

"They ain't all gonna fit in there," he drawled.

"Alayna!" Ada Mae called, waving a liver-spotted hand toward the men urgently. "I'll transfer you," she said into the telephone, punched a few keys and deftly answered the still-ringing phone.

"Ain't no more room back there," Dirty Hands said to Alayna, then turned around and hoisted a few more boxes onto the empty hand truck, treating her to a prime view of the sweat stain on the back of his uniform.

"Oh, yes. She's standing right here, Ms. Stinson. I'll put you through."

Ada Mae glanced at Alayna.

"Where have you been? I didn't see you slip out, and I have no idea where *he* could be." She rolled her eyes significantly before continuing in her fluttery, old-lady voice. "These men are delivering documentation Ben Richards requested from Cybex. This woman Denise Stinson has called for you three times. She's on the phone again now. I'll put the call through over there." She pointed to a phone in the waiting area.

"No," Alayna shook her head. "I'll be in the War Room. Give me two minutes." She turned to the deliverymen. "Come on, guys. You're with me."

She jogged up the halls, pushing down the rising nausea tumbling her stomach as she stepped into the stuffy War Room. Immediately she understood what Dirty Hands was talking about. There was no way all that stuff would fit in this small space and leave any room to work.

"Get it in here the best you can," she told the

workmen. "I'll figure it out later." The telephone rang, and Alayna bent to answer it.

The room swayed and blackened like an amusement park ride, but she grabbed the phone with one hand and the back of a chair with the other and made it all still again. She took a deep breath, hoping her head would clear.

"Ms. Stinson, Alayna Jackson. I'm so sorry to have missed your earlier calls," she said, forcing her voice into a tone of bright encouragement.

"Well, I'm glad to finally get to talk to you!" a cheerful voice answered. "Are the guys from Business Archives there yet?"

"Ma'am!"

Alayna turned. This time her stomach *and* the room rotated like a merry-go-round on fast-forward. Alayna pressed her eyes shut.

"Ms. Jackson? Are you still there?" Denise Stinson sounded a million miles away.

"Yes."

"I guess they're there, but I need to tell you—"

"It ain't gonna all fit in here, lady. There's more on the truck!"

"There's another room just down the hall—" Alayna heard herself murmur, but the words sounded submerged in deep, black ink.

"Ms. Jackson, I think most of what you need is—"

"Where?"

"Around the corner. I'll show you just as soon as I—" She turned again, accompanied by another gut-wrenching head-spinning blinder of pain and weakness. This time she reached out, clawing air, looking for anything to lean against . . . anything . . .

"We've clustered the good stuff in the boxes labeled—"

And damn if the phone didn't drop from her fingers like a hot potato and the room gave up its half-assed efforts and decided to whirl like a kid's kaleidoscope, multicolored, gray, then black. And damn if the next wave of weakness didn't blur the faces and figures around her and hush the sounds of them down to the pulse of her own blood rushing in her ears as loud as surf on the beach.

"Alayna!"

His voice came from somewhere too far in the distance for easy acknowledgement, and as she filled her lungs to shout out, she felt herself falling. Firm fingers dug into the flesh of her arms in restraint.

What was it with Ice and his damn *hands?*

"Let me go—" she muttered, furious with him, these stupid documents, Martine, Mama for dying, these loud delivery men, and the whole damn situation.

"You're going to pass out."

"I am *not*—" she insisted, pulling hard away from him, breaking his grasp to spin like an electronic top toward the edge of the worktable. "Mind your damn bus—"

Her knees buckled.

She heard the sharp *thwack* of her forehead as it collided with the sharp rim of the table and felt an excruciating stab of bright, hot pain. Then the floor leapt up to catch her, and a big, blank, black deep claimed her mind.

Alayna knew she was probably in an ambulance because of the siren's shriek and the rocking jostle, even though her head ached like fire. The simple effort of blinking was almost too painful to repeat, and thinking was out of the question. Someone muttered, "She's coming around," and she caught a glimpse of a very young-looking white man in a blue uniform. Another man sat beside him on a little shelf of a seat, her blue handbag tucked ridiculously under his arm.

Ice.

He looked like a drag queen with a poor sense of accessory. And as usual he was a mess, a crimson patch of what looked like drying blood marring the whiteness of his shirt.

"What . . . happened to you?" she croaked.

"Shut up and lie still," was his snappish response as the young paramedic pushed her shoulders back onto the gurney and started shining a light in her face.

Her head hurt too much to argue, so she closed her eyes again to make Ice Man and his whole scene disappear.

"Uh-huh. I see. Go on."

The familiar voice grated like a pumice stone on tender skin. Alayna opened her eyes.

It didn't take more than a second to realize she was in a hospital room. She knew the smell all too well: industrial strength cleanser striving to overpower the smells of human illness and decay.

"Look, given the circumstances, I think it would be best if you stayed put. Well, tomorrow, I guess. It's a nasty lump, size of a golf ball. No. She needs rest and quiet, not . . ."

She tried to sit up, but a pain ricocheted through her head like a bullet in a bad western. She touched a bandage so thick that it was obvious somebody had gotten jiggy with the gauze, but still, she could feel the lump swelling underneath.

"I've heard enough," Ice hissed into his cell phone, sounding far from cool. "Yes, stay there. For the good of all, apparently."

He snapped the thing shut, exhaled loud irritation and turned around.

"Good, you're awake," he said, but his tone said, *What the hell did you do* this *for?*

When he approached the bed, she saw the dark stain of blood ruining his shirt at about the place her head might have rested if he'd tried to help after she and the table had had their little encounter. It was a funny smeary half-circle, almost like he'd deliberately pressed himself against the wound, trying to staunch the blood's flow. From the looks of it, there'd been a lot of blood to staunch.

She reached for the gauze again, but Ice snatched her fingers.

"Leave it alone," he muttered, sounding like a worried father. He kept his own long warm fingers clamped over hers as he sat down on the bed, taking up more space than his share.

She thought he wanted to say something, but no. Just fixed those gray marbles on her face and stared at her, which was nothing new. Only now he'd added a new-piece-of-the-puzzle expression to his limited repertoire. Apparently, he was giving it a test drive.

Hard as it was, Alayna held her tongue. He could

look at her funny for a little while, if she'd bled *that* much on the man.

"You want to talk about it?" he asked after a while.

"About what?" Alayna said, sounding like something had crawled down her throat and died.

Ice let go of her long enough to pour a cup of water from a little pink pitcher on the table, making no comment about either the way her hands shook as he gave it to her or the fact that she held on to the cup with both hands like a small child. He waited until she'd sipped to her heart's content before continuing with, "About what happened."

"Nothing happened. I tripped," she lied, going for forceful and coming up faker. "Don't worry about me. My sister will be here soon enough, and you can get back to whatever you have to get back to."

At the reference to Martine, Ice got up and showed her his back.

"Your sister and I decided it would be best if she let you rest tonight," he said at last. "You'll see her in the morning."

She tried to imagine it: the Freezer and the Furnace. In a conversation. A World Wrestling Federation match was more likely. Still, she wasn't prepared for the feeling of relief that swept over her at the idea of not having to look at Martine for a little while longer. A heavy sigh lifted her chest, and her eyelids dropped over her eyes in gratitude.

It was a struggle to open them again, but when she did, Ice was smiling a slight, secret smile.

"What?"

"A concussion," he said as if someone had conferred an M.D. on him since she'd blinked. He glanced at his watch. "I've got to go. I'll tell the nurse you're awake on the way out."

He grabbed his suit jacket and squeezed her fingers again.

"I'll be back later. Okay?"

"Okay," Alayna heard herself murmur like some kind of feeble little flower, dependent on the sunshine of his smile. But if he heard it, nothing showed in his expression. When she blinked again, he was gone.

An ancient-looking doctor came in, shined a light into both her eyes, asked her a few very dumb questions ("What's your name?" "What day is it?" "Who's the president?") that hurt her head more than the answers were worth. He made a bad joke about tables winning matches with flesh every time, and when Alayna looked at him like he'd bought his degree at a discount store, he muttered about keeping her for observation and that her boyfriend could take her home tomorrow.

Before she could ask him who the hell he was talking about, he was gone, too, and she was drifting back into sleep.

In her dreams, Mama walked right up to her and wagged an accusatory finger in Alayna's face, over and over again until Alayna woke, nearly crying in frustration and someone was shining that damn light in her eyes again. When she blinked again, Ice was there, sitting quietly in the bedside chair, wearing sweats and tennis shoes and reading what looked like a computer specifications manual.

"Hi," he said. "How's your head?"

"Go . . . home . . ." was all she remembered saying before closing her eyes again for another round of Mama's finger swishing in her face like a metronome.

"I tried . . . Mama . . ." she murmured.

"I know," someone answered, and a warm hand stroked her cheek. "Go to sleep now."

It was what she'd been waiting for. Permission.

When she opened her eyes this time, the room was filled with bright morning light and the bedside chair was so empty that she would have doubted it had ever been occupied, except for the little vase of sunny flowers on the nightstand beside her.

I've heard of knocking yourself out for something, read the card, *but this is ridiculous. BJR*

The most disgusting feeling in the world is taking a shower, then slipping on yesterday's dirty underwear and court suit. Twice she tried to call Martine to ask for a bag of clean clothes, but there was no answer at home. Maybe she was already on her way.

Feeling funky, Alayna dragged herself out of the bathroom and sank into the chair to wait.

The second most disgusting feeling in the world is sitting in a hospital room, abandoned by your kin. When the sun climbed toward noon and still Martine hadn't presented herself, Alayna had to keep her throat tight and her eyes wide to stop herself from dissolving into a hiccupy display of hot, salty tears that would have embarrassed the average two-year-old. The hospital people—everyone from the doctor to the nurse to the nursing assistant who was ready to change the bed—kept asking who was coming for her until she was so damn irritated that she almost didn't care if anyone was.

Then, looking ridiculously healthy and handsome and cool and calm, the Iceman cameth.

"Ready?" He even smiled a little when he said it.

"I've been ready," Alayna snapped. "Is Martine with you?"

"No," he said, and, reading the look on her face, he hurried to add, "she had some . . . errands. I'm taking you home."

"Thought you might want these," he said, handing her two pieces of mail as she settled her shaking body beside him in the black car. The first was her pay stub; she'd forgotten that yesterday was payday and the first pay period to reflect her new salary. The second envelope also had the look and feel of a check. Alayna ripped it open.

Five thousand dollars, payable to Alayna M. Jackson, drawn on the account of Hughes Weston and Moore. Cash money for college tuition. More tears stung her eyes. She folded the check quickly and made a great study of the ugly gray downtown sidewalks, scrolling out the window.

"Something wrong?"

He'd put on his pity-party hat and kid gloves again: she heard it in his voice. Alayna reached down deep, past the tears, past the hopeless futility of it all, and yanked at the edge of her attitude until a bit of it wiggled free.

"You talked to my sister? Martine?"

"Yes."

Suddenly his voice was as flat as old ginger ale.

"And?"

"Brass balls run in the family. Apparently."

Something memorable about his own damn balls was on the tip of her tongue, but he stopped her with, "Save it. This is the way, right?"

Chapter 12

This time, when Alayna saw the greenish Honda station wagon parked in the driveway, she pretty much knew what she'd find inside, but her stomach did a nervous little flip anyway, and the ache in her head whammed away like it was getting paid by the pound.

Going back up those steps and into the house under the new regime would be the worst mistake she'd ever make. She knew it just as certainly as she knew night followed day, as the Pips followed Gladys Knight. But could she really just turn to Ice like he was her own private driver and say "The airport, on the double?"

And if she did, where would she *go*?

"Thought she said she didn't have a car." Ice murmured, opening the door and sliding out. Before Alayna had pulled her thoughts or her limbs together enough to touch the door handle, it was open and he was there, holding out a warm, steady hand.

She took it, furious with herself for needing it, but

there it was, and there he was, and what else was she supposed to do?

Rap music shook the rafters as they mounted the stairs to the porch together like an old couple using each other's bodies for mutual support. Alayna reached into her purse for her keys, feeling the Ice's eyes on her still-quivering hands. He was about to take over, like the guys in those old, old movies that still came on PBS sometimes, when she stopped, turning to him with eyes wide with determined desperation.

"I—I think I'm going to do something," she blurted out. "Something . . . well, look, would you just . . . just back me up, okay?"

On Ice, puzzled looked like no.

"Look, it's nothing bad. I just can't . . . I just need to teach my sister a lesson. Give her a little of her own medicine so she'll understand. Play along, okay? Or at least, don't contradict—"

He nodded suddenly, locked and loaded, all somber and serious and grim again. "What's the game?"

In only one night, it was like she'd never lived there. Jamal's jacket lay over the edge of the living room sofa, his shoes against the door. A big laundry bag full of dirty boy clothes rested against one wall, and a stack of CDs spilled out of a backpack on the floor. The smell of something warm and spicy filled the house.

Jamal himself appeared a second later in his sock feet, sucking at the corner of a slice of toast.

"Martine! Your sister's home!" he called over the music in the general direction of the kitchen.

Martine yelled back, "Coming!" and Alayna heard

the oven door slam. A second later, Martine was standing beside Jamal, her eyes sweeping first over Alayna, then Richards.

"Ouch!" she muttered, looking at the big white bandage on Alayna's forehead. "That had to hurt."

Her eyes swung back to Ben.

"So . . ." she said with a maternal cool. "The famous Mr. Freeze."

She cut her eyes to Jamal, and the two of them smiled one of those smiles that meant that everything Alayna had ever said to her sister about Ice had now been passed on to Jamal Preston.

Alayna should have been paying him, because Ice went to work immediately, earning every version of the name anyone had stuck on him. He regarded the teenagers coolly for a moment, then picked his way across the messy living room and shut off the CD player. "Alayna doesn't need that crap right now."

Another look passed between Jamal and Martine. The one that went *Excuse you?*

"What . . . what is going on here?" Alayna asked faintly when Ice returned to his post as Official Backup Dude.

"Nothing. Jamal's nearly all moved in. Just a little more stuff to find a place for. We did the shopping this morning. You know, Alayna, first of the month?" Martine waved the checkcard to Alayna's bank account before pocketing it. "And I'm going to run a load of laundry. You know, family stuff." She smiled at Ice. "Jamal and I are engaged. We're expecting our first child in December."

"You told me. Last night, remember?"

Alayna glanced up at him. He already knew this?

What else did he already know? What did *he* know that she *didn't* know?

"May I have my checkcard, please?" She'd meant it to sound "Maya Angelou" and was shocked as shit when it came out "Brandi." Ice's fingers curled around her shoulder.

"I just told you, I already did the shopping—" Martine began.

"Now."

Alayna took a step . . . into Ice.

The man right on top of her like a peel on a banana, his chest right up against her back like he was scared of something. She'd asked for backup, but clearly he didn't understand the idiom.

White people.

"You won't be needing it anymore. Next month you and your husband will have enough money from your jobs to buy your own groceries. See, if we're all going to live here together, we'll be making some adjustments to who pays for what. That's the first one."

Martine's lower lip did an ugly curl.

"This is just like you, Alayna. It's all about control, money being one of your favorite methods. I don't understand why you're so—"

"You say you want half this house? Fine. You can have it. You have half the electric bill, half the water bill, half the taxes, half of everything. You can pay half to fix the washing machine next time it breaks down, and—"

"Why stop at half, Alayna?" The Freezer moved even closer and cupped his other palm around her elbow like he'd been welded there.

"Shut up," Alayna hissed, jerking her head up at

him so suddenly that all of her brains shifted from one side to the other. The room stuttered on and off, like a faulty Christmas light on a fading tree.

When Ice's arms circled her waist, she got it. All his weaving and dodging was in service to the monumental effort of trying to keep her from falling flat on her ass.

And considering what had happened the last time she'd resisted his aid, Alayna gave up and rested her head against his chest for a long second, during which Ice rubbed her shoulder as uncertainly as a man rewarding an untamed animal.

"Alayna?" Now Martine sounded worried. Was it because her sister looked like a survivor of Smackdown, or because a white man had just wrapped his steadying arms around her, and Alayna had allowed it?

"You know," Ice continued, "I really think you should stick to your first plan and let these young people have the house to themselves. Three's a crowd. Or so I've heard."

"My first plan?"

"That's right," he continued. "You needed your suitcase, and didn't you want to change your clothes?"

"What are you—"

"See, Martine, Alayna's been telling me for days about how this place really isn't right for her anymore. Too big for a single woman with the whole world open to her, but just right for a young family. You know even before your engagement she was thinking of selling it, or maybe signing it over to you and getting an apartment—"

Martine's face lit up with thirteen flavors of

Delight, a few dozen of Joy and a round of "Hip Hop Hooray."

"Would you, Alayna? Unless you're gonna give me that college money, it might take us years to raise the money for someplace else."

"No, you can't have the college money. You shouldn't have that money and you know it. But you can have the house," Richards said like it was his to bestow. "But like she said, you'll have to take care of it. Pay the taxes. Electricity, water. These old houses . . ." He looked around appreciatively. "They last forever, but the upkeep. Upkeep's a bitch. What do utilities cost on this place, Alayna?"

Martine's smile faltered a little.

"We could manage," Jamal volunteered, managing to sound both masculine and sure. "It'll still be cheaper than renting a place. And it's fully furnished, right?"

The temperature dropped to Kelvin-scale as Ben Richards gave the boy one of his chilly little smiles.

"Fully furnished . . . Okay. Sure, why not? Go on, Alayna. Get your things."

But he held her shoulder, keeping her stock still under the rock of his steady hand. "And, oh. The card."

He held out his hand for the checkcard, still curled in Martine's pink palm.

"But . . ."

"Now."

Jamal and Martine exchanged uneasy glances.

"The bills are paid." Alayna said in another pathetically weak voice. "All of them. Right out of my account."

"And you have food," Ice added, firm to her faint, managing to sound doubly determined for reasons of his own. "That gives you thirty days to raise the money for next month's expenses. Card."

And he snapped his fingers impatiently.

Martine looked at him like he'd lost every marble in his head. "Alayna," Martine began. "You gonna let this . . . *man* . . ."

"Give it to him."

Martine poked out her lip and rolled her eyes, but she handed it over.

"After you're married you won't need Alayna's health insurance plan anymore, either," Richards went on, sounding like he was reading from a pre-pared checklist. "Probably won't even be eligible. But you've got that covered, don't you, Jamal? Health insurance for your wife and your child?"

"Sure . . . I guess," Jamal said, matching Ice man to man, even with his eyes bugging out of his small, round head.

"Great. Alayna, if you're up to it, you start the pro-cess Monday. It'll take about thirty days to drop Mar-tine. What's the family plan cost? Three hundred a month?"

Alayna nodded. When Martine and Jamal exchanged a nervous glance before looking at Ice like he was the last apocalypse, she couldn't help feeling a new respect for the man.

"Good thing you already have a car."

Jamal cleared his throat. "Uh, that's my grandpar-ents' ride."

"Oh, well, you're young. You don't need a car." Richards paused a moment. "But you will need child care. Not too early to start thinking about that. It can get expensive."

Jamal's face relaxed into a smile. "My grandparents will help with that."

"Your *grandparents?* Don't you think they'll be a little old for that responsibility? They'll need you to look out for them pretty soon. And don't count on Alayna. Alayna's going to be pretty busy." His arm slid a little more possessively around her. "With me."

Martine's jaw hit the floor and her tongue rolled out of her mouth like the red carpet of a Hollywood premiere. Ice couldn't leave bad enough alone, because when he spoke, his voice was soft and deadly. "Guess who's coming to dinner."

It was worth silence, worth submitting to his embrace, worth even the pain in her head screaming like a car alarm just to see the dumbstruck look on her sister's face. Alayna turned her head, pressed her face deep into his shoulder and made a miserable effort to keep from busting out laughing.

But when Martine's birthday luggage was packed with Alayna's things and loaded in Ice's trunk, it didn't seem so funny anymore. Not when Martine clung to her neck, her eyes filling with tears, thanking her with a gratitude that was the most sincere emotion Alayna had seen from the girl in days.

Alayna could only look at her with wide-eyed misunderstanding. She wasn't giving them anything but a hard lesson, was she?

And it wasn't funny when Jamal called Ice "sir" and shook his hand, looking all grave and adult. Or when Ice took Alayna's arm like she was in police custody or something, fastened her back into the sleek black car, and they pulled away from the house on Magnolia Street, the only home Alayna had ever known.

"What was all *that*?" Alayna demanded.

"What?" He was more interested in finding his sunglasses than in talking, patting first a little hold on the dash designed just for the purpose, then the space between their seats, before remembering they were perched atop his head. "I backed you up. Like you asked me to."

"I asked you to back me up, not throw me out!"

Ice sighed like Atlas and resettled the weight of the world—plus one teed-off black woman—on his broad shoulders.

"Calm down. You're going to make yourself sick. Just because they let you out of the hospital doesn't mean—"

"I'm fine."

"You are not."

"I ought to know how I am."

Annoyed, he reached across her, flipping down the mirrored visor in front of her. "Look."

Ugh. Her brown skin had lost its golden sheen, looking instead as though she'd been lightly dusted with flour. She'd thumped her head just close enough to her left eye to turn the skin beneath it an ugly shade of yellow green that tomorrow would blossom a nasty purple-black. Top it all off with a lovely three-by-three-inch square of white gauze and complementing tape and you had your garden variety my-man-beat-me-up African-American beauty. All she needed was a TV talk-show explanation: "See, what had happened was, Malik, he trying to creep with this other woman, and I said 'nuh huh' and slapped him and he got mad and busted me in my face."

Alayna shoved the mirror back into its hiding place. "You've made your point."

Ice nodded. "Thank you. Now," he paused a moment, gathering steam, "I have something to tell you that you're not going to like, but it has to be said before we make our next decisions."

We? Our?

"Let fly, Ice," Alayna grumbled.

He let the clause four violation pass, which made sense, considering what he had to say next.

"You're wrong, Alayna. You're dead wrong. They've made a mess, let them clean it up. It's not your job—"

"*I'm* wrong!" Alayna jerked her head toward him so fast that the pain was like a lightning bolt inside her brain. For a flash of a second everything went white, then black, then back to normal.

"Calm down," Ice repeated. "Calm down. Your impulse was correct. You need to get out of there. You have to get out of their way."

"It's impossible to stand in Martine's way. She's determined to get what she wants and she doesn't give a damn who she steps on in the process. She wants to get married, she wants to be a mommy, fine. Forget that neither one of them has a job, neither one of them knows the first thing about utility bills and health insurance and childcare! Forget that they can't take care of themselves—let alone their baby—"

"They'll learn. Or they'll fail . . . and they'll still

learn. But they won't do either if you're always there to bail them out."

"I'm not going to bail them out! You heard me say I was cutting off the money! If they want to be grown, let them be responsible for their own cable bill and their own food and—"

"And you're going to live in the house without electricity because they couldn't pay their share?" He shook his head. "You wouldn't have done that. And I'll bet you my next *two* paychecks that Martine knew that. Very well."

"So, you kick me out of my own *house*?" Her voice rose in betrayal, cracked and fractured to a sob.

"I analyzed the situation and then . . . I backed you up. That's all."

"Analyzed. Sure. Right. What about that other . . . stuff?" She blinked quickly, but the feeling of aloneness had taken hold and wouldn't let go. "Like anyone would believe you and me were . . . anything other than what we are."

But he was listening to the sounds, not the words.

"Are you . . . *crying* . . . again?"

"Shut up," Alayna sniffed, turning her face toward the window. "You're making my head hurt."

He closed his mouth and didn't say another word for the rest of the drive.

They cruised through downtown and then up Peachtree Road into a fashionable midtown neighborhood where high-rises, bungalows and stately mansions clambered against each other for a view of Piedmont Park. Richards paused beneath one of the tallest buildings, dipped a little white cardkey into a security station, and they submerged into an underground garage.

"Where are we going?"

"You have to stay somewhere, don't you?"

"Oh, no. I'm not—"

"It'll only be for tonight—"

"No. I'll just stay at a hotel."

"I'm not wild about it either. Trust me." He turned toward her, presenting a pair of worried, smoky eyes. "But you've had a head injury and the doctor specifically said someone should—"

"What? Watch me sleep! Jesus! Because that's all I need, some sleep! Just to lie down for a minute in *peace!* What's the big—"

"Calm down."

"Stop saying that, okay!" Alayna practically yelled even if it did make her brain throb wildly in her skull. "I don't want to calm down! I want to go *home,* you hear me? I want to go home! I . . . want . . . oh . . . *shit,*" she muttered as more tears fell fast and hot and heavy. "I don't have a home anymore. I . . . don't—Shit, shit, shit." More tears fell and no one and nothing was going to stop them this time.

"Alayna," Ice murmured after the worst of the sobbing ebbed. "If the same stuff that's in you is in Martine, she might just rise to this challenge. Besides," his voice grew suddenly wistful, "I just thought you might like a little peace for a change. A little *freedom.* Some time when you don't have to be responsible for someone else every waking second."

"Stop it. Stop being *nice* to me, okay?"

"Can't. Don't tell anyone. I like to keep it hush-hush but," he leaned close so that the words were little more than a hot rush in her ear, "I'm a nice guy."

Chapter 13

She didn't notice how fabulous his condo was until much later, for two reasons. First, her head hurt too much, and second, its charm was buried under so much clutter that it was impossible to tell anything about it on first glance.

They paused briefly in a pretty lobby decorated with elaborate floral wallpaper and a great big urn of the real deal, while Ice conducted a low-voiced, cryptic conversation with an older man at the concierge desk. Something about needing help today and an overnight visit.

Then there was a long, slow elevator ride up a lot of floors, a short stint of a long, empty hallway, and finally he led her up a few steps to a small, but exceedingly messy, loft bedroom furnished with a single bed and chest of drawers in masculine dark woods. A dark blue recliner and a monster-sized television set consumed the corner of the tiny room, along with enough old newspapers and magazines to keep a recycling center busy for days.

Ice scooped a box of crossword puzzles out of the seat, parked her in the recliner and pulled the blue comforter off the hastily made bed, ripping off the pale blue sheets deftly and replacing them expertly with fresh white ones.

"Doesn't your maid do that?"

"I'm sure she would, if I had one." He glanced around the room and added, "Which from the state of this place should be fairly obvious."

"You can afford one, or do you just *like* clutter?"

"Love it. Here."

From the smallest piece of the College Luggage he pulled an old T-shirt and a pair of shorts and tossed them at her—a little before she was ready.

"I asked your sister to put a few comfortable things in here. Unless you want to sleep in *that*." He gestured toward the funky, rumpled gray suit.

"You think of *everything*," Alayna muttered, pulling the shirt from over her face where his throw had landed it. She stood up slowly, shrugging out of the suit jacket with effort, and sank down on the bed, certain that lifting another finger would be more than a loving God could ask her to do.

"Need some help?"

Alayna shot him a dirty look.

"Nothing I haven't seen before."

"You're not seeing mine, so get lost."

"You're welcome. You hungry?"

"No."

"Good. There isn't any food anyway. We eat out a lot."

"We?"

And *bammo whammo,* he was as uncomfortable as

a size 14 squeezed into a size 4 gown for a formal event. His face turned a strained shade of purple. Now he was ready to leave.

"I mean, I." And that old familiar abruptness Alayna knew so well was back in his voice. "I'm going to go order in a few things and make some other *arrangements*." He put a quirky little emphasis on the word, and if Alayna hadn't felt so exhausted, she probably would have concluded he was a southern-fried Jeffrey Dahmer, planning to get the right seasonings to complement his plans for her demise. "I'll check on you in a few minutes."

"Don't bother."

"Just to make sure that T-shirt finds its way over your head."

He probably did come back, but she didn't know it. She changed slowly, crawled beneath the clean white sheets of the little bed, and closed her eyes. When she awoke the sun had set, the room was dark and she was quite alone.

She sat up slowly. Her head still hurt a little, but the heavy sledgehammer ache of earlier had diminished to the weight of a construction hammer. She slid her feet to the floor and stood up, steady, then struck out for one of the two doors in the nearby wall that might lead to a bathroom.

It was a toss-up. Monty Hall, gimme door number one.

A closet. Filled with men's clothes that didn't look to be Ice's taste or size.

Alayna closed the door and tried the next one. Success. The bathroom.

A comb on the counter leaked a few slimy, silvery-blonde hairs. A toothbrush, razor, deodorant all left where they were last used in a kind of practical disorder.

Alayna found a bowl brush behind the toilet and some cleanser under the sink and gave the toilet a thorough swish before doing her business. She'd never known a man yet who could clean a bathroom.

Alayna washed her face, found her own comb in the bag Richards had left on the floor by the bed, swept her hair up into a lank, but serviceable, ponytail, and went to find her host.

He was sitting on a deep leather sofa in the loft den just outside of the tiny bedroom from which she'd emerged, eating Chinese food directly out of its paper container watching basketball. "Ooh!" he grunted as a Hawk missed a shot. "Play-offs my ass. This team sucks. Just sucks . . ."

He stopped, gazing at Alayna, a lo mein noodle sliding off his chopstick. He licked his lips and swallowed once so hard it looked like he was choking on an egg roll.

"What?" Alayna asked, self-conscious under the ogling. Okay, she still looked pretty rough, but, come on. She crossed her arms and felt her breasts, jutting like firm ripe pears beneath the light cotton, loose and braless and very visible under the thin white fabric.

In the time it took her to scurry back into the bedroom and hook them up, the sweaty men on the television and his food had reclaimed Ice's attention and he was following *their* tautly muscled bodies with interest. She sat down on the other end of the sofa, appropriately lifted and separated, her arms still folded over her chest.

"You look better," he said at last.

You mean because I put on a bra ... or do you mean ... ?

"What are you eating?"

"Egg rolls, fried rice, pork lo mein, uh, barbecue spareribs and sesame chicken." He slid the containers toward her, and she could see he'd already stuck a fork or chopstick in each. "Want some?"

"Your eating habits are a disgrace," Alayna muttered, wrinkling her nose at the picked-over offerings.

"What's wrong with them?"

"Nothing but grease. Not a vegetable in any of this—"

"There's green onions in the fried rice."

"That doesn't count and you know it." She sniffed the chicken. Delicious. "You didn't get any steamed rice?"

"Uh ... yeah." He rummaged around for a bag at his feet. "I didn't even open it."

"Good. Something you didn't drool all over. Thank you."

"Finally," he muttered and pretended to watch his basketball game. But Alayna knew better. From the corner of his eye, he watched every forkful of rice and chicken go into her mouth, watched her sip down a glass of water and a little diet soda, watched the three times she reached up to touch the lump on her forehead, because every time, his hand zipped out to push hers away. Watched the way she glanced around the apartment, checking out the wide-screen television and the CDs lining the entertainment center—mostly jazz and classic rock, but some unexpected artists like Luther Vandross and the Temptations, the papers surrounding a small computer in the corner, the dirty shirts and ties draped over the back of the chair. And when she got up to peer down into the living room below, she felt his eyes traveling from her butt to her heels, doing a little checking of his own.

For a gay boy, he sure was interested in the female anatomy.

"Who boxes?"

"Huh?"

Alayna pointed toward a punching bag on a stand by four stunning floor-to-ceiling windows that show-cased a magnificent park view. Or they would have if they'd been cleaned in a dog's age.

"Who boxes? You? Or your roommate?"

He joined her.

"Me. And I don't have a roommate."

Alayna looked over at him.

"Look, Richards, it's nice of you to put me up like this. It's friendly. You didn't have to do it, and I appreciate it, okay?" She paused. None of this was registering exactly. He was just staring at her appre-hensively with his eyes darting around in his head. Like he was too busy trying to think of his next lie to listen to what she was saying. "And your business is your business. I don't care, and I'm not going to dis-cuss it at the law firm. As far as I'm concerned, this whole weekend is clause two, and I intend to keep it that way. Honest."

"Discuss what?"

"Anything. Everything. Like I said. I don't care—"

"Care about what?"

"You're really something, you know that?" Alayna muttered. "I don't care that you live with another *man,* Richards. If you don't want to call him room-mate, fine. Call him your boyfriend or your significant other or your lover—"

Ice sprang away from her like she had the cooties. "*Lover?* You think I'm *gay?*"

She'd been pretty sure of herself until he wrinkled his forehead and snapped his neck at her like a bleached, full-grown Gary Coleman.

"Well, aren't you? I mean, there's obviously some-one living here other than you. It's obviously a man, that's clearly his room. You must be very much in love, because when he calls you freak out." Alayna shrugged. "Joel pegged it a long time ago."

"Joel? Joel Mitchum?"

Alayna nodded, and Ice scrunched his lips together and started pawing his scalp like something was crawling in it.

"He said from the first that you were gay, just in the deep, deep closet."

"In the deep, deep closet," Ice repeated blankly. "And you . . ."

"Well, I confess I wasn't sure. You don't—" Alayna struggled for the words—"seem . . . all that gay to me."

"Thank you," he muttered, but he didn't sound like he was exactly doing handstands about it.

"In fact," she continued, studying him carefully now. "A couple of times, like just now—"

"No, you're right," he interjected quickly. "I'm . . . what you said. That's it. Just don't tell anybody, for God's sake."

Alayna stared him down. Martine had given her a lifetime's experience with lies and liars, and right at this minute, Ben Richards was exhibiting all the classic symptoms. He couldn't seem to figure out what to do with his eyes, and his voice had a suspiciously untrustworthy waver in it.

"If that's not it, what is it?" Alayna asked slowly. "What's your deep, dark secret?"

"It's not a secret anymore. You're onto me."

"But the way you looked at me—"

"All men appreciate a beautiful woman," he said, giving her his eyes for just the briefest second before he shrugged away from her, flopped down on the couch, and buried his face in his hands. His shoulders lifted in a long, hard sigh of exasperation.

"I won't say anything."

"Right," he said dubiously.

"I won't say anything. I won't say anything."

"Right," he repeated dully.

He wasn't making any sense, and Alayna was on the verge of pressing the point when Ice held up his hand. "Enough," he barked.

"Well . . . can I use your phone?"

His eyes slid back to her. "Why? To share this latest little bit of information with your sister? Or can't you wait at least a day before you call to check on her?"

Bye-bye, Nice Guy. Back to Mr. Ice McNasty.

"Look, I thank you for everything, I truly do. But mind your business, okay, Richards."

"Your nose is pretty deep in mine right now." He rose and paced over to her. "What is *your* deal, huh? Smart, attractive woman without a man in sight from all appearances."

"I'm too busy for dating and you know it."

"Not *one* friend she can call in an emergency."

"Friends are a luxury I can't afford."

"Why not? Because you were breaking your back for Martine? Or because you're scared to death?"

"Scared to death? Of what?" Alayna spat. "What on earth do I have to be afraid of?"

"Beats me. Men? Rejection? Yourself?"

"At least I'm not hiding what I am in a damn closet."

"Aren't you?" he snorted. He had his ugly face on now, nostrils wide, lips in a pale snarl, a funny crimson flush in his cheeks.

"Oh, forget this," Alayna muttered, storming into her temporary bedroom. She bent with quick, determined fury, yanked up the travel bag, and ignored the whooshie of wobbly weakness that turned both her stomach and the room for a flash of an instant. *Throw up later,* she told herself firmly. *All that matters now is to get the hell out of this lion's den as fast as feet will fly.*

"What are you doing?"

"Leaving." She pounded barefooted down the few stairs to the lower level muttering a TGFA prayer: Thank God for Adrenaline. But between the heft of the bag and the effort of running, she was winded before she remembered the direction of the front door.

"Where are you going?"

"Anywhere but here. I don't have to stay here and take this bullshit from you."

He overtook her easily, with a smirk that crossed the border into smug on his face, then stationed himself in front of the exit like he'd just done something significant.

"No."

"Get out of my way, Richards," Alayna hissed menacingly at him like she meant it.

"No."

"Get out of my way!"

She swung the bag at him with all the strength she possessed, but on a good day she wasn't Sampson, and today, even Delilah would have won their arm-wrestling match. Of course, he ducked, but not before she caught his glasses with a Gucci corner. They smacked on the floor with a multisyllabic tinkle that sounded like more than a couple of pieces. *Good,* she thought furiously, even though the effort of the swing had cost her her balance and the energy of her anger had demanded all of her fragile strength. She fell hard against him, thumping the sore spot on her forehead against his chin, as he too lost his footing and crumpled against the condo's door.

"Jeez, woman," he panted as bag and woman slid with man to the floor with a thump. "Go. You're wearing a T-shirt with a hole under the arm, you don't have on any shoes, you don't even know where your purse is, but if you want to go," he held her closer, "be my guest. Just know that a black woman looking like you look right now could get arrested in this neighborhood for vagrancy, or worse. And good luck getting Martine to bail you out. You could call me, but," he paused just a fraction of a fraction, "I'll probably be out with my boyfriend."

She would have said something if she'd had breath for words. And she would have struggled out of his grasp if she hadn't been nearly blind with fresh pain and nausea. But she was too winded and tired and woozy to ask why was he looking at the hole in the arm of her T-shirt anyway? And just what kind of racist neighborhood was this? And just where had he put her purse, the thieving, rotten . . .

"I . . . I . . . don't feel good . . ." she muttered into his chest, all weak and needy. Again.

"I know. My fault. Time to stop fighting, Ali. Truce, okay?" he said softly. "Come on." He struggled unsteadily to his feet, managing to pull her up too without releasing her, which was a good thing, since her brain and her feet didn't seem to have reconnected just yet. "Back to bed."

At two in the morning, furious grunting sounds—*Ugh, ugh. Ah . . . Hrmmpf*—followed by the sounds of fists slapping leather awakened her.

At first she thought Ice's male playmate might have come home and that what she was hearing was the noise of rather violent intimate coupling. But remembering the punching bag, she took a chance that she wouldn't see something she really didn't want to see and crept toward the loft.

Sure enough, there he was: Ice in all his glory. Shirt off, a tiny little pair of gray athletic shorts on his trim hips and gloves on his hands. Laying the punching bag to waste in the room below. As he danced around the swaying bag, she could see the muscles rippling in his stomach and arms, and a fine patch of brown hair mat his chest before diving down into the tight shorts in a thin straight line. For just a second, Alayna's imagination followed that line, dove down to the bulge between his legs. She remembered the feeling of being cradled in those strong arms, held tight against the rock of his chest. A strange feeling of warmth made her breasts tingle and her heart pound as she got a flash of herself pinioned beneath him, arms wrapped tight around that strong back while those trim hips twisted and pivoted in a very different dance.

She snapped herself out of the fantasy, unnerved by her own thoughts. Good-looking though he might be, Ice was the wrong color. As many good-looking black men as there were in Atlanta, there was no reason to be thinking about doing the nasty with this dude. But when she looked back at Ice, his body and hair were slick with shimmering sweat and the overwhelming feeling of desire was still there. A longing to grab a towel and run it gently along the sculpted muscles of his shoulders, belly, forearms, back . . . and let whatever happened after that, happen.

As if to second her emotions, Ice swung at the swaying bag, hissing angry words between his clenched teeth.

"Gay! Damn it! Gay!"

While Alayna watched, unseen, he pummeled the bag until he nearly staggered with exhaustion. He gave the bag a final slam, then backed away from it, wiping his dripping face with his arm.

"Shit," he muttered, then turned toward the kitchen, a frustrated, sweat-wet Adonis, if ever she'd seen one.

Lord, I'll take one just like him, she thought, her eyes glued to his tight haunches as they disappeared out of view. *In black.*

Chapter 14

"Stop that. If you keep picking at it, it won't heal," he said over an egg breakfast that must have been ordered from a nearby diner. He'd slid it out of the Styrofoam onto a dark green plastic plate, replaced the plastic fork with a real one that looked reasonably clean, and offered it to her on a battered little dinette in front of the condo's huge windows. She could smell fresh coffee perking in the kitchen behind them.

"Who anointed you my father?"

"Back to normal, I see. Probably some kind of medical miracle."

He had barely looked at her since she'd come down in what she supposed was his lover's bathrobe—an old maroon thing that smelled of camphor and peppermint that she'd found looped on a hook on the bathroom door. She caught a quick glimpse of Ice's rumpled hair, dirty T-shirt and shorts before he jerked the newspaper back close to his face. He looked so tired that she wondered if he'd slept at all after his boxing match.

"Where are your glasses?"

He reached into his pocket, tossed a handful of bent and busted pieces onto the table, and resumed looking at the newspaper.

"Oh," Alayna murmured, struggling with the debt of an apology she knew she owed but felt reluctant to pay. "But if you hadn't—"

He crumpled the paper and tossed it aside.

"I have something for you." He fished into the pocket of his shorts and flipped a little white card onto the table.

CRC. Corporate Rental Company. Temporary furnished housing at affordable prices, it read in bold navy letters. Beneath it was the name Ivy Banks followed by a phone number.

"I used them while this place was being renovated," he said. "They have properties all over the city, a couple within walking distance of the office, if you like. It's cheaper than a hotel for long-term arrangements and—"

"Am I cramping your style, Richards?" Alayna asked sweetly.

Satan probably smiled like that just before taking a soul to Hell. He rubbed his knuckles across his chin while he calculated, and Alayna noticed for the first time the light brown hairs dusting his fingers and the back of his hands. Ice was pretty Neanderthal: hair always sprouting from his chin, on his chest, on his hands. She wished she hadn't been so distracted by muscle during the wee hour boxing match. He probably had bear skin rug growing out of his back, too.

"I'll take you over this afternoon if you're up to it."

"We could go now as far as I'm concerned."

"Good idea," he interrupted, rising with a nonchalant stretch. "I'll shower. You eat."

"Fine. Great," Alayna hesitated. "You . . . you haven't—"

"Heard from Martine?" he finished as though reading her mind. "Martine's fine. She's got Jamal. Don't worry about her, worry about yourself, Ali. Looks like all you've got is me."

That sobering thought was still chasing around her brain an hour later when they climbed into the car. And Ice was swigging yet more coffee from his heavy-duty tankard, only now he was whistling like he was happy or something.

"Could you stop that?"

She couldn't see his eyes behind those cool black shades, but she could see his teeth. All thirty some of them. White. Grinning.

"Why? Bothering you?"

"Duh."

He whistled louder, then, like he was proud of himself for being so annoying. Alayna had to talk to herself to keep from slapping him upside his head. Knowing Ice, though, he probably would have liked that, too.

Finally the whistling stopped and he spoke. "Here you go." He pulled up in front of a small storefront office in a downtown strip mall. He stretched toward the backseat and settled her travel bag in her lap.

"Aren't you coming?"

He shook his head. "My coach has turned to a pumpkin. Call me on my cell when you find one you like and I'll bring the rest of your suitcases over."

"Off to meet your Prince, Cinderfella?"

Another Happy Man turned Nasty Man smile. "Something like that," he snarled. "Good-bye, Ali."

If there hadn't been a police car parked in front of the donut shop on the corner, he probably would have left black skid marks on the pavement only inches from the spot where her toes touched the ground.

Alayna hitched the travel bag onto her shoulder and turned toward the realty office. She opened the door with one hand and pawed deep into the black pit of her purse with the other. The slim black cell phone leapt to her hand like a magnet.

She dialed the number to the house on Magnolia Street, planning on a casual, "What's up? Just thought I'd let you know I'm moving from Richards' to an apartment tonight. Need my own space, you know? Everything okay with you two?"

Perfect. Or it would have been. But the phone just rang and rang, until she heard the voice of the nugget-headed boy on *her* damn answering machine saying, "Hey there, this is Jamal—and Martine—" Tiney's voice pounced into the greeting for this additional tidbit of information, "And you've reached the home of the Prestons. We're not here right now—or we're busy, if you know what I'm saying—" Jamal laughed a little "Mac Daddy" laugh and Martine squealed, "Stop it!" before closing with "leave us a message and we'll get back to you ASAP. BEEP!"

Alayna lost her little speech and something closer to "You'd think you could wait until I got myself a new *phone number* before you just erased me off this thing. What if someone calls for me, huh? What if—"

But before Alayna could compose her mouth to

cuss them out on voice mail, a perky little blonde chick in a fuchsia sundress and matching lipstick—both too bright for her pale skin—was waving at her like an SOS. Alayna tested out a smile, approaching Fuchsia Lips and a desk decorated with about two dozen of those little toys that came with children's meals at places like McDonald's and Burger King.

"Hi there! I'm Ivy Banks," the woman in the fuchsia sundress drawled in an accent so thick she didn't have to add "And I'm a hick-come-big City to catch me a man." There was an annoying lilt at the end of every sentence she spoke that would have made even the most startling of exclamations (My God, I think he's dead!) sound like a question (My Gawd, ah think he's day-ud?) Other than that, she was about what Alayna would have expected, if she had given some thought to what an "Ivy Banks" might look like. Around Alayna's age, trim and pretty in a pert, white girl cheerleader kind of way. The sort of woman who would marry a doctor, have three sons and spend her thirties in a minivan.

Assuming she wiped off that awful pink lipstick.

"Great! Great! Great!" Ivy Banks repeated with her fuchsia lips when Alayna announced her business. She was trying her best not to stare at the big gauze patch Ice had made a huge production out of changing before they'd left his apartment this morning ("What did you do, dunk your whole head under the shower?") and failing miserably, since every few seconds her eyes darted between the patch and the blackening eye. "First, Ms. Jackson—do you mind if I call you Alayna? Thanks, such a pretty name. Now first, let's find out a little about your needs and preferences.

A few short questions, nothing too terrible! We've got some really prime units available right now, so I know we can find something great, great, great just for you, y'know?"

She turned toward a computer terminal and began typing with the expert speed and confidence of someone who knew secretarial work, murmuring, "Just putting you in the system here . . ." as she worked. A few seconds later, she flashed Alayna another vivacious sell! sell! sell! smile. "How'd you find out about us?"

"A colleague of mine. Ben Richards?"

Alayna wouldn't have thought it possible, but in the next instant, all the sunshine drained out of Fuschia Lip's face.

"Ben Richards?" she breathed, clutching the pale skin at the base of her throat. "There must be some mistake. Ben Richards? Lawyer? Tall, good-lookin' and uh . . ." She wrinkled her nose, searching for a politic conclusion for the sentence. "Difficult? You work with him?"

"Worse. I work *for* him."

"I'll pray for you," Fuschia Lips muttered, shaking her golden curls from side to side. She frowned into the computer a moment, scratching at her teeth with the lurid, pink fluorescent pen. Apparently the woman had a fatal attraction to this color. "Uh . . . he didn't . . . have anything to do with . . ." She squinted at the white bandage on Alayna's forehead.

"Of course not!" Alayna said, surprised by the suggestion. "Why?"

"I'm sorry. I didn't exactly mean . . . forgive me. You're right. It's just . . . a guy with a temper like that . . ." She shuddered. "You should have seen how he threw things around this office last year when he was a client. He's just about the last person I would have expected to get a referral from!"

"What happened?"

"Oh . . ." Fuchsia Lips flashed a nervous look up at her, as if realizing for the first time this conversation might have an impact on their transaction. "Nothing really. Just some kind of misunderstanding, y'know? About a year ago he reserved a two-bedroom for a month while some work was being done on his place? But there was some kind of foul-up and when move-in time came, we only had a one-bedroom unit in the building he wanted." Fuschia Lips rolled her eyes. "Hit the roof and bounced back! We offered him a two-bedroom in any other building we manage—and there are at least two dozen of them—all over the city. No. He wanted the Mitchell Arms. It's over near Grady Hospital, y' know? It's a nice enough building, a good location if you're a doctor or something, but we've got much nicer units in Buckhead. He finally took one of our downtown spaces—much smaller— but it had two bedrooms. But not before he threatened to sue everyone from me to the corporate owners."

Ivy Banks managed a grin, but her eyes still had that shook-up look of someone remembering having the bejeepers scared out of them.

"Well, apparently, he's over it now," Alayna offered, trying to sound only mildly interested. A building near the *hospital*? Why had Ice been so insistent about *that*? Was he sick? AIDS? No. No one who ate like Richards ate, and worked out like Richards worked out, and was built like Richards was built had anything like any AIDS. No. Maybe the boyfriend? That phone call she'd overheard—the one where he'd nearly taken her head off—and his diner disappearance floated back to her. Might be.

Tough. Poor Ice.

Fuschia Lips piped up again. "And what was really weird about it was when I asked him who else would be staying with him, he said, 'No one.' Now, why does a guy who lives alone need two bedrooms, y'know?"

Fuschia Lips's big blue-marble eyes danced with curiosity—not that Alayna could blame her. Still, Alayna made a mental note and filed it away under B for Busybody even before she'd recalled the clause four prohibition on gossip. Once a woman like this had you in her mouth, you were stuck there. Today Ice Man, tomorrow Alayna M. Jackson.

"I can't imagine," she said innocently enough, though she couldn't help imitating Fuschia Lips's slumber-party way of talking about the man. "What do *you* think?"

"What do I think? What else is there *to* think? Gay as a birthday party!" Fuschia Lips laughed, a bright, tinkling tone with just a hint of catlike hiss beneath it. "The second bedroom was for the *boyfriend*. You've seen Richards. He's what? thirty? thirty-five? And drop-dead gorgeous? And a lawyer? And still single? Gotta be. Surely you've seen signs?"

"Not really. I don't know him that well." *I just spent the night in the boyfriend's bed.* She didn't care to give that too much thought. "I was thinking about a studio," she told the woman. "Fully furnished, of course, but keep the cost low."

Fuschia Lips wasn't quite ready to let it go.

"But it was really confusing," she continued. "See, I thought, I mean, he seemed so, well, I thought he was kind of . . . *interested,* y'know?" She wiggled her eyebrows at Alayna, acknowledging her as a fellow foot soldier in the unspoken code of suggestive gestures. "He has this . . . this way of *looking* at a woman, y'know?"

The memory of Ice's hungry eyes riveted on her breasts flashed in Alayna's mind again. In the next flash, she saw him at the punching bag, but in the next, he was driving away in an all-fired hurry to meet someone.

Net result: inconclusive.

Fuchsia Lips interrupted, her voice sad and almost wistful with missed opportunity. "But then, when that other stuff happened with the bedrooms and he got so nasty and mad about it, well. It was clear he was hiding something, and that's the only thing it could be, y'know?"

Alayna frowned. "But if he's got a boyfriend, wouldn't he still only need one bedroom? I mean, it's an intimate thing, right?"

Fuchsia Lips surveyed her blankly, brains a-smoke over that one.

"Maybe they need space?" she offered after a while. "You work with him. Don't you need space?"

"A girlfriend could need space, too, though."

"Then why say he lives alone?"

Why indeed.

Maybe it wasn't a boyfriend. A relative maybe. Someone older. A father, an uncle, even a brother or cousin. Someone with some kind of medical problem. But then, why all the lies?

Ice, you're a puzzle. That's what you are.

Fuchsia Lips asked a dozen more questions—this time all related to fully furnished studio apartments—then stopped, grinning with satisfaction.

"I got a *perfect* little place for you! It's *soo* cute—too cute for most of our clients—but you . . . you're gonna love it, love it, love it!"

Fuchsia Lips was right. Alayna loved it, loved it, loved it—"it" being a charming, spacious, one-room apartment on the second floor of one of the converted plantation-sized houses that still clung to the periphery of Atlanta proper. Hardwood floors, high ceilings, an old-fashioned eat-in kitchen with the original brick still on the walls, and the pièce de résistance: a little nook of a living room, with built-in bookshelves and a window seat stuffed with large, soft pastel pillows. Six long windows curved toward the street outside, washing the entire place with sunlight and brightening the sunny yellow walls. Everything was a clean, pristine white: the bed frame, the side tables, the cozy two-seater dinette set hidden behind a white counter ledge separating the tiny kitchen from the rest of the room.

"And that's not the best part," Fuchsia Lips chirped, opening doors and straightening peachy pillows and generally showing the place to its best advantage, like a hyperkinetic spokesperson. "The best part is it only costs—"

A knock on the still-open door interrupted her, and both she and Alayna turned toward the sound. Fuchsia Lips broke into a grin as wide as the Grand

Canyon, and the temperature in the cute little place suddenly jumped about a thousand degrees.

Lord, have mercy.

A tall block of African-American cheesecake, wearing dark blue sweats and a white T-shirt so tight every plank in his washboard stomach rippled like amber waves of grain, oozed across the threshold. A basketball was tucked under his arm, and he was sweating slightly, glistening really, a moist sheen on caramel colored skin. His dark hair was close-cut and conservative, but an impish little black mustache chased the outline of his full lips.

"Sorry," he said in a deep voice that vibrated like a soul back-beat. "That you, Ivy?"

"It's me, Linc!" Ivy Banks bounded into his field of vision, looking liable to climb this brother as fast as her name suggested. Alayna steadied herself against the kitchen counter, feeling a little like a creeping vine herself. A Martine-ghost started whispering in her head, "Girl, that man's da *bomb!*"

"You going to be here a few minutes?" he asked. "My company sent the rent check to me again." He rolled a pair of dark brown eyes in mock aggravation at the perfidy of the Accounting Department. "I'll run up and get it. Saves me a trip down to your office later."

"Sure. Run on up, Linc. I'm just showing this unit to—"

But Da Bomb's eyes had already found, considered and digested Alayna. He stepped into the apartment, the smile on his handsome face compressing into a frown of concern.

"Pretty lady," he growled, "please don't tell me some brotha messed your face up like that. 'Cause if you do, I'm gonna be forced to hunt him down like a dog and—"

"Oh no, it wasn't a brother—," Alayna answered quickly, surprised by the sudden violence in the man's voice.

Da Bomb's face crunched down a level into something surpassing rage. "Black, brown or *white*—" and there was a nasty little hiss on the last of the options. Alayna frowned. This brother was fine, but he wasn't the Protector of Negro Women Everywhere. And he sure didn't know her well enough to get snippy and snarly about it.

"It wasn't a *man*," Alayna corrected, her irritation only barely concealed. "I tripped, bumped my head on the edge of a table and . . . it's a long story." *And it's not any of your damn business anyway*, she added with a flash of eyes and a determined fold of her lips.

Da Bomb's eyes shot to Fuchsia Lips, as though seeking confirmation, but Fuchsia Lips lifted her shoulders in a dubious shrug and kept her little pink mouth shut.

Not one of them said a word, and it got real quiet in the cute little place for a while.

"Well, I suppose an introduction is in order here," Fuchsia Lips said when the lengthening silence finally breached her comfort level. Alayna could almost see her gearing her voice back up to its perky, get-the-job-done style. "Lincoln Warren, Alayna Jackson. Alayna-Linc, Linc-Alayna," Fuchsia Lips repeated in a storybook singsong. "Has a nice ring to it, doesn't it?" Then, with a smirk of mischief on those bright pink lips, she stirred the pot a little. "Alayna might be your new neighbor. Linc lives upstairs."

"You new to Atlanta?" Da Bomb named Linc said, going for a kinder, gentler tone of voice.

"Hardly. I've lived here all my life. But I'm in transition right now, so I need an apartment until things sort themselves out."

That set off Round Two. Linc looked at Fuchsia Lips, Fuchsia Lips looked at Linc, and then they both looked at Alayna, interpreting the meaning of the words *transition, things,* and *sort themselves out.* Coupled with the state of her face, they were clearly chalking her up as a battered woman on the run, in spite of all her assertions to the contrary.

Whatever.

"Well, you've found the right place," Linc rumbled in that smooth-as-honey voice of his. "They did a good job with the restoration of this building, so it's comfortable. Modern. Nice people, the rent's not as outrageous as some of these furnished places—sorry, Ivy—" Ivy laughed a little but let the man talk. "And I'm right upstairs. You need me, just holler. You'll be safe here. I'll see to it."

"Safe? From who? You?" Alayna quipped before she could stop herself.

He had light brown eyes, almost hazel, as liquid as melted butter. When he laughed, they lit up like candles in his smooth brown face.

"Depends. Do you want to be?"

Alayna rolled her eyes, sorry she'd spoken. The very last thing she needed now was to start some kind of fling with the Player-Who-Lives-Upstairs. And the whole thing was Ice's fault. She'd gotten into a bad habit of saying the first thing that came to mind—thanks to him and his stupid clauses and contracts.

"Jury's out," she muttered.

Linc held her with his eyes for a long, serious second before he laughed again. "You're something else, you know that?"

"Yeah. I know that," Alayna agreed, massaging attitude to its nth advantage. "And if you know that and I know that, then there shouldn't be any problem, right?"

"Right." Linc clicked his heels together and lifted his hand to his temple in what would have been a precise military salute, except for that persistent and contagious smile of his that totally ruined Alayna's concentration. When she slipped up and grinned back at him a second later, the satisfied expression on his face was almost enough to make her wish she hadn't.

Almost.

Fuchsia Lips watched them as if her commission were coming from a successful love connection, not a rental.

"So, Alayna," she said at last, when the flirtation paused long enough for them to remember she existed. "You want to look at some others or . . ."

Somehow, Alayna managed to tear her eyes away from Mr. Lincoln "Da Bomb" Warren long enough to answer. "Will you take a personal check?"

Linc flashed his dazzling whites again as he took her hand.

"Welcome to the neighborhood," he said, "pretty lady."

Chapter 15

"**Y**our timing is lousy."

Ice sounded static-y, distant and pissed. As usual.

"You've done this before. You know how long this stuff takes," Alayna began, looking around the apartment. Her apartment. The signed lease lay on the little kitchen ledge beside the two keys secured on a CRC key chain. Linc had edged out when Fuchsia Lips had whipped out the serious paperwork, rumbling "See you later" in a voice that had had the effect of sounding both casual and meaningful all at the same time. Alayna would have bet good money that he practiced that come-hither-go-away-with-me approach on a tape recorder somewhere, but then Fuchsia Lips was shoving legal documents under her nose and she had better things to think about.

And now that she was alone in the place, her place, Ice was acting like a fool.

"I don't think I can get away right now," he muttered like the whole call-me-later-I'll-drop-off-your-stuff plan had been her spur-of-the-moment imposition instead of his very own baby from Jump Street. "No. No, I can't make it. I'll have to drop your things off tomorrow after work—"

"Fine." Alayna didn't bother to conceal her irritation. "I'll just pick up my Jeep from the office and—"

"You shouldn't be driving yet and you know it," he interrupted testily. "Get this straight for the last time, Ali. You've had a head injury. A *head* injury," he repeated as though she had difficulty remembering which part of the body that was. "Serious enough to knock you *out*—"

"What's with the 'Ali' stuff?"

He sighed like she was working his last nerve—instead of the other way around. "After the greatest boxer who ever lived. It's a compliment."

"It's a clause violation," Alayna corrected. "You better dig up your scrap paper and check yourself, because if I'm gonna be 'Ali,' you're gonna be 'Ice.' And I don't think you're going to like that."

"I like it fine."

Alayna recognized the tone—do what you want, I'm going to do what I want anyway—and sighed. There were gum wrappers on the street worth more than their damn contract. All she needed was to get invited to Sunday dinner with Ice and his lover and the whole thing was history.

"Look," she began, adopting a let's-be-reasonable-adults tone. "You're right. You've driven me around enough for one day, so why don't I just get a cab out to your place and—"

"No!" he shouted, and Alayna jerked the cell phone away from her ear.

"No need to shatter my eardrums, Richards. I already have a *head* injury," she muttered, thanking God for the opportunity to serve the words back to him on the same platter of idiotproof emphasis. "I don't need to go deaf, too."

He must not have liked the taste of that dish, because he didn't respond. Instead, he just took a nice, long, extra-deep breath. "Look. I've got to . . . I'm not going to be home for a while."

There it was again, the evasive, ask-no-questions-I'll-tell-no-lies voice. Too bad it didn't have a good enough beat to dance to. She was just about to tell him she knew what he must be going through, but he kept talking so fast she couldn't squeeze a "but" between his words.

"So, tomorrow afternoon," he was saying. "Maybe around lunch, we'll—"

"I need my clothes, Richards."

"You'll have them tomorrow."

"But what am I supposed to do without my things! What am I supposed to *wear!*"

A burst of static over the line magnified his exasperation as he sighed, "For God's sake, Ali! Go shopping. You got a nice fat bonus. Spend it."

"What do you know about that?"

Nasty Man laughed. "Martine. She told me everything. You don't have any secrets, not anymore. And Weston must have been desperate. I'm obnoxious, but I'm not worth five grand."

"Don't underestimate yourself, Richards," Alayna seethed. "You're more than obnoxious, you're—"

But the connection fizzled and broke, and he was gone before he got to hear the truth about himself, Alayna Jackson style.

And that, in a nutshell, was how she found herself sitting in the food court of the Lenox Mall on a Sunday afternoon, wearing sunglasses indoors and picking at a plate of fruit salad, people watching. Watching and wondering what on earth had possessed her to buy two new blue dresses and a summer suit in a regal purple—that weren't even on *sale*—and worse, to have picked up a little something for Ice, as well.

Take that, Martine. Now when you ask me about the money, it won't be there. I spent it. Or at least some of it. On myself.

The thought should have had some comfort in it, or at least had an ounce or two of vindication tucked somewhere in its bags, but Alayna got not one drop of either one of them. Instead, a nagging itch of guilt scratched the back of her brain. Like she'd spent her last dollar on a sack of magic beans and was seriously considering spending her last quarter on a book for the village idiot.

She didn't want to feel that feeling, so she stuffed it into a mental drawer labeled Never and concentrated on the people around her instead.

It wasn't even all that hot yet, but every couple in Atlanta was strolling through the mall like they needed air conditioning. Old couples, young couples, white couples, black couples. Copycat couples who carboned each other right down to their matching tennis shoes, and couples who proved the old folks didn't lie about opposites attracting. Tentative couples on their first dates and arguing couples who needed to make this date their *last* before they wound up on an episode of *Divorce Court.*

A young couple, no more than twenty years old, ambled by holding hands and talking like they had a desperate need to pour their life stories into each other's ears. A straggly goatee sprouted from the young man's chin, and he wore dime-store flip-flops below a rumpled pair of shorts. His girl wore her shorts and flip-flops with a tank top that revealed a shapely midriff and a belly-button ring. They seemed happy and well suited to each other, a couple of college kids maybe, on their way to enjoy a flick at the multiplex.

"Look! Look!"

The instruction was hissed and urgent, and Alayna turned. Two older white women hunched over ice cream sundaes at a table behind her, conversing in loud whispers.

"*Look* at them!"

Alayna looked. Sure, they were dressed kinda sloppy, but that was the style, ratty and pierced. And you have to wear tank tops if you want to show off your tattoos.

"I don't understand it," Woman One murmured to Woman Two disapprovingly. "He'd be a nice-looking boy if he'd shave that scruff off his face! Why a nice-looking boy like that would need to date one of them I don't know."

Them? Alayna had to take another look at the kids before she caught it: the young woman was black, the young man, white. Funny. It was the kind of difference she usually noticed before anyone else in the room, but she hadn't. Not this time. They were just too alike for it to make much difference.

"It's all the rage with the young people—this interracial stuff," Woman One continued in a meant-to-be-heard hushed voice. "They're everywhere! They think it's cool!"

"Rebellion, that's all it is," the other agreed. "They outgrow it and go back to their own kind."

"Well, I'm glad it wasn't popular when my kids were growing up. If my daughter had dated a black boy, I'd have just died!" Bigot One paused, probably to stuff chocolate syrup into her fat face. "Her father probably would have shot him! Her, too."

"God just didn't intend that sort of thing," Bigot Two said as if she'd just asked Him about it yesterday and His response had been most emphatic.

"Can you imagine kissing one of them?" Alayna could hear the woman's shudder. "I'm not prejudiced as long as everyone stays in their place. I don't care if you're black, white, or green but—"

"I wouldn't kiss one if my life depended on it."

"Ignorant," Alayna muttered loudly enough for the big ears of Bigot Ladies everywhere to hear. Without looking back at what she knew would be their astonished clutch-the-pearls-Doris expressions, she scooped her trash onto her tray and left the Food Court, wondering what Ice would have said if he'd been sitting in her seat. Maybe an interracial couple wouldn't have pressed his buttons. Maybe it would take a pair of boys holding hands.

She saw him again, pummeling the stuffing out of that punching bag, hissing the word *gay* over and over while he gave the leather hell. Not exactly a Zen affirmation. And then there was the way he'd looked at her for that two seconds when she'd come out of the bedroom without a bra. Like it'd been a long time seen he'd seen even the outline of a breast up close. Like he'd missed them. Like he might even be a little curious about hers in particular.

But that was ridiculous, from basement to attic and on every level in between.

She made her way slowly through the mall, telling herself she was too damn tired and headachy to worry much more about him now anyway. Tired enough to try her first night in another strange bed, in another strange place. A creepy-crawly of nervousness jitter-bugged through her stomach at the thought of being alone in the small apartment. At least at Ice's house there had been *someone* there. Too bad that someone was Ice.

She dismissed him from her mind again, giving him his own special drawer and his own mental label: a great big question mark.

She almost didn't see them. Wouldn't have except for the sound of the laughter, its familiar tones perk-ing her ears, making her crane her neck through the nearby shoppers.

And sure enough, there they were. Martine and Jamal. Walking along hand in hand, laughing—laughing that same funny-bone-teary-eyed-roll-on-the-floor laugh—and talking, looking totally compatible and right together. Happy, healthy, not a care in the world.

What came next wasn't gradual, wasn't the slow dawning of a realization but a one-two punch of clar-ity knocking her right between the eyes until she was swaying back and forth on the spot like Ice's punching bag.

The first understanding was that she, Alayna, had been replaced.

And the second was that Ice was right. She really *was* all alone, and absolutely scared to death about it.

"This all?"

The sun was hugging the horizon as Linc dropped her store bags in the entranceway and looked around. He'd been heading out as the cab had deposited her and her shopping bags outside the cute little place, had happened to look over just as her knees had gone a little wobbly and things had gotten a little dark around the edges. A short rest on the concrete had been looking like an option until Linc had hopped out of his shiny SUV.

"Oh, there's more," she replied, hoping he wouldn't make a big deal about how fast her butt hit the nearest chair, or the sigh of relief that escaped her lips. She focused on his question. What were the words to describe Ice these days? Boss? Nurse? All-purpose Annoyance? "A friend is going to drop off some things tomorrow and the rest . . ." She forced a breezy no-skin shrug out of her shoulders. "I'll have to go home and get the rest."

Linc's perfect black mustache hard-lined on his straight lip. "No way," he said, shaking his head. "Not by yourself, you won't. I'll go with you. Or better yet, the police—"

"For the last time I am *not* running from a boyfriend!" Alayna shouted, propelled to her feet in exasperation. The whirl of breath and motion made her head start to swim like yesterday all over again.

Linc lunged for her, but she waved him away. He watched her sink back into the chair, brown brow knitted with concern, but all he said was, "Uh-huh," and changed the subject by giving the place the formal look-see.

"This is a nice unit," he said, checking the windows, peering behind doors, like chief of security or something. He pulled open the empty closets and peered inside as though he was expecting to find an intruder. "Nice."

"Yeah. All I need now is some food in the fridge," Alayna muttered, annoyed by the way he'd taken possession of both the place and of her. He was like Ice in that way, treating her as though she were a little lost lamb in need of a shepherd. Okay, so she *was* a little lost at the moment, but he didn't have to know that, did he?

She touched her forehead, feeling the wad of gauze and the still cresting lump beneath it. The thing was just as sore as it could be, and she could almost hear Ice saying—

"Don't touch it."

She looked up and Linc was beside her, pulling her hand away from her face. "It won't heal if you pick at it."

Great. Black Ice. Alayna sighed.

"Look. Thanks for the help, but I've got a big day tomorrow and I'm really tired, so why don't you . . . ?"

"You eat?" he asked. " 'Cause there's a little bistro

down the block. Nothing fancy, but it's good food. I'm not much of a cook when I'm on the road, so I go there a lot. We could go over and get us something."

Alayna took in his carefully pressed slacks, crisp shirt and the distinct aroma of some masculine cologne that wafted from him like wind. "Looks like you were on your way out."

Linc looked a little guilty, like he'd been caught on the creep. "Nothing important," he said, not quite truthfully. "Anyway, we could call it your welcome dinner."

"Did you say 'on the road'?" Alayna cocked her head at him. "What do you do, exactly?"

"Sell drugs," he said, matter-of-factly swinging those liquid-light eyes at her. He waited until a sober expression had consumed her face before adding, "For a pharmaceutical company. A little industry humor."

"Very little," Alayna said dryly, but he'd already seen her smile. He sauntered closer to her, all of his perfect teeth gleaming, grace and muscle and assurance at his complete command. All hunter. All man. There weren't any question marks on the Linc Warren score sheet. He had the confident charm of a brother who *knew* he could get a woman to do just about anything he wanted . . . with enough time and the right bait.

He smiled at her like he'd already made a decision and if she was a good girl, he'd let her in on it.

"Got a better idea. You rest here and I'll go get it. Then you and me can sit right here and get our grub on, okay?"

Alayna grinned directly into his face, smiling promise and attraction until Linc was nearly salivating expectation. "I don't think so."

Linc's self-satisfied expression slid off his face like eggs off a greased griddle. "Why not?"

"Well." Alayna ticked off the fingers of her left hand in succession. "First of all, it's late. Second, I'm still sort of recovering from this." She let her fingers graze her forehead again quickly but removed them before anyone could object. "Third, I work for a guy who will have me hustling from nine to nine tomorrow, and fourth I just met you a couple of hours ago. You seem nice enough, and you're certainly"—she paused, pondering the effect of compliments on the male ego before plunging ahead anyway—"good-looking and all that."

Linc accepted this as the fact it was and allowed her to continue without so much as a blink.

"*But* I really don't know a thing about you, so . . ." Alayna opened the front door wide and showed him the hallway with a slight nod of her head. "Thanks for everything, Linc. Really. Now . . ." *Hasta la vista, baby.*

Whether it was the suspicion in her face, or the black eye and its companion forehead gauze, or the way her lips turned down, or the combination of all of them, she didn't know, but something made him look serious. And even sexier. He nodded, folding his upper lip deeper under his lower one so that little black mustache seemed to make a double frown.

"No problem. Another night," he said and accepted her invitation into the hallway without further insistence. "How's tomorrow?"

"No."

He must have liked rejection, because the grin suddenly returned wider than ever. Yeah. He was a hunter all right. Probably the kind who liked to play with its food before he devoured it.

"Okay, pretty lady. I'm on the road Tuesday until Thursday. Mark me down for Friday night?"

And before she could think of an excuse to say no, he walked his six-plus-feet of fineness out of her apartment, turning back just before one foot hit the stairs toward his evening plans.

"I'm one of the good guys, Alayna," he said like this was Hollywood and it was time for his close-up. "You know, the good guys? Decent brothers *do* still exist."

"For the last time," Alayna threw up her hands in aggravation, "no one *hit* me!"

But he responded to that with little more than a final flash of teeth and jogged down the stairs.

Alayna watched his firm buttocks until they disappeared, then closed the door, locking it tight. She pressed her back against the door and looked around the pristine white emptiness, praying for the strength to survive her first night of solitude.

Chapter 16

Ice dripped his glasses-less self into the War Room just before lunch wearing a dark blue suit that didn't do a thing for him and a pair of bleary slate eyes above a puffy set of matching gray bags. He held his briefcase in one hand and a stack of bound papers tucked under his arm. In the other hand, he balanced the ubiquitous coffee tankard, steaming with heat and obviously very full. He dropped the stuff on the table, slumped in the chair opposite her and rubbed his face.

Even with a big fat bump on her head and her left eye purple as a plum, Alayna *knew* she looked better than he did.

"What happened?" she said. "Get run over by a truck after you stood me up yesterday afternoon?"

He grimaced at her, his eyes sweeping over the new suit, but he kept his lips zipped. Finally he slid a series of transcripts across the table at her.

"Last week's interviews," he muttered, and went back to head rubbing and nose pinching.

Alayna pulled the precarious stack toward her and

flipped. The topmost one, on which she recognized the name of Cybex's chief software designer, was three inches thick—easily four hundred pages long. Ice must have talked to this guy for nearly eight hours straight to have a record this thick.

"So. Are our clients really software thieves, or what?"

He stuffed a fist in his mouth, trying and failing to press back a yawn. After a quick gulp of coffee, he answered in his lawyer voice, "A jury toss-up. It looks to me like these two companies independently developed very similar software, but one of them, our client, did a better marketing job and thus consumed the lion's share of the profit," he yawned again, dropping the going-to-court tone. "At least, that's what all Graves's people say, anyway."

"So we're the good guys?"

"It's the other side's job to prove we're not."

"So now we need to serve some discovery on them and find out what they've got that proves we're not the good guys," Alayna finished.

"Yeah, and get through all of this." Ice shrugged toward the mountain of boxes that filled the tiny room and sighed, pulling at his eyes again. "I don't think there's a smoking gun in here, but we've got to get through it anyway. I'm beginning to think we're approaching this the wrong way, anyway. I think it's the hearing we ought to be worried about, not the trial. If we can beat them on the law, there'll be no need for a trial." He pinched his nose again, hard enough to leave deep pink marks where his glasses normally would have been. "I want you off the documents, if you're up to it. Time to dig deep on that constitutional stuff."

"I'm up to it, but what about . . ." She glanced around the room at the mountain of unopened boxes piled up around them.

"I've got the critical ones. Denise Stinson set them aside. And I talked to Graves and Weston." For the first time, Alayna noticed his lips did a little twist of distaste when he said the man's name. But before she could compose a question, he said, "We really need a temp to help with the documents—we really need another lawyer on this case too, but Weston's got to bust my balls on this one, so we're not going to get either one." Sarcasm dripped from the words, and Alayna quirked an eyebrow at him, wondering what exactly his grievance against Boss Man was.

She didn't get a chance to ask before he continued. "But he says we can have Trixie. She's been asking for a change of pace and some overtime, so—"

"Trixie?"

"Trixie," he repeated in a tone so flat that, if she hadn't been looking at him, she would have barely recognized it as his voice. "You'll have to supervise her of course, but she's better than nothing."

"Not much," Alayna muttered and waited, expecting some kind of rebuke, but Ice said nothing. Not a word of sarcasm, nary a smart-ass remark. Alayna looked him over again. He really did look terrible, like he'd had the weekend from hell. Which, when Alayna remembered everything he'd done for her, at least, he probably had. And if something had gone wrong with his significant other, too. . . .

Something tender snuck up and tapped her on the shoulder, and before she knew it, she was abandoning the fine art of giving him shit and reaching for the box hidden beneath her chair.

"What's that?" he asked, eyeing the bright paper and fancy ribbon suspiciously.

"Open it and see."

A mischievous smile crept across his face. "For *me*? Oh, you *shouldn't* have," he said in Ice-ese, taking it gingerly from her hands. He held the box to his ear. "It's not going to explode or anything, is it? Maybe I should call the Bomb Squad first?"

Yeah, he was all right.

"Open it, fool. Before I take it back!" Alayna snapped, but the hard words didn't stop her from grinning at him, or him from grinning back.

Ice played the part of the excited toddler to the hilt. With eyes now glinting with anticipation, he ripped the fragile paper gracelessly aside and pulled the glasses case out of the box. He looked up at her, questioningly, but didn't open them.

"To replace the ones . . . that broke," Alayna explained.

"You mean the ones *you* broke," he corrected her, giving her some eyebrow attitude of his own. "Picking frames for someone else is risky business."

"Chill, Ice. Same brand, same style. Went to three different shops in the mall to find them. And they didn't have black, so . . . well, open them."

He did. A moment later he'd settled the tortoise-shell frames on his face and was squinting naked-eyed at her through their empty panes.

"You'll have to put your prescription in it." Alayna

leaned across the table, prodding at his ears and nose, adjusting, while those smoky eyes, exposed through the lensless windows of the frames, followed her soberly. She studied him critically a minute, then nodded her satisfaction. "I thought so. The brown looks better."

"I liked the black."

"You might have liked them," Alayna let her finger swish beneath his nose, just to remind him who he was dealing with, "but they didn't like you. Made you look like a nerd."

"Maybe I *want* to look like a nerd."

"Don't be contrary," Alayna rolled her eyes. "No one *wants* to look like a nerd. Not even you. Go get the lenses fixed."

"Can't. Too much work."

"Can't work if you can't see," Alayna muttered, turning back to the transcripts. When a solid minute passed and he still hadn't left, she looked up at him. "I said go."

He grabbed his coffee and rose reluctantly. "You're an extremely bossy woman, Ms. Jackson."

"Deal with it, Mr. Richards."

He still didn't leave, not until he found his good-guy tone. "You didn't have to—"

Something warm spread up and out of her. Gratitude, maybe. Appreciation. Or something else. But Alayna smiled at the man in spite of herself because of it.

"You're right, I didn't," she heard herself saying . . . and sounding like she meant it. "But you *are* a nice guy, so . . ."

"Say what?" His grin almost consumed the dark

shadows under his eyes. What nice teeth he had. Nearly as white and perfect as Linc's.

"You heard me," Alayna grumbled, wiping the smile from her face in a hurry. "And don't expect me to say it again. *Ever*."

He laughed a little, then slouched toward the door.

"And if you're not back in"—she flipped her wrist to consult her watch—"two hours, I'll come down to the garage and wake you, okay?"

He left with a flush of red in his cheeks and a big goofy smile on his face, like he'd been caught thinking about what color panties she wore. Alayna watched him go, then grinned herself all the way to the library and into the Georgia Constitution, without giving the impending presence of Trixie McCoy another instant's thought.

"It's . . . cute . . . I guess." With a heavy *plop,* Ice dropped seven of the eight remaining pieces of the College Luggage—he let her hold one—and stepped into the place, his brow crinkling in critical appraisal.

"Don't sound so enthusiastic."

Ice folded his arms across his chest and didn't say anything at all for a long time. To his credit, he didn't go around opening every door and poking his nose in every drawer, either. But his eyes made a thorough sweep of the room, and if there was even a bump in the surface of the smooth white bedspread, those twin gray eagles had noticed it.

"I'm surprised," he murmured at last. "I wouldn't have expected you to choose something so . . ."

"So . . . ?"

"Feminine."

Alayna rounded on him, her hand slipped to hip. "*Excuse* me?"

Ice put up his hands like a criminal on *Cops* and backed away from her in sham surrender.

"Hey, you picked it, not me. It's so . . . frou-frou. You don't strike me as the girly-girly type."

"What were you expecting? Wood paneling? Flannel sheets? A spittoon?"

Ice laughed. It had taken him three hours, but he'd gotten the glasses fixed and he looked a thousand times better. Alayna had no doubt he'd also caught himself a nap in that time, too, but she wasn't going to mention it—unless he kept on pissing her off.

"No, I wasn't expecting *that*," he continued, still chuckling to himself like he'd stumbled into the funniest little joke he'd heard for a while. "I just meant . . . I don't know. The way you dress, the way you always wear your hair back off your face . . . so utilitarian. So *practical*. So, I just thought you'd prefer something more—"

"Manly," Alayna finished, slamming into the kitchen to pull two glasses from the cupboard.

"I didn't say that, either."

"You didn't have to."

"You're putting words in my—"

"I always heard gay boys appreciated well-decorated spaces."

"Maybe they do, but I," he began, but a set of firm, confident knuckles applied themselves vigorously to the door at that instant, interrupting him. Alayna hurried out of the little kitchen, pushing Ice, who had the nerve to stand slightly in her path, roughly aside.

There stood Linc in dark slacks and a short-sleeved

shirt of some clingy fabric that showed every cut on that perfect physique, smiling wide and taking great pains to keep one hand hidden rather dramatically behind his back.

"I'll tell you right now, pretty lady, you work too much! I been knocking since six o'clock and—" His cognac eyes fell on Ice, standing like a big blue-suited block of something foul in the center of the floor. "Oh," Linc muttered, and Alayna heard the guarded shift of his tone from the intimacy of black on black communication to whites present formality.

Don't bother, it's just Ice, she wanted to tell him, but that would have been like saying, *Don't worry, it's just my pet tiger.*

"I'm sorry, I didn't realize," Linc said stiffly, then stretched a hand toward Ice. As he leaned toward the man, Alayna saw the effusive bouquet of peach-colored gladiolas clasped in his other hand. "Lincoln Warren."

The two men shook, and, if Alayna wasn't imagining things, proceeded to size each other up with the same careful, catty head-to-toe scrutiny they usually accused women of. Finally, Linc tore his eyes away from Ice long enough to remember the reason for his visit and drew his arm from behind his back.

"For you. Housewarming present."

"They're beautiful," Alayna lied, pretending that showy glads were her most favorite of flowers. "How thoughtful!"

She shot Ice a *somebody*-thinks-I'm-a-girl look. He scowled and touched his middle finger to the bridge of his new glasses—either flipping her off or as a reminder of just how "girlish" she'd been when she'd smashed them. Alayna ignored the Ice Block and made a great, noisy deal of arranging the long-stemmed display beside the tiny cluster of daisies Ice had given her in the hospital.

"You're not the boyfriend, are you?" Linc snarled in a voice with just enough civility shellacked on top to avoid a barroom brawl. Alayna glared over at him, but he wasn't looking at her. Neither was Ice. They only had eyes for each other. It was like she wasn't even there.

"Boyfriend!" Ice scoffed in a tone that made Alayna mentally condemn him and all his offspring to eternal Hell. "Right. I wasn't aware there *was* a boyfriend. I'm the *lawyer*."

Linc shot Alayna a questioning who-you-suing look.

"My boss."

"Oh. Right. Good," Linc muttered, sounding like he believed that was the extent of Ice's relationship with her about as much as he believed that the horrors of slavery had dissolved with the Emancipation Proclamation. " 'Cause if I ever get within striking distance of the fool who—"

"Linc, I told you," Alayna interrupted, speaking as slowly and carefully as a schoolteacher disciplining a child who refused to listen. "I hit my head on a *table*."

Linc waved her away, staring straight at Ice, who kept his face as blank as Stone Mountain and his arms crossed like swords.

"I heard what you *told* me," he snapped. "And I'm sure Richards would agree, it sounds like some abused-woman-cover-story bullshit."

An icicle dripped from Ice's face. "No, Mr. Warren," he said coolly. "For the record, she tripped over some boxes and hit her head on the table. At the office. I saw the blood and everything. Rather clumsy, our Alayna."

Thanks, Ice. Did you have to put it like that?

They stared at each other again, then Linc cast a confused glance at Alayna, but there was nothing she could do but grimace I-told-you-so at him.

"So, *Linc,* may I call you Linc?" Ice began after a pause long enough to drive a double-wide through. "Lived here long?"

A muscle tightened under the smooth brown facade of Linc's skin. For a flash of a second, Alayna smelled sulphur.

"Actually homebase is Jacksonville, Florida," Linc said smooth as icing. "But since I have a lot of business in Atlanta and its environs—"

"Linc's a rep for a pharmaceutical company," Alayna interjected.

He tossed a smile at her, but his eyes corrected any misapprehension she might have had about his needing any further assistance from her. Alayna folded her lips and made herself a fly on the wall.

"I spend about half my time in and out of here and the other half in Florida," Linc continued, still smiling spite in Ice's face. Alayna knew the subtext only too well: *Yeah, I'm educated, yeah, I've got a good job. What did you think? That I was the janitor or something?*

Alayna had said something similar herself, back long ago when Ice was a stranger.

"Odd territory," Ice said flatly, and Alayna recognized that tone, too. She'd never seen Ice cross-examine a witness, but she'd watched Weston do it a thousand times. Ice's voice had that same trust-me-I'm-here-to-trap-you edge. Distrust was a natural part of an adversarial legal system, and it was also a natural part of being black, a good bit of the time. But since they weren't in court, and Ice wasn't black, what was *he* tripping about?

For a split second, she wished she really spoke White People Language instead of perpetrating it in the office day after day. Maybe then this would make some sense.

"You've found me out," Linc said slowly. "Actually, I'm not a rep. Not anymore."

Alayna turned, yanked fully into the conversation by this admission.

"No?"

Ice's setup was buried beneath that one word, and if Linc wasn't careful . . .

"No," Linc said calmly. "Actually, I'm a regional sales supervisor. So you're right, it's odd territory, supervising and managing the actual sales forces in four states. Keeps me on the go, but the money's great, I like to travel, and the company pays for apartments in Atlanta, Columbia, Chattanooga and a few other cities, so I'm well taken care of."

Psyche, Ice. Score one for the brother.

"I'm sure," Ice sounded faintly disappointed. "You must miss your family in Jacksonville. Your wife—"

"Nope. Not married. Single and free to mingle. And there's a whole lot more mingling to do in Hotlanta," he said, giving in to the luxury of a grin. "You know what I'm saying, man?"

Ice couldn't have scowled any deeper if his life had depended on it.

Round two goes to the brother, too.

"I know what you're saying," Ice repeated mechanically, then his eyes swept toward Alayna. "I should get going. Will you be okay?"

"Don't run off on my account," Linc insisted. "Really nice meeting you. And don't worry, man. I'll keep an eye on her. Both eyes, actually. If you know what I'm saying."

"Yeah," Ice muttered, and to her great surprise, he leaned down and pecked her cheek good-bye.

"Thanks again for these," he murmured, touching the glasses. "See you tomorrow."

And before Alayna had recovered herself enough to either thank him or wish him a good night, Ice beat a hasty retreat down the stairs and into the evening heat.

Linc stared after him for a minute, then cocked his head toward Alayna in query.

"What's with you and the White Boy?" he asked casually enough, but now *his* arms crossed his chest. It was a clear signal from black man to black woman: You better have an explanation for this and it better be good.

"You sound . . . happy," Martine said.

The unpacking was finished, if it could be called unpacking. Clothes, shoes and luggage stowed in the closet, Mama's pictures arranged on the bookshelves, toiletries in the bathroom. Done. Personalized . . . in a pathetic hour and ten minutes. Her photos looked silly on the shelf with the decorator's selection of hardback books, her clock radio silly on the bedroom nightstand, even her toothbrush was silly in the brush stand. Maybe Ice was right. It was a cute little space, but she was just a perpetrator in it. A perpetrator with cash, but a perpetrator all the same.

Thinking of Ice brought back that little kiss. Innocent enough. Or it would have been. If they'd had it like that. Which they hadn't. The only reason he'd done it was to get under Linc's skin. But why on earth had he felt the need to do that?

God only knew, Alayna thought, dismissing him from her mind again as she tried to get settled for a quiet evening. But the window seat was uncomfortable, and there was nothing on television but lawyer shows. She squirmed on the pastel pillows, wishing for the ancient brown sofa at home and the soft spot near the bolster that curved in anticipation of Alayna's butt.

Thinking about home led her straight back to thinking about Martine, and her hand reached for the phone like it had been endowed with a mind all its own. After all, she had a new phone number, she told herself. It was the perfect opening. The perfect excuse.

"So, what are you doing?" she asked her sister, once the business of relaying the number was accomplished.

"Nothing, laying on the couch, trying to eat something." Martine sounded sick and spiritless. "Do you like it? Your new place?"

"Yeah!" Alayna said, a little more enthusiastically than she'd meant to. "It's only ten minutes from the office—I could probably walk—"

"Yeah. Well. Like I said. You sound . . . happy."

"Is that a bad thing?"

Alayna could hear her sister's grimace of annoyance, and she regretted the words. This flammable relationship couldn't stand a lighted match, let alone even the suggestion of another round of flame-throwing accusations.

"That whole deal with that Ice guy," Martine said, picking up the yarn of conversation and rolling it down to the edges of their last face-to-face encounter. "That was some kind of routine you guys hooked up, wasn't it?"

"No," Alayna lied.

"Yeah it was, too," Martine insisted, her voice growing more and more powerful, more and more certain. "He ain't your type."

"How do you know?" A sudden wash of apprehension swept over Alayna. Martine hadn't guessed about Ice, had she? Because if Martine even suspected Ice was gay—

"Well, he's white, for one thing."

"Oh, that," Alayna sighed. "So?"

"So?" Martine couldn't suppress a giggle. "Come on, Alayna. You can't stand white people. Complain about them all the time. Won't even call them by their names if you can help it. 'Boss Man' and 'Ice Man' and ain't nobody ever going to forget the way you blasted that Greta Chick. What did you call her? 'Lawyer Barbie'—"

"That wasn't because she was white. It was because she was dumb. And things change," Alayna protested. But that didn't stop the truth from seeping out of her sister's words and squirming into her gut. Hadn't she just two seconds ago called Ivy Banks "Fuchsia Lips" in her mind? And what about Ice? The guy had let her stay at his house, changed her bandages, driven her all over town, and she couldn't recall a single time she'd called him by his first name.

"And if he's your man, how come you didn't move into his place?" Martine challenged, tugging at her story like a dog smelling meat. "I know you, Alayna. How you hate to spend money."

"He offered, but . . ." she continued, feeling like lightning would strike her down at any minute. "I've always wanted my own space."

"Mmmpf. Never said so before. You're the original homebody, and you know it," Martine grumbled. "You ain't kidding nobody. And even if you *do* got a thing going with him, it won't last. You don't know the first thing about keeping a man, Alayna."

"Really?" Alayna said sharply. "And you do?"

"I know enough to pay attention to what I look like."

"What's that got to do with anything?"

Martine sighed my-sister-is-an-idiot, and Alayna could almost see her eyes roll up to her hairline in irritation. "Look at yourself," she let out a snort. "*Dullsville. Boring.* You so frumpy you make Plain Jane look fly!" A sound in the background distracted her. "I gotta go. You're still coming to graduation, right?"

"Yeah," Alayna sighed.

"All right."

A second later she was listening to the dead air of an ended call. Twice in one day, someone had gotten on her case about her style, or apparent lack thereof. What had Ice said? Something about her practical hair and her utilitarian clothes.

Disgusted, Alayna slid off the window seat.

In the bathroom mirror, she stared at her face. Beneath the white gauze was a two-inch gash, sewed tight by stitches slicing the now-receding swelling just above her left eye. It was ugly, but not as ugly as the gauze. Alayna threw the patch into the garbage and leaned forward, squinting at her reflection.

Imagined without the lump, it was a nice enough face. Brown skin the color of walnuts without blemish from forehead to chin. A nose—a little flat and fleshy around the nostrils—but okay. A pair of dark brown eyes fringed by a decent flock of lashes, though one of them was still bruised and dark. Full lips that looked kinda pale and a little dry, but not cracking or scarred. Not supermodel gorgeous, but far from lizard-butt. Alayna let her shoulder-length hair out of its clip. It was black and relaxed to fashionable straightness, but without any style. No cut, no color, no curl. And she'd worn it the exact same way for as long as she could remember, pulled straight off her face in a ponytail, or tucked up in a bun.

Hair. It was as good a place to start as any.

She grabbed a comb and a pair of sharp scissors, found her old curling iron and some rollers in a haphazardly packed cosmetic bag. Instant gratitude for all those years she and Martine had been too broke for the salons surged to the top of her mind. With the pages of *Ebony, Jet* and *Black Hair Secrets* open on the floor around them, they'd whiled away many a Saturday afternoon styling each other's hair. She wondered if Martine remembered. It hadn't always been argument, struggle and strife. Sometimes being sisters, being two girls raising themselves alone, had been fun.

Alayna cut a deep part at the back of her head and brushed half her hair toward her face. Even alone, there were worse ways to spend an evening than playing beauty shop.

Chapter 17

"My goodness, Alayna. I hardly recognized you!" Ada Mae Potter's hands fluttered toward Alayna for a moment, as though she'd had the impulse to feel the thick black curls framing Alayna's face. And Alayna wouldn't have minded, but the old woman reclaimed them long before her fingers ever actually came near enough for touch, restoring them to the order and calm of her switchboard. Alayna thought she read something in the woman's eyes, something like uncertainty, something like unease.

Prickly. That's what Ice had called her. Apparently, Ada Mae Potter thought so, too. At least enough to worry about how Alayna might react if she touched her without expressed written permission.

"Your hair. It's lovely," she continued kindly. And there was nothing but sincerity in her voice. "And is that a new dress?"

"Yes," Alayna said, self-consciously smoothing the fabric around her hips. "Bangs are better than that bandage, I guess."

"Much. But it seems to be healing nicely, and you look very pretty. That color blue suits you. Sapphire, isn't that what it's called?" She smiled encouragingly, and Alayna felt an irrational gratitude surge in her heart. It wasn't like she needed this old white lady's praise, but it was nice to hear something nice all the same. "A touch of lipstick and you'll be quite stunning," the ancient receptionist concluded, then lowered her voice for a different tidbit. "Oh," Ada Mae chuckled a grandmotherly chuckle. "Trixie's looking for you."

"Where's Mr. Freeze?" Trixie asked almost the second Alayna entered the War Room. She, too, looked Alayna up and down, trying hard and failing miserably to pretend no interest in new dresses and black eyes.

"He'll be here," Alayna replied.

"I gotta go if Weston needs me," Trixie reminded Alayna, wrapping the shapeless red rag of sweater she always wore tightly around her skinny frame.

"Then let's get started. We just need to—"

"I know," Trixie snapped. "I may not have a college degree, but I was indexing documents before you were *born*. Back when we had to do it all by hand. What's the case about?"

Alayna told her in as few words as possible, planning to make this encounter one of the longer ones of their forced companionship. Trixie seemed to have the same idea, because she nodded once, her bright blue eyes glittering like medical sharps.

"Okay, so it's about computers and stuff—I got that. But other than that, it's just a garden variety theft case, right?"

The woman's reaction was so similar to her own first-blush take on the complexities of the law of intellectual property that Alayna almost laughed.

"Yep."

Trixie grimaced. "Lawyers. Why use one word when you can use sixteen thousand?"

Alayna sank into a chair beside her. "Did Weston volunteer you for this or . . . ?"

The woman's beady marble eyes snapped to her face. "I wanted to do it."

"Why?" Alayna asked, instantly suspicious. Trixie had been ace-boon coon with the unfortunate Greta Jennings and made no secret of just how much she'd hated Alayna's guts since Lawyer Barbie had resigned.

And true to form, Trailer Trixie shut down faster than a Carribbean food stand when the health inspector steps up for some roti.

"Because," she replied testily. Translation: *None of your damn business.*

Alayna would have bet money that a couple of days with Ice would send Trixie back to Weston with her hurt feelings in a paper bag, but no such luck. By her second day on the case, Ice was in love. Like she'd known the case for months, Trailer Trixie dived into the tedious work of summarizing, numbering and cataloging box after box of legal documents with gusto. She speared each piece of paper with those sharp rat teeth of hers and digested it as if corporate documents were her entree of choice. And even better, from Ice's perspective anyway, she asked him no questions whatsoever. Just filed, stamped, cataloged and summarized, all in silence, though Alayna occasionally looked up to see those too-bright, too-beady eyes crawling from his profile to hers like something with too many legs.

Which might have been another of God's strange blessings, because Trixie distracted her just enough just by sitting there to limit Alayna's thoughts of Martine to every *other* thought rather than every *single* thought. She'd gone to sleep a concerned sister and awakened an addict in the throes of detox, shocked by the depth of her jones, shaking with the urge not for drugs or alcohol or sex but with the fierce and almost overwhelming desire to call home and check in.

Alayna exhaled a quiet sigh of inner turmoil. Nosey as he was, Ice looked over at her anyway, watching her face like he expected her to say something. Then he gave her one of those inscrutable Ice smiles, unfolded himself from his chair and stretched like he needed to wrap the whole room in his arms.

"I need some more coffee," he announced like this was something new and significant that deserved special commendation. "Want some?"

"You making?"

"What do you think?"

Of course he was. He always did. Dumped whatever was in the office coffeepot straight down the drain, even if it was full to the brim and the person who had just made it was still standing right there, stirring in her creamer. Dumped it *all* and started over from scratch. It was one of the little things that made him oh-so-popular around this law office. That, and he'd be just as likely to tell that poor coffee stirrer to get out of his face as say good morning.

But the truth was, Ice made great coffee, a thousand

times better than anyone else's. He might not know how to open a bag of pasta or how to pick his dirty shorts up off the floor, but the man could *brew*. If his legal career came to an end tomorrow, there were coffee bars that would pay top minimum-wage dollars for his services and be glad of it.

"You know how I like it," Alayna said, flicking the skin of her wrist at him. "Got it?"

"Thanks for the visual . . . *again*," he said in the same yeah-yeah-I'm-not-an-idiot-you-don't-have-to-tell-me-that tone he always did when she gave him the arm reminder. He quirked a querying eyebrow at Trixie, who was getting a tennis neck from following the volley of their conversation.

"Yeah," she growled, rising. "But I'd better come with you. Since I'm not *lucky* enough to have skin that serves as a visual aid."

Then she laughed a gravelly laugh that sounded like pebbles in a blender and stuffed her knobby fingers into the stretched-out pockets of her red sweater.

Something about the way she said the words "lucky" and "skin." Something about the laugh. Like flame to a pilot light, fury leapt to life in the pit of Alayna's stomach and sprang to her brain. She opened her lips, mouth set for the I-don't-have-to-take-any-shit-from-you tone of voice, but Ice was in line ahead of her.

"Get a tan."

Alayna swallowed her incendiary sentence with a snort, staring, like Trixie, at Ice like he'd just sprouted a second head. But he just stood there, the only one in the room who knew for sure whether his words were a slam, or a joke, or just an observation.

"Well, if you're coming, come on," Ice muttered, yanking the door open impatiently and preceding her into the hallway.

Trixie pulled a pack of cigarettes and a chipped Bic out of her pockets, then followed him without another word. If she said anything else that wasn't strictly necessary for the remainder of the day, Alayna didn't hear it. But every time she looked up, those weasel-like blue eyes were darting from Ice to herself and back again.

"Does it hurt?" Alayna paused just long enough for Trailer Trixie to add, gruffly, "if you don't mind me asking."

Biting back a tart response in favor of one more appropriate to the circumstances—their desperate need of this woman's help with sixteen tons of documentation—Alayna shrugged and muttered, "I'm flesh and blood, just like you."

"Blood," Trixie sniggered a little, showing a mouthful of small, tar-blackened teeth. "You can say that again. Surprised they got that carpet cleaned up as well as they did. But then I guess we can thank Richards for that."

"Ice?" Alayna shook her head. "Doubt he cares about the carpets. You've seen his office. Pigs live better."

But Trixie didn't seem to be listening. She stared at Alayna, her mouth a wide-open ring of surprise. "You heard about how he freaked out, right? I mean, *some-body* told you."

"Told me what?" Alayna frowned distrust at the

woman and raised her guard a couple of notches, just in case. "Who freaked? Weston?"

Trixie rolled her eyes. "Weston would only freak if you bled on his wallet," Trixie grumbled. "No. Richards. The Freezer. Ice or whatever you call him. Freaked out. Started hollering for 911, ice packs, first-aid kits. Insisted on holding you. The paramedics had to pry him off you." Then she graced Alayna with a cagey little smile, like she was happy to have been the bearer of this somewhat dubious information.

"You're exaggerating," Alayna scoffed.

"If I'm lying I'm dying," Trixie said soberly, raising her hand in an oath. "Ask anybody. Damn near the whole firm saw it. Big fat hullabaloo, that's what it was."

Knowing the whole firm watched her bleed all over the floor while an uptight lawyer had a meltdown wasn't exactly the kind of news Alayna liked to hear. But somehow Trailer Trixie's words tinkled with truth's little ding-a-ling bell. Or maybe for some reason she could imagine this scenario, the heroine out cold with a big bloody welt on her forehead while the hero screams for medical assistance. Melodrama. The stuff of all Martine's favorite television shows.

"Well," she said at last. "You know lawyers. Got to be the center of attention."

Trixie cackled until Alayna thought she might cough up a lung.

"Funny," she muttered, still hacking. "You know who you remind me of? That girl on that TV show." She crinkled her nose in an effort to watch it on the memorized screen behind her eyes. "You know who I mean. The one who always puts her hand on her hip and wiggles her neck." She made a vain and ridiculous attempt at imitation, poking out her lower lip and glowering while her head wobbled on its stem. "It comes on that channel with all the black people shows. I never actually *watched* it, but I've seen the commercials. Y*ou* must know."

Sure. All black people watch those silly sitcoms, while eating fried chicken and sucking down Colt 45. All black women have two or three kids by the time they're twenty, don't care how wide their asses get, and will gather poor white waifs like you to their ample bosoms and love you up like you're Scarlett O'Hara and this is Tara.

"No. I *don't* know."

Trixie's mouth clamped shut while Alayna gulped air like a drowning man, praying to the Holy Trinity for calm and strength. Trailer Trixie didn't say another word, like she knew any sentence that started with a reference to her "black friend" or "the black girl she knew once" would be finished in Kingdom Come.

"Oh, come on, Ali," Ice muttered. "I don't have time for this bullshit." He stuffed a mouthful of French fries into his face, chewed twice and washed them down with another swig of coffee. Alayna shook her head. It was a wonder he hadn't choked to death.

But they did smell good . . . and he'd made a nice big puddle of ketchup right in the center of the little basket they'd come in, so that the ends were nice and red and tangy. The salt and the sweet probably tasted delicious. She leaned closer as he scooped up about six more and tossed his head back, the better to snap them up whole from salty tip to tomato-ey ends.

"We need help, she volunteered to make a little extra cash. That's it. You know what your trouble is?" he continued. "Everything's a conspiracy to you. You're *paranoid.*"

He slid the fries toward her, nodding invitation. Alayna was on the verge of declining, but the things were talking to her, wafting their enticing smell under her nose like the ultimate distraction. And to make matters worse, Ice picked up a nice long one, re-dunked one end deep in the ketchup and leaned toward her, waving it seductively under her nose.

"This fry is out to get you, Alayna," he intoned. "It's a part of a vast conspiracy—"

"Oh, shut up," Alayna muttered, slapping his hand away. "This coming from a man with so many secrets, he can't even keep track of them all."

Ice ate the French fry, wiped his hands and mouth with a greasy napkin, then pushed the rest of the basket toward her.

"Okay. So maybe Trixie doesn't like me. So what?" he muttered, showing her some crushed potato parts. "What's she gonna do? *Gossip* me to death?"

"That could hurt you plenty around here. Probably already has," Alayna added, giving in to the siren call of the French fries. "Maybe Weston wants her to give him and the partnership committee the 411 on you."

"I thought that's what you were for."

"Me?" Alayna started. "Why would I—"

Ice laughed. "Got ya. I'm not worried about this. I'm surprised you gave it any credence at all."

"Oh. Excuse me. I forgot who I was talking to. The

big bad white boy. No one can hurt *you*. You're immune."

"White, black. Black, white. What does *that* have to do with anything?"

"Everything."

"Nothing. Christ, Ali. Sometimes I think you're just as racist as the people you complain about."

"Me!"

"Yeah, you. You don't speak to half the firm—"

"Look who's talking—"

"You've got a chip on your shoulder about discrimination that you're just dying for someone to knock off—"

"Now wait a minute—"

"You see the KKK in every white person you meet—"

"I do not—"

"Then why do you care? How can what they say hurt you? How can it *hurt* me?"

"White people. You don't believe snakes crawl 'til they bite you on the butt. That's your problem."

"Black people," he said, mimicking her tone exactly. He even stuck a hand on his hip. "See snakes where there's nothing but string."

"Fine. Think that. Think no one can hurt you. One day you'll find out what I already *know*. That they *can* and they will if you're fool enough to give them the chance." The French fries were habit forming and she reached for another couple, ignoring the don't-eat-'em-all look on Ice's face. "There are people right here in this firm who would just as soon stab you in the back as give you the time of day."

"And if you're looking for a backstabber, Ali, you'll

find one. Every time. And don't forget, they come in all colors, backstabbers." He paused, blinking at her soberly too long for comfort. "So do friends," he said, locking those slate saucers on her face.

To her knowledge, Alayna had never blushed. Sure, sometimes her ears felt hot like someone had turned on the heat in her brain, but other than that, no. Blushing was for little white girls with skin like porcelain dolls. Or for goofy white men who didn't know how to say what they meant or mean what they'd said. Blushing was for people who had something to be embarrassed about.

But Ice stared at her so seriously for so long that she finally felt just about as nervous as a bride. No. Nervous as groom. Brides didn't get nervous. They got *determined*.

"Preach on, Ice," she said to him finally just to cut the tension. "Just don't expect me to pull out the blade after Trailer Trixie does in your shot for partnership."

And it worked, because he shook his head and muttered, "There's no reasoning with you. Look, I've got to get out of here. I gotta meeting out at Cybex." And indeed he was already throwing things into his briefcase with the random disorder that was his habit in all things. "I don't know if I'll be back. I want you to start on the first draft of the brief on this constitutional thing—"

"The brief? Me?" Alayna stopped mid-French-fry crunch. Pulling the cases was one thing—even reading them and figuring out which were the strongest. But drafting the brief? "I don't know, Ice. I can handle the research but"—she shook her curls—"it's a pretty complicated argument."

"Hey. You wanted more responsibility. 'As much as I can handle,' you said. So . . . stop wasting your time worrying about Trixie, and *handle* it." He leaned across the table and patted her cheek. *"Got it?"* He snapped his overstuffed briefcase shut and struggled into his jacket. "I got to make like a train whistle and blow."

"What?" Alayna couldn't help grinning.

"My father used to say that . . . a long time ago," Ice said.

And even though he was grinning that I-think-I'm-pretty-damn-cool grin, there was a touch of sadness in his eyes that hadn't been there before.

He leaned over like he was going to kiss her good-bye again, but he changed his mind mid-lean and just squeezed her shoulder instead.

"Toot-toot," he muttered and left.

She stood in the cluttered office after he was gone, thinking through their conversation . . . and eating the last of the fries, since Ice had been kind enough to leave the remains in their little paper basket, smack in the center of his desk.

He was dead wrong about Trixie McCoy; she knew it. That was the trouble with talking to white people about racism, of talking to men about sexism, the problem with talking to anyone who never lived under an -ism of any kind in their entire lives. Until there were crosses burning on the front lawn, they not only didn't have the vocabulary for it, they couldn't even see it.

Finally, she decided to just take the damn French fries and head back to her own work space, rather than standing here in the middle of the floor in Ice's.

And of course, as she closed his door behind her, who else came swinging up the hall but Trixie, the smell of cigarette smoke clinging to her like her own personal cloud. Her eyes flickered over Ice's door, and she licked her lips like she had the perfect smart something to say, until Alayna gave her a heavy-duty scary sister face. Instead, Trixie twisted her own face into a sneer and ambled back down the hall toward the War Room without saying a word.

Chapter 18

God doesn't care too much about the prayers your mouth and your mind make, but He must love the little ones you make in your heart.

Because when the setting sun and a job well done released Alayna from Hughes Weston and Moore that evening, she found the secret longing of her heart sitting on the steps outside her apartment building.

The girl had barely straggled to her feet when Alayna's arms went hard around her, feeling her slender shoulders, smelling the familiar scents of bar soap and Intensive Care lotion and the coconut-y oil sheen Martine always sprayed on her hair. *Family*, Alayna breathed deeply, nestling her chin against the girl's warm neck, *no one else smells like them*.

At first, Martine patted her back, trying to play like she didn't want or need a hug from her sister. But she finally gave in, and Alayna was encircled as Martine hugged back, squeezing for dear life.

"What's this for?"

"Nothing," Alayna said too quickly, blinking back

the tears already blinding her. "Just a bad day at White Folks, Inc. I guess."

"No, I mean it." And Alayna thought she heard the little catch of emotion beneath the light tone. "You haven't hugged me in . . . I don't know how long. What's up?"

"It hasn't been *that* long."

"Yeah it has," Martine muttered, pulling away. What's the matter with you? and a host of other as yet unasked questions were written all over her face.

"What are you doing here?"

But Martine was too busy to answer. Too busy giving Alayna's dress a thorough up and down and the new bangs a critical smirk.

"What did you do to your hair? Cut it?" She grabbed a fat black curl at Alayna's chin and pulled it until it sprung back into place. "Hmmpt. Get the back trimmed at a salon . . . and maybe some highlights. Your color was always a little drab. But . . ." She shrugged a bit, refusing to say the obvious: Alayna looked good.

"Thanks," Alayna said, conducting an appraisal of her own and finding far less to compliment. Martine looked thin and sickly in spite of her efforts at calm and cute. "You all right?"

"Just sick to my stomach. As usual. Girl, I heard about morning sickness, but this is ridiculous." She shrugged toward the building's door, her face brightening with curiosity and excitement. "Can we go in?"

Alayna led the way. When they reached the apartment, she opened the door and ushered her sister inside, quickly flipping on lights, yanking down blinds and checking messages like this was a routine of months or years, instead of only a couple of days.

Martine was too busy to pay Alayna's bustlings much mind. Her eyes crawled from the window seat's fluffy pastel pillows to the bookshelves adorned with the pictures from home to the tiny kitchen alcove and finally to the big white bed, where Alayna had just dropped her purse and the heavy black satchel she usually carried instead of a briefcase. Martine's lips and eyebrows made another little contraction of approval before settling on Alayna's face, which was glinting with fresh curiosity.

But before Martine could launch her offensive, Alayna initiated one of her own.

"Where's Jamal?"

"Working. His job started this week."

"Where?"

"Delivering pizzas."

Alayna suppressed a remark about how many minimum-wage jobs it took to support their household and poured her sister a glass of water from a little Lucite pitcher—courtesy of Corporate Rentals—instead.

"You don't look so good—"

"Yeah, well look who's talking," Martine quipped, but she was smiling a little. "It looked kinda green on Saturday, but I didn't think you'd get a full-blown black eye out of it. Makes you look like Ice took a closed fist to you."

"Yeah. I've been getting that a lot." Alayna handed her a glass. "Drink this. I read somewhere it's important for you to stay hydrated."

"I know that, Alayna," Martine rolled her eyes. "For a second I thought I had the wrong apartment. You're acting all . . . weird and stuff. But it's you all right. Just can't stop, can you?"

Still, she drank it down thirstily, handed the glass back, accepted a refill.

"So. How did you get here?"

"Bus."

Alayna frowned. "It's late, Martine."

"Well, we don't have a *car* . . ." And this had that hint of request buried deep within it, and Alayna halfway expected to hear ". . . unless you'll give us the Jeep." But instead, Martine concluded with a relatively tame, ". . . and I figured you'd drive me home."

"So what did you want to talk to me about? Is something wrong?"

Martine's eyes shifted, signaling the end of their smooth ride. Alayna took a seat on the bar stool beside the girl, strapped on an imaginary lapbelt and prepared herself for turbulence.

"Does something have to be *wrong?*" Martine's lips crunched together in annoyed disgust. "Maybe I just came to visit. See how you were. I mean, you still got a great big knot on your head and everything."

"Did you?"

"Yeah!"

But then Alayna knew her too well, well enough to read every blink, every widening of the eyes and sniff of the nose. She knew the tones of truth, the smell of a lie, and the brief silence that preceded deceit. The brief second of hesitation before Martine had said "Yeah" had told Alayna everything she needed to know. She folded her arms on the counter, and waited, staring at the girl with eyes that said, *Nice try, sister girl. Nice try.*

"I did!" Martine insisted. "Sort of. I mean, I also wanted to know if you're still coming to graduation."

"I'm still invited, aren't I?"

That got another eye roll, this one more dramatic than the first. "You're my only family, Alayna. Cut it out," she sighed. "You bringing Ice Man?"

Ice? Oh yeah, her boyfriend who wasn't her boyfriend who was still sort of her boyfriend for certain purposes. A state of affairs that had the same circular truth as Martine's not-pregnant-pregnant story to Jamal, Alayna thought, feeling a little ashamed of herself for coming down so hard on the girl way back when. Especially since she was now going to sit here and pull a lie as big as a whale out of her butt and offer it up for general admiration.

"Uh . . . he . . ."

" 'Cause if he's not, Nalexi needs another ticket, and—"

"Give it to her then," Alayna agreed quickly . . . too quickly probably. "It's okay. Ice—I mean *Ben*—will understand."

Calling him by the name his mama had actually given him felt strange, like she was speaking a foreign language. Ben. Ice didn't look like a Ben. He didn't act like a Ben either, but then, what mother on God's Green Earth would look into the face of her newborn son and ask the nurse to put Overconfident Jerk on his birth certificate?

Martine either chose not to notice Alayna's quick insertion of the man's given name or had lost interest in Alayna's love life altogether because her next words were, "Get me a graduation present?"

"Not yet. What do you want?"

Martine's eyes darted around the apartment again. For a second Alayna feared the girl would say *This place* and set off an argument it would take a couple of burly cops to settle. She imagined the look on Ice's face when she presented herself at work the next morning with another black eye courtesy of her own baby sister. He'd probably just shake his head and swear off rescuing damsels in distress for the rest of his days.

But instead, Martine said simply, "Money. Cash, if you got it."

Which was exactly what Alayna should have expected in the first place, if Ice thoughts hadn't entered the picture.

"Fine. I'll put what I was gonna spend in your card."

"Well see," Martine's skinny hindquarters shifted on the bar stool. "The thing is, we, I, want it now."

"Now?" Alayna left Ice in the tundra and snapped her total attention to Martine. "Why? You guys can't be in trouble already?"

"We're not in *trouble*, Alayna! Jeez!"

"Then why?"

"Look, I just *need* it. Okay?"

"For what?"

"I just do."

Martine's eyes said she was bracing herself for the coming tirade about responsibility and frugality. But considering Alayna's whole life had been spilling and rolling like the contents of a cereal box in the hands of a chunky child, all she did was smile. She would have hugged the girl again had Martine not had that sour, demanding look on her face.

"If you can't do better than that, you'll have to wait until Sunday," Alayna said cheerfully. "I know what you're up to, and I don't think you should be blowing money on parties for your friends. You guys are going to need every penny when that baby gets here. Put it in your savings account and—"

"Yeah, yeah," Martine grumbled, cutting her off. "I didn't think it'd work, but it was worth a try." She shrugged off the defeat and launched her next missile without segue. "You aren't really gonna take me off your health insurance, are you?"

Alayna paused. Ice had urged her to start the paperwork, but Alayna hadn't even made it to Personnel yet. Visiting Personnel was like issuing a press release at Hughes Weston and Moore, since, ironically, the department was run by the biggest loudmouth the joint had.

"Eventually," she said slowly. "Why?"

" 'Cause see, they don't get no benefits at the Pizza Shack until they been there a *year*." Martine shook her head with dubious disbelief. How dare Pizza Shack choose not to invest in employees who keep their jobs all of twenty minutes? The nerve. "And until I get something better than the video store—"

"Tried to tell you this, but no. You guys thought you had it under control," Alayna chided, flipping back to instinct, automatic pilot, the conditioning of ten years of pseudo-maternity. "You and Jamal take things like health insurance for granted when the truth is you gotta *earn* benefits with hard work and—"

Martine showed her a traffic cop palm. "If you're gonna be like *that* about every little thing I ask you for, just forget it," she muttered, sliding off the stool and giving Alayna a full view of her wasted figure. Martine had always been slim—except for her behind, which puckered out from the rest of her like a little Africa—but now even her bottom had shrunk to bone.

"Jamal was right!" she railed. "We ain't got nobody to help us. We got to do this ourselves, no matter *what*."

"You got to have insurance!" Alayna grabbed her sister's shoulders and planted Tiny Butt back onto the stool. "'Specially in your condition. I'll leave you on it as long as I can, but once they find out you're married, well, you should probably go back to that doctor. See what they think about the morning sickness."

"I *know,* Alayna," Martine spat in the voice she usually reserved for the chronically stupid. "I'm *going.* Friday. That's why I *asked* you about the insurance."

"You could have called for that."

Martine sighed. "Like I said, Alayna. I wanted to see . . . your place . . . and . . . all. It's nice," she finished quickly, before Alayna could conclude that she might be *missed* or anything like that. "Jamal and I coulda got a cute little place like this if you and his grandparents woulda come up off our college money."

"No, Martine," Alayna said, but the smile had returned to her face again. "Come on. It's late and you need your rest."

"There you go again."

"Fine. *I* need *my* rest. I'll drive you home."

Martine inspected Alayna carefully.

"Sure your man won't mind?" Martine peered around the apartment like she might have missed something in its tiny accoutrements.

"What man?"

"Ice. *Ben.*"

So she *had* caught that.

"Oh," Alayna said quickly. "Him. We have so much work right now that we won't . . . hook up . . . until the weekend."

Martine grinned. "Oh. You won't hook up until the weekend? Sure you're hooking up at all? I don't see you doing the nasty with no white boy." Her nose crinkled in mischief. "What's it like?"

"Like any other man," Alayna answered quickly. "Now—"

"You know what they say . . . about how they got little—"

"Martine!"

"Well! I'm just curious, that's all. He *is* a white man, after all."

"Don't let his skin tone fool you. Ice ain't white. He's just Ice. Frozen water. Everybody knows about water. You can see right through it."

"But is it big or—"

"I'm not discussing this with you, Martine," Alayna said, drawing chalk lines of finality around the words. "Now come on. I got a big day tomorrow."

Chapter 19

Friday morning, Ice decided to break loose some Hell around the office and prop it up. And Alayna damn near missed the whole thing.

She overslept; trying to be pretty added time to the morning routine, and it was after ten before Alayna was hurrying up the corridor toward the War Room, walking the length of it in a narrow light blue skirt purchased the day before in a spur-of-the-moment-people-working-my-nerves spree. The door to Ice's office was closed, but that was neither unusual nor unfortunate. It simply meant Ice was here, Ice didn't want to be bothered, and Ice was ignoring the firm's open door policy and being Icy.

After all, he was above office decorum. He was the Ice Man, million-dollar-almost-partner guy. More power to him.

But just as she cleared his doorway, Ice the Immune's door flew open, rebounding on its hinges with a sudden burst of sound and light. Trixie came tumbling out into the corridor like he'd thrown her there.

"Mind your damn business!" Ice shouted from the interior, then the door slammed closed, echoing down the corridor like the crack of a gunshot.

Heads appeared around corners, poked out of cubicles and offices as secretaries, lawyers and paralegals leaned into the hallway to find out what the fuss was about.

Poor Trailer Trixie gripped that lank red sweater more tightly around her and stared, stunned, looking for all the world like a flat-haired, raccoon-eyed refugee from a frigid war zone.

"My God!" she exhaled, turning eyes as bright and round as a photo of the Earth from space at Alayna. "My God! How-how—"

"What happened?"

"I—I was tryin' to help—," she stammered, seeming willing to accept help even in Alayna's particular shade of brown in this moment of need. "And—and he just—"

Alayna's hand was already on the knob when Weston rounded the corner, his moon face pinking with anger.

"What the hell's going on, Trixie?" he demanded, giving Alayna a scrunchy face of disapproval. "Who's slammin' doors and screamin' and hollerin'—"

"Me," Trixie interrupted, but she pulled herself together a little, squaring off to the man with near defiance that might have passed as "attitude" had her face not been so pink with distress. "Richards pissed me off. Let the door go a little harder than I meant to. Won't happen again. Sir." She cast a quick don't-blow-it glance at Alayna, enlisting her in a conspiracy that, as yet, Alayna knew nothing about.

"Well," Weston grumbled. "If it's going like that, maybe you need to come back to typing—"

"No!" Trixie exclaimed too quickly, and a kind of beaten-down Deference took Defiance's chair in her tone. "I mean, no. Sir. Alayna will smooth it out, won't you?"

"I'm sure it's nothing," Alayna said quickly, watching Weston's face. "We're under a lot of pressure here. All of us. Lot of work, tight deadline."

Weston stared from one to the other like he knew he was buying a sack of baloney, but if he didn't take it there'd be no meat today.

"I got a client in my office," he muttered. "And you guys are out here acting like kindergartners." He pointed a stubby finger in Trixie's face. "You do what The Freezer tells you to do or I'll put you back behind your desk."

A dark and concentrated loathing possessed Trixie's face for an instant before she muttered, "Yes, sir" and scuttled down the hallway imitating a police officer breaking up a disturbance with her "Nothing to see here, move along" mutterings to the sundry faces of the assembled crowd. She looked back only once, cutting her eyes in another urgent glance between Alayna and Ice's closed door.

The whole thing had the stink of a setup.

He was slumped in his chair, which was swiveled toward the paper-strewn credenza behind him, showing her little more than the black bolsters of the headrest and the very tip of his head.

"Hey," she said cautiously. "Ice. It's me."

"What do you want?" he snapped.

"What's the matter? Trixie finally piss you off?"

"She didn't piss me off," he muttered, two-tongued and slurred. Alayna edged a little closer to the back of his chair.

"Then what did she do?" she continued lightly. "Ask too many questions? Eavesdrop on your phone calls? Tap into your e-mail?"

No answer at all.

"I got it. She tried to seduce you."

That should have been funny, but Ice just sighed. "She doesn't have the right . . . equipment . . . as they—we—say," he said as convincingly as a prediction for August snow. But he still wouldn't turn, wouldn't look at her. As inappropriate as a belch at tea with the queen, her pocket analysis of the man's sexuality tallied up another two cents in the hetero column and another dollar on the what's-the-real-secret bottom line.

"Then what the hell's the matter with you?" she asked, taking the don't-piss-a-sister-off tone—since nothing else worked anyway. She swung his chair toward her so she could stare him dead in his face.

Or rather, what was left of it.

Someone had split his bottom lip into two swollen bubbles with the business end of a fist. He was pressing a makeshift ice pack of a few cubes wrapped in a bloody handkerchief against it, but it didn't appear to be doing much good. His lip looked like it had been pumped with air.

"Good God, Ice!" Alayna breathed. "What in the *world* . . . ?"

"Not you, too," he muttered. "I'll throw *you* out of here next if you're going to start moaning about a doctor."

"You don't need a doctor, you need a *keeper*," Alayna grumbled, taking the handkerchief from him and setting to work mopping at the lip like a corner Cut Man during a Title fight. "Honestly. Can't leave you alone for a second. Now, shut up and hold still."

He dodged her fingers like a petulant "got a boo-boo" baby until she squeezed his face in a vise and held it.

"It's fine . . . damn!" he said, and he winced as Alayna's fingers finally made contact with the damaged skin around his mouth. He grimaced, then closed his eyes and his mouth as the cool of an ice cube addressed his lower lip.

Child, adult, man or woman, there's something intimate about touching someone's face. First of all, you have to get pretty damn close to them to do it, and then there you are, looking into their eyes. And face skin, unlike hand skin, or arm skin, or skin almost anywhere else on the body, always has a delicacy to it. A vulnerability. Touching Ice on the face wasn't any different. He must have shaved before he'd gotten smacked, because his skin was smooth and thin—almost papery—over the bones of his jaw. And when her fingertips brushed against his lips, they were surprisingly soft. He opened those pearly grays suddenly and fixed her with a look that flipped a switch inside her and set off a chain reaction of funny, uncomfortable twitches from tits to crotch.

"I thought you knew how to fight," she muttered, hoping her blouse concealed the fact that her nipples had sudden perked up and made their presence known. "Who hit you?"

"A table."

"Very funny." Alayna folded her mouth in disbelief. "Only your table really did have four fingers and a thumb. How's he? The other guy?"

"Fine." He rubbed his rib cage a little, and for the first time, Alayna noticed that his shirt was a dirty mess, missing buttons and pulled loose from his belt like it, too, had been the victim of a major tussle.

"What? You owe Lenny the Shark some money?"

"No."

"Pick a fight with a street gang?"

"I didn't pick anything," he muttered, pulling the ice out of her hand. "If you must know, I didn't even see him. Parked my car and was on my way into the building and," he paused, his eyes shifting from her face to the window, "some guy in a ski mask jumps in front of me and slugs me. He . . . uh . . . swiped my wallet. Then he was gone."

"You were *mugged* in the parking lot? This morning?" Alayna grabbed the telephone. "You call the cops, right now—"

"NO!" Ice snatched the phone out of her hand and slammed it into the cradle. "You sound like that stupid Trixie again."

Alayna quirked an eyebrow at him. "Calling the cops doesn't sound stupid to me," Alayna said slowly. "In fact, *not* calling the cops sounds stupid to me. If someone jumped *you,* who's next? Me? Ada Mae Potter? Ice, you've got to—"

"No. Uh . . . he's gone. It was just . . . me . . . he wanted."

Alayna eyed him dubiously. "*You*? Why?"

But that got nothing but silence as an answer. For all his even, steady gaze, the falsehood stank to high heaven.

"More clause two, Ice?" she said softly. "Someone beats the hell out of you and—"

"It was just one shot. I wasn't expecting it—"

"What will you tell me next? It's some kind of *gay* thing—"

Something dark stirred in Ice's eyes, and he stood up, slowly uncoiling himself from his chair like a long, pale snake.

"What did you say?" he hissed.

"Gay. Fairy. Queer!" Alayna coated each word with contempt before hurling it at him, watching the rage in his face degenerate into fury as she let fly every nasty invective she'd ever heard for a homosexual male.

"Shut up!" Ice roared as his hand circled around the nearest thing—his coffee tankard—and he threw it with all his strength. It sailed across the room and collided with an unspectacular slam against the opposite wall.

Alayna rounded on him with both barrels loaded.

"What the hell is your *problem*? Who did this?" she demanded. "What is the deep, dark secret? What are you *hiding*?"

"Nothing!" he shouted. "Now leave me alone!"

He started for the door, but Alayna had anticipated Ice's famous escape move. She put herself between him and the exit, chin raised in challenge.

"No! No *running*. Not this time. This time you're going to *say* something!"

"About what?" he growled through gritted teeth.

"About what's going on with you!"

Had he been in a better mood, he probably would have laughed, or at least that's what she read in his face as he measured his six-foot-three, God only knew how many pounds against her slender five-foot-six. One shove—it didn't even have to be hard—and she'd be on the floor and he'd be out there.

But as she expected—though his fingers were curled into fists at his sides—he did no such thing. Instead he stepped backwards away from her, took a deep breath and closed his eyes to coax his composure back. When he spoke again, he was safely back in civil decibels.

"Ms. Jackson," he began, letting her know right there that she'd pushed him close to his absolute limit. He hadn't called her that in weeks. "Clause two—"

"To hell with clause two!" Alayna hissed. "You know what? You . . . you play one of those double standards. You want to be all up in my business, you want to share and be concerned and helpful, but let someone get within a mile of your shit and—whammo! It's clause two!"

"We made an agreement," he said, trying to keep his voice level and detached. Like that was going to spare him her anger or something.

"You know, you're really good at telling other people about themselves but pretty lousy at listening to the truth about your own damn self."

"And what might the truth about my own damn self be, according to you?"

"That something's *wrong!*"

He squeezed his temples, squinting, then exhaled heavily. "Don't be so dramatic," he muttered. "Other than this case and you driving me crazy, nothing is *wrong*."

"Really? Then how do you explain *this?*" She grabbed his face, pinching until he winced again and pulled away. "And how do you explain *that?*" She nodded toward the brown, streaked wall and the contents of the mug puddling black on the blue carpet.

"She calls me names then wants to know why I got mad," he muttered.

"Stop it, Ice. You're not gay and we *both* know it."

His mouth opened in immediate denial, but Alayna shut it with an upturned palm.

"We *both* know it," she repeated firmly. "So the only question is, what are you hiding that's so important you'd rather the whole world think you were gay than admit it? Who are you protecting that you'd tell me some bullshit about a mugger—"

"I told you. I'm *gay*." His voice dropped to a whisper that might have been a hiss had his thick bottom lip not prevented that. "And you don't know what the hell you're talking about."

"I know enough not to believe you. You can say that to anybody else you want, but I *know* you, Ice."

"You know me? That's funny. What do you know about me? What difference does it make to you? What do *you* care anyway."

"You're right. I don't care!" Alayna exploded. "But only because you won't let me. Dammit man, I'm trying to be your *friend* here! I'm trying to understand what your problem is—what's so wrong in your life that you'd let people think you're gay, that you're crazy, that you're the biggest asshole to walk the earth rather than tell a single living soul—"

He started moving then, but she grabbed his arm, stopping the exodus with a sudden vehement rush of words. "What is it? Who's sick? Who's dying? Who are you protecting with all of your strength?"

"No one. No one's sick. No one's dying. My God, what—"

"Stop it. You think I'm stupid? You think I don't know about drop-everything-and-come-home phone calls? You think I haven't told all kinds of lies to keep strangers out of my family's final business. I told you I used to sleep in my car—"

"It's nothing like that—"

"Why can't you just *tell* me? Maybe you don't think you can tell anyone else, but you can tell me. Because if you're going through anything like the hell I went through when my mother died . . . I'm *with* you, Ice, not against you! And I care because I *know* beneath all your bullshit there's a decent human being who cares about people! And I care because I . . . I—I—"

The fine hairs of his forearm were warm beneath her hand, and the rest of him was very close to her now, close enough for her to curl the fingers of her other hand around a shoulder, or lay against his pale, tired cheek. She wanted to do just that: put both of her hands on him. Pull him into her arms and tell him everything would be all right in God's own good time. To just hang on until then. Hang on for dear life.

He seemed to read it in her face, because his expression softened a little and the tension in his body eased just the tiniest fraction. Those steel eyes begged for the finished sentence.

". . . because I . . ." she faltered.

Could have been her imagination, or the twitching trick of a fat lip, but she thought she saw the faintest hint of a smile lift Ice's kisser. Like he'd read a chapter of her mind and was pleased with its contents.

It didn't stop him from acting like an asshole.

"Because you have got this whole thing totally wrong," he grunted.

Bad tactic. Big mistake. She loosened her grip, let him go.

"I must have lost my damn mind to think there was anything beyond this Ice Man bit you like to play. To think that we might have been . . . friends . . . or something. . . ." She sighed in resignation and frustration. "But you don't want any friends, you don't need any friends. You don't need any comfort. You don't need nothing from nobody. You're the *man*. Nobody can hurt you. Only us flesh-and-blood folks can be hurt. Only us flesh-and-blood folks got weaknesses or need a shoulder or a hand. But not you. You're gonna be the hero or the asshole with nothing in between. And you know what? I don't need *either* one of them jokers."

"Alayna—"

But her hand was already on the doorknob.

"Call me if you ever decide to be a real human being, like the rest of us mere mortals. I got work to do."

She left him standing there, just like he liked to be: alone.

Chapter 20

"**D**id y'know that I been married to my old man for thirty years?"

For hours after the encounter with Ice, Trixie took a clue from Alayna's expression and didn't say one word to her, though those rabbity blue eyes followed her every movement as she slammed around the War Room, looking for God only knew what.

Alayna glared at her, wondering what had brought on both her sudden recovery and her unexpected choice of topic.

"Oh yeah?" she muttered. Subtext: "So what?" She gave up on the boxes and flipped the switch on a laptop stationed at the end of the long table.

"Yeah," Trixie continued with another asthmatic chuckle. "Got married young. Too young. Everyone said no way was this going to work. Too different, y'know?"

Alayna just stared at her.

"Fought with him every damn day of them years, too. Lazy, fat fart," she grumbled on, pursing her lips like the man was lazing and farting right here in front of them. "But let me tell you, when hard times hit, there ain't a better man. Not to me anyway."

Her pale eyebrow arched at Alayna. "You get what I'm saying?"

Alayna stared at her. The woman looked a *little* less Reb-ish than she had ten words ago, but not that much. "Look," she said at last. "I don't know who sent you here or what you think you're going to accomplish, but let me tell you right now, it's not going to work, okay? So why don't you do us both a favor and drop the let's be girlfriends routine, Trixie. The day you and I are friends is the day there's a Sister in the White House and you're playing my Mammy on TV."

Trixie's face skipped pink and went right to purple. "You're a piece of work, Alayna."

"Takes one to know one," Alayna muttered.

"A piece of work!" Trixie repeated, her voice raised in anger.

"At least I'm honest. I'm not playing this game with you, Trixie. Put all your cards on the table or go home. You've hated my guts every since Greta Jennings and—"

"Greta Jennings was a lousy lawyer," Trixie said stridently, poking a bony finger under Alayna's nose. "Everybody knew that. She didn't want to be a lawyer and she was bad at it and she was right to leave. But she was just a *kid*—and a damn nice kid at that—just trying to find her way! And you! You were just jealous—"

"Jealous! *Please!*" Alayna sucked her teeth in annoyance and showed the woman her back before the impulse to break her wagging finger became too strong to resist.

"Jealous because she had a degree. Jealous because people liked her. Jealous because she had *friends* here—"

"Friends who had to constantly cover for every mistake she made—"

"You didn't have to treat her like the dirt under your nails," Trixie continued, wound up to a nasty fury, "just because you were smarter than she was! But no. You stuck her in a box, slapped a label on her and did everything you could to get her out of here."

"She was incompetent!" Alayna nearly screamed.

"Did that give you the right to call her a stupid Barbie Doll?" Trixie shouted back. "No. I don't like you for that. Putting everybody into your little categories. You ought to know better. Of all people."

Then she sat back down and closed her lips, started gnawing on the contents of a thick personnel record. Snort and slam and mutter as Alayna might, Trixie did a pretty good job of pretending that she couldn't be bothered with looking up.

Linc's message had been to meet him at a place called Pedro's at seven. "Wear your sexiest dress and your dancing shoes, Pretty Lady," he'd said, in a chocolaty, delicious voice on the answering machine. " 'Cause we're gonna step *out!*"

At first she'd rejected the idea out of hand, but the alternative was a night alone with the television set. What was the point of having a new hairdo and a closet bulging with cute new clothes if no one ever saw them? And now, with Trailer Trixie reading her the riot act and Ice holed up in his office with an ice pack, she was thankful that Divine Providence had taken hold of her tongue and turned a certain no into the kind of maybe a man like Linc Warren understood as yes.

At seven o'clock on the proverbial dot, there she stood with her hair freshly styled, smelling like half the Macy's perfume counter (the salesgirl had caught a whiff of a scentless woman and decided to make her month's commission), and wearing a new red dress that was about as close to sexy as she was willing to step at this moment—a slinky little sheath of a sleeveless thing with a jewel neckline that skimmed the breast tops and a hem that stopped about three inches shorter than traditional business attire. With a black jacket, it *might* pass muster in the office, but never in court. The sandals were little shiny black strappy things that had made it absolutely essential to get a pedicure and polish, which had also meant her nails had had to get the treatment too or they would look naked. Those painted feet in those shiny shoes couldn't go anywhere but on a date.

She'd been standing in the entranceway to Pedro's for about five minutes, feeling increasingly self-conscious as every dude sauntering into the place gave her the face, tits and hindparts inspection and a few women scowled the you-think-you-cute ugly face at her. But just as a couple of the ho's looked like they might be ready to fight about it, Linc walked up, looking terrific in a smooth black double-breasted suit, white Chinese-collared shirt and sleek black Italian loafers. He looked mmm mmm good, but he smelled even better.

"Hi there," he murmured, taking her hand and pulling her close enough for a little peck on the cheek. An instant later he stepped away, his black eyes roving over her. "Where have you been all my life, girl? Gorgeous. Absolutely gorgeous. I gotta get you inside before you cause an accident."

Linc leaned across the table, rapt with attention.

"You kidding me? Boss Man came down the hall—"

"Yep—"

"And the secretary. Trailer Trash Trixie—"

"Trixie," Alayna corrected, still smarting with the woman's words. Maybe she owed the chick her proper name after all. Then again, maybe not.

"Man." Linc tossed back his head and laughed. "That's one crazy office, and one crazy white boy. Sleeping in his car, disappearing for hours at a time, getting into fights with garage-roving street gangs—"

"Crips!" Alayna joked, trying hard to rejoin the spirit of the thing since she'd violated about half the clauses in the contract in less than thirty minutes of conversation. But the way Ice had been acting lately, he didn't deserve more than a moment's guilt and not more than a second's consideration. Besides, she had to talk to somebody, and Martine wasn't home today. Alayna wondered vaguely if that was a good sign or a bad one. That doctor's visit was today, but it should have been over hours ago.

And somehow, she couldn't bring herself to relate

what had happened afterwards, or the choice words Trixie had tacked on her door like Martin Luther or some silly white girl vengeance squad. The possibility that the woman might even have a *point* was too sensitive for any serious consideration.

"Yeah, right," Linc rolled his eyes. "Why they always gotta be some black kids? White kids roll people, too, you know. And your White Boy, he crazy. He's certifiable. He don't mess with you, does he?"

Linc's voice had that protective edge in it again.

"No," she shook her head, making the stylist's elaborate cluster of curls swing in vehement denial. The woman had crimped and burnt every strand like she was getting paid by the hair instead of the whole head as a unit. "He's rude to me, but, he's rude to everyone. In fact—" she stopped. On the tip of her tongue were the words *he's better with me than anyone else,* but she didn't want to reopen the what-is-he-to-you can of worms with one more person today. And she didn't want to revisit Trixie's odd, opposites-attract love story or why Ice was competing with Martine for Every Thought status in her mind.

But Linc was waiting for her to say something.

"Even Boss Man complains about it," she added.

"But he takes it?"

Alayna shrugged. "Ice is good. Brilliant, even. Makes the firm a ton of money. Period. Weston's gonna have to make him a full partner, whether he likes Ice or not."

Linc blinked his liquid brown eyes at her soberly. "Full partner. A brother who acted the way this dude is acting would have been history long ago. I don't care how brilliant he was or how much money he made for the firm, you hear what I'm saying?" Linc's expression darkened. "The rules are always different for them. Always were. Always will be. And you watch your back. Trixie sounds like a setup to me. You don't want to be the one to pay for all this shit, you know what I'm saying?"

Alayna knew what he was saying, having said it herself only a few hours ago, unleashing the wrath of the Red Sweater in the process. But listening to Linc say it made it sound like a lie. Another uncomfortable sting of uncertainty needled her brain.

Linc wasn't paying that any mind. He reached across the table, snatched the garlic bread off the side of her plate and grinned like a fox who'd just paid an illicit visit to the hen house.

"Forget about the Ice Man, the Freezer Boy, whatever. I've done my share of grinning in white people's faces for the week, now I had enough of 'em. Don't want to see one, don't want to talk to one, don't want to talk about one."

"That might be hard. They're everywhere, you know."

"Not everywhere. We work together, but we sure as hell don't play together. And now, Pretty Lady, it's time to *play*."

On the word "play," the smile drained from his face in a statement of reversed priority. Whatever he had in mind was serious business to Mr. Linc Warren. Maybe a little too serious, Alayna thought nervously, knowing damn well that when it came to play, the other kids had driver's licenses and she was still riding a Big Wheel.

He took her to one of the black nightclubs Alayna

had heard so much about but had never actually entered, a trendy watering hole of glammed-up African-American wannabe gods and goddesses bumping bodies and business cards under a swirling splash of colored lights. There was nary a person paler than beige in the joint.

Her sexy red dress was nothing in this place of bare midriffs and plunging necklines and skirts so short they could have been sold as panties. Every woman in the place was beautiful, tall, short, thin, wide, dark-skinned or fair-skinned or somewhere in between. Every last one of them was working what God had bestowed 'til it liked to drop dead with the struggle. Still self-conscious about the deep scar on her temple and the makeup-defiant bruising still visible under her left eye, Alayna stared at them, feeling as uncomfortable as a little old lady at church without her Sunday wig, until Linc dragged her out on the dance floor.

The loud music pounded away any lingering self-doubt. Linc grinned at her, moving his hips seductively.

"Come on, Pretty Lady," he urged, practically shouting over the thumping beat. "Let loose. Don't be shy."

And she did, gradually letting the music sweep her out of herself, moving her hips and legs around, the pounding rhythm shaking loose everything but itself vibrating inside her. She closed her eyes, making even Linc and his broad shoulders and dazzling smile disappear, caring for nothing but the music and the movement of her own body. And while those video hip-hop dancers didn't have to worry about their job security, Alayna was pretty sure the casual observer wouldn't have guessed that the curly-haired woman in the red dress had never danced outside her own bedroom in her entire life.

Cut after cut of heart-shaking groove, and Alayna danced until the back of her dress was wet and clinging to her body and Linc was palming the sweat off his face with his hands. When an old-school slow drag finally replaced the rhythmic jive, his smile eased into a groan of relief.

Alayna slowed and stopped, ready to move off the floor, noticing for the first time her feet aching in the strappy new shoes.

"Oh no, you don't. Not yet," Linc growled like she was about to walk off with something that belonged to him. He took her hand and slid it around him. A second later, his fingers were around her waist. Another second more, and he'd pulled her close against him, not seeming to mind her damp clothes or the light smell of funk competing with the Macy's perfume counter. "One more."

And that was nice too, only Alayna couldn't help feeling a little wary. Linc moved so fast. Too fast. And then, there was the thought of Ice, which popped into her mind the second this man's arms went around her. Like some kind of mental chastity belt.

Alayna tried to push the man's image out of her mind. But he was just as persistent in imagination as he was in person. Just lingered there with that look on his face. That look that had been on his face just before she'd banged out of his office and sworn she'd never say word "Q" to his sorry, stick-up-his-butt self again.

And what the hell was she thinking about him for anyway? Here she was, out with a perfectly nice man.

A *black* man who understood what it was like to always be in the minority. A black man who knew the frustration and resentment of working twice as hard to be thought half as good. He was handsome, smart, had a good job, knew how to treat a woman, hadn't asked for a penny from her pocketbook or an ounce of sympathy for his sob story. Hadn't asked her to drive, hook her own ride or lift a single finger all evening. Hadn't shown her any of his fingers either.

Woman would have to be a damned fool not to try to hang on to a brother like this . . . and here she was thinking about some stupid white boy who had told her three different times—with increasing volume—that he was gay. Gay as bird. Gay as a birthday party. Gay as the Easter Parade.

A stupid white boy who'd never been followed by a store detective for no damn reason, who'd never been told "the position is filled" as soon as he showed up for the interview. A stupid white boy who didn't know what it was like to look in someone's eyes and know they hated you just because of the color of your skin.

Linc beamed down at her, and if he suspected that there was another man on her mind, it wasn't written in his face. He didn't even mind that when the dance was over, she wanted to go home, or that her end of their lively conversation trickled down to the occasional distracted mutter. He didn't mind anything . . . until they at last arrived back at their building and he escorted her to her door.

Everything from the way he leaned against the door as she found her key to the bedroom smile on his face made his intention clear: He expected the evening to end inside her apartment, with the two of them making love on the big white bed.

And everything inside Alayna was saying no. No way. Not yet. So when she turned to him, with the steel of decision in her voice and said, "Thank you, Linc. I had a really great time," she wasn't at all surprised to see his smile slip a couple of notches.

He rebounded quickly and, like the first-rate salesman he was, sweetened the deal a little.

"Me, too," he said softly, gathering her into his arms. "But it doesn't have to end," and he closed his eyes, lowering his mouth toward hers.

He began gently, only brushing his lips against hers, then following up with long and strong kisses until finally he slid his tongue into her mouth and pressed her tightly against him, his hands sliding from her waist to her bottom, massaging it gently. Alayna closed her eyes, wondering if maybe she'd been just a little too hasty, enjoying the warmth and strength of him, giving in just the slightest bit. . . .

Then there was Ice again. Just behind her eyelids, staring at her, just to the left of seductive and far to the right of appropriate. And then she started wondering about how his lips would feel and, once his motor was running, whether his hands would slide first to her butt, or her breasts or somewhere else altogether.

Ice-thoughts totally wrecked any possibility of a Linc groove, and, as a side effect, made her absolutely furious.

She pried herself away, suddenly wanting nothing

more than to be alone in the apartment with a stiff enough drink to talk herself down from Ice Heaven before things got any more out of control.

But first there was Linc. Linc who was looking at her like she'd lost her damn mind. Linc, who probably wouldn't take too kindly to: *yeah, while I was kissing you I started missing that white guy and wondering what it would be like to be kissing him instead.*

"Linc," she said, sounding all breathless and shaky and stupid. "I like you. I really do, but like I told you, I hardly know you."

So what? flickered in his eyes.

"I'm sorta . . . old-fashioned, Linc. So, not yet, okay?"

He blinked a couple of times as this information registered in his brain, but his face said he didn't exactly buy it as truth. Alayna had the feeling it had been a long, long time since any woman had told Lincoln Warren no. If any woman ever had.

But finally he shrugged, smiled. Stepped back out of her face and into his own space.

"I didn't figure you for one of those religious girls, not dressed like that. Not since you agreed to go dancing. Most of those women don't drink, don't dance, don't do nothing but eat, breathe and sleep with Jesus—" He laughed a bit, tickled by himself. "You know what I mean."

"It's not a religious thing," Alayna said quickly, pushing back the grin that threatened the sincerity of her whole speech. "I need to *know* you."

He spread his hands in what-you-see-is-what-you-get display.

"*Really* know you," Alayna insisted, rolling her eyes. "Seriously."

"Serious, huh? Serious?" He leaned in close again, demonstrating just how serious he intended to take the whole conversation by planting a nibbling kiss on the side of her neck. "Very, very, serious."

But Ice was in and he wasn't budging now. So the moment Linc's lips touched her skin, Alayna felt a nasty little shiver of distaste course through her. Linc seemed to mistake it for excitement, because he gathered her close to him again.

"Stop that," she muttered, pulling away from him, her voice brusque and sure this time. "I mean what I'm saying and you need to listen to it."

"I do?"

"You do."

"You sure?"

Alayna nodded. "I'm sure. Very sure."

He pasted a grave expression on his face for a half second. Then another smile stole across his features.

"So what are you telling me, Alayna?" he said with a mock exasperation. "That you ain't gonna gimme none until you're in love, or something?"

Hollywood has nothing on the human brain for making movies, and the brain's faster and doesn't charge ten dollars for a ticket, either. In the time it took him to finish the sentence, Alayna imagined herself in bed with Linc, then rewrote the scene, imagining herself in the same bed with Ice.

Hootchie, she chided herself, shaking both the images away.

"Yes . . . no . . . well . . . maybe," she told the man

waiting beside her, sounding about as convinced as lukewarm coffee.

Linc gave her a smug little smile, then traced her lips with a long brown finger. "Well. I'll let you have this round, Miss Alayna. In the interest of being a gentleman and all. But like the man said: I'll be back." The finger dropped from her face and he cocked it at her. "See you tomorrow, Pretty Lady." Then he sauntered slowly into the darkness and disappeared up the stairs.

Chapter 21

The next morning, Alayna sat down in the window seat with the newspaper and a cup of coffee. Glorious beams of pure May sunshine filled the room, wasting their radiance on Alayna, who barely noticed them as more than light by which to try to make her fuzzy brain function enough to get back into the office in another couple of hours. She shifted her butt on the hard pillows, trying again to make herself comfortable in this pretty space, and tucked her feet up under her. When she turned to the end table to set the cup down, she noticed the blinking red light on the answering machine for the first time.

"Hey. Where are you? With the Ice Man? I went to the doctor. Call me."

Alayna nearly spilled coffee all over herself. Great. While she'd been out dancing and dreaming and making up sex shows starring two men in two different flavors, her sister might have had an emergency.

She dialed quickly, fingers shaking, guilt already running a rampage in her mind, but of course, on a

Saturday morning the day before graduation, no one was there. She dialed the cell phone, too. Nothing.

Almost as soon as she had left a quick message, her doorbell rang.

The little white clock on the bookshelf read a hair before 10 A.M. Alayna said a quick prayer of thanks for the inspiration that had urged her to get up and get ready as soon as her bleary eyes had opened. She crossed the little room in six quick steps and opened the door wide.

She expected Martine, or possibly Linc, though somehow rising this early on a Saturday morning after having been out until two didn't suit his image.

But it wasn't Martine . . . and it wasn't Linc.

Ice stood in her doorway, looking beat-up and annoyed.

"What are *you* doing here?"

"That should be obvious," he grumbled. "I'm here to see you."

Typical.

"Why?" Alayna muttered, moving aside to let him in. "You were going to see me in a couple of hours anyway."

"Not alone."

Alayna looked him over suspiciously, but his expression wasn't giving anything away.

"I didn't think we had anything else to say to each other."

"Wrong. Coffee?" he asked, edging past her into the tiny kitchen, dumping the contents of her fresh-brewed carafe and setting about the task without a word.

"So what do you want?" Alayna prompted when the silence began to work her nerves.

"Be nice. I'm a guest."

"An uninvited one," she corrected quickly. "If you've got something to say. . . ."

He ignored her, measuring out a careful scoop of coffee and sifting it gently into the basket. He reached into the refrigerator like he lived there, pulled on the pitcher of cold water and poured an even two cups' worth into the machine.

"See," he said as though speaking to the machine. "The trick is in the water. The colder the better."

"I'll remember that."

"And you have to measure carefully—"

"Right. Great. Out with it, Ice."

"You can make it next time, then. I drink mine—"

"Black. I noticed."

He smiled then, like her words fit with some secret joke he had going. Apparently he'd just gotten a haircut too, because the skin around his ears and at the base of his neck looked a little more pale and visible than it had before.

Alayna rolled her eyes. "Well?" she demanded. "What?"

"I've been thinking about our last conversation," he said, at last coming around to the point of the visit. "And you're right."

He grimaced like the word "right" had been ripped from his body without proper anesthetic. Alayna couldn't suppress a victory tour of self-congratulation.

"Well, I *know* that."

"Wait, there's more."

He came close to her then, until their bodies were only inches apart. His hands landed on her shoulders, gently . . . and there was something gleaming in his eyes that made Alayna's heart start knocking wildly in her chest. And that look was on his face. The look she'd seen when she'd closed her eyes under Linc's embrace. The look that made her push away the attentions of a gorgeous man who was actually interested in her, for . . . for . . . what?

"Alayna, Ali," he began. "I think it's time for me to—"

But it was a like bad television show, where the writers have pulled out every stop to keep the tension high and the possibility for resolution low. Because at the exact moment he was going to say something that might have actually been worth listening to, a quick rap on the door separated them. Linc's head appeared between the door and jamb, last night's wide grin still plastered on his face.

"Alayna? You decent?"

Why didn't I lock the damn door? Alayna wondered, but it was too late. Linc didn't wait for an answer. He strolled right on in.

He was wearing another white T-shirt and a pair of dark blue shorts, showing off a pair of beautiful brown legs dusted with black hair. He held a basketball under his arm. As his liquid brown eyes swept over her, then Ice, then back to her, the grin faded deep into his mustache.

"Richards. Nice to see you again." He hardly sounded like he meant it, but the two men shook hands anyway.

"Warren."

"Sorry to . . . *interrupt* . . ." He tossed the word at Alayna like a question, but continued with ". . . but I just thought I'd see how you were doing. That was a pretty late night last night." And this time he used his grin as a weapon. "She was a dancing *fool!*" he said, chuckling locker-room confidential to Ice. "I'm surprised this girl right here can walk this morning."

"You two went out last night." Ice's eyes swung between Alayna and Linc. A crazy, completely irrational twinge of guilt surged inside her, and she almost spat out something completely stupid like *Well, I wasn't going to sit up in here waiting for you,* but Linc was already in the game.

"Dinner and dancing," he answered proudly, while Alayna was still choking back what lawyers called "admission against interest"—or in layman's terms, a confession. "Gotta treat a lady right, you know what I'm saying?"

"Yeah," Ice muttered tightly. "Dinner and dancing. That's one way of doing it."

"Heard you had a little trouble with some kid who wanted your wallet."

Ice's gray eyes shifted a little, encompassing Alayna in his grim stare.

"Yeah . . . ," he muttered. "Caught me by surprise."

"Yeah. I bet."

The skin around Linc's eyes cinched in suspicion, but he addressed his next remark to Alayna.

"So. Looks like you gotta work today."

"For a few hours," Ice interrupted. "I've got a big case. Ali's invaluable to me."

"Ali?"

Ice smiled one of his nasty-nice lip jobs.

"She's a champ, right?"

"You box?"

"I do."

"How about basketball?"

"I've been known to play that, too."

Linc looked Ice up and down, guess-timating height, weight and build and, knowing Linc, probably the circumference of the man's balls, too.

"You got time for a little one-on-one?" he asked slowly. "There's a hoop behind the building. But . . . I guess you probably have to get back to the *office*, right?"

If Linc had been going for subtlety, he'd failed big time, because even Alayna caught the challenge in his voice. He might as well have called Ice's Mama a double-wide and finished it. Alayna took a nervous glance up at Ice, half ready to throw herself in between them if necessary . . . and half curious about what would happen if she didn't.

But Ice's face creased into an ear-wide grin. A second later, he'd forgotten all about Alayna, coffee and whatever it was he was going to say and was pulling his white polo over his head to reveal that pale, hairy, tightly muscled chest.

"Let's go, man," he said, stretching out his hand and showing far too many teeth for any normal person to be comfortable with. But Linc shook it willingly enough . . . and showed a few teeth of his own.

You would have thought they'd challenged each other to a duel on the field of honor with all the hand-shaking and smiling and preparation they'd made.

"Ex*cuse* me?" Alayna asked, hands on hips, staring at them both like they'd completely lost their minds.

But Ice had already thrown his shirt across her bed like it belonged there, and he was following Linc, bare-chested and ready, out of her apartment and down to the parking lot below, leaving Alayna standing in the middle of the floor, staring after them like a complete and total fool.

She was still standing in the middle of the floor, waiting for her mind to make itself up enough to tell her feet where to go, when the phone rang.

"Hey."

Martine sounded terrible. Weak and sick. Even the sassy back-talking edge was gone.

"Bad night," she replied to Alayna's questions. "I was asleep when you called. Gonna have to call in to the store today, can't make it."

"What did the doctor say?"

"Dehydrated. Wants to see me again in a week. Gave me some stuff that's supposed to help, if I can keep it down."

"Do you want me to come?"

"No," but it wasn't very convincing. "I'm just gonna try to sleep. Graduation tomorrow."

"I'll have my cell, so if you need anything— anything at all—"

"Okay," Martine said, sounding already asleep again. "Hey, Alayna, where were you last night?"

A flush crept to Alayna's ears.

"Out dancing. At Paradox."

"You, at Paradox? Cool," she murmured. "I'm tired now."

"Get some rest. I'll call you later."

Then she hung up.

* * *

Alayna managed to distract herself for a full hour before giving in and going down to the basketball court.

The May sun was climbing toward its zenith, and even in her sleeveless tee and light cotton slacks, Alayna was sweat-through-hot almost as soon as she stepped onto the asphalt.

Ice had to be roasting with those khakis on, and Alayna noticed dark stains of sweat making patches on his hips. Both he and Linc were bare-chested now, sweat streaming off their bodies, Ice, hairy and Neanderthal, Linc a smooth cocoa. In a way they were perfect complements: a yin and yang of toned, healthy manhood in contrasting shades of black and white. They were even almost the same height.

However, there was nothing yin-yang-Eastern-meditation about their game. As Alayna approached, Linc elbowed Ice hard in the solar plexus and sank a lovely jumper from the top of the key. He didn't seem to have a problem with the foul until he caught sight of Alayna standing on the sidelines, arms and lips folded in disapproval. But Ice wasn't much better. He knew Alayna was standing there, so he stopped short of deliberately fouling Linc, but there was a vicious intensity to his game that smelled foul anyway.

And they were equally guilty of the high crime of showing off.

Alayna watched for a few minutes, then stalked back toward the building with curiosity congealed and disgust on low boil. She ignored Linc's calls of "Where you going?" and Ice's "We're almost done" and returned to the welcome cool of the air conditioning, which, it appeared, was her only friend this morning.

Dumped by two men. For a game. Or for each other, if you wanted to look at it that way. They were probably *both* gay.

A freshly reshowered, freshly redressed Ice came looking for her in the library two hours later, holding coffee in her favorite mug like a peace offering.

"No thanks. I've had mine for the day. Back at *home*. Hope you had a nice time. Some of us had to get to work," she told him and promptly showed him the back of her head. He ignored that, took a sip of the coffee himself, and pulled up a chair beside her. The unnervingly fresh smells of soap and shampoo radiated from him.

"Look, Alayna—"

"We have a lot of work to do, Ice, remember? You have seven depositions next week—"

"What do you know about that guy Linc?"

The question was sharp enough to scratch glass.

"I mean," Ice said, backing down from the challenge in her face. "Is it . . . serious?"

Serious? I just met him a minute and a half ago, idiot, she wanted to snap, until she noticed jealousy's cousin, distrust, floating around in those clear gray eyes.

"What's it to you?" She tossed him some shoulder and waited.

Ice frowned himself into a scowl, sloshed the coffee all over her papers and leaned over her chair, one hand on each of the armrests like he was going to scare her into some kind of confession or something.

"I don't like him."

"Well, whoop de doo. He doesn't like you either. Lord, let there be peace on earth. Amen."

"I'm serious."

"So am I," Alayna muttered. "And since you'd rather hang out with another man than talk to me—"

"So now you believe me?"

"No," Alayna said bluntly. "But you had your chance to speak the truth and you wimped out. Blew it. So unless you're ready to put your money where your mouth is, I'm taking your word about yourself from here on out."

"Now wait a minute—"

"I know what you think," Alayna exploded, feeling the heat of oppression mingling with the steam of righteous indignation in her brain. Martin Luther King, Malcolm X, Jesse Jackson and all their saints and apostles gathered behind her as she spoke, nodding their amens. "That all black men are trifling, or players or criminals—"

"I just said I didn't like him."

"The man took me *dancing*. And that doesn't make him trifling, and that doesn't make him a player, and it doesn't make him anything but a man who took me dancing! You got that?"

Her index finger found his chest in three sharp pokes right along the sternum. It couldn't have hurt him, but he stared at the instrument all the same.

"You know something, you've got a whole set of assumptions about white people, about white *men*, that don't have much basis in reality."

Alayna rolled her eyes, then converted her finger to its alternate use, pointing out the obvious.

"Excuse me? First of all, I haven't said one derogatory thing about white men. And second of all, any conclusion I've reached about your kind is based on the hard, cold facts of my personal experience."

"What hard, cold facts?"

Alayna paused. It was one thing to read him, but it was something else altogether to start rattling off names and dates and stuff.

"Look, it's probably better if we don't get into all this," she muttered at last. "Because the last thing I need is for you to take something I say the wrong way and the next thing you know . . ."

He nodded.

"See, there you go. Assumption number one: whitey is out to get me."

Alayna glared at him. "I never said that—"

"You don't have to. I'm not stupid, Alayna, and I'm fairly observant. You keep your guard high—"

"That's because—"

"Of assumption number two: whitey can't be trusted. Not one of us. Never."

That was when Alayna considered using all her fingers to give him something to match the purple welt on his lip. Then sanity prevailed and she put her digits away before she put someone's eye out.

"Look at you. Are you trustworthy, Ice?" she said, letting her voice tell him he was tiptoeing way too close to the tulips. "*Are* you?"

Ice let that one sink in, sink deep, penetrating the silence between them. From the blank expression on his face, Alayna fully expected him to lock his lips, turn on his heel and march out of the library like a remote control robot, so precise and mechanical that she'd hear the gears grinding as his long legs kicked out toward the door. That's what he always did when he didn't get what he wanted, made some snide remark and got the hell out of there. His lips were already puckering with the words.

She shook her head. "Don't bother. I have work to do. I'd like to get out of here at a decent hour."

"Plans with Linc?" he asked with a malicious little smile.

"Yes. Not that it's any of your business. Clause two, and all that. Remember?"

She thought he'd leave then, but to Alayna's surprise, he pulled his chair closer to hers and got right up in her face, right in her space, right where there was no escape any place. But instead of saying something foul, he leveled those startlingly clear baby grays right at her and said in the softest voice she'd ever heard him use, "Is he who you want?"

A little chill of fire raced up her bare arms, sank into her skin, twanged a couple of heartstrings, then dived a free fall into her stomach.

Alayna swallowed hard. Ice yelling and screaming, she could handle. Ice trading one-liners and looking ready to kill, that was normal. Ice looking like any second now he was going to press those thin lips of his on her mouth—right here in the library at Hughes Weston and Moore—was something else altogether.

"Thought you were . . . gay," she stammered, trying to find something else to look at, which was hard because he had blocked out everything else with that big, hunky body of his.

"No, you didn't."

She looked up then, reading some kind of Big Decision dancing in his eyes.

"What—" she asked suddenly as half her stomach took a jittery, brakeless elevator ride from her abdomen to her shoes—and the other half leapt to her throat. "What do you intend to do?"

When his eyes slid down her face to focus on her lips, she knew the answer to that one.

"I intend to—" he began fiercely but stopped short, his eyes fixed on a spot over her shoulder, utterly arrested by whatever had entered his field of vision. Alayna turned, too.

Weston.

Standing at the library door in a loud pink golf polo, his ears pinker still, staring at them like he'd just seen something that scared him into his next lifetime.

"Everything okay here?" he asked, muddy brown eyes darting from one face to another.

"Fine," Ice muttered, and then he did something Alayna had never seen him do in Weston's presence. He lowered his eyes.

"I was looking for you, Richards," the older man said, his voice still wary, still careful. "Need to get an update on this Cybex thing. Partnership vote's coming up soon, you know."

The nice-nasty smile snaked across Ice's face. "Partnership. Yeah."

"Not that it's any big deal. You *are* your father's son, after all. A credit to any law firm. Talk to Judge Richards lately?"

The unpleasant smile went nowhere as the father's

son answered, "This morning, in fact. He sends his regards. As usual."

Suspicion fled Weston's face long enough for him to look immensely pleased. Like he'd been told the president said hello.

"Well. Come on down to my office for a minute, will ya? I'm sure Alayna can finish up . . . whatever . . . capably without supervision. Right, Alayna?" Weston said. The eyes that he leveled on her glinted with deep distrust.

"Yes, sir," she said quietly, even while rage was screaming like a teakettle in her ears. "More than capably."

Weston nodded once, then jerked his head toward the door. Ice followed like the little robot she'd suspected he was all along.

The right, good girl, play-by-the-rules thing to do would have been to follow instructions. Stay right there in the library working on her brief. Wade through the reams of computerized legal research. Wait.

But with all of her alarms tingling and the next scene of this drama about to play only a few feet away, she got right up out of the chair. Because sometimes "being good" is about the same as being really, really, stupid.

"Look, I'm not saying there's anything wrong with it. And I'd feel the same way if she were white, believe me—" They were in the firm's small kitchen, murmuring near the coffee machine. Weston spoke in a low voice, hurried and troubled, as though he knew damn well he was in deep doo-doo just breathing the subject. "I'm trying to look out for you here, Richards, you know that, don't you? I just don't want any of the other partners—or clients—to think you're . . . well—"

"I'm . . . ?" Flat as ice, as smooth and as dangerous.

Weston's pause was long and uncomfortable. "Having an office affair with—"

"With . . . ?"

Another uncomfortable pause. Alayna pressed as close to the door as she could without being seen. She could hear them both clearly—and even see part of Weston's khakied girth. Ice was invisible.

"With Alayna," Weston said as though resigned to the down and dirty. "And don't bother to deny it, son. I've been around this block a few times myself and I know that if it hasn't already happened, it's just a matter of time before . . ." He left that one alone and picked up the conversation a yard down the line. "And don't get me wrong, Alayna's a wonderful girl. Smart, capable, pretty little figure, lovely face. Especially lately. Seems to be blossoming right before our eyes. Any man would find her attractive—"

"But?" Ice interrupted.

"But . . ." Weston paced out of her view. "But there are those in this firm who wouldn't be entirely . . . comfortable . . . with that situation. Especially not now when we're reviewing you for partnership decision. You're not very popular with some of the men already, Richards. But you've made them so much damn money—and the Cybex thing! Well, the Cybex thing is *huge!*" Weston was fairly chuckling with glee now. Alayna heard his hands slap flesh and guessed that he'd just clapped Ice hard on the back. "You like

Alayna. Fine. Be discreet, be careful and have fun. Have some fun for me while you're at it. 'Cause if I were just a few years younger . . . But wait a month. Wait until you're *in*, boy. You understand me?"

There was a long pause before Ice answered.

"I understand you. Perfectly."

She didn't hear the rest, if there was any more; she'd already whirled around and hurried silently to her office. A rage more violent than any feeling she'd ever known filled her mind, covering a horrible sadness.

And to think ten minutes ago . . .

Idiot, she muttered to herself. *Idiot, idiot, idiot.*

Chapter 22

Did he come back to tell her what Weston had said?
No.

Did he come back to the library at all?

No.

Did she see him again?

Sure, when she went looking for him, to remind him that the next day, Sunday, was Martine's high school graduation and that she wasn't available. Did he look at her again with those smoky, I-want-to-ravage-you-on-this-very-spot eyes?

Hell, no.

He said, "We got a meeting with Graves tomorrow." Seeing her face, he added quickly, "I can't discuss it here, but—"

And when she told him no and why, he sighed, "Crap. We are so behind," rolled his eyes and went back to what he was doing.

Without another word. Without an explanation. Without anything. As though the conversation in the library had never taken place.

Alayna left him, her thoughts a swimming mess. Longing bumped up against distrust, doubt shouldered hard with fury. The loudest and most insistent of them all was something like fear, but every time she asked for its identity, it got angry and evasive and hid in one of the darker corners of her mind, whispering like an incessant proselyte, inviting every other emotion to its temple to pray.

Which was probably why when Linc thoroughly trashed the guy at dinner that night—from his game to his name to legal claim to fame—she listened in encouraging silence, even if she couldn't quite make herself join in. And it was probably why she said yes when he suggested a movie that evening, and other than the fact that Wesley Snipes was in it, she couldn't have told you one thing that happened in a single frame.

And it was probably why, when he slipped his arms around her when the show was over, she did her level best to kiss him back passionately and to kick thoughts of anyone or anything else to the furthest curb of her mind. *Handsome, employed, interested, successful* ran a continuous loop in her mind. And she'd be twenty-eight in September. Not getting any younger . . .

But her heart's core kept hearing Ice's "Is he who you want?" and wasn't convinced.

"Is the second date the charm, Pretty Lady?" he asked when she finally wriggled away from him.

"Who won the basketball game?" she asked suddenly. "You never told me."

Linc grinned.

"Who else? Everybody knows white boys can't jump. Now, uh," he pulled her into his arms again, "as stimulating as this conversation is, I had a different kind of stimulation in mind, you know what I'm saying."

He kissed her again and again, and Alayna did her best to fake the feeling, but even Linc could tell it wasn't happening for a second night. With a puzzled look on his face, he mounted the stairs to his apartment, and Alayna slipped behind the door to try to sleep alone in her big white bed.

Lying there alone in the dark, she tried not to think about Ice and Weston, about Martine and Jamal, about Mama and Daddy, Linc and herself, about all the missed chances and opportunities of this ridiculous experience known as a life. Nothing worked. Nothing had ever worked. For all her efforts, hopes, prayers, faith and crossed fingers, nothing. In the end, God did exactly what he wanted to do and you either got with His program and lived miserably ever after or went to Hell. Maybe both.

You tell God I'm not playing anymore, Mama. If I don't get to be happy, if you got this deck stacked against me everywhere I turn, then at least let me be miserable someplace else.

Alayna turned on the lights, got up and pulled a piece of paper and pen from her work satchel. She wrote a check and a short letter, folded them and left them on the counter, waiting for two things: an envelope and the moment for their proper delivery into the appropriate hands.

Then, feeling somewhat more at peace even though

she'd written a declaration of war, she crawled into bed and stared at the ceiling until fatigue caved in to sleep.

The next day belonged to Martine and Jamal and the two hundred other graduating students, who, with their clans and kin, stuffed themselves into the sweltering gymnasium of McPherson High School for commencement festivities.

To say it was a madhouse would have been an understatement. The stands were jammed belly to belly and butt against butt, and still barely accommodated all the well-wishers. The public address system kept winking out, and occasionally a student's name died unheard. At other times the families made such raucous cheers, did such lewd dances, and sang such loud songs after their graduates' names were called that it was impossible to hear the names of the next several students at all.

When Martine's time came, Alayna stood up, tugging slightly at her dress, clapping and cheering, joined by Martine's many friends and her many friends' families, making a decent enough sound to avoid the ultimate of high school humiliations: unpopularity. Martine tipped across the stage in her cap and gown and a pair of too high heels Alayna didn't recognize, which meant Martine was probably spending her part-time paychecks and not saving them for the bills that would come due again in a couple more short weeks. Ice was right, they needed a few months, probably. Long enough to know what it feels like to have creditors calling and to get a couple of disconnect notices from Georgia Power.

Ice. Just the thought of the man poked a hurt deep inside her. The old folks used to say, "When you curl up with a snake, you got to expect it to bite you." They also said, "A leopard can't change his spots." Those old folks. They had a million of them. A million ways to call you a damn fool without actually saying the words. And even as she sat here in this sweltering heat, calling herself a damn fool with every phrase and euphemism on the round blue planet, that little voice in her heart kept talking about him, talking *to* him. Kept missing the man so fierce she was sorry she'd ever given him a moment's brain time from the get-go.

No wonder the old folks also used to say, "Let sleeping dogs lie." It's better not to take a stick to something you don't even *understand,* much less know how to feed, train or housebreak.

Alayna brought herself around to clapping vigorously, if not exactly enthusiastically, when Jamal Preston did his walk down the stage, peering around the crowd for his people. From the activity in a front-row bleacher across the way from her, she suspected that the stout woman in the too-tight yellow suit might be his grandmother, and the skinny, balding, dour-looking man beside her, his grandfather. If those were the Prestons, they looked resigned to the inevitability of their grandson's next steps: marriage, then parenthood.

Her attention was distracted from the Prestons when a skinny young man in an old man's suit released a bright halo of festive, multicolored balloons right next to her. A woman who had to be some grad's mother stood up, tears of pride streaming down her face. Alayna watched them, a stranger in a strange land. And suddenly, it didn't seem like such a bad thing to want a family, and a home, and a man to love you.

The thought twisted the painful knife Ice had stuck in her back. The next thing she knew, she was crying like there'd been a death and birth in the family in the same split instant.

Because, of course, there had.

When the "congratulations" were said, the hugging was done, and Alayna had begged off accompanying her sister and the Prestons to the obligatory after-graduation meal, she made her way back to the car.

A beige envelope was just lying there, quiet and innocent, on the cracked black passenger seat of the Jeep. Some clever delivery boy or girl must have dropped it through the gap between the window and seal Alayna always left—to let some fresh heat in, she supposed, judging by the temperature inside the old car.

Alayna struggled inside, rolling down the windows with the old-fashioned crank handle with one hand, ripping the card open with her other hand and teeth.

An invitation.

To the wedding of Martine Jackson and Jamal Preston at the state courthouse on Friday. Reception to follow at the couple's home, 555 Magnolia Street.

Alayna studied it a moment, turning its weight over and over in her palms until it delivered its full message.

Wedding. Friday. Courthouse. Reception.

Of course. The final nail in this coffin. The deal

sealer. She thought of her own letter still resting on the counter at the cute little place, and remembered.

She needed some envelopes.

That was how the envelope, complete with check and letter, ended up in the bottom of her big, black bag on Monday morning. Delivery was another matter.

It's easy to think about quitting, easy to write up all kinds of elaborate "fuck you and this job" letters of resignation, sign them and seal them up with a lick and promise into a crisp white business No. 10. It's something else altogether to tender the same, put them into the hands of your boss, surrender them, *do* it. Quitting is irrevocable. Quitting without the first plan about what you're gonna do with your life is either an act of faith or absolute lunacy. Quitting without the first plan about what you're gonna do with your life over a stupid *man*, well, that was something only a woman would do.

And then there was the lure of the law to distract her. The chance to write a major brief from top to bottom on a complex legal issue. The chance to match her brain cells against the Georgia Legislature and the state Supreme Court. The kind of opportunity she'd always wanted—always known she could handle—but had never been given.

Until Ice.

So . . . didn't she owe it to him to finish that much of the case before . . . ?

And if not to Ice Man or Boss Man, didn't she owe that much to their clients, Alan Graves and Cybex?

All of which just made the little "quit and go to law school" voice mutter so insistently in the back of her brain that she had to check her bag for the letter and start the whole resignation analysis process all over again.

And, somehow, the brief got longer, and longer, and stronger and stronger, until Thursday morning when there was nothing else to do to the draft but drop it on the only clear spot in Ice's cluttered office, the seat of his black chair.

There was little chance of running into the man, since he'd been locked in the main conference room all week, conducting depositions. At the end of the day, he ducked out of the building almost immediately, and if he did come back, it was at some ungodly hour when even the cleaning crew had gone home.

Alayna suspected that was exactly what he was doing, from the to-do stickies she found in her chair every morning. Her chair was always littered with yellow Post-its: "Pull Document # T-14657. Let me know what it says about a former employee named Tubbs." "Think we can file the brief first of next week?" "Check on Trixie. She should have finished by now." And so on. *Ad nauseam*.

And speaking of Trixie . . . she was a document *machine*.

After only a couple of days, Alayna was amazed to find the War Room nearly empty except for half a dozen odd boxes. And most of those were the new stuff their opponents had sent in response to Ice's requests for information.

"Where is everything?" Alayna asked, trying to sound unimpressed. But her voice betrayed her.

Trixie barely glanced up.

"Sent it back to Cybex," she snapped in a you're-still-on-my-shit-list voice. Maybe deservedly so, Alayna reluctantly conceded . . . mentally. Only mentally. Since Ice had decided to hightail it back to the safety zones of he-who-would-be-Partner-dom, Trixie didn't have to divide her energies between spying and working. Maybe that alone was the reason she'd gotten it done so fast.

"But what about—" Alayna began, certain there was something the woman had forgotten.

Trixie must have read her mind, because she hitched a bumper crop of Annoyance to her cigarette-puckered lips and sighed.

"We've copied everything crucial, and damn near everything that wasn't. The hard copies are filed and stamped, and I've stored them next door, just to separate what's done from what's in progress."

"What about—," Alayna began again, but again Trixie interrupted with a grumbled explanation.

"Scanned." She patted the laptop in front her with a yellowed claw. "All of it. In numerical order, with cross references based on the key words," she said with just the faintest hint of pride. "I was afraid I wouldn't be able to figure out this doc management software, but turns out," she snapped a couple of bony fingers and grinned, "you *can* teach an old dog a trick or two."

"That's amazing," Alayna murmured, appreciating the woman's skills in spite of herself. "I gotta confess. I didn't think you could . . . ," she began, but the beginning of that sentence just made the woman's smile widen.

"Surprise, surprise," Trixie replied in a perfect

Gomer Pyle Southern whine that almost made Alayna laugh until she reminded herself that laughing with Trixie would be tantamount to staying on the plantation after the Yanks had burned it to the ground.

She should have just gone on and laughed.

But instead, in the effort of swallowing down a chuckle, she opened her mouth and said something far worse.

"You should apply for Joel's spot," Alayna heard herself saying as she poked a curious nose into an open box that smelled suspiciously dank. "Or mine, after I—"

Alayna snapped her mouth shut immediately, grasping at the air to try to cram the words back inside. All the while, Trixie stared at her with that aha!-I've-got-you-my-pretty look on her witchy face.

"After you what, Alayna?" she asked innocently, smiling like either a fanged predator or a grotesque imitation of a teasing best girlfriend. "After you quit? Gonna marry Richards? Gonna go to law school? Both?"

In the mad, brain-racking scramble between Trixie's questions and her response, Alayna couldn't clearly see the impact of her admission. If the scrawny woman told on her to Weston, he'd take Alayna's resignation letter now as good as later. Ice might protest, but then again, he might not. After all, the brief was done. And at heart, he might be more like Weston than she'd ever realized. Green was the only color that really mattered to the Boss Man. Green and more green. Why not let Trixie earn her commission with a nice big fat secret to report to her greedy leader?

But in the end, more from habit than anything, she

lied. Kept her secrets at least partially secret for another day.

"Neither." It came out, huffy, snobbish, more condescending than angry, and Alayna was a little surprised at the tone. She'd never really listened to herself before. "I was just complimenting you, that's all. You don't have to make such a big deal out of it."

And she watched the smile drain from Trixie's face.

"Too bad," she said gruffly, licking her dry lips in an I-need-a-hit nicotine craving. "Richards keeps talkin' 'bout what a good lawyer you'd make."

This was news, and from the mirror of Trixie's face, Alayna knew she'd revealed as much.

"He stops in sometimes. See how things are goin'," the older woman explained. "Keeps talkin' 'bout how we're not gonna need all these documents and depositions. How you're gonna win it on the brief."

"He's just being—"

"Nice?" Trixie shook her head. "Remember who we're talkin' 'bout. What's the matter? Don't think you can do it?"

"Of course I can," Alayna snapped.

"Then go on to law school, Alayna. I won't tell Weston."

"I'll go to law school when you get a paralegal certificate, Trixie," Alayna scoffed, peppering the words with unlikeliness.

Only Trixie had a few dozen years' experience with cross-examination techniques herself and knew Alayna just well enough to set the trap. A look of pure you-think-you're-so-damn-smart crossed her face as the woman said, "What you think I'm workin' overtime for? My health? Tuition, baby. Tuition."

She stood up and jammed her hands into the pockets of that red rag for her cigarette case and lighter.

"See ya on campus, Ali," she muttered around a cancer stick, then swept out of the War Room like it was Diva's Night at the Apollo and she was Diana Ross.

Ice must have stopped the deposition to read the brief, because the thing was back in her chair when she returned to her office.

"File it," said the top stickie. "We'll talk about the notes later."

Notes.

The brief was covered with them, stickies in four different colors, marring the pristine whiteness of the paper like the flags of warring nations. Alayna sighed, certain that the rewrite would take a year, until she realized that the stickies were just the things he needed to know about the legal theory behind the argument in order to persuade the court at the hearing. As for the substance of the brief itself, he had only one comment, written on the last blue sticky on the last page: "Excellent. You're as smart as you are beautiful. Ice."

The words made her furious even while her eyes filled with tears. This was so like him. He had to make everything as hard as he possibly could. And he'd even stooped low enough to get Trixie McCoy into the act.

Chapter 23

"**Y**ou'd better go change."

Alayna glanced up at Ice, stilling her heart's happy dance with a stony glare and the reminder of how the Boss Man had backed down his rap. Funny how frank interracial dialogue and I-wanna-get-next-to-you went out the window when partnership and big bucks were on the line.

"Why?" she grumbled, marking it down as a favor that she was speaking to him at all. Maybe she should have quit yesterday, right after he'd approved the brief. But no. She wanted to stick around and see what happened at the hearing. Stick around and have Pretty Boy Floyd here in her face, acting like a week hadn't passed since he'd left her in the library with her heart pounding out "Do Me, Baby" and her face turned up for a kiss that never came.

Made her want to slap him clear into the next galaxy. But instead she scowled hard at him and pretended that whether he came or went made no never-mind in her world at all.

Ice did his Lake Placid imitation and ignored all the attitude he was getting like he wasn't getting it.

"The wedding." He tapped the pane of his watch. "Starts in about an hour."

"How did you know that?"

He reached into his jacket, and for the first time, she noticed how well-dressed he was today: a sleek gray single-breasted number, white shirt, pale blue tie, the whole ensemble fitting him to perfection. And in his hand was a familiar-looking beige square addressed to Benjamin Richards, Esq. care of Hughes Weston and Moore.

"I assume you're invited. You *are* her sister, after all."

"But why did she invite you?"

Again, she heard herself, ugly words, snide tone. No wonder just the slightest "ow-ee" of hurt squinched his face.

"Perhaps she still thinks we're . . . involved," he said slowly. "Or maybe it's just because she's figured out I dragged you kicking and screaming into your newfound freedom and is intensely in my debt. Or maybe it's to thank me for keeping you so busy here you don't have time to go driving by Magnolia Street every hour on the hour to check on them. Or maybe she's discovered my secret—"

Alayna gave him a thumbtack sharp don't-tell-that-lie-no-more glance, but he waved it away.

"—that I really am a nice guy."

For that he got an eyeroll and raspberry exhale into his smiling face. She had to remind herself again that he didn't deserve it, or she probably would have smiled.

"Missed you, Ali," he said softly, but before she could remind him that remark was over the line, outside of his jurisdiction and in excess of the four corners of their written agreement, he reversed on his own with, "So are you going to change, or what?"

"What are you, the fashion police?" She backed off the ugly tone a few inches, so it almost sounded like teasing. It was all the encouragement he needed. He sat down on the edge of her work space and grinned at her like he'd discovered *her* secret.

"I saw that Macy's garment bag you snuck in here this morning. Go. Put it on."

When Alayna just eyebrowed in response, he continued. "No need to take two cars. You know how parking is around the courthouse. Besides, I want to talk to you. About Cybex and Graves. About the future."

Alayna uncoiled herself from her chair slowly, feeling every inch of a cobra on the attack. "You're making a lot of assumptions here, Ice," she said softly when her long stare into those gunmetal eyes had done its work. "That I want to hear anything about Graves and Cybex. That your future and my future have anything to do with each other. And how do you know I don't have a date?"

The arrogant little smile slid off his face. "Do you?"

Alayna hesitated. Linc had wanted to go, but he was four hours away in Columbus all week. Even though he planned to hit the road right after his noon appointment, with summer weekend traffic, there was no way he'd make it back in time for a four o'clock ceremony that would be over in ten minutes and a reception filled with rowdy teenagers that Alayna doubted she'd attend for more than a hot second.

Still, for just an instant, she felt a hot flash of guilt. The same niggling feeling she always felt about Linc, whether he was standing before her in the flesh or just a thought in her mind. After weddings, resignations, deed transfers, permanent apartment searches and Ice-purges, Linc would be the next thing in her life up for serious reexamination.

"Oh, all right," she grumbled, pretending not to feel the fluttery anticipation buzzing in her stomach at the prospect of Ice's company. "I'll be ready in a few minutes."

She didn't have the first clue why she'd bought it, the silky little piece of summer-sky blue. Spaghetti straps down to a low neckline, a flouncing scalloped bottom, a flimsy little shawl with azure fringe. Impractical. Made for nothing more important than the dubious job of looking pretty. And it had cost too much—way too much—but Alayna had bought it anyway, chipping steadily away at the remains of the bonus check not taken by rent and security deposit, acting like she wasn't going to return the whole five thousand out of her savings account in another week anyway. Acting like she was going to have a job at all in another few days.

But, after all, Martine was getting married. Today. And it was time for a whole list of new decisions.

Finding a real place to live—not a temporary rental of someone else's furniture.

Transferring all the bills out of her name and into the names of Martine and Jamal Preston.

Deciding on the new meaning of her life.

One thing was sure, the woman who had bought this dress was a different woman from the one who had lived at 555 Magnolia all her life. The woman who had bought this dress was the woman who had gone dancing, and had giggled on the phone late into the night with Linc, had felt a little passion, a little pain. The woman who had bought this dress was ready to make a statement, even if that statement was nothing more substantial than "I'm cute."

She stared at the shimmery froth for a moment more, then pulled off her white blouse and stepped out of her blue skirt and slipped the little dress on over her head. Off came the panty hose and boring blue pumps, and instead, she pulled the tube of fancy perfumed lotion from her black satchel and squeezed a generous dollop into her palm, rubbing it deep into the bronze skin on her legs and thighs and heels until they glowed. Then she eased a delicate pair of silver sandals onto her feet.

At the mirror, she let her curls out of their clip and dumped the collection of cosmetics and styling implements onto the restroom counter, praying for a peaceful process. It was time to start the arrangement.

Ice came to his feet so fast he rammed his knee against the War Room table.

Take that, she thought as his avid eyes swept over her: hair piled in curls off her neck, a pair of silver earrings sparkling near the loose tendrils at her ears. Lashes and brows enhanced, lips penciled and sticked. Perfume. And the dress.

"Wow," he breathed, and that look was on his face

again, only now she was on guard against it. The God-I'm-so-hot-for-you-I-can't-stand-it look. Or more accurately, the God-I'm-so-hot-for-you-I-can't-stand-it-but-I'm-not-going-to-do-a-thing-about-it look. Instead of bringing comfort, the look made her wish she'd told him to go on ahead alone.

"When you go change, you really . . . change."

Alayna grimaced. "If that's supposed to be a compliment, it needs some work."

"You look beautiful," he said softly. "Breathtaking. Stunning. Gorgeous—"

"And that's overkill."

"You've got this fixed so I can't win, don't you?"

"And just what were you hoping to win?"

He sighed his surrender then. "Just as hard-hearted and suspicious as ever, I see. Ready?"

"No," Alayna said grimly. "But let's go get it over with anyway."

They were late.

The chapel, if it could be called that, was a tiny, windowless government block of a room on the third floor of the courthouse, dressed for the occasion with a little white trellis twined with plastic flowers and a square of green carpet the size of a doormat. There were no chairs. Civil weddings were strictly an in-and-out operation. Lingering was not encouraged.

The judge, a short, dark-skinned Sister Alayna didn't recall ever having seen before, was just beginning the traditional words when she and Ice added themselves to the number of the dearly beloved. All heads swung toward them, partly because they were interrupting, and partly, Alayna suspected, because they were such an odd couple, Richards tall and gray and grim as an undertaker, Alayna a mist of blue flounces. And the race thing, too, probably. Her sister gave Alayna a long, slow look, head to toe, appraisingly. Then she poked out her lower lip, rolled her neck a little and cut her eyes at her future husband. Alayna knew the look: *Alayna thinks she cute.*

After an odd beat as the energy of the room accommodated two new entrants, Sister Judge resumed.

Martine must have spent most of her savings on her dress—a little pearl suit dress that said Neiman Marcus like the price tag was still attached, topped off with a tiny cloche hat like she was Jackie Kennedy or something. Next to her Jamal had GQ-ed his tuxedo with a long, coat-length jacket and a round, no-tie collar. With a fresh skinnier-than-thou haircut, he looked shiny as new money and nervous as hell.

Alayna looked around. She recognized a couple of Martine's friends from school and a few guys she supposed were part of Jamal's crew, but the stout lady in the yellow suit and the dour old gentleman were conspicuously absent. Apparently the Prestons intended to hold to their resistance, at least until they looked into their great-grandbaby's eyes.

In the presence of God and this motley assembly of a few teenagers, Alayna and Ice Pop, Sister Judge did her thing. When she got to that time-honored line about objections, Ice, who made it a point to keep one of his big heavy hands on Alayna's shoulder or elbow or somewhere, wound his fingers into hers and squeezed so hard, she almost slapped him.

In a fast flurry of words, soft-spoken promises, and

desperate need for organ accompaniment, it was done.

Martine was married, Alayna blinked back a few tears, and Ice waved a handkerchief under her nose. A real, live, freshly starched piece of bona fide linen— no wadded tissues this time. And best of all, he kept his fat mouth shut.

"Come on," he muttered after she wiped and blew her last. He nodded at the crush of young people gathered noisily around the bride and groom, and the judicial assistant who was already trying to push them all out the door before the next ceremony began. "We'll congratulate the happy couple at the reception."

Pulling up to Magnolia Street was almost too painful to stand. Too many emotions. Too many memories. But mostly, a weird sense of finality and separateness that took Alayna completely by surprise.

How could her home of a lifetime become a place she dreaded to even *enter* in only a few short weeks?

They sat in the car for a moment, silent, watching the lights inside, listening to music floating out to them. The place was already bustling with even more teenagers—apparently the ones who had preferred to skip the solemnizing and get straight to the party.

As they watched, a long white limo pulled up, depositing Martine, Jamal, Nalexi and half a dozen more boisterous teens, who disappeared quickly up the porch stairs and into the house.

"You don't have to do this," Ice said softly after a while.

"I do, and you know it."

But she didn't move, just sat staring at the house for a long time.

"This was always my home," she said at last. "Always. Even when everything around it and inside it was pressing on me . . . pressing on me like . . ." She sighed. "It was always my home. And now . . ."

She stared at the peeling paint, the gabled front porch, the new windows installed and paid for, the hanging boxes of flowers Martine planted every February. She could almost see the live Christmas tree in its usual place in the wide front window, hear her father's step on the porch and her mother's voice in the kitchen. She closed her eyes, seeing the rooms inside as they had always, always been.

"Okay?"

"Of course," she nearly snapped, but she managed to pull her voice out of its tailspin with a sigh. "It's just . . . complicated."

He nodded.

"Resentment, gratitude, doubt, relief, guilt and pride . . . shake well. Yeah. Complicated," he muttered.

"What do you know about it?"

He smirked. "We have a lot in common, you and I. Come on. Let's do this . . . then . . ." He hesitated, as though the words had suddenly become difficult. "I still want to tell you about Graves and Cybex . . . but mostly . . . well, I've got something to show you."

Inside was the prom . . . with a wedding theme. Big white bells and streamers, at least a hundred little white votive candles all over the place on homemade holders on which "Jamal and Martine forever" had been written in neat golden script. The smell of barbecue wings filled the house, and next to a big punch bowl on the dining room table was a three-tiered wedding cake complete with two little black-faced figures. Beside it was a smaller table, laden with brightly wrapped boxes.

If Ice had any idea how out of place he looked among young black teenagers half his age, he didn't show it.

"Martine spent all the money in her savings account, plus her graduation money on this. I can just *tell*," Alayna seethed. "What are they going to do at the first of the month?"

"Their problem. Not yours," Ice said. "Let's go wish your sister and her new husband happiness. That's what we're here for, remember?"

They found the new Mrs. Martine Preston in the small kitchen. Martine wore an apron over her wedding suit, and the yellow oven mitt was getting a workout. It was like behind the scenes at a short-order diner. Alayna caught a glimpse of her sister's face. Her lips were pressed tight together, and the skin under her eyes looked pinched and chalky, as though it was taking all she had to keep from upchucking right then and there.

"Finish up and get this food out there, girl!" Martine commanded a little moonfaced girl with a bad weave Alayna didn't recognize. "Can't have no party without no food—"

Then her eyes found Alayna and her escort. The apron slipped over her head faster than a heartbeat and found itself wadded on the counter.

"Alayna!" she exclaimed. "I'm so glad you came."

As Martine gave Alayna a long, hard embrace, the whole place got a little quieter, as though most of those present had heard some version of the Martine-Alayna saga and were eager to catch the latest installment.

When Alayna was released, Martine gushed, "Mr. Richards!" and presented Ice with her cheek, like she was Joan Collins on *Dynasty* or something.

"Mrs. Preston." He kissed the proffered skin with aloof formality, being a perfect Ice Man . . . if you weren't looking at the glint of mischief in his eyes. Alayna could tell he was getting a kick out of this, out of Martine's pretensions, the eyes of the spectators, the stillness of the room. He knew his role: fish out of water, the sister's weirdo friend, and he played it with just the right edge of indifference and attitude. Alayna wished she could just sit back and watch him, but she had to play her part in the game.

"I've brought you something," he said.

Martine's face lit up like Christmas.

"Jamal!" she called into the living room, practically bouncing on her toes with excitement. "The Ice Man—Mr. Richards brought us a present!"

Jamal materialized out of a cluster of young men behind them, shook Richards' hand and waited. Then, with a flair for the dramatic that reminded Alayna of the moment of revelation on one of those whodunit television shows, Ice reached into his jacket and produced an envelope. He held it, hovering slightly in the air between them, as Jamal and Martine stared first at the envelope and then each other, smiling widely.

"Thank you!" Martine squealed, grabbing it. "Thank you, so much!"

In her impatience, she nearly ripped the envelope to

shreds trying to open it. She pulled out a single sheet of paper.

"It . . . looks like . . . a bank statement . . . ?" she said in a puzzled voice. "Oh my God! It's one thousand dollars!"

"Yes. For your baby."

"That's wonderful!" Martine breathed. "Thank you. That means we can buy the crib we saw in the catalog and—"

"No." Ice gave them an icicle smile. "It's a trust account, not a savings account. You won't be able to pull the money out. It's held in trust for the baby, gathering interest until the child is eighteen. Over time, this money could grow to more than enough to cover his or her entire college education, if he or she is so inclined. Alayna's the trustee . . . in case our . . . friendship . . . is short-lived."

Martine and Jamal stared at him, disappointment competing with gratitude competing with wariness on their faces, and Alayna nearly had to put her head on his chest again to keep from cracking up laughing. Of the hard lessons ahead for the Prestons, learning to manage money was clearly going to be among the hardest.

"Thank you," Martine stammered. "It's a very thoughtful—"

"And generous—" Jamal added.

"—gift," Martine finished. The expression on her face said that a thousand dollars *now* would have meant far more to her than $80,000 in the future.

"My pleasure."

Martine's face swung toward Alayna. "And what did *you* bring me, big Sis?"

"You'll have to come by the firm next week, Tiney," Alayna said, matching the Ice Man's calm. "I'm giving you what I promised I would, title to this house."

"I know but . . ." She shifted a little. "I thought—"

"It's paid for," Alayna said, feeling tears stinging her eyes. "Mama always said it was ours to do with as we saw fit. You and your family can do what you want with it."

"Hey, Tiney!" someone yelled from the living room. "You . . . your sister . . . you got another . . . guest."

Martine frowned, disentangled herself from Jamal and moved toward the door, her husband trooping dutifully after her. Ice quirked a query at Alayna, who shrugged a response and prepared to follow her sister and her new brother-in-law into the crowded living room.

The familiar rumble of a deep, melodious voice reached her ears before she even saw the rest of his good-looking self.

"Stay here a second," she murmured to Ice and hurried toward the sound.

"Hi. You must be Martine. And you, my brother, are Jamal. Congratulations. I'm a friend of Alayna's."

Linc had the slightly rumpled, more than a little hassled look of a man who'd driven 300 miles fast as a bat out of hell. He kissed puzzled-looking Martine on the cheek, and handed her a little box wrapped in silver and topped with an ornate white bow. An instant later, he locked Jamal a soul handshake, complete with a little press to the chest like he intended to be a part of the family for a long, long time.

He stepped toward Alayna as soon as the first flounce of her dress appeared, his lips puckered for a kiss of welcome.

"Linc! I thought you couldn't make it!" Alayna exclaimed, that nasty guilty feeling twisting her guts already. "So I—"

By the way his face froze, hardened and glazed over with a barely concealed dislike and distrust, she knew Ice hadn't stayed in the kitchen like she'd asked him to. That he was right behind her, probably with that possession-is-nine-tenths-of-the-law look on his face.

Linc straightened up to his full height, his upper lip all but disappearing behind the little black mustache.

"What's he doing here?" he rumbled in a voice a full octave lower than usual and as many degrees meaner.

"He was *invited*, Linc—"

"By who? *You?*"

"Listen, Linc—"

"I ain't listening to nothing, Alayna. What's the deal? Me on Tuesdays, Thursdays and Saturdays? Him on Monday, Friday, and Sunday? What kinda player are you, huh?"

"It's not like that—"

"I'm sick of this shit. I'm sick of this, okay? For the last time," Linc muttered, control and restraint tight in his tone. "If it ain't like that, just answer me one thing straight up. What is the deal with you and Home Boy, here—"

"Home boy?" Ice interrupted coolly. "Gee, thanks, Warren. Most people find me too stiff to be a home boy. I'm flattered."

Linc reached for him in a move halfway between a

lunge and a leap. Jamal saw it coming, because he stepped in front of him, clapping him on the shoulder and murmuring something about peace while Alayna turned around quickly, put herself right in Ice's line of vision and hissed, "Shut *up*. Please."

A mutter of interest swelled and died in the room as a few dozen pairs of teenaged eyes got hip to the two "old guys" with Martine's sister.

"This isn't the time or place for this," Alayna said quietly. "Both of you need to check yourselves because—"

"I'm not used to playing second to a white man, Alayna. So for the last time, what's with you and this guy?"

"And for the last time he's my boss," Alayna snapped. "And he's a friend. He was *invited* to this wedding, and he has as much right to be here as you do. We were both at the office, we were both going to the wedding, so he gave me a ride."

Linc shook his head. "You must think I'm real stupid," he grumbled, sounding like murder and looking like war. "All these hours you say you're *working*—"

Entitlement. That was what she heard in his voice. An ugly take-you-for-granted-because-I'm-the-black-man certainty that reduced her to the label *my woman* with the same possessive ownership as he might have said "my dog," "my car" or any other inanimate thing. And the tone resonated through her not just because she hated being its subject so much but because she recognized it from her own repertoire of judgments and assumptions. "My job," "My role," "my responsibility," . . . "my sister."

Lord, forgive me. I didn't know, she thought

quickly, then arranged her mouth to spit some of Linc's self-righteous fire right back at him.

"You know something, Linc. I don't have to take this from you. It's not like we're *married*. We're not even—"

"You're *black*, Alayna. In case you'd forgotten it."

"This is not a conversation for my sister's wedding."

"Why not? She probably already knows you can't be bothered with a decent brother who *works* for a living. No. You gotta cross the color line—"

"Stop it, Linc—"

"All that crap about being 'old fashioned,'" he snorted. "Is that what you call it?"

"I said, stop it."

"That what you call it when you're playing darky to his Massa Overseer—"

And that was when the bell sounded and Ice came out of his corner, pushing her and Jamal aside, stepping fully into Linc's face.

"I think somebody needs to teach you some manners, Warren," he hissed nastily.

"Oh yeah? You think you can handle it? Then just step to me, Ice Man."

"Stop it!" Alayna shrieked, pulling Ice away from Linc and holding him. "Enough! Both of you!"

Volume, fury, pitch . . . her words had them all, and the small room stilled to silence. Alayna held Ice's wrists tightly, knowing full well that in another second he would push her aside, and—unless every last one of these teenaged boys jumped in to prevent it—there would be no stopping these two from causing each other some serious damage. She glanced up at his face. Ice was angry, just out-and-out mad. A vein ticked purple in his cheek, looking ready to explode.

"Don't do this, Ice," she whispered, pleading. "Please."

But he didn't seem to hear her. His eyes were on Linc, as though measuring the steps between where he stood and the other man's throat.

Alayna followed his eyes.

Jamal still stood in front of Linc, not touching but blocking with a sort of masculine grace. Alayna remembered the boy was an athlete, said a quick thanks to Heaven and promised God and all the angels never to say another foul word against his skinny head as long as he kept these two fools she'd brought to this reception from making a worse spectacle than they already had.

But when her eyes found Linc's, she understood. His eyes were locked on her hands, wound into Ice's, holding him, restraining him, touching him.

Choosing him.

And Linc's eyes said there wasn't going to be a fight. Not today. Because there was nothing here worth fighting for.

"Look at you, Alayna," he muttered, oozing disgust with every word. "I never understood how Sisters could do this. Abandon the black man. Your brother in the *struggle*."

"I'm still your Sister in the struggle, Linc." Alayna snapped her neck just enough to let him know this Sister still knew from whence she came. "I'm your sister in four hundred years of fighting oppression, bigotry and discrimination. But, Linc, I've got no reason to hate this particular man," she glared challengingly at him. "And neither do you."

Linc shook his head.

"Whatever, Alayna." He was almost laughing now, like the whole thing was six degrees beyond ridiculous. "Go on. Have your white boy. Justify it any way you want. Just don't come crying to me when he's through with you"—he shot another ugly spear of loathing at Ice—"and he will be soon enough. Don't come to me, because I won't be there. I swear I won't."

Then he turned on his heel and strode out of the place without another word.

Stupid dress, stupid shoes, stupid hair, stupid men, stupid, stupid, stupid *life*.

Two dozen black teenagers stared at them like this was the best show they'd seen in life, and they couldn't wait for what would come after the commercial break.

"Ali." Ice tried to put those big paws on her shoulders like he'd won her at the county fair.

"Shut up," she murmured, swatting them away without looking at him. "Just . . . it's time for us to go."

She nodded thanks at Jamal, kissed Martine's cheek and moved out of the living room, keeping her head high and her eyes on the screen door, so she couldn't see the expressions of the kids around them.

On the porch, she thought she was safe, until she heard some tactless teenager exclaim in a voice a little too loud for the proximity of the subject, "Dang! Did you *know* your sister was a player, Martine?"

Chapter 24

"I don't care what you want to say, I don't want to hear it," Alayna said when she was buckled beside Ice in his sleek black ride. "Just take me home and don't say a word to me, okay?"

Ice frowned, but she shot him such an evil look that he folded his lips, started the car, and for once, did what he was told. Even the weather knew what kind of mood she was in. An evening shower rumbled in the sky, strewing clouds across the sunset. A few hard droplets spattered the windshield as they left the leafy neighborhood and merged onto the asphalt jungle of fast-food restaurants and grocery stores, headed back into the traffic and noise of the center of town. Ice turned on the wipers, and soon they were beating out a steady rhythm, keeping time with her thoughts: fool, *swish,* fool, *swish,* fool, *swish,* fool . . .

Fool for taking this stupid job.

Fool for busting her head on that damn table.

Fool for starting this game with Linc.

Fool for thinking she knew what the hell she was doing from one minute to the next.

And most of all, fool for sitting here next to *this* fool again, having revealed so much of her heart.

They'd been driving for a long time when she realized he wasn't anywhere near her apartment building. They were circling the southeastern part of downtown, near the old Grady Hospital and the low, institutional-ugly buildings that surrounded it.

"I told you to take me *home!* Where *are* we?" Alayna asked, but Ice didn't even look at her. She saw a muscle twitch slightly in the tight profile of his jaw, then he angled the car into the parking lot of the Atlanta Alzheimer's Care Center.

He killed the engine and sat still for a moment, not looking at her, engaged in an eleventh-hour debate with himself. A thousand questions jumbled to the front of Alayna's mouth, but she dammed them at her teeth and kept her eyes on the man at the wheel.

"I've wanted to tell you a thousand times . . . but . . . it's not my secret. Took me a while . . . but guess I finally found a loophole."

He popped the locks and turned toward her suddenly, showing her brilliant gray eyes and an expression she'd never seen in them before. They pleaded for compassion, for understanding, for acceptance. And whether he knew it or not, that one desperate, begging look was enough to drain any harsh or smart-ass remark from her brain for as long as his face wore it.

"I don't have an umbrella," he said at last in a soft and slightly scared-sounding voice. "We're going to get wet."

* * *

In the short dash from the car to the doorway, where a receptionist nodded recognition and buzzed them through a locked security door, they got soaked.

"To keep the patients from wandering away," he explained, shaking the sopping suit jacket he'd offered as a rain shield and wadding it up under his arm. His tone said he appreciated the necessity of locks and guards but didn't like the system particularly.

Once inside, though, it was clear a great effort had been made to make a cheerful impression. They entered a bright common room, decorated with comfortable armchairs, side tables covered with assorted books and magazines, and even a large floral arrangement on a central table. Childish but colorful murals painted the walls. The room's sole occupant, a tiny old man in a wheelchair, sat near the windows, staring out into the downpour in apparent fascination.

"Ben! Thank God!" exclaimed a young nursing assistant who had been moving at breakneck speed down the hallway. She waved at him, approaching rapidly on white tennis shoes that squished on the waxed linoleum, pert features crunched into a frown. "I was just about to page you! We had another *incident*."

She said the word hesitantly, as though trying to minimize its impact, but Ice reacted like she'd called him an asshole anyway.

"*What?* When?"

"Just now," the girl said urgently. "And the director wants to see you—"

"Yeah, yeah," he muttered in his the-director-can-go-straight-to-hell tone. "Where is *he?*"

The little NA looked suddenly nervous.

"We . . . we had to . . . we had to put him in restraints again."

"You *what?*" Ice roared.

The girl pinkened and jumped away from him, frightened. In a restraint of her own making, Alayna took Ice's arm and pulled him out of the girl's space so she could squeak out, "He was violent. You know the rules—"

"Where is he?" Ice repeated furiously.

The girl pointed up the corridor.

"Medical," she said. "But the director—"

"Can kiss my ass," Ice muttered and charged up the hallway, pulling Alayna after him.

Two-thirds of the way up the corridor, he shoved open a heavy door and led her into a long room that could only be "Medical." It looked every inch like the emergency section of a hospital, complete with all kinds of equipment and a couple of examining tables separated by curtains. A young male nurse, his skin the color of bitter chocolate and his head afire with tiny, peroxide-dipped braids, moved around doing this and that and, it appeared, keeping an eye on Medical's only patient.

Though his hair was white and his body was considerably more frail than Ice's, there was an unmistakable resemblance any stranger on the street could have caught. The same intense gray eyes, same frowning, firm mouth. The same air of authority. Alayna had an immediate image of this man thirty years earlier in his black robes, presiding over a complicated case. He would have been formidable enough to scare the Greta Jennings ilk of the practice half to death. Even now, as Judge Douglas Richards lay on the examining table, wrists bound to its sides by white cloth ties, his sharp gray eyes wandering the room, he had the manner of a man who expected not to be trifled with.

Alayna glanced up at Ice, who released her hand as he advanced toward the bed, his face still suffused with anger. She watched him, a whole new window into the man opening before her eyes. All the sudden exits and disappearances, the strange hours and phone calls, the door slams, the lies—even the split lip—started to make sense.

"Hey! You're not supposed to be in here—" Mr. Nurse said before he registered who the intruder was. "Oh, it's you, Richards." He, too, looked uncomfortable, as though he expected the reproach to come. "Look, I—" he began, but he was cut off with a growled, "I told you not to do this anymore, Malcolm," as Ice started loosening the restraints at the old man's wrists with the calm expertise of a trained medic. "I told you not to—"

"Hey, man," Malcolm shook his weeny braids and sighed defeat. "If you'd seen him swinging like he was half an hour ago, you'd—"

"I'd have removed him from the situation. I wouldn't do this."

Mr. Nurse shook his head. "It's not that easy and you know it," Malcolm said, and Alayna had the feeling Mr. Nurse had been around on the day Ice's Daddy had popped him one across the mouth. "He's gonna hurt somebody. He can't help it, but he is, Richards."

"Exactly," agreed a supercilious female voice from the doorway behind them.

There was a rumble of thunder then, and the lights seemed to dim just as Alayna turned, making her think of one of those old-timey movies that heralded the arrival of the villain with thunderclaps and low light. A severe-looking black woman wearing a red suit, her hair in tight, iron-gray curls, appeared at the entrance, her red-rimmed mouth set in thin, fighting lines.

"Mr. Richards. I'm glad you're here," she said coldly.

"You won't be, Mrs. Aubry." Ice kept his attention on the father, whom he had now freed. "How you doing, Dad?"

The older man's eyes skittered over Ice as though he had never seen him before in his life.

"Where's Ben? Where's my son?"

"I'm Ben," the son responded mechanically, as though he'd introduced himself to the man a thousand times. "Sit up. We're going home."

Judge Richards obeyed the instruction, glancing around quickly, as though determined not to miss a detail.

"Who's the pretty nurse?" Judge Richards asked, gunmetal eyes flickering over Alayna with intense interest.

"I'm wondering that myself?" Mrs. Aubry interrupted before Ice could answer. She'd been giving Alayna the big disapproving eye for a while, clearly making an unpleasant assumption based on the slinky blue dress and flippy shoes. "You know this area is strictly off limits, Richards. Family only."

"She *is* family," Ice snapped.

Mrs. Aubry frowned. "She doesn't look like family to me," she sniffed.

"Well," Ice gave the woman a look that could turn stone to fire. "The legal definition of family grows broader in nearly every court decision. At this moment, Ms. Jackson falls within the definition of family as I understand it, but if you care to *argue* the point—" He left the sentenced unfinished, but the flash in his eyes and the shrug of his shoulders said in unmistakable terms, *Bring it on.*

Mrs. Aubry glared at Alayna as though the entire situation were her fault, consulted an internal legal counselor and wisely decided against litigating the matter.

Judge Richards didn't let go so easily.

"Who's the sexy *girl?*" the old man repeated irritably.

"This is *Alayna,* Dad." Ice put an extra emphasis on her name as if the old man would register its significance. "The one I've been telling you about, remember? Alayna, this is my father, Douglas Richards."

"Hello, Judge Richards." Alayna approached him cautiously, laying her hand over his briefly in greeting. His skin was as soft as well-worn leather, but his eyes were as sharp as eagle talons. They roved over her, hair to hips, before he muttered, "You know my son, Ben?"

"Yes."

"He's a lawyer. Damned fine one, too."

"I know."

Douglas Richards nodded abruptly. "Good. Good. You're not as dumb as some of these people around here, I can tell. Now, young lady. Find my son and tell him I'm ready to go home."

"I'm right here, Dad," Ice interrupted. "I'm Ben. And we're going home—"

"Not yet," Mrs. Aubry interrupted. "I need a word with you, Mr. Richards."

"Then start talking, because we're leaving," Ice muttered.

"Not until we've spoken," she countered, squaring off in the doorway like a lady linebacker. "In private."

"All right. See you, Malcolm," Ice said to Mr. Nurse, who chuckled slightly, shook his braids sympathetically and left.

"And your . . . friend. . . ."

Alayna would have gladly excused herself, if only to avoid this woman's imperious gaze. But Judge Richards had her hand pinched between his now and seemed to have forgotten about her. His long, pale fingers were surprisingly strong. Extricating herself would either require an insultingly obvious tug or permission neither of the Richards men seemed inclined to give.

"She isn't going anywhere," Ice began. But another sharp crack of thunder overrode him, shaking the sky. Heavy rain began to smash dangerously at the windows, demanding the right to dry itself inside.

The face Ice swung toward Mrs. Aubry tightened to dangerous, too.

"If that's your choice, fine," Mrs. Aubry said testily. "I warned you, Mr. Richards—"

"And I warned you," Ice hissed. "You do not have grounds—"

"Oh, I have grounds! In the past month we've

had no less than six—*six*—violent outbursts involving your father. He nearly broke Julie Kominski's nose."

"He did not break her nose. You know as well as I do that the circumstances of that incident were extremely unclear."

"Be that as it may, the nonresidential facility is not designed for patients who require this level of care! You were informed of that when he was accepted."

Ice's fists were clenched at his sides. In a minute—it was clear to Alayna anyway—the son was the one who was going to need to be removed from the nonresidential facility. Maybe Madam Directrix shouldn't have been so quick to see Malcom leave.

"I was *not* informed that your recourse would be to tie him down like an animal," Ice shouted at the woman, but she seemed utterly unimpressed by the volume of his rage or the tracks of his tears, or anything else.

Go 'head with your bad self, Alayna thought, admiring the woman's gumption. *Just hope you got yourself a tranquilizer gun hidden in that suit somewhere, Sister.*

"What do you want me to do? Let him punch out my staff?"

Ice didn't have a legalese response to that, so he didn't respond at all, just tightened his grip on his father's arm and stared at Mrs. Aubry like she'd dyed her nose hairs green.

Mrs. Aubry sighed, bringing herself under control like a tired mother on the verge of child abuse.

"Mr. Richards, I understand how difficult this is for you, believe me," she said, rinsing some of her hard edges in the washy tones of pity. "But I'm terribly sorry. It's time to either admit your father to the residential facility or find him another placement. His disease has progressed past the point—"

"No."

"The daily program's not serving him. He needs a more intensive care than—"

"No."

"Mr. Richards, you're not helping him with this attitude. What if he hurt someone? What if he hurts himself?"

"He won't."

And with his harsh finality, Ice effectively killed the sympathetic approach. Mrs. Aubry drew a deep breath, shook herself and gathered her strength for the last word.

"We'll refund the balance of this month's fee," she said softly. "Don't bring him back on Monday. I've already filled the slot. Unless, of course, you want to put him in the residential program. I've still got those two openings."

"I wouldn't bring him back here if this center were the last on earth, Mrs. Aubry," Ice said coldly, taking his father by the arm with one hand and grabbing Alayna with the other. "Come on, Dad. Alayna and I are taking you home."

"He asked me to. Long time ago. Before . . . when he still . . . Swore me to secrecy . . . it's hard to explain. You have to understand our relationship." Ice eased his father into one of the small dinette chairs and turned it toward the condo's huge windows. Outside, the trees in Piedmont Park below bent under the force of the storm.

"My mother died when I was seven, and it's just been me and Dad ever since. My earliest memories are of going to court with him." A little pleasant-memory smile crimped his lips, then faded. "After Mom died I used to go there after school a lot and watch. He took care of me himself, never shunted me off to a boarding school or hired a nanny or anything. Must have been hard on him, but I never knew that. Not then."

"I guess you were pretty close," Alayna offered when Ice's long pause stretched from hesitation to difficulty.

"Yeah." He patted the old man's shoulder gently, but whatever else Ice wanted to say was still wandering the maze of emotions inside him. Alayna settled herself into her chair, letting Patience beat down the other feelings swirling in her own uncertain heart. A time for every purpose under Heaven, the Good Book said. After Ice found his way through the words inside him, she'd have her chance.

Her hips had no sooner hit the chair when the father's soft, strong hand clamped down on hers again.

"You know my son, Ben?" Judge Richards demanded, gray eyes riveted on Alayna's face.

"Yeah. Helluva guy."

"He's a lawyer."

"I know."

"Tell him I'm ready to go home now."

"You are home, Dad," Ice said dully. "You are at home, and I'm Ben."

Doug Richards ignored him. "My son will come to get me soon," he told Alayna as though confiding an important secret. "We're going to have dinner."

"That sounds wonderful, Judge Richards."

Now the old man's steely eyes were fixed on her. "You know my son, Ben?"

Alayna shot Ben a querying look.

"That's his drill. Same round of questions. It's pretty common with Alzheimer's patients," Ice explained, rubbing his face irritably. He stripped off his wet shirt like he was furious with it and tossed it onto the first available surface—the arm of a nearby sofa—then stalked toward a cordless phone on a side table.

"I'll order some dinner and—" he began wearily.

"And it'll take until next month to get here in this weather," Alayna quipped, tossing her head toward the windows as another crack of lightning claimed the sky. "I'll make us something."

"What?"

"What have you got?"

"Nothing." A sheepish embarrassment flickered over Ice's face. "See, I don't . . . I don't really shop—"

But Alayna had already left them for the kitchen.

The refrigerator was a disgrace. Desperately dirty and nearly empty except for a few stored containers of takeout, some orange juice, half a bag of potatoes that looked like peel-today-or-put-in-the-garbage-tomorrow, a dozen eggs, and a few slices of bread. The freezer wasn't much better. Huddled sadly against a thick coat of ice were a wilting box of toaster waffles, one lonely TV dinner and a couple of different brands of premium high-fat ice cream.

Ice crept in behind her, looking even more sheepish and embarrassed at the non-contents of his kitchen.

"How's your cholesterol?" Alayna asked, shaking her head at the ice cream.

"One sixty nine," he muttered. "Heart rate 60, blood pressure 105 over 63. Thanks for your concern. And I told you. There's hardly ever food here. I don't shop because I can't cook."

"You've got eggs, you've got potatoes, juice and bread." She started opening cabinets in the messy little space until she found what she was looking for. "You've got grits—what a good Southern boy you are," she said lightly and was relieved to see the gloom and fatigue lift from his face, if only for a second. "You may not have dinner, but you have breakfast. Get dry. I'll stir this up."

His hands lit on her shoulders again, and he turned her toward him.

"Forget that. I need to explain this to you," he began, his voice suddenly urgent. "You called me untrustworthy and you were right. But I want you to *understand* why I misled you."

"I already do," she murmured, tracing the cut on his lip with new understanding. The pressure of her finger made something wild and passionate light in his eyes, and Alayna's heart started thudding so hard that she knew in another few seconds they'd both abandon food, Judge Richards, the rain and the tacky filth covering this kitchen's floor for the feeling of skin against skin. Just seconds until everything they'd both been holding back burst forth and was hidden no more. She could almost read the countdown in his eyes. Three . . . two . . .

"Whew! You stink!" she said, stepping away from him and fanning her nose with a fluttery, shaking hand. "Got yourself all worked up and funky back there, huh?"

He smiled a smile that said he knew he'd been deflected and would play along, this time.

"Shower," she commanded, trying hard to make·it sound like a requirement when they both knew she'd been one second from falling into his arms, funk and all. "I'll make us all something to eat, then you can tell me anything you want. Go."

The little smirk smile was back.

"So, I'm allowed to talk in my own house after I shower?"

"For a while."

He snorted loudly but sauntered out of the kitchen in obedience.

"Okay, Dad?" she heard him say in the living room. "I'm going to take a shower. Alayna's in the kitchen making you something to eat."

"Yeah, yeah . . ." the old man muttered grumpily, as though his son's words were life's most supreme annoyance. "Go ahead, go ahead."

She heard the punching bag absorb a short but furious round of grunted blows before Ice's feet carried him up the stairs.

"He was diagnosed about eight years ago," he told her later after he'd wolfed down most of the eggs, a serious helping of fried potatoes and four slices of toast. It was fortunate that his father's appetite was light and Alayna's nearly nonexistent. Ice ate enough for all of them. Alayna mused a moment about the financial impact he probably had on all the local take-out restaurants, then focused fully on his story.

"Stepped down from his seat on the federal bench shortly after that," he continued, draining the juice, too. "For a while I thought he'd die just from depression alone. Dad was proud of his accomplishments—he hated giving up his seat on the court. But he was already starting to forget things. Little things. Minor things, really. The names of his law clerks or of the lawyers appearing before him. But I guess if you have a reputation for a mind like a steel trap . . . he just couldn't stand the idea of becoming some stereotypical, doddering old judge. So he quit. Left Washington, left his friends, his career, his reputation. Came to me here and made me swear that I'd keep his secret no matter how bad it got."

"Did he ask you to keep him here, with you?"

Ice's face crunched into a nasty frown.

"I know where you're going, and I'm not shuttling my dad off to a nursing home—"

"Did I say you had to! *Listen,* Ice!" Alayna reached out and pulled on his ear. "That's what these are for."

He grinned for the most fleeting of seconds, then sighed.

"No," he muttered. "That's my idea. I know it doesn't make any sense but . . . I can't. I won't. Even though . . ." He reached over and helped the old man guide a forkful of eggs toward his mouth. "He hasn't known me consistently in months. And now he gets his days and nights confused. Wakes up at about three A.M.—the time I'm just getting to sleep most of the time—and wanders around the condo all night. I can't coax him back to bed and I can't go to sleep myself either. I'm afraid of what might happen. He thinks the closets are his chambers, the bathrooms are courtrooms . . ."

"And the hitting?"

"New." He sighed, a heavy, heart-dragging sigh.

"What will you do now, on Monday? I mean, that woman—"

"Mrs. Aubry."

"She didn't sound like she was kidding."

"Private nurse, I guess. Hired one a while back to help out when I have to work late, weekends. But Dad doesn't like her. She comes near him and he's ready to fight. Lately, he just takes to people or he doesn't. He seems to like you."

Was there the glimmer of suggestion in the words? Or was it just her imagination? Ice's expression was innocent enough, so she shook away her suspicion with a bright, "Who wouldn't?" and got another weary smile.

"Why couldn't you tell Weston you need to work from home for a while?"

"Weston." Ice nearly spit out the man's name, as though just saying it was poison. "Weston wants Cybex as the firm's next big client."

"I thought Cybex *was* the firm's next big client."

Ice shook his head.

"Just for this case. See, Alan Graves and I go way back. He called me about this matter because of our growing expertise in technology cases. But Weston wants it all. All of the company's legal work. From employment contracts to product licensing to slip and fall cases—everything. The whole enchilada. So he made this deal with Graves. Hughes Weston and Moore does this infringement trial for peanuts—"

"And gets all of the company's business if you win," Alayna finished. "Sounds like Weston." She shrugged a nearly bare shoulder. "What's wrong with that? You brought the business in. You'll make partner for sure."

"If I can behave," he muttered bitterly, but before Alayna could ask him if that was even physically possible, he added, "keep my fondness for a pretty black paralegal under wraps. Be more polite and deferential to the other partners. Keep working with a shoestring staff to maximize profits."

"Do what you gotta do, right?" Alayna muttered, and it was all there again, her fury with him for his silent acquiescence to Weston's fatherly advice. The ugly truth between them surfaced. For all their smoldering glances and heart-skipping chemistry, when the choice was Alayna M. Jackson or partnership, the boys at the firm won hands down.

And she got so wrapped up in feeling her own pissed-off self-pity that she almost missed the ire snaking through his next words.

"That son of a bitch Weston—and the others. Smug, self-righteous parasites. I'd rather shovel shit than partner with any of those fools. Weston and his ilk are exactly the reason Dad didn't want anyone to know," he continued, his voice hard with anger. "For all the talk about what a great man my Dad was . . . is . . . was"—he frowned over the verb and then let it go with a sigh—"he wasn't very popular when he was on the bench. Some of his decisions were groundbreaking. Race relations, affirmative action."

"I've read a few of them myself," Alayna said quietly.

"Who hasn't?" Ice rubbed his hand through his hair, making it stand up in spiked frustration. "A lot of his former colleagues in the legal community would love to know he's . . . he's . . . like this."

"So what are you going to do?"

"About what?"

Alayna rolled her eyes. "About *him*," she jerked her head toward the judge. "About Weston? About the firm? About your situation?" *About me?* she thought impatiently but had the good sense to keep those words in thought rather than deed.

Ice threw up an expression as blank as a roadblock and tried to wall himself off from the words. Alayna tossed her head at him, letting him know with a shake of frizzed curls she had no intention of backing down.

"You're gonna have to do something, Ice. He's not a precocious seven-year-old you can take with you wherever you go. And you can't go on like this, Ice."

"Have to."

"If you make partner—"

"I wouldn't have their partnership if it came with a solid gold office," he grumbled. "I've indulged Weston this long because of Alan Graves and Cybex. The second this case is over, I'm taking a chunk out of that slimy fat fuck. *Watch* me."

Thank God for small favors, Alayna sighed. *He's a crazy jerk, but at least he's not in league with the devil.*

"And after you tell off Weston and get yourself kicked out on your butt? Then what?"

"I have a plan," he muttered.

"It's not going to work."

"You haven't even heard it yet," he snapped.

"If it involves trying to care for your father yourself, I don't have to," Alayna shot back. "It's not going to work."

"It will, somehow," he said, rising so quickly that the table shook. He paced away from them, staring out at the continuing downpour, his face as dour and gray as the dripping weather.

"He's not going to get better."

"But he might not get any *worse!*"

As if to prove his son wrong, Doug Richards let a fragment of egg slide off his fork and land with a plop on the front of his pale blue shirt. He stared at it for a moment, as if he'd never seen anything like it before and wasn't entirely sure what to do about it.

"Here," Alayna said gently. She showed him the napkin first, then shook it open and scooped the wayward bit of food off of him as the old man watched in amazement.

"You know my son, Ben?" the judge asked her again, his silvery eyes glittering.

"Yes. He's a piece of work." Alayna rolled her eyes dramatically and threw an eyebrow toward the sky to make her take on the words plain.

Judge Richards laughed. "You *do* know him," he chuckled. "Indeed. Yes, indeed."

Ice Man Ben turned toward the exchange just in time to catch her floor show, then had a devil's time trying not to smile.

"He's a lawyer," the old judge continued, grinning mischief at Alayna.

"Damn good one, too, I hear. He could make partner. Be a mucketey-muck around the law firm. Unless Graves is smart enough to make him a better offer . . ." and she quirked a querying eyebrow in the son's direction and got back a lip twist she read as how-did-you-know-that but no words in response.

"He's going to come and get me. We're going to have dinner."

"Where? Mad-Cow Burger Box?"

A snort of laughter from the window.

"You're pretty," Judge Daddy observed, as though he'd recently been appointed to an expert panel on the subject.

"Thank you, sir."

He looked over at Ben. "Hey, you. Boy. Don't you think she's pretty?"

"Beautiful."

Alayna laughed. "Lawyer double-talk from both father and son. Girl could be up to her neck in b.s. if she spends too much time around here."

"I like her," Judge Richards pronounced, glaring hard at Ben. "Better than that ugly lizard of a nurse you usually bring round here." He rolled his eyes in pronounced distaste. "She can stay."

For a long while, the only sounds were the sounds of rain beating against the window glass and Doug Richards' fork, chasing bits of fried potato around the edges of his plate. The old man had forgotten what he'd started with those three little words, but one look at his son's face told her that Ice was working them through fourteen different mathematical computations. When he came up with an equation he liked, the son's sober gray eyes searched her face, making that nervous thumpitty-thing start in her heart all over again, loud, irrational and utterly untrustworthy. She glanced toward the rain-driven windows, but even Mother Nature had decided to participate, sending lightning to light the sky like a forked tongue and another big thunder boomer to shake the silence.

Lousy weather to ask a man and his ailing father to drive in.

Especially since her heart was wailing out a chorus from the musical *Dreamgirls*. "I'm staying, I'm staying . . ." it sang. "And you're gonna love me."

"She's staying, all right," Ice muttered as though reading the sheet music in her brain. "Because she's crazy about me and she knows I'm crazy for her, too."

Chapter 25

"**L**et's get one thing straight, okay? I'm not going to be your . . . your . . . chocolate plaything," Alayna insisted as Ice pulled her into his bedroom the second after he'd coaxed the Judge into turning off his light.

All he'd had to do was profess his undying love, and her resolve had gone totally out the window. He'd probably known that from the beginning, probably why he'd said it. And here she was scrambling to recover just a shred of dignity before it was too late altogether.

" 'Chocolate plaything'?"

Those two heavy hands came down on her shoulders again, but this time with a purpose. The rat already had the zipper to the shimmery blue dress halfway down.

"You know what I mean," Alayna shrugged him off, but all that did was loosen the flimsy garment that much more. "Sucking my toes here and at the office its back to Me Boss, You Work—"

"What office? I told you. I'm finishing the case and that's it," Ice muttered, burying his lips into the side of her neck as the dress slipped off her body into a flouncy puddle on the floor. "Besides, that's not what I had in mind."

"Had in mind?" Alayna repeated. That didn't sound good at all. She wanted to resist, but her fingers disobeyed, peeling away his shirt, feeling the rounded muscles beneath his skin. She wound her arms around his neck, pulling his face close to hers. "Exactly what *do* you have in mind?" she asked, struggling to sound as insistent and determined as a woman wearing nothing but a push-up bra and lacy panties could possibly sound. But the words came out as a husky assertion of desire, and Ice didn't answer.

Instead, his mouth crushed down on hers, demanding reciprocation, swallowing every objection mind or mouth might make. When his tongue caressed hers, Alayna felt a spark of electric passion ignite inside her. She could have powered the whole city of Atlanta with that kiss, thunderstorm or not.

What else was there to do but give up, give in? Cave. Wrap herself around him and call it a night.

After all, if she was going to be honest about it, giving in to him was what she really wanted to do anyway.

It must have taken him a second to get that she wasn't fighting him, wasn't even putting up a token resistance like some virtuous heroine in a dollar-ninety-eight grocery store romance. When the realization reached him, when he really felt her hands caressing his back and her lips returning his passion with all the fury and flame in her body, his kiss changed. Stoked by her response, his first hot fire matured, turning from eager red to a steady blue blaze.

If you've ever wanted a man so much you could have crawled up his body, dove under his skin, built a permanent home in the funk of his armpit and a vacation lodge from the lint between his toes, you know how it felt.

She'd been too lost in the feel of him to realize they were moving until her back brushed against the bed and Ben Richards' lean length was stretched out atop her, his face buried in the side of her neck, his fingers cupping her breasts. She could feel his solid weight, smell him, and for the first time she understood what it meant to be swept away, past the point of caring about anything but the sensations of skin on skin, lips on lips.

She reached up and took his face with both hands, pulling him so close there was nothing between them but the smallest fractions of air and space, no sounds but the sounds of breath, no sensations but the feel of their bodies, colorless in the darkness, finding each other. He wasn't white anymore, just a man, a man surging with desire for her. He wasn't Ice, he was Fire . . . friendly fire, licking eagerly at her lips and neck and breasts, consuming her.

His hand caressed a bare brown thigh, and Alayna felt a warmth spreading through her, touching every part of her body. She sank her hands into the soft silk of his hair, then pressed her fingers into his shoulders. His mouth moved off hers, traveling over her face, down her neck, nuzzling the soft skin between her breasts, and Alayna heard her own breath, ragged with passion whistling through her teeth. She forgot the longwinded lectures she'd given Martine about condoms, diseases, and unwanted pregnancies and just said, "Yes."

No.

Ice rolled off her with a hoarse "Wait," and she heard a drawer opening in the nightstand beside the bed, then Ice cursing impatiently as he pawed its contents in the darkness.

"Where . . . ?" he grumbled as the pawing continued and Alayna grew colder and colder in the absence of his embrace. "Shit."

The next sound was the thud of various papers and objects hitting the floor as Ice lost his temper with the process and resorted to more violent means of finding what he was looking for.

"What—" Alayna began.

"Aha!" he breathed, jubilantly. "I knew I still had a couple of them in here. It's been too damn long . . ." he murmured, talking more to himself than to her as she heard the sound of snapping latex.

"Remind me to get some condoms," he murmured, sliding back beside her and gathering her into his arms again. "Where was I?" And before she could form the words to any of the even dozen smart remarks marching to the front of her brain, he was busily reheating what he'd left on the back burner and turning a few new dials in the process. Within minutes, she'd forgotten the words, forgotten the interruption, forgotten everything but that single word that would unlock a long-secret place inside her forever. She said it again: "Yes . . . yes . . ."

And he knew exactly what she wanted.

She'd heard it would hurt—everyone said that about the first time—but when he jabbed himself deep into her with a hard, determined thrust, the burning was so intense that she shrieked with as much surprise as pain.

He stopped, nearly pulling out until she locked herself around him, drawing him back, slowly taking him fully into her body again.

"Jesus, Ali! Why didn't you tell me?" he murmured, his breath hot and annoyed in her ear.

"What did you think? All black girls give it up in their teens?" Alayna snapped back, attitude interrupting the steamy sex vibe. "Because I wasn't that kind of teenager. I had *responsibilities*—"

Another heavy rush of hot air filled her ear, this one flavored with exasperation.

"Black, white has nothing to do with it—"

"Oh. So you think *all* women just—"

"Shut up, Ali."

His arms tightened around her, binding her to him like ropes. Then his lips found hers again, only this time he was planting little butterflies on her face instead of hard, heavy tongue sandwiches.

"So now you're going to get all soft and gentle," Alayna muttered, pulling away just long enough to find his eyes in the darkness. "Just because I'm—I was a—a—"

"Virgin. And yeah. I'm going to get all soft and gentle," he snarled, sounding totally teed off that he'd been forced to admit it. "So just shut up and let me love you, okay?"

And he did, in a serious slow-jam put-on-the-Marvin-Gaye-then-call-Teddy-Pendergrass style until

Alayna was practically crawling up him. A feeling of pleasure unlike anything she'd ever known spread from her loins to her chest then seemed to shoot through the top of her head and the tips of her toes.

No wonder women lost their damn minds over this stuff. Gave up freedom and jobs, and all their self-respect and—

She gasped and sputtered and squirmed out a loud exclamation of utter pleasure, and he stopped, waiting, letting the spasm have its way with her. And when she could see and hear and think again, she thought he was finished, he'd been still so long.

But oh, no. Not Ice. Nowhere near.

The man was just a *freak*. A freak who would stick his tongue anywhere, a freak who spent and started up all over again like he had reserve supplies buried under his skin. When he stuck his tongue under her armpit, Alayna couldn't stop herself from squealing with laughter.

"What?" he murmured as she pulled his face away. But she could feel the smile on his face and hear it in his voice.

"It's gross!"

"Wasn't bothering me. But, since you object, I can think of a better place . . ."

And the face dived down her body, parted her thighs and made itself comfortable until she was so warm and soft and wet and delirious that when he slid himself back inside her, there was no pain, just gratitude that finally the itch his tongue had stirred would be satisfied.

And now she grappled with him, lifting her hips to meet his thrusts, rubbing his back and buttocks, urging him on until, wet with sweat and winded, he whispered, "You win," and, spent, collapsed, gasping, against her breasts.

He rolled onto his back in the darkness, pulling her into the crook of his arm.

"Thanks."

"For what?"

"Trusting me."

"Yeah . . . well . . . it was just time. I'll be twenty-eight in September."

"Oh. So it's got nothing to do with me," he said nastily. "It was just 'time.' Why didn't you get your friend Linc to do the job? I'm sure he's capable."

Alayna smiled in the darkness. Sometimes the Green-eyed Monster was a woman's best friend.

"Go to sleep, Ice."

"Yeah," he murmured, already fading. "Dad gets up early. I love you, Ali."

It's hard to explain how something can be both expected and unexpected at the same time. And just as hard to explain why as much as she wanted to say it back to him, the words got stuck in her throat and wouldn't come out. She could count on one hand the people she'd said "love" to . . . and all but one of them was dead.

And being hot for a man didn't mean you loved him, did it? Thinking about him all the time and wanting to cuss him out one minute and cuddle up with him the next? Talking to him in your heart when he wasn't in sight and saying the first stupid thing that came to mind when he was—those weren't exactly standards in the gospel of love, were they? Alayna thought of Martine and the tenderness and responsibility, the irritation and aggravation the girl had always stirred. But Martine was her sister: loving her was like a bad habit, an addiction, a circumstance.

But so was Ice, in a different kind of way.

Love. For all the composing and conversing people did about it, the word sure didn't have an easy definition.

She thought it all the way through—not even omitting Trixie's comments about her own "lazy, fat fart"—but when she'd finally worked through it enough to figure out what to say in reply, he was snoring loud enough to give the thunder outside some serious competition.

Yeah, Mama. I probably do love him, sloppy, obnoxious fool that he is.

Then she nestled her cheek against the furry warmth of his chest and, little by little, allowed herself to sleep.

Sometimes months—even years—go by on a level track with barely a rattle in the routine. Days come and go, looking pretty much the same as their predecessors. The sun rises and sets, the seasons change, the bills somehow get paid and time marches on with very few changes in the faces or the scenery, and your heart's greatest challenge is dealing with the boredom of it all.

And other times, changes come so fast and thick, there's barely time to adjust from the mountaintop before Time's Roller Coaster has plunged you back into the valley, and barely time to experience the valley before you're climbing toward the sky again. And your heart's greatest challenge is the possibility that it might just break apart under the strain.

Later, Alayna knew, they would all look back on this as the time of the roller coaster and thank God for blessings that appeared as disasters and sorrows kissed by angel's wings. But in the living . . . it was hard, hard traveling.

She and Ice were both resting in the deep, dreamless sleep that blesses the sexually satisfied, when a telephone's cry split the dark silence.

Ice shuddered awake and dove out of the bed, shaking Alayna loose from his arms with rude impatience. With the first light of dawn filtering through the windows, Alayna could see him as he bent, naked, to retrieve his pants from the floor.

Nice ass.

Pale.

But nice.

He pulled the ringing cell phone out of a pocket of his trousers puddled on the floor and flipped it open, turning toward the bed, completely unself-conscious as he gave her the total full frontal.

The matted brown chest hair she knew, along with the thinning line that led to his navel. Then came . . .

A couple of big walnuts and a long, pink banana?

Alayna shuddered. Grateful as she was for all the wonderful feelings his organ had brought her, from here on out, Ice needed to keep his clothes on.

"What—what—Do you know what time it is?" he hissed, and Alayna followed his eyes toward the red digits of a nightstand clock. A shade before 5 A.M.

"Oh, all right," he groaned, thrusting the phone at Alayna. "Someone named Nalexi . . . ? She's hysterical. I can barely understand her . . . Something about your sister . . . ?"

"There's not much we can do . . ." the young emergency room doc was saying to Jamal and Nalexi when Alayna arrived with Ice and his father in tow. "This early in the pregnancy either the bleeding will stop on its own . . . or it won't."

"And the baby?" Ice asked, sounding as urgent as if he were the father. He kept a tight hand on Judge Richards, who had been awakened, irritable and resistant, from a sound sleep to make this journey. Hastily dressed in khakis and a clean polo shirt, the old man's gray hair stood in a fluffy bed halo around his head. The judge seemed subdued and sleepy but was otherwise docile enough.

Alayna was his composite opposite: dressed in her rumpled party dress, shaking with anxiety, too nervous to stand still, almost too nervous to speak. A thousand should-haves lined up in her brain, clamoring for first shot at building a guilt complex. Should have gone to the doctor with her, should have checked on her more, should have helped with the wedding reception, should have—

"She'll either lose it or she won't." The young doctor sighed. She was blonde and attractive in a Greta Jennings sort of way, the sort of woman Alayna might once have nicknamed "Dr. Barbie." But right now, the young doc looked as grave as GI Joe. Her mind was so focused on her patient that she didn't even seem to notice the strangeness of Alayna holding

hands with Ice holding hands with his dad. "That's
small comfort, I know, but it's the best I can do." She
sighed. "I'm sorry."

Jamal looked like the thunder and lightning that
had shaken the trees the night before had personally
cracked open a new hole in his existence, and
Nalexi . . . well, one look at the girl's tear-streaked
face, mascara running wild and free down her cheeks,
and Alayna knew she'd misjudged her. Misjudged her
something fierce.

She dropped an arm around the girl's shoulder and
squeezed, suddenly thankful that Martine had such a
friend to confide in. Alayna herself had never had a
friend like that, she realized with a sudden, sad jolt.
Had that been why the trust these girls had in each
other had been so hard to understand?

"Can we see her?" Jamal murmured, his voice soft
and determined in the stunned silence that had over-
taken them all.

"Sure. But one at a time, okay?"

The doc turned, ready to lead the way.

Jamal studied Alayna for a moment, then with that
maturity of his that never ceased to surprise, he said,
"You go first, Alayna. You're like a mother to her . . .
and I guess a woman needs her mother at a time like
this."

Jamal locked eyes with Ice, searching for something: confirmation, validation. They must have
found a place of mutual agreement, because Ice nodded twice, lending the young man his encouragement
and more.

"Are you sure . . ." Alayna began, but Jamal's yes
was calm and grave and completely certain.

"Go," Ice said, kissing her forehead. "Jamal and I'll stay here with Dad."

And when Alayna looked back, the three men—Ice, his father, and Jamal—were sitting together in the waiting room, offering their stoic comfort to poor little Nalexi, who sobbed like Martine's baby was her very own child.

Staring back at them, a thought hit her with a force beyond the passion of lovemaking, or all the wordplay and arguing, the roundtable rows of who was a racist and who wasn't. At times like these, when the world was upside down and life hung in the balance, it rarely seemed to matter what color the people around you were. It just mattered that they were people . . . and that they gave a damn.

The doctor led Alayna through a maze of white curtained stations to where Martine lay, swathed in a white paper gown and gauze, her eyes wide with fear.

"You think God's punishing me?" she blurted out almost immediately, in a tiny little girl voice Alayna barely recognized.

"No, baby," Alayna whispered. "No, I don't."

"You were right . . . I was . . . so mean . . . manipulating him . . . but . . . God knows my heart. I love him. I really do. And I'm going to be a good wife to him. I swear I am. And I'm ready to learn to be a good mother, too . . . I am—"

Alayna smoothed her hair back off her forehead, stroking at the little wisps around her sister's temples, just like she had done when the girl was a skinny collection of limbs, growing fast and full of questions.

"I'm sure God knows that, too."

"Then why, Alayna? Why . . ."

The tears started then, great big chest-racking sobs. The kind only a stone can listen to without being moved, the kind no woman who has ever loved like a mother can bear without wishing there were a way to take on the pain herself instead.

"I—don't want—to lose—this baby, Alayna. I—don't want to . . ." Martine sobbed.

"I know . . ." Alayna murmured. "I know . . ."

And there was nothing Alayna could say and next to nothing she could do. Nothing but hold her sister close and let her cry until her eyes were empty and her heart was sore, whispering over and over, "It'll be okay, it'll be all right," in desperate petition to God that the words would prove true.

Finally Martine raised her head and stared at her sister, inspecting Alayna's sex-mussed hair and yesterday's flouncy party dress. Alayna watched with relief as a mischievous grin of understanding crept across Martine's tear-streaked face.

"So . . . you and Ice have *fun* last night?"

Alayna flushed.

"I guess so. Yeah."

Martine nodded her approval.

"The other guy was good looking, but Ice's more your type. He's a real asshole—"

"Great," Alayna rolled her eyes. "My 'type' is a real asshole—"

"But you gotta *respect* him for it," Martine asserted, swinging her head on her neck in Gospel amen. "I like him in spite of his crazy self."

"Yeah. I like him, too."

Martine's smile widened a little more.

"Come on, Alayna. Just *'like'*?" And even under the circumstances, Martine managed a sassy, I-can't-believe-you roll of her eyes. "Never mind. Your face tells the story. And I'm glad," she said, her expression growing serious. "I know you promised Mama you'd take care of me, but I bet she wanted you to take care of your own damn self, too. I mean . . ." New tears glimmered in her eyes. "Imagine how Mama must have felt . . . knowing she was . . . leaving. Dying." The word came out a small whisper of breath, and Alayna realized with a jolt that it was a word her baby sister had never said before. "She must have been worried sick about both of us. Whether we'd be okay. Whether we'd be happy. Not just me, you know. You were her baby, too—"

You were her baby, too.

The simple truth of the words soared into her ears like an arrow quivering in a bull's-eye, and finally Alayna understood. Her mother's last words—the ones she'd never finished. *Promise me . . . you'll take care of . . .*

Yourself.

A wave of tears filled Alayna's eyes as the obvious-ness of their Mama's intentions swept over her, wetting her afresh with love. Martine was right: Alayna had been her mama's baby, too. Of course her dying wish would be to see both of her girls happy, healthy and beloved.

"Thank you . . . for saying that," Alayna muttered, hugging Martine tightly. "Thank you—"

But Martine wasn't listening. Over Alayna's shoulder, a slit appeared in the curtain separating Martine from the other emergency room admittees. Jamal stood in that crack.

"Sorry . . . I just . . ."

The teasing smile ghosting around Martine's lips hitched, faded, then dissolved. Fresh tears puddled in Martine's eyes at the sight of her new husband's anxious face. Jamal looked from one sister to the next, then cleared his throat in query.

"It's okay, Jamal," Alayna said, squeezing the girl's shoulders once more, managing to smile a little while she did it. "This is really your place now. Not mine."

He accepted that statement wordlessly, crossing the room to his wife in the space of a second. Alayna gave them a last backwards glance as she retreated. Jamal rocked Martine in his arms as they cried together.

This was a personal matter now, a private affair between Martine and her husband. No others needed. Alayna wiped her face with her hands and hurried back out to the waiting area, where she had personal matters of her own.

Ice leapt out of his chair as soon as he heard her shoes clicking on the tiled floor, concern crumpling his face into an ugly scowl.

"So . . . how does it feel to be the only man who's visited both the Jackson women in the hospital?" Alayna managed to say, but her voice came out all shaky and forced and utterly unbelievable.

"I'm honored," he said in that serious, flat tone of his, and when he wrapped his arms around her in a long, comforting embrace, Alayna suspected he was telling the straight-out truth.

* * *

They let Martine go home an hour later when the worst of the cramping was over and the bleeding hadn't stopped.

"Are you sure you and Martine want me there?" Alayna asked when Jamal insisted she join them at the old house. "You sure you don't want to be alone together—"

"It's not about what we want. It's about what we *need,*" Jamal said, making the distinction in a voice quietly wise and ponderously adult. "Martine needs you . . . and we have the rest of our lives to be together."

Even Ice blinked a little at that one, but he agreed when Alayna suggested he and his father return to the condo, extracting only a kiss and her promise to join them there herself soon.

The house was a mess: the detritus of Party, Interrupted cluttering every surface from bathroom to front porch. While Jamal helped Martine to the bedroom they now shared, Alayna changed her clothes, said a thankful prayer to the gods of Filth everywhere, and made her hands as busy as her mind.

"You don't have to—" Jamal began when he emerged from the bedroom an hour later and found Alayna on her hands and knees, scrubbing a tacky puddle of spilled soda off the kitchen floor.

"I gotta do something," Alayna muttered, wiping her sweaty face with a soapy palm. She shrugged toward the dirty floor. "*This* is something."

Jamal squatted beside Alayna on the old linoleum and pulled the sponge from her hand.

"I got this something, then," he said. He nodded

toward the bedroom's closed door. "Y'all got things to discuss."

Was it the emphasis he placed on the word "things," or the way his eyebrows rose in inscrutable, unspoken commentary that made the back of Alayna's neck get all prickly and her lips lock down like the penitentiary after a breakout? The expression on her face made the little nugget-headed Man-Boy grin.

"Good luck," he muttered, then ducked his skinny scalp toward the soda-stained floor like his life depended on Spic and Span.

Alayna cocked an eyebrow at him, but Jamal wouldn't look at her, wouldn't say another word. Still, even while he rubbed at the floor like a janitor on probation, Alayna caught a glimmer of an idea that Jamal Preston might be more than equal to the challenge that was Martine. Perhaps her sister *had* picked the right man for herself . . . whether she realized it or not.

And since when did the Queen of Sheba reside at 555 Magnolia Street?

Martine reclined on the big bed with her legs elevated and a new gold-fringed afghan draped around her shoulders. A big tumbler of juice, sipped through a straw, and an expression of magnanimous largess on her wan face topped off the effect.

Lord, Alayna thought, making a mental note to warn Jamal at a later date. *This boy keeps it up, Martine will be spoiled so rotten she'll stink on ice.*

Queen Martine smiled and patted a spot on the bed beside her in invitation.

"How you doing, Tiney?" Alayna asked.

The majestic smile slipped a little, and for the

briefest of seconds, emotion tumbled and swirled on Martine's face. Sadness, fear, doubt and even the barest flash of relief danced their nanosecond across her sister's face. Then Martine took a deep breath and said, "Jamal and I been talking about the future . . . and we've made a decision."

"Okay . . ." Alayna sank onto the proffered spot and stared into her sister's eyes, waiting.

But now that the moment was come, Martine seemed to have lost her way. Her eyes darted around the room, looking for a place to light while she made whatever momentous announcement their "discussion" had yielded. When nothing in the room suited the purpose, she gave up and met Alayna's even gaze.

"We gonna move to Alabama," she said at last, the words coming out in a breathy rush, as though she expected Alayna's objections to begin immediately. "Jamal's gonna go on to Tuskegee. Go on to college. We'll get ourselves one of them apartments. Married student housing." She said these words proudly, like escaping the undergrad dormitories was an accomplishment or something. "When he gets done with school, he'll get a job and we'll sell my house here and buy a place of our own. We talked it over, and if you want, you can rent my house from me until I'm ready to sell it. I'd give it to you cheap, since you're my sister and all."

My house. Not *our* house. Not *Mama's* house. *My* house . . . as though she'd poured the foundation herself. *Give it to you cheap* . . . Alayna couldn't stop herself from chuckling, which made Martine squirm like an army of ants were goose-stepping down her back.

"That it?" Alayna asked when she stopped laughing long enough to speak.

"Yeah, that's it," Martine replied, and now the eyes that found Alayna's face were steely with challenge. "And I don't see what's so funny about it. I mean . . . yesterday at the wedding reception—which you *ruined* by the way—you said you'd give me the house as a wedding gift. And I'm counting on that promise—"

This time, Alayna's laughter ended in such a heavy sigh of relief it almost gave away her part in this game. The face of the woman-girl before her was still too pale, still too taut with both physical and emotional pain, but there wasn't a doubt in Alayna's mind: Martine was going to be all right.

"I said I'd give you my half of the house to raise a family," Alayna said lightly, giving her sister the response her unreasonable demands so clearly deserved. "I didn't say I'd turn this place over so you could fritter it away decorating married student housing, bossing your husband around and getting your nails done! I won't give you a penny for that mission, and you got a lotta nerve asking me to!" Alayna laughed again. "Rent! Girl, you must be crazy!"

"I need that rent money!" Martine cried petulantly, crossing her slender arms over her chest in a pout. "I have to have some income if I'm gonna go to school too—"

"I didn't hear one word about you going to any school in what you just said! But when we sell the house, your share will be more than enough for both of you to go to school, get a car . . . and have a nice down payment on a house of your own somewhere, too, when the time comes, if you're careful with it—"

" 'My share'?" Genuine befuddlement creased Martine's impatient young face. "What are you talking about 'my share'?"

"Your half. Your portion. Your share, dummy," Alayna repeated, thumping her sister's forehead like it was an unripe cantaloupe. "*Now* is the time to sell this house. Put it on the market. Tomorrow if you want. We'll split the proceeds fifty-fifty. You take yours, I'll take mine, and we both go on and do what we gotta do."

Cagey, calculating suspicion played across Martine's face.

"How much will I get? What's the house worth?"

"Fifty, maybe sixty thousand. Apiece."

Martine caged and calculated a little more.

"If you'd honored your promise, I'd get a hundred grand."

Even though Alayna was propped uncomfortably on the edge of the high bed, her hand found her hip bone, and her finger found its favorite swishing place in front of Martine's nose. "If you don't take what I'm offering, girl, I'll take a page from Ice's book and put your share in trust until you're thirty-five. Get it?" She flattened the finger into an outstretched palm. "Now, do we have a deal?"

Martine took her hand like she half expected it to evaporate.

"Deal . . . I guess," she muttered. "But what are you going to do with fifty thousand dollars?"

"I'm going to law school."

The words were out of her mouth before the thought formed in her brain. But when Alayna's heart leapt up in affirmative agreement, like a wallflower asked to dance at the senior prom, there was no point in throwing on conditions like *maybe* or *might*.

"Yeah," she repeated, savoring the feel of the words on her tongue. "I'm going to law school."

She lifted her eyes to Martine's face and found nothing there but a big, sloppy grin of pride and approval.

"So . . . you're finally going to do it?" Martine murmured.

Alayna shrugged as if she weren't smiling so hard her face might crack in two.

"If Greta Jennings could do it, how hard can it be?"

And Martine laughed, and Alayna laughed, and they kept on laughing until tears were rolling down their cheeks: tears of sisterhood, tears of release and tears of gratitude for the painful, perfect perversity of God the Most High.

When day turned to dark again and the bleeding hadn't stopped, there wasn't any doubt.

Martine had miscarried: the baby was gone.

Chapter 26

It was a new experience: being welcomed at the end of a day with a passionate kiss and the warmth of a masculine hug. New to have someone's eyes riveted to her face when she spoke. New . . . and nice.

And the condo looked good, too. He'd spent the day making an effort, or so it appeared, because she could see the floor and there weren't clothes littering the furniture. And a nice meal from a restaurant several steps above his usual junk food fare was on the table, along with candles and a pretty bouquet of mixed flowers that said *florist,* not *grocery store,* without being ostentatious.

Ice seemed to appreciate her efforts, too. She'd stopped back at her apartment after leaving Martine and Jamal to shower and put on something pretty, spritz on a little more perfume and rearrange the frizzy, crinkly mess that the rain had made of her hair—because the way his eyes roved over her said dessert wasn't just going to be a slice of cherry cheesecake. She had something for *that,* too, thanks to a trip to the nearest drugstore and a short and only slightly embarrassing conversation with the pharmacist. Who knew condoms came in so many styles, colors, sizes and even flavors?

But mostly it was the talking, the give-and-take of insults and information, of escalating, passionate exchange by degrees serious and silly, intellectual and idiotic. Unfettered by secrets at last, being with Ice was as natural as breathing air and ten times more fun.

He was sympathetic and silent for the long, sad narrative about Martine and Jamal, appropriately supportive of the college decision ("At least one of them will get an education") and downright philosophical about the future of 555 Magnolia Street ("When it's time to go, it's time to go").

But when she told him how weird her apartment felt now, he started acting like himself, because she got "I told you it was too frou-frou" in sardonic reply. She told him about how she'd decided to look for something more spacious ("What do you want now—a barn?") and by the time that was finished, they were arguing like he'd never put his face between her legs and howled like a wolf.

She told him everything . . . or nearly everything. She didn't tell him about her plan to resign, not being sure exactly where that plan now stood in the face of recent developments. And she left out all the facts of her latest encounter with Linc.

Because of course, when she'd gone home, she'd seen him on the stairway, headed down from his apartment to the street, dressed for an evening of serious play, Lincoln Warren–style.

"Linc," she'd begun, planning to try to explain the whole ugly thing one last time. "Look—"

He'd flashed her a bad-bulb smile that had flickered on and off in an instant, then he'd cut his eyes over his shoulder.

The woman following him down the stairs had been gorgeousness personified: perfect cinnamon skin, sleek black hair, long, thin legs topped by a firm behind, covered in a dress just south of hootchie.

"How's it going, Alayna?" Linc had asked, and she'd noticed the nasty little edge was still in his voice.

She'd paused, watching the woman's eyes flick over her with just enough curiosity to be polite, but not enough to suggest either jealousy or interest. "Fine. I was hoping to . . . finish . . . our conversation. From yesterday. But I see you're busy."

He'd shaken his head soberly.

"Oh, yeah, well. I think we were finished anyway, don't you?" He'd turned back to the woman, taking her hand. "Come on, Simone. We got places to go and people to see!"

Ice didn't need to hear that, especially since Linc was right: It was finished anyway.

Dessert wasn't cheesecake.

It was another slice of all the passion Heaven allows mere mortals . . . as sensual and beautiful as the night before. With two differences: First, this time Alayna played the aggressor, and second, she learned how to slip the condom over the pink banana before easing astride him and going for her very first ride.

Alayna watched his face register pleasure as she

moved slowly against him, learning his rhythm. His hands caressed her back, guiding her forward and back along him. When she rotated her hips, putting some soul in her thrust, his eyes closed and his breath came in short gasps, followed by a slow smile of absolute contentment. She repeated the movement again and again, thrilling in the play of excitement in his clear gray eyes. And in concentrating on pleasing him, her body warmed with the heat of her own pleasure, too.

"Torturer," Ice groaned, reaching up to pull her mouth to his.

Then she felt herself turning, their bodies still locked together, and he was over her, possessing her body completely again, rocking her toward a moment of absolute surrender to his power, and she wanted nothing more than to give him all of it, bones, sinews, sweat, blood as she strained against him, arching toward each shuddering thrust of his hips.

She felt his body spasm with the release of his passion, and her own body echoed in its own quivering waves.

He collapsed against her, sighing release and exhaustion, his long, hard-muscled body slick with sweat. For a long time, he was still except for breath, his chest filling and emptying in the slow rhythms of sleep or something close enough to it to accept a summons in its behalf. Alayna entertained herself: playing her hands in his wet hair for a moment, mopping his temples with her palms, tickling the skin at the nape of his neck and rubbing her cheek against the sticky, scratchy skin of his cheek.

"I love you, too, Ben," she murmured as though

he'd just spoken the words just seconds before, not nearly twenty-four hours ago.

Ice's head popped up, wobbling with surprise and accusation. He looked like a jack-in-the-box prototype for serious, color-challenged little boys.

"What did you call me? And what took you so long?"

"I called you Ben. It's your name, isn't it? And it took so long because I had to think about it," she said coyly, smiling secretly at his irritation. It was a nice thing to know—that it mattered to him whether or not his feeling had been reciprocated. The kind of information a woman might have need of a few stops further down the romantic line.

"Obviously," he grumbled, but instead of using the confession as a prelude for greater intimacy, he yanked himself upward and started fumbling with his crotch. An instant later, he pulled the condom off himself and chucked it across the room, where Alayna was sure she'd step on it on the way to the bathroom. "Of course, I *knew* you loved me, but I'm glad you finally got around to admitting it."

"You *knew* it!" Alayna blustered. "How could you know—"

He jabbed a finger toward her face.

"The eyes. They never lie."

Alayna rolled them at him, for good measure. "Don't get nasty or I'll take it back."

"You can't take that back," he muttered, grabbing her and pinning her down with a gruff kiss. "You said it, I heard it. It's like a contract—"

"Oh Lord," Alayna sighed, squirming beneath him. "Not another contract! That's the very *last*—"

But Ice was already reaching for the light on the nightstand.

"Get up. We got business to discuss." He took both of her arms and parked her in a sitting position, his naked gray eyes gleaming with excitement. "Okay. After this hearing—or at worst, after the trial—we're leaving Hughes Weston and Moore and starting our own firm—"

"*What?*" Alayna gave him the mouth-down-eyes-up look that black women everywhere had to perfect before they got their first visit from Miss Menses. "Our own firm? Did you throw your brains out with that condom?"

"Very funny," he muttered.

"It's not funny at all," Alayna snapped, adding a neck roll and the ever-popular chest poke to her efforts. "I thought you might join Graves at Cybex, but not—"

"I'm a *trial* lawyer. I go to *court,*" he explained, giving her back a finger of his own, which he thumped unceremoniously against her forehead like he was trying to reactivate some bad brains. "If I become in-house counsel, I'll never see the inside of a courtroom again. End up pushing papers all day—"

"But you'll have a reasonable schedule, at least! And starting your own firm is a huge financial risk! What if you don't get any clients—"

"I have one client already," he announced, Smug and Sure running hand-in-hand across his face. "It's Cybex."

"Cybex!" The forehead thump wasn't necessary now, since he could have blown her over with the lightest of whistles. "You're going to *steal* Cybex from Weston?"

Ice laughed a selection from "Evil Villains of the Twentieth Century" and grinned.

"Right from under his nose. Alan's already agreed to sign with me after this trial. Call it a tribute to our long friendship."

Buggy eyes. That's what she had. Buggy eyes blinking like she couldn't control them. And a fishy mouth opening and closing soundlessly, to match.

"Weston's gonna eat you alive," she said at last.

"Might." Ice stretched languidly and dumped his arm around her shoulder as casually as if he'd just suggested they flip on *Late Night* with Leno. "But I doubt it. This sort of thing happens all the time. Lawyers leave, they take their clients with them. And it's his own fault." He paused a moment, muscles in his face working seriously, and she knew he was working on the words to tell her about the conversation they'd had about her.

"I heard him . . . and you . . . talking . . . that day in the kitchen," she admitted, tripping his story a little further up the line.

Ice stared at her a full minute, and Alayna waited, reminding him in her silence that if he thought he'd cornered the market on long, lingering looks, he still didn't know who he was dealing with.

"Chocolate plaything," he chuckled at last. "Now I get it. Should have known. Is that why you didn't say anything to me all last week?"

"Your gums weren't flapping much either, Freezer Boy. Here I am thinking you're playing along with

Weston, waiting until after the partnership to make your *moves*." She wiggled her shoulders, tossing the word back to him in disgust. "And I decided right then and there I wasn't staying around there long enough to be *moved* on—"

"Listen." He grabbed her face, squeezing her cheeks together just hard enough to shut her up. Alayna batted his hand away, but while she was rubbing her jaw and shooting some evil sparks in his direction, he got the space he needed to say, "The only reason I didn't say anything was I realized I might be putting you at risk. It would be just like Weston to fire you for something like this—"

"Who's suspicious now?" Alayna muttered, but he ignored her.

"I didn't want you to get fired. Not until I had someplace for you to go. And now I do. I'm leaving, I'm taking Cybex . . . and a few *other* things that belong to me."

And he had the nerve to grin an utterly up-to-no-good grin.

"Now I *know* you're not talking about me, Mr. Man. 'Cause slavery's been over for nearly two hundred years and—"

"Just *listen* to me," he said, all eager-beaver and buck-toothed. It wasn't like him, all this salivating emotion, like an attitude he'd borrowed just for the occasion. Familiar as it was, she couldn't nail it down. "You love me, right?"

"You're all right," Alayna said slowly.

"Good enough, considering I don't have time to wait around while you think about it another twenty-odd hours. And since you love me, you'll move in and we can work together and sleep together and take care of Dad together and—"

Bam, slap, clink.

A prison door slammed shut, the metal-on-metal clang echoing down cavernous corridors. In the next cell, great big ugly girls who looked like dudes, girls with hairy underarms and the extra time to lift massive weights bigger than her whole damn body. It was like waking up on an episode of *Oz.*

"Wait a minute . . . wait just a—"

"Just *listen*, Ali—"

And while she stared at him with her eyes rolling back in her head and her tongue lolling on the ground, clearly catatonic, he just kept talking. Kept singing her whole life with his words, killing her softly, locking those heavy-duty, high-security, consecutive life sentence iron gates until he made Peter, Peter Pumpkineater's wife's unfortunate habitat look pretty damn appealing.

Work together, sleep together, live together, take care of Dad together. Ice in the morning, Ice at night. The twenty-four/seven of Ice-dom, Ice-ness, Ice Cream, Ice Machine . . .

But I just escaped from this jail, something inside her whimpered. *I just escaped from living for someone else. I just broke out of caretaker hell. . . . You can't mean to send me back, Lord? Just for falling in love with some dude? 'Cause I don't know if I love him THAT much—*

"Keep it hush-hush. On the down low. But we still need to meet with Trixie—" she heard him say, and that pulled her out of her coffin long enough to exclaim, "Trixie? Trixie *McCoy?*"

"I want her to join us. Take over the para-legal/secretarial stuff while you're—"

"Trailer Trixie?" Alayna repeated. "What do you want with *her*?"

"Here we go again," Ice muttered, shaking his head. "Why not? She's just as miserable at Hughes Weston and Moore as you are—"

"*Trixie?*"

"What?" Ice asked, turning toward her. "She's experienced, efficient as holy hell and ambitious. What more do we want? You can't do all this stuff anymore. Not and go to law school and help me with Dad and—"

"You've completely lost your mind! First of all—"

She showed him all ten of her fingers, ready to tick off her arguments in succession:

Trixie will tell Weston.

Trixie will tell *everyone*.

Trixie hates my guts and she'll take yours on a plate, too, if you're serving.

And what makes you think I want to live here.

How do you know we even *like* each other?

But see, the thing about loving a lawyer is it's hard to win an argument. Especially when said lawyer knew every last bit of her personal business.

She'd already decided to quit the firm—which she'd told him; and she did want to go to law school—which she'd told him. And she did need to move—which she'd told him. And looking for a new place would be an unbelievable hassle, especially for a sister without any appreciable income—which he'd probably figured, since there was no telling how long it would take for 555 Magnolia to sell. But she did have experience in caretaking. A lifetime's worth.

Which she'd told him.

That one made her stomach flip with resistance. But how on earth do you tell someone who's just spent the day with your sister in the hospital that while you're happy to accept his help with yours, you don't want to take care of his family?

"The question is really whether you should take day classes or night ones—and where," Ice continued, loud-talking, shooting down every objection she made and showing too much spit in the process. It suddenly snapped into her mind exactly who he reminded her of: the original spitmeister, Alan Graves. No wonder they'd stayed in touch all these years. Deep down, Ice was closer to geek-a-rama than he'd care to admit.

"I think you could get in anywhere," he said, giving her the ADD vote of confidence, "but it might not be a bad idea to start in the fall at Georgia State while you wait to get admission to Emory—"

"Wait . . . wait, just a minute!" Alayna interrupted, finally tired of the rush of foregone conclusions and judgments. She sat up so abruptly that the sheet fell away from her body, and for a second Ice was as distracted by her breasts as he had been the first time he'd seen their outline through a T-shirt. She had to grab him by the face and stare hard into his eyes to be sure he was listening . . . and even then it was a crapshoot.

"I'm not sure I can take care of your father, Ice. I'm not trained to—"

"It's easy. And he likes you," he said, and she got

the distinct impression he knew he was wrong. "I'm tired. We'll talk about it some more in the morning. We're meeting Trixie for breakfast—"

"She's going to tell Weston. I'm telling you, Trixie McCoy is nothing but—"

"White trailer trash," he said flatly. "And everyone knows how *they* are, right? Honestly, Ali. Give it a rest."

Then he rolled over and started snoring almost instantly, like he'd accomplished something.

She lay awake for a long time, long enough to know exactly when the darkness of night turned to the dimness of a dream, but at some moment between awake and asleep, Mama flitted in and sat down beside her. She looked at Ice's lax, snoring mouth and pale, hairy chest and sighed a sigh that Alayna guessed could only mean one thing: *Sorry, baby, either way you move on this one, you're fucked.*

Chapter 27

"**I**'m in," Trixie said before Ice had even finished laying down the deal. "You bet."

They were sitting in Ice's diner in the half hour between early lunch and late breakfast, concealed in Ice's favorite corner booth.

And since it was a humid, sunny Sunday, Trixie had left that ugly red sweater draped like a surrogate over her chair outside Weston's office. Without it, Alayna could actually see the rest of the woman's attire: a pretty sheath patterned with little baskets of blue cornflowers. Alayna was wearing the exact same dress in purple.

Ice sat with his arm practically around Alayna's shoulder in an attitude of possession that would have turned Tanger Gina's orange hair green if she'd been there to see it. But apparently the girl was off today or on a long break, because she hadn't yet bustled up with a bushel of fresh smiles for her favorite customer. Alayna kept trying to nudge him off, but Ice wouldn't leave off the public display of affection. For someone who swore he wanted what was private to stay that way, he was as obvious and open as a street hooker at the Million Man March. Alayna could have sworn everyone in the joint was staring . . . but every time she looked, no one was.

Except Trixie. She was staring. Staring at Ice as he outlined this "plan" of his in short, direct sentences that made Trixie's flat blue eyes dance like Muppets. From time to time, those marbles flickered over that big, pale, hairy-knuckled hand as it cupped Alayna's bare shoulder . . . but then she might have been interested in the smooth brown fingers that plucked it off every time, too.

"Maybe you didn't hear him right—"

"I heard him. I'm in," Trixie muttered defiantly. "Teach Weston a lesson. Greedy little bastard."

"But the money—"

Trixie shook her head. "I can deal with the salary if Richards will pay for school. That's the big thing. I want that certificate—"

Alayna folded her lips tight and snorted in a deep, loud breath of determination. There was only one way to crack a nut this hard.

"I know Weston sent you to spy on us."

The woman glanced quickly at Ice, who just eyebrowed back. Then Trixie reached for the cigarette burning black-and-gray smoke out over them. She took a long, deep drag before saying in that frog-throated voice of hers, "So?"

"You admit it?"

"Weston wanted to figure out a way to keep Cybex . . . and sack Richards. At first he thought you'd do the trick. Piss him off so bad he'd lose his cool . . . and he'd be able to easily get rid of both of ya." She rolled her eyes. "*That* didn't work. So he offered me the slot. Told me to see what I could find out."

Alayna shot Ice triumph in a glance.

"I took a page from *your* book," Trixie continued, jerking her head at Alayna. "Asked for cash on the barrelhead—"

"How did you know about that?"

"You think Gloria Dupinski in payroll was gonna cut a check that big and not tell a soul?" Trixie's flat-tire lips bubbled a cackled laugh. "Please. The whole firm knows about that one."

Alayna waved the bonus check breach away.

"Stick to Weston. You told him what? That Ice and I—"

"I didn't tell him *shit,*" Trixie drawled, poking out her lower lip to its ugliest and most threatening advantage. "I took his money and put it in my pocket and went on with my damn business. After ten years with that son of a bitch, I'd already earned it, yes I did."

"Then—?"

Trixie wheezed out a chuckle that sounded like a cat upchucking a particularly large hairball. She and Ice exchanged another private glance, and for the first time, Ice's silence registered in her nostrils with the aroma of fresh bull crap.

"Alayna, for a smart girl, you're dumb as dirt, y'know?" Trixie laughed, sounding almost kindly in spite of herself. "Any fool could see what was up with you and Richards. Weston's a prick, but he's got *eyes.* . . . No. I didn't tell him nothing. But I did tell *somebody* something—"

"I knew it!" Alayna pounced.

Too soon.

"I told Ben there that Weston was a snake in the grass and to watch his damn back and yours too, since you were too busy calling me trailer trash to listen."

First class fooled. Signed, sealed and delivered.

Alayna shook Ice's hand off her shoulder and gave him some you-could-have-told-me dagger eyes as she tried not to let either one of them see the steam coming out of her ears.

Because in about two seconds, she was gonna have to apologize . . . to Trailer Trixie.

Alayna crunched her face into a reasonable facsimile of sincerity and opened her mouth, but all that came out was, "I . . . uh . . ."

And Trixie wheezed another pneumatic chuckle and sat back, looking fairly well satisfied.

"It's done, then," Ice muttered and finally put his digits to an appropriate use by reaching across the table to squeeze the pale flesh of Trixie's ropy hand. Then he pulled Alayna's on top of it and grinned.

"Ladies, to the birth of Richards and Associates." He rubbed his hands together as if he were stoking the fire in his eyes. "Okay, Alayna, Goddess of the Constitutional Argument. What do I have to do to make Friday's hearing our final appearance as employees of Hughes Weston and Moore?"

A single hour's hearing. If they won, in all probability there would be no trial. If they lost, they'd be back again in a couple of short weeks for several grueling days of testimony and exhibits and a parade of witnesses climbing up and down the witness stand. Questions and cross questions, Alan Graves leaning across the table to whisper suggestions, Trixie watching with attentive interest and Ice live and onstage as counsel for the defendants.

The idea was to never get there. To end it at the hearing on Friday and tell off Weston as a victory party.

By Thursday, Weston and Graves were sitting in on Ice's practice sessions: two of the Devil's best advocates, ascended from the Depths for the sole purpose of peppering Ice with questions. Ice stalked the War Room restlessly and more than once, he turned to her. "Ali?"

And she offered him the best suggestions she could . . . before slipping back into the thoughts circling her brain like aircraft on standby, waiting for permission to land.

Tell him no.

Tell him NO.

TELL HIM NO.

Tell him no. But was there a way to yes to just the man and no to the rest?

Tell him. Tomorrow, the little voice in her brain whispered urgently. *After the hearing's behind us. Tell him, quit, and for once in your life, take care of your own damn self.*

"Alayna?"

She started, recalling herself before an impatient *What?* fell out of her mouth. Graves and Weston were staring at her like they expected rubies of wisdom to fall from her lips.

"Oh," she said, trotting out her own smart-as-shit voice. "I think you reply to that kind of inquiry by reminding the court that precision is at the heart of any legislative act. Unless it's very clear what conduct is prohibited, the law is not only useless, it's dangerous. That's why the Supreme Court in its wisdom defined 'overbreadth' as basis for constitutional attack of legislative action nearly two hundred years ago."

Weston nodded a little, but the excitable Mr. Graves burst into a round of spontaneous applause. "Jeez, Richards. Why don't you just let her do the hearing? You stay home and get some sleep, dude. God knows you look like you need it."

He was right. Ice had puffy gray circles under his eyes again. Judge Daddy was night-roving.

Ice managed an eat-shit smile, rubbed his forehead wearily and said in a flat, remote, utterly detached tone, "Gentlemen . . . lady . . . I think we can win this thing on the law."

Weston beamed.

"They'll appeal—"

"But it'll take at least a year before the high court will hear it—" Ice interjected.

"And in that time—" Graves picked it up.

"No trial, we got a good shot to get the injunction dissolved and—"

"You're a genius, Richards," Graves said.

"True. So is Alayna."

Weston's smile faltered a bit, but he covered it by showing all of his teeth to Alan Graves.

"Want to sign the papers now?"

Graves shot a quick glance at Ice that only a man too busy counting his money could miss, then licked his lips. "Let's just see what tomorrow brings, hey?"

Tomorrow.

* * *

After a nearly sleepless night alone in her cute little place, debating and redebating the words she'd use to tell him, Alayna rose before dawn, showered quickly and slipped on her most conservative going-to-court blue suit. Putting on perfume and jewelry was automatic now, as was firing up the curling iron and sweeping a little eyeliner beneath her lashes and a little lipstick over her lips. The scar on her forehead was almost completely gone now, the remaining indentation neatly covered by a fringe of bangs. The bruising around her eyes was nothing more than a hint of shadow.

She stared at her face for a long time, until the features were odd meaningless blobs, and the colors—brown, pink, black, white—were just interesting groups of related shades. *God must see us all like this*, she thought, *just multicolored blobs, another funny-faced human in the process of being.*

It was the exact same courtroom as a month ago, before the same crusty old judge, same bushy-haired woman representing the opponents. Same everything, except Trixie McCoy, decked out in a dark blue box of a suit that, on her bony figure, made her look like a knife in an envelope.

Ice excused himself for a quick and cordial conversation with opposing counsel, leaving Alayna to babysit Graves and Trixie. Instead, she busied herself with the preparatory acts of laying out copies of the brief—including Ice's personal coffee-stained, stickie-covered copy—a clean yellow legal pad and a pen. Trixie, it seemed, served at least one purpose: Graves took her on as his gabbing buddy, and soon the two of them were engaged in a nonsensical conversation about the weather. When it degenerated into the difficulties of frying eggs on various hot surfaces that weren't intended for the purpose, Alayna totally tuned them out and tuned back into Ice.

He looked tired—as tired as she'd ever seen him—and that was saying something. Tired enough not to protest last night when she'd told him she wanted to go home. Her home. The cute little place. He hadn't raised an eyebrow . . . or an insult. Maybe he was tired enough not to freak out about the coming I-don't-want-to-live-with-you-and-your-dad discussion.

He was tossing a final, insincere comment at the bushy-haired woman and turning to give Alayna a what-are-you-looking-at? face, when it happened.

A shrill beep rent the subdued stillness of the sober room. Everyone, Alayna included, touched their pockets, purses and briefcases searching for the device that was the source of the sound, and when, in relief, they found that some other fool was the offender, they quickly muted their own cell phones and beepers so as not to be a source of future interruption once the judge was present.

Everyone, that is, but Ice.

He froze stock still, midstride between the opponent's counsel table and their own. Frustration, fury and fear in equal parts claimed his features as he reached into his trouser pocket and pulled out the device.

Alayna handed him his cell phone before he asked for it, and he took it, not even seeming to see her. He was out of the courtroom at a fast walk, face on the phone, dialing.

"What was that about?" Graves's face was the dictionary definition of *befuddlement*.

"I don't know," Alayna answered, not altogether truthfully. She'd seen the digits on the pager when Ice had dropped it for the phone: 911-911-911 was all it said.

Trouble. Big trouble.

He returned a few seconds later. The little color that had been in his haggard face was gone. His hands shook slightly as he stuffed both phone and pager into his pocket.

"I have to go," he said, which wasn't a surprise, but the tone was. She'd heard him annoyed and irritated a thousand times, frustrated and concerned at least a hundred. But underneath them all had always been that smooth confidence. Whatever it was might have been heavy, but He Could Handle It. He could always handle it.

No.

Panic had crept into his voice and spread to his face. It had eaten his confidence for breakfast and was working on devouring any other scraps of self-certainty he had lying around. Ice was terrified.

"Ben . . ." Alayna grabbed him just as he sagged against her like a deflated balloon.

"My God, man!" Graves rushed to her aid, seizing Ice by the arm, with Trixie, her beady eyes wide with fear, trampling his heels. "Richards, what is it? What's wrong?"

"I-I—" Ice stammered, but whatever he might have

said got lost as a burly bailiff, fresh from the WWF circuit, cried out at the top of his rather substantial lungs, "All rise! This court is in session. The Honorable Judge William Childress, presiding."

Ice put his hands flat down on the counsel table in front of them, tried to steady himself and shook his head.

"I can't do this," he muttered. "Graves, you're going to have to—"

Moonwalk across the stage . . . naked . . . in front of a raucous crowd at the Apollo Theater.

Graves looked at Ice like that was exactly what he'd proposed.

"I'm no litigator! I've never argued a motion in my *life*—" he began, then stopped short, listening to Ice's breath, too fast, too shallow, hitching in time to his eyes darting around the room.

"You better sit down, Ben," he murmured. "You look like—you look like—"

Ice waved the man away. "I gotta go. *Now*."

"We'll get a continuance," Alayna made her voice decisive. Decision made, no arguments. "Just tell the judge—"

"What's the problem over there, Richards?" snapped Childress, annoyed at the whispering sounds from their corner and the flurry of flesh pressing toward Ice, shoring him up.

At the sharpness of the man's voice, something snapped to attention in Ice's eyes, calming him slightly. Alayna caught just a glimpse of him as a kid, sitting in his formidable father's solemn courtroom, soaking in the drama of it all. He took a full breath and straightened up.

"Your Honor . . . I've just learned of a family emergency," he said, sounding eerily professional even though he looked for all the world like an Unseen Hand had taken a sledgehammer to his foundations. "The movants seek a continuance—"

"What's the nature of your emergency, Mr. Richards?"

Ice's mouth opened and closed for a few seconds, like he was trying to say something but couldn't. Finally, he choked out, "I would . . . prefer . . . not to divulge that . . . Your Honor."

Judge Childress frowned. Opposing counsel was on her feet in a second.

"Your Honor," she began in her clipped, gonna-please-the-court voice. "A continuance would prejudice the interest of my client immeasurably. While we have every sympathy with Mr. Richards' *alleged* family difficulties"—she put a doubtful emphasis on the word just to be nasty, since anyone could see the man was all shook up—"a continuance of this matter jeopardizes our ability to continue preparation for trial. As the court is well aware, the necessity for trial at all is affected by this hearing—"

"The court is aware of that, Ms. Bell. And with the current state of the calendar," Judge Childress intoned with noticeable irritation, "I won't be able to schedule this again for another two or three months." His eyes snapped back to Ice. "I have your brief, Richards, and while I've read it and I find it clear as to your position on the law, I do have some—"

But Ice had stopped listening. He grabbed Graves by the tie and jerked the man into his face.

"Ali wrote the brief," he hissed.

"That's great, Ben," Graves choked. "But—"

"No!" Ice repeated, shaking him like sense was rattling around in there somewhere. "Ali wrote the brief. She can do the hearing—"

But before Alayna could shape her lips into no, Ice was addressing the judge.

"I have to go, Your Honor. It's . . . it's . . . a matter of life and death. My colleague Alayna Jackson will handle the hearing—"

"*What?*" Bushy Hair began, swinging her head toward them so fast the frizzy mass bounced on her back like barefoot boys on a flatbed. She continued, sounding like a fractious child challenging parental preference for a calmer sibling. "But Your *Honor*—"

"It's permitted provided my client agrees—" Ice roared and shot Graves a vision of knuckle sandwiches to come.

"Your . . . Your Honor," Graves cleared his throat and started again. "Your Honor. As—as—vice president for business affairs and general counsel for Cybex, Incorporated, I—I have full authority of the company's legal matters and . . ." He glanced from Ice's tense face to Alayna's surprised one, took a deep breath and said, "She can do it."

"Thank you, Alan," Ice said, and he looked for a second like he was going to grab the man and kiss him full on the mouth.

But instead, he gave Alayna a twist of the lips that never reached the worry in his eyes, turned on his heel and made for the exit.

"Someone oughtta go with him," Trixie muttered in her gravel-under-a-tire voice.

"Yeah. Hurry," Alayna said, but Trixie wasn't asking permission. She was already squeezing past Graves and scurrying her skinny-legged self up the short concourse to catch Ice by the hem of his gray suit jacket just before the courtroom doors swung closed behind him.

Alayna watched them, wondering if he knew that for all her smart-assed remarks and dagger-eyes, he'd just taken her heart out of the room with him.

The room's silence finally reached her ears, and she slowly turned her eyes from the heavy wood doors to the rest of the empty courtroom. They were all staring at her—judge, opposing counsel, Graves, all of them. Waiting.

"I know this is highly irregular, Judge Childress," she said softly into the still chamber. "But I'll do the best I can. Would you like me to present our argument, or would you prefer to ask your questions?"

The judge swept some measuring eyes over her and said, "Why don't we cut to the chase, Ms. . . ."

"Jackson."

"Ms. Jackson. I've read your brief, but there are a few things I don't quite understand . . ."

It wasn't any different from sitting around in the War Room with Ice, Weston and Graves . . . in fact, the man asked most of the same questions they had. When he was finished, the judge nodded at her a little and turned to Bushy Hair.

"State your case, Ms. Bell. I'm listening."

Alayna wasn't . . . listening, that is. Her mind kept running back to the look on Ice's face. Whatever had happened had scared him badly enough to smack down Smug and replace it with Scared. And had she not seen it herself just now, she'd never have believed such a thing was even possible.

Something was desperately wrong with Doug Richards and his son knew it, knew it the way that only people who have a connection beyond words knew it. Just like Alayna knew that Ice was in bad shape, too.

Somewhere out there, the judge's gavel fell. Alan Graves's exuberance started yanking her shoulders.

"You hear *that*! I *knew* it! I *knew* it! Richards is gonna *freak*!" he said excitedly.

"What—"

"Didn't you hear him?" Graves jerked his head at the swirl of black that was the now-disappearing judge. "Geez, he just said how impressed he was—"

But he was interrupted by her bushy-haired opponent's outstretched hand.

"Good work, Ms. Jackson," she said, managing a smile that appeared to be draining her heart's own blood. "We'll appeal, of course, but . . . Judge Childress is right. You really *should* go to law school." A crisp white card appeared out of nowhere and a second later was pressed into Alayna's palm. "We really could use you at Marker and Boorin. Call me."

Alayna slipped the thing into her pocket unseen, muttered something reasonably polite to the woman and turned to Graves.

"We've got to find him," she said, already throwing all the shit back into the briefcase in a jumble Ice himself would have envied.

"Sure, sure. But where—"

"Just shut up and drive, Alan," Alayna snapped, jabbing the briefcase into his soft gullet hard enough to ensure he'd keep his mouth closed and do what he was told.

Chapter 28

Ice's condo was total chaos.

Three police cars with their lights flashing were parked at the front entrance, an even dozen officers were searching the grounds, an ambulance and even a fire truck sat lazily at the corner.

Someone had some serious pull at city hall . . . or the kind of disaster that makes the five, six and eleven o'clock news was in progress.

"What's going on? What happened?" Graves demanded of a female officer in a uniform a size too small for her blossoming behind.

"Some old guy with Alzheimer's wandered away from his keeper," she drawled, shifting her weight from foot to foot. "You live here?"

Alayna started running: up the manicured lawn toward the entrance, through the lobby, to the elevator doors, where she pounded on the button until the thing nearly broke under her hand. When Graves caught up, his well-meaning, goofy face said *confusion* even worse than normal.

"The 'old guy' is Doug Richards," Alayna explained before the questions started, then stared her boyfriend's first big client hard in the face.

Graves blanched.

"Doug Richards? You don't mean—"

"Yeah. Ben's father."

"For the hundredth time, I thought he was sleeping!" a woman in a floral uniform top shrieked as Alayna and Graves elbowed and explicated their way into Ice's place.

She was young, with a medium build and height and probably white, though her skin had a suspicious yellow cast that would have been worth Alayna's further investigation under other circumstances. But the chick's mouth wrecked the whole thing—two gold teeth front and center with a big old gap between them. Made her smile like a baddie out of James Bond.

"This place is like a pigsty," she continued rabidly, "and I thought it was high time to *at least* wash up the breakfast dishes—"

"You thought! You thought—" Ice hissed, fury snaking through each word. He leapt from his place on the cluttered sofa and lunged at the woman, feral and furious. "I pay you to watch *him,* not do the goddamned dishes—"

"Mr. Richards, we know you're upset—" a calmer male voice interjected, and Alayna saw a little man with a thick hump of skin on the back of his balding white head give Ice a hard push back into his chair just as she and Graves stepped into the living room. Trixie immediately lay one maternal hand on his shoulder in pseudo-restraint, but the other was clamped barfly tight around a cigarette. She took a drag—the quick, nervous puff of the seriously stressed-out—but otherwise kept her eyes riveted on the bald man.

"But we need you to stay calm and help us think of places to *look* for your father," Bald One continued, walking his voice down the narrow line between comforting and condescending.

"He could be anywhere by now," Ice muttered, sounding sick with defeat. "Piedmont Park, the MARTA station, halfway to Lenox Mall—"

"We're checking all that—" The man turned suddenly, showing her a surprisingly compact body that didn't jive with the roll of flab at the back of his head. "Hey! What are you doing here? Who let these people in—"

A voice at her side filled the void.

"Alan Graves." Graves extended his hand toward the man, with an assurance Alayna had always suspected must be in there somewhere. "I'm Mr. Richards' personal attorney, and this is his fiancée, Alayna Jackson. I'm glad you're already on this matter. Judge Richards is something of a legend in the legal community."

The bald man's eyes swept over them, displaying only a modicum of interest. He gazed at Graves slightly longer than Alayna, calculating his pain-in-the-ass factor, then said, "Detective Groggan. We're trying to target the search. We figure he's got around half an hour on us, but he might have been confused—"

Ice sunk his face in his hands.

"Judge Richards is not confused. At least not in his

own mind," Alayna said softly, moving quickly around the cop to Ice. Trixie surrendered willingly enough, her eyes catching Alayna's long enough to deliver a furtive prognosis: not good.

Alayna touched Ice's shoulder. He sat up and looked up at her.

His face was something special and significant being razed by fools, plundered by war, raped by savages. Just looking at him made a pain flare in Alayna's chest that was a neon advertisement for heartaches everywhere.

"You told me that the first time I met your father," she added in a gentle tone she barely recognized as her own voice . . . and certainly not a voice she'd thought herself likely to use with the Ice Man.

"Yeah," Ice sighed. "He always knows exactly what he thinks he's doing." He cocked an eye at the gold-toothed nurse. "Tell me again. What was he talking about this morning?"

"Like I said: nothing special," Golden Gap said impatiently. "He was actually kind of quiet. Not like when he thinks he's in court or something. Said he wanted to retire to his chambers. Do some reading. I took him to his room, put him in his chair and that's where he was when I left him." She lit them all with a glimmering yellow smile. "He must have been hell on wheels in his day."

"He was," Ice and Graves said with the same simultaneous awe and respect, but in the beat after their chorus, the woman snapped her fingers and said, "A brief! Just before I left his room, he started going on about an important brief. Searching through that mess of newspapers and magazines up there, muttering about going to hearing in the morning—"

"I've been talking to him about the case—" Ice interjected. "He seemed sort of interested . . . in a way."

"That's it?" Detective Groggan sounded like he'd been cut out of *Law and Order* and pasted into Ice's living room. "Not much to—"

Ice sprang to his feet. Alayna grabbed after him, aiming to slow his frantic roll long enough to answer the questions bubbling on the police detective's lips, but he was too fast. He tore out of the room, racing up the stairs three at a time.

She found him in the old man's walk-in closet, pulling out clothing like Doug Richards might be hiding in it.

"Go to my closet!" he shouted, still tossing clothing maniacally. "Look!"

"But—"

"He hid in the closet once, remember? I told you that story, didn't I? Look!"

You didn't tell me any such thing, Alayna thought, but she kept the words in her head and with a quick nod of understanding, hurried off to Ice's bedroom, where she found nothing but a bunch of blue and gray suits in a bunch of different fabrics, a million white shirts, a rack full of ties. No Doug Richards. Nothing even remotely close.

Ice joined her just as she had given up on the closet and decided to visit beneath the bed. Any other time, her butt swinging in the air, stretching the fabric of her dark blue skirt, would have gotten a few different kinds of rises out of him. But he simply said, "I don't believe he could have left the building. Joe's working the desk. He *knows* us. He and his wife have watched Dad for me in a pinch. He would never have—"

Groggan appeared, scratching the hump of fat on his neck in irritation.

"I told you we checked this house thoroughly already, sir," he sighed. "And the concierge . . . one Joe Schultz . . . says he didn't see Mr. Richards leave. But he was away from his desk for a while helping another resident unload some groceries—"

"I think he's still in the building," Ice repeated, his voice edged with a scary, desperate, I-don't-hear-you determination. "Dad barely understands how to work the elevator anymore, and unless he just stumbled into a stairwell he wouldn't—"

"But he might have, Ice," Alayna said softly and watched his face change as the truth hurt him. "And if he went down to the parking garage—"

She let the sentence die, but he knew. If Judge Richards had gone down to the garage, he could have easily reached the street. And if he'd wandered into the street . . .

"We've a couple of officers searching the garage now. And others going door-to-door through the building asking if anyone's seen anything. A number of your neighbors have volunteered to help, but we need to give them some guidance. And that's why I asked you if your father has any favorite places. You know, a place with some significance that he might have—"

Ice shook his head.

"I told you—he's not cogent most of the time.

When he gets these ideas that he has to go to court or his chambers, he ends up in broom closets and recycling chutes and—"

The words broke on his face like dawn.

"In this building, the garbage chutes are in little closets just before you round the curve to the elevators. Two on every floor—"

But Groggan was already on his radio, issuing curt instructions.

They found him several floors down in the trash disposal area, holding some discarded papers and muttering between two blue recycling cans about the shoddy quality of what passed for legal work.

Ice's voice shattered with relief when he and Alayna joined the gathering crowd of searchers around the old man. Ice sunk from his quivering legs to his shaking knees. "Dad . . . Dad, you scared me to death," he murmured, pulling the old man into his arms. "You . . ."

Doug Richards jerked away from him, gray eyes glittering threat, hand raised to strike.

"Get off me! Who *are* you?"

Ice stretched his arms toward the man, almost pleading for recognition, then his shoulders contracted in on each other with the sting of the rejection. He tried to stand, but his legs would no more obey his brain than his father would rush to his embrace. A painful, pitiful silence fell over the collected observers.

"I'm Ben. Your son," Ice managed, as hollow and empty as the nearby trash chute.

"You're not Ben," Judge Richards snapped. "I

know my own son. You just keep away from me now. All of you—"

"You heard the man," Groggan interrupted, scattering the search effort with the robust energy of his voice. "Go on. Get!"

Judge Richards nodded approval at him.

"I like you. You're not as dumb as some people around here," he muttered, casting a disapproving eye at his heartbroken son.

"Don't be so hard on him, Your Honor," Groggan said grimly. "You don't know what he's been through. I got some people here who want to make sure you're okay—"

"Of course I'm *okay*—"

"I know that, and you know that, but neither of us is going to get any peace until *they* know that—"

And as if on cue, the EMT crew arrived, pushing aside police and bystanders to do their thing, and Doug Richards transferred his objections to them.

With Alayna's help, Ice struggled off the floor, far more in need of the attention of the EMTs than his father. Detective Groggan started clearing out his people and calling in the officers who'd spread out to search. But there were still neighbors and others standing around, gawking like they were waiting for someone.

"Thank you all. Thank you very much," Alayna murmured. "Ben . . . and I are very grateful. Very . . ." Alayna tugged Ice away from the center of activity by the sleeve of his rumpled shirt. He moved like everything alive inside him had been cut to ribbons.

Graves watched, concerned. Trixie dabbed at her

tear-soaked face with her arm, muttering over and over, "Poor man, poor man."

"You want me to . . . ," Graves began in a hushed voice close to Alayna's ear, but she shook her head.

"He's okay. They'll both be okay. Go, Alan. He'll call you tomorrow. And Alan?" She kissed his cheek, which turned crimson, then purple, then pale again. "Thanks."

Graves nodded. She could tell he felt bad about it, but the truth was he was glad to leave. This scene had gotten way too heavy. He quirked a brow at Trixie, asking.

Trixie snorted back a noseful of something Alayna hoped she wouldn't have to see and squared her shoulders in preparation for Alayna's personal rebuff.

"If you wouldn't mind, Trixie," Alayna said softly, "I'd really like you to stay a while."

Shock, then relief, then a kind of purposeful determination mottled the woman's baggy face.

"Y'all get on down to the hospital. Get Richards there checked over while you're at it. I'm gonna go on back to the house and get rid of that bad-toothed nurse," she grumbled. "Neither one of them needs to see her ugly mug again in this life."

Alayna nodded, managing to give the woman a slight smile of thanks before she scurried away.

"I should have . . . I should have . . . found a safer place for him . . . long time ago . . ." Ice muttered almost to himself. "I just thought . . ."

"You did what you thought was right."

"What I thought was right," he repeated sarcastically. "He could have wandered into the street. He could have gotten hurt. Worse . . ."

"But he didn't," Alayna murmured as she pulled him close. "He didn't. And from now on," she sighed uncomfortably as Doug Richards' full weight settled on her shoulders, "we'll *both* be around to keep an eye on him—"

"He . . . he . . ." His voice cracked with emotion, and she felt the tears there long before she saw them rolling down his cheeks. And she knew, in a realization that felt like physical pain, that she'd never be able to leave him alone with this burden. No more than she would have left Martine alone and in trouble. You just don't do that and use the word *love* . . . even if it means you lose a part of yourself.

But Ice was working himself around to an acceptance of his own.

"This . . . that plan was . . . crazy . . . just . . . I can't even make him know who I am. How could I ask you to—? This . . . isn't going to work, is it?"

"I don't know."

"It isn't," Ice asserted, anger rumbling in the words. He inhaled deeply, pushed himself away from her and wiped his face in his hands. "Okay. I'll call Mrs. Aubry this afternoon," he said quietly. "I'll beg her to accept him as a residential client if I have to . . ."

Alayna sighed. "Ben, sweetheart, after the things you said to her, I'd say 'begging' is pretty much what it's going to take."

Chapter 29

"I knew you could do it," Ice said almost twenty-four hours later, when he'd recovered himself enough to care about such unimportant things as Weston, money, and the future of his career.

They were in his father's room with boxes, plastic bags and suitcases, beginning the job of organizing Judge Richards' move from Ice's condo to Mrs. Aubry's Alzheimer's center. Ice struggled over almost everything he touched, but he was doing it . . . doing it with a decent showing of that I-can-handle-it confidence Alayna knew so well.

"I need to call Weston today—"

Alayna shoulder-shrugged him into silence. "He can wait. Let's get your father settled first." She abandoned her garbage bag long enough to quirk a "time-to-talk-turkey, turkey" brow at him. "And we've got a few other things to settle about this 'Richards and Associates' idea, anyway."

"Not this again—"

"Yes, this again—"

"Alayna—"

"Ben!" Alayna snapped. "I've still got reservations, objections, questions—"

"Reservations, objections, questions . . . ," he grumbled, grabbing a stack of freshly laundered polo shirts from the clothes rack and tossing them onto the bed in a messy heap. "*Now* what?"

Hand to hip. Finger to face.

"You're taking a Sister for granted, you know that?"

"Impossible," he snarled, nasty as he pleased. "You talk too much for that."

"Well, you worked out *Trixie's* compensation plan. She got her duckets, but me, I haven't heard word *one* from you about mine!" She curled her lip at him like he was the original Slave Labor Boss, and she folded her arms across her chest. "How much, Mr. Ice Man?"

He rolled his eyes.

"Oh, I get it. I'm talking about independence and love and freedom. But for you it's all about the money, honey."

Alayna blinked at him, flashing a mouthful of suspiciously sunny teeth.

"Girl's gotta pay the rent."

And there went those magnificent grays, full of challenge and menace, looking downright uptight. *Finally, Ice Man returneth*, Alayna thought with relief. *Thank the dear Lord.*

"The rent?" he barked, wadding up another stack of his father's clothes. At this rate, the poor man would be wandering around the Atlanta Alzheimer's Residence Facility looking like a rumpled tissue. "Not this again. I've offered you rent-free—"

"Yes. I've heard your offers—you just haven't been listening to my answers." She waved the whole subject aside with a flutter of her fingers. "We'll come to that in a minute. Stick to the salary, please."

Ice frowned. "Now?"

"Well, we could wait until later, but . . ." She sauntered toward him, doing what she hoped was a pouty, sexy, come-get-me pose. "I'm feeling awfully *generous* toward you right now."

He grinned, a real, live, honest-to-God facecracker. It was a damn shame, the effect just the suggestion of the *possibility* of sex had on men. Girl-children should have been born with a label attached, fixed on their undersides like those tags on mattresses: *Caution, you are dangerous to the opposite sex. That's why they'll do anything possible to keep you unaware of your power.*

Alayna made a mental note—*Explore uses of pure unadulterated sex appeal*—and tossed a flirty set of eyelash bats into the mix.

Too much, apparently.

"The salary might be on the low side at first," he grumbled, backing away from her like he knew he was being manipulated.

"Then no deal," Alayna snapped back, abandoning sex as a weapon and returning to the solace of her black Hefty. "I got an offer from Marker and Boorin to consider anyway," she lied. Truth was, she couldn't find that woman's card anywhere, but there was nothing like a little healthy competition, right, Mr. Basketball Man?

"Hmmm." Ice scratched his face a little. "Marker and Boorin? Good firm."

"Yeah. And they *pay*."

"Yeah, but *I* don't work there," he said smugly.

"Another plus," Alayna said light as cream pie and just as sweet. "Face it, Ice. You've got too many personal problems."

He probably hadn't meant to, but his laugh exploded out of him, a big old belly-shaking, foolish-sounding thing. He sunk onto his father's little bed, holding his stomach, then stretched out, still sniggling like there was a feather under his chin. Alayna grinned at herself. She'd made a funny.

"Look at who's talking," he managed after a while. "Okay, okay. Suppose I offer a little bonus? Something to keep you happy until the cash starts rolling in."

And to her surprise he pulled a small velvet box out of his pocket and started laughing again—no doubt at the stunned Cheerio in the center of her face where her mouth had been.

"What the hell . . . ?" Alayna took a step toward Man With Box as though pulled by invisible magnets, mentally adding another sentence to the Girl Child warning label: *The programming of this model can be damaged or destroyed by the words "I love you," velvet boxes and assistance in times of crisis.*

"You don't really deserve it yet, but . . ." said Prince Uncharming, another I-need-to-be-slapped grin on his face. "But what the hell?"

Alayna snatched it out of his hands. "I deserve it just for standing around here *talking* to you, you big, loud jerk," she breathed, finding it tough to put full spirit behind the insults. Under the circumstances.

You got to hesitate just a second before you open a

little velvet box. Just a second to take a big old fairy-tale breath. A second to savor the "happy ending-ness" of it all.

Because inside that little velvet box, of course, was a great big diamond. It even caught a ray of sunlight and started refracting the hell out of it, just to make sure everyone knew what they were dealing with.

"I got it the day you got pissed with me and told me to go to hell," Ice said, admiring her face admiring the rock.

"Which time?" Alayna muttered, still unable to tear her face off the thing. Her finger itched to give it a test drive.

"The last one . . . I think." He paused, and a glimmer of apprehension snuck into his face as he studied her. "Well?"

"Well . . ." Alayna repeated, struggling not to let on just how pleased and impressed she was, for fear he'd make this sort of extravagance a bad habit. The thing was the kind of rock you'd expect to see on a movie star or royalty or at least on some eighty-year-old dowager with blue hair and a double chin. And if you even *consider* marrying a man, you can't have him throwing perfectly good money down the drain just to show off. "It's pretty, but—"

"But what?" The skin between his brows was puckered with anger. Her gentle suitor had that ready-to-throw-your-ass-out-the-damn-window glare in his eyes again—which meant he was quickly gaining ground on the road to emotional recovery.

Tell him now, you fool. You won't get a better chance, a voice in Alayna's heart counseled. *Right now.*

"But . . . I'm not ready to marry you," she said, keeping her tone as loving as she could, considering what she was saying. Alayna closed the box gently and covered Ice's fingers around it.

He scowled at her as she grabbed a fresh trash bag and bent, scuttling a pile of *Time* magazines into it with her foot.

"Why?" he demanded, pissed his plans had been uprooted yet again. "What's the matter?"

"Well," she began slowly, still concentrating on the work before them. "I hardly know you."

"You know me just fine and you know it," Ice growled. "What else?"

Alayna caught a quick glance of Muhammad Ali on the cover of one of the *Time*s and scrounged to fish it out of the pile.

"Second of all," she told the Champ, dusting him off a little before tossing him to his biggest fan, "if we're starting a new firm, that ring is way too extravagant. I know Cybex is a good client, but we'll have a lot of start-up expenses, Ice. Even after Martine and I sell the house on Magnolia Street, I can't be wearing all our cash flow."

A smile crept across his face.

"Oh. You've got a point," he murmured, stuffing the ring back into his pocket. "What was I thinking? You'd probably just pawn it anyway, right? Isn't that what you black people do with your valuables?"

"Watch yourself," Alayna warned, but she was grinning now.

"What would you prefer? A cigar band? A Cadillac? Fur coat? Gold teeth? Tell me what you want."

She should have held on to Ali just a few seconds more . . . so she'd have something in hand to bop him upside his head with. But instead, with empty hands, she said simply, "Partnership. As soon as I pass the Georgia State Bar. Richards, Jackson and Associates—"

"Richards, *Jackson* and Associates?"

"You heard me."

"Does this mean you'll marry me eventually?"

"Don't know," Alayna said slowly. "Pretty serious contract, marriage. Just *thinking* about marriage is serious. And you're white. That makes it even more serious."

"Well, excuse me for breathing—"

"You're excused. And there's still a lot of people out there who don't like mixed marriages—"

"Who cares what they think? I don't."

"Neither do I. But our kids might."

Oh, Lord. The word "kids" made a devilish grin spread across his face. He sauntered toward her, all fingers and lips, like he was ready to start the baby-making right then and there on his Daddy's narrow little bed.

And to stop that, Alayna *had* to whack him one, hard enough to knock his glasses a-slant, but not hard enough to break them.

"Pay attention! You want to talk to me about marriage, I'd say we need some ground rules."

"Ground rules?" He grimaced at her, what-you-talking-about written all over his face.

"Got any paper?"

He glanced around the room. They were surrounded by paper: newspaper, magazines, crossword books, paper, paper everywhere. All already claimed by words.

"You're serious?" he asked. And even though she nodded, heart-attack serious, he didn't make a move for either pencil or pen. Just frowned ugly at her, lip curled, eyes dark. "What? Love, honor and cherish?"

Alayna snorted. "You'd better, or you'll be loving *yourself* late at night. No. First of all. I want a long engagement—"

"How long?" Ice interrupted.

"At least a year—"

"A *year?*"

Alayna snapped her neck and executed an Olympic 10 hand-on-hip slip before staring him down with, "Look. I've been through a lot of changes in the last couple months and I don't need to jump feet first into anything until I know what the hell I'm doing. And you, too. You don't know your ass from a hole in the ground right now. Changes at home, changes at work. And if you think I'm gonna let you just plop me in here the second your father's gone, well . . ." Alayna sighed and shook her head. "You need to go sit down somewhere and *think* about yourself."

Ice appeared to be enjoying the floor show, because instead of the usual round of protests and counter-arguments, he just laughed. "Okay, okay, Miss Thing," he said, but it sounded all clipped and stupid, and Alayna nearly lost her groove to bust out laughing. "All right. A year. Is there more?"

"I'm not moving in with you, that's for damn truth."

Laughing Boy shut down mid-"ha." "Never?"

"Not until you learn to clean up after your own damn self and cook a decent meal. I am *not* going to be your maid, Richards. Not in this life. You need one? Hire yourself one."

He grimaced at her, but his eyes were dancing with enjoyment and gratitude. This was heavy, hard work, packing up Doug Richards, abandoning a decision, revealing a promise. What better way to get it done than have your girlfriend insult your hygiene and reject your marriage proposal?

"Okay," he muttered. "Fine. But now I got one." He approached her, pulling the slick edge of the heavy bag out of her hand with Intensity branded on his face. "Wear the ring," and before she could think, he pulled the glittering monster out of the box and took possession of her commitment hand. A second later, he'd forced the thing onto the appropriate finger, where it fit like Cinderella's slipper and sparkled like the jewels in Snow White's evil stepmother's crown. "It was my mother's," he said, hiding his emotion with more Mr. Gruff and Master Grim. "I had it put in a new setting . . . for you."

Alayna stretched out her fingers and gave them a hard once-over. Lord have mercy, did that ring look good on her hand. So good, she knew she'd miss it fierce, if, in the end, she had to give it back.

"Well. I guess I can wear it . . ." she said, trying to sound casual and unimpressed. It wouldn't do for Ice to think she liked it or anything. Wouldn't do at all. "If it means that much to you. Now . . . just incorporate all the clauses from our working agreement—"

"*What?*"

"Hello?" Alayna knocked on his forehead with

three ashy knuckles. "Are we talking long distance? Have I got a bad connection?"

Ice swatted her fingers away and pulled her into his arms, like some Hollywood hero at the end of a big love scene: *fade-out, kissing.*

"Don't you want me in your personal matters, Ali?" he murmured, all romance and syrup.

Alayna cast her eyes to Heaven and sighed.

"Not that part, Ben Richards. How can I keep you out of my personal matters when you *are* my personal matter—"

And the disrespectful so-and-so started kissing her before she could even finish the sentence. *What a jerk,* Alayna thought. *Thank God for him for me, Mama.*

Then she wrapped her arms around his neck and got down to the business of loving him.